PICKED OFF

The Brie Hooker Mystery Series by Linda Lovely

BONES TO PICK (#1)
PICKED OFF (#2)

PICKED OFF

A BRIE HOOKER MYSTERY

LINDA LOVELY

HENERY PRESS

Copyright

PICKED OFF
A Brie Hooker Mystery
Part of the Henery Press Mystery Collection

First Edition | June 2018

Henery Press, LLC
www.henerypress.com

Cover art by Stephanie Savage
Author photograph by Danielle Dahl

This is a work of fiction. Any references to historical events, real people, or real locales are used fictitiously. Other names, characters, places, and incidents are the product of the author's imagination, and any resemblance to actual events or locales or persons, living or dead, is entirely coincidental. Las Vegas was chosen as the home of *Picked Off*'s fictional Sin City Aces football team because the city had no pro football team when the book was written.

Trade Paperback ISBN-13: 978-1-63511-342-6
Digital epub ISBN-13: 978-1-63511-343-3
Kindle ISBN-13: 978-1-63511-344-0
Hardcover ISBN-13: 978-1-63511-345-7

Printed in the United States of America

For My Writers' Police Academy "Family"

ACKNOWLEDGMENTS

I owe continuing thanks to the owners of Split Creek Farm in South Carolina and Morning Glow Farm in Wisconsin for all information related to goat dairies. Split Creek Farm also was kind enough to host the book launch for *Bones to Pick,* while Six & Twenty Distillery provided mystery fans with tastings of fine local spirits akin to those my character Paint Paynter will offer when he expands his product line beyond moonshine. Of course, after attending, author Polly Iyer did threaten to sue me due to her new addiction to Six & Twenty's Carolina Cream.

For information dealing with fantasy football, I need to thank friends Chris Christensen and Matt Goddard. I also should give a nod to my great-nephew Braden Mann, a kicker for Texas A&M University, whose talents have certainly increased my interest in watching the sport. Any errors in football references are mine alone. Educating someone like me who is a total pigskin dummy is a daunting task.

My good friend Kay Kirkley Barrett, Esq., former City of Clemson Attorney/Prosecutor, provided insights into how my character Iris Hooker, Esq., might spend her workdays. I also want to thank Howard R. Lemcke, another member of the legal profession, for his winning charity bid to have a *Picked Off* character named for him. Mr. Lemcke has written a riveting true crime book of his own, *In Her Own Backyard: A Perfect Husband, A Perfect Marriage, A Perfect Murder*, based on a murder case he tried as a prosecutor for the State of Utah.

Grateful shout outs are due to the Henery Press editorial team, including Maria Edwards and Rachel Jackson, who helped improve my manuscript, and illustrator Stephanie Savage for her cool covers. I also owe thanks to Rowe Carenen of The Book Concierge for her efforts to reach new audiences.

Major thanks to my critique partners—Donna Campbell, Danielle Dahl, Charles Duke, Howard Lewis, and Robin Weaver—for their support, excellent suggestions, and, most of all, their friendship. However, I need to single out horse-and-mule wrangler Howard for his suggestions. Howard spins great tales about how he's learned his equines' many peccadillos.

As always thanks to my husband, Tom Hooker, who couldn't be more supportive. I value his feedback on early drafts, and his help in talking through plot dilemmas. For this series, he has even lent his surname to the main character, Brie Hooker.

With incredible thanks, this book is dedicated to the Writers' Police Academy, celebrating its tenth anniversary in 2018. The determination of founder Lee Lofland and Dr. Denene Lofland to help crime writers "get it right" through hands-on learning experiences makes this annual event at a real police academy a fun adventure for both writers and fans of crime fiction. I've been lucky to be included in the volunteer "family" that helps with this event.

ONE

I shrank into a tight crouch and crept along the fence line. The gate sat twenty-five yards away. It felt like a mile. My nerves jangled. Who could blame me? Yesterday's assault would have scared the beans out of a bowl of chili.

Mist shrouded the hilly field in the skimpy pre-dawn light. A dark silhouette moved. He was awake, alert.

Could I reach the gate before he noticed?

The wind whistling down from neighboring mountains favored me. It whisked sound and scent away from the enemy—a one-time friend who'd turned into an animal I could not recognize.

My arm ached from lugging my heavy load; the cold of the metal handle pierced my glove. If forced, I'd use my burden as a club. Duncan's choice. I scuttled ahead. Ten yards closer.

A rooster's crow broke the silence. I held my breath. Would the sound prompt Duncan to turn? No. Something else captured his attention.

Five more yards.

Duncan stamped the ground. Cold? Or did he sense my approach?

Don't turn around, please.

My icy fingers found the gate hasp. Last night I'd sprayed WD-40 on the hinges, hoping to silence its rickety creak. I lifted the hasp and pulled. The gate no longer creaked, it emitted a low groan. Not low enough to escape Duncan's senses.

Holy Swiss Cheese.

I ran. The metal pail banged against my calf.

I reached the trough, dumped the pail's contents, and sprinted back toward the gate.

Duncan pounded after me. Too close. I could hear his snorts over my panicky wheezing. I jumped outside the pen and jerked the gate closed.

Duncan squealed in frustration and butted his hairy head against the wire fence.

"Ha. Beat you today, you rancid chunk of Braunshweiger." I shouted in victory.

Okay, Brie. Stop yelling cheese and meat curses at a stupid billy goat. Duncan's not an alien life form, just a horny buck intent on boinking anything that moves.

Once I'd walked beyond Duncan's spitting range, I upended the pail I'd used to carry his high-energy feed. Like he needed more energy. I parked my behind on the bucket for a short rest. I'd completed deliveries to two of our billy boys—Duncan and Jordan—and escaped clean.

It galled my butt that our male goats had taken to spitting at me, Brie Hooker, the vegan. Hardly seemed fair. I fed them. Didn't even eat any of their animal-kingdom cousins. Why me?

Behind his fence, Duncan, our Nubian buck, was putting on quite a show. His long pink tongue squirmed in the air as if he were slurping imaginary ice cream. His eyes rolled, and he blubbered. That's the noise our horny bucks emitted to express undying affection for nearby does.

Fortunately, the wind carried most of Duncan's racket and smell away. Up close a billy goat's odor could choke a rotting zombie. Thank heaven, our boys only smelled during rutting season.

When I came to live at Udderly Kidding Dairy last spring, the bucks were affectionate, non-odiferous gentlemen. Aunt Eva said shorter days and less light triggered rutting madness. If we didn't need their randy assistance to breed our does, I'd keep the boys' pens noonday bright year-round.

Enough wishful thinking. We were expecting two-hundred people for tonight's shindig. The goal was to raise money for Carol Strong's campaign for South Carolina governor. And, I had to admit I was looking forward to meeting her son, Zack, quarterback for the Sin City Aces. He was flying in for the party.

I was a big fan. What wasn't there to like? The football star was an exceptional athlete, articulate, and did I mention handsome?

While Hallow's Eve was still a week away, tonight's Halloween-themed event was a costume party. I hoped my friend Mollye, who tended to be a tad scatterbrained, had kept her promise to pick up my Little Bo Peep costume.

I still remembered our first meeting. Mollye explained her mom added an "e" to her name to make it six letters—a lucky number.

While I didn't know if the nonessential letter had improved Mollye's fortunes, I felt super lucky she was my pal. When we were kids, Moll boarded ponies at my aunts' farm, and we were inseparable during my summer vacation visits. Our friendship always renewed itself with ease. Now that I lived at Udderly Kidding Dairy we had ample opportunities to join forces and stir up trouble.

Hmmm. Maybe I should plan an alternate outfit in case Moll forgot my costume. I could wear the newest in horny goat protection—a heavy-duty rain slicker and hazard gloves.

As I hung my slicker on a peg outside the milking barn, I spotted Eva standing with head bowed on the hill where she'd scattered her twin's ashes. She often went there to commune with Aunt Lilly, whose unexpected death brought me to Udderly. Without her twin, Eva needed my help to manage her farm and its four-hundred goats. The arrangement was meant to be temporary. But it had been months since Eva or I had broached the subject of an end date. We both had our reasons.

I yoo-hooed and pointed toward the cabin. I hoped Carol would be on time for breakfast. I was starved. My body clock had tuned itself to farm routine—up before Riley the Rooster crowed, in bed before network TV broadcasted adult-rated fare. Life was soooo exciting. Truthfully, the calm felt sort of good after last spring's near-fatal adventures.

As I neared the cabin, Carol's brand-new Cadillac bumped down the farm's gravel drive. Socks, one of our five Great Pyrenees guard dogs, woofed and ran to join me, apparently unsure I was smart enough to know we had company.

I waved. Carol, a state senator, was my aunt's oldest Ardon County friend, and Eva really missed her when the legislature was in session. I waited as she exited Big Car—Carol's name for it. The Caddy was one of Zack's many expensive gifts. Now that she was running for governor, Carol fretted that Big Car made her look like a fat cat politico, but she hated to appear ungrateful.

"Hey, Carol. Eva's headed our way. Come inside while I put on coffee and start breakfast."

Carol patted Socks' head, while deftly moving in circles away from the huge body trying to rub on her. She lost the battle. Socks butted her thigh with his face, drool escaping his happy lolling tongue. Then he did a shimmy and plastered his entire body against her leg. Streaks of slobber and white fur clung to her black slacks.

Carol just laughed and scratched the big Pyres' cheeks. No wonder Carol was one of my aunt's favorite people.

"I'll wait for Eva," she said. "I see her chugging down the hill. Want to make sure her chunky self doesn't need CPR."

I laughed. "Won't tell Eva you said that."

"Then I will," the sassy redhead quipped.

I'd heard Eva tell how Carol had saved her sanity. When she arrived in Ardon County as a nineteen-year-old bride, Carol, also a married teen, became her friend and confidant. As Eva's husband became more abusive, Carol assured her that wasn't the way marriage was meant to be. She was helping Eva plan an escape when my aunt's brute of a husband vanished.

These days Carol seemed to kid Eva more than ever. I think she realized the jibes reminded Eva of her twin. As long as I could remember, my aunts delighted in trading barbs. When Carol wasn't around, Eva directed most zingers at her live-in help—*moi*. I was slowly getting the hang of counter-punching.

The minute I entered the cabin, Cashew, my seven-month-old puppy, ran excited circles around me. I gave her a quick pat and promised to pay more attention after I brewed coffee.

Eva and Carol entered, jabbering like agitated crows. Carol picked up Cashew, who had a knack for hoodwinking visitors to fawn over her.

"What do you want for breakfast, ladies?" I asked. "How about oatmeal with blueberries and walnuts?"

"Ha," Eva answered. "Make mine eggs over easy, thick bacon, and buttered toast."

"I'll have the same," Carol said as she opened the fridge to get cream for her coffee. When the state legislature wasn't in session, she visited Udderly enough to act like family.

"What's with the Post-It?" Carol asked and then read the note. "The aliens have surrendered. Quit beheading Martians."

I rolled my eyes having already seen the sticky refrigerator barb. "That's Eva's culinary critique of last night's menu. I served braised Brussels sprouts. She prefers to call them Martian heads."

Carol chuckled. "Good one. I'm not a fan of the little green hockey pucks either. But I know you're a fabulous chef, Brie. I wanted you to cater tonight's fundraiser—especially since Udderly Kidding Dairy is hosting. But I owed the owner of Red's Bar-B-Q. He's a long-time supporter, and he provides eats at cost."

"Not a problem. With carnivores in the majority, you better serve more than veggies. I only try to convert meat-eaters in small groups, and I don't give them knives."

Carol smiled. "Hope we have a good turnout. I need money for a final campaign push. Zack offered a big donation. But if I accepted, I couldn't scream about the out-of-state super PAC throwing money at my opponent. Everyone knows the PAC's run by the oil lobby. My stand against off-shore drilling doesn't endear me to them."

Eva huffed. "Everyone knows our paper's numbnuts owner is a major contributor to that PAC. If off-shore drilling gets the green light, Allie will make a pot load of money. The *Ardon Chronicle* lets her vent. Real estate and energy investments are her gravy."

I jumped in to thwart Eva's familiar rave about the local press. My aunt had good reason to bear a grudge. Allie'd used the newspaper's horse-pucky headlines to snipe at Eva for decades—ever since my aunt's husband disappeared. The publisher employed every trick from innuendo to unnamed sources to label my aunt a murderer.

"We're thrilled Zack's coming, but how in the world did he get a weekend off?" I asked.

I'd been surprised a pro quarterback could take any time off in the height of the season.

"His team played Thursday and the next game's a week from Sunday, so Zack scored a weekend pass," Carol answered. "He'll fly back to Vegas Sunday morning."

Aunt Eva smiled. "Can't wait to see Zack. I remember when he threw the touchdown pass that cinched Ardon High's state championship. I cheered so hard I had laryngitis for a week. I love that he's living his dream. Quarterback for the Sin City Aces."

Carol's fingers fidgeted with her coffee cup. "I still worry his dream could morph into a nightmare. The possibility of injury is bad enough, but you wouldn't believe how many weirdos and gamblers send threats. If he gets sacked or a throw's intercepted, it's as if they think Zack did it on purpose."

Her eyes squeezed shut. "This Halloween tomfoolery must be getting to me. Not sure it was smart to plan a campaign event with a Halloween theme. The *Chronicle* will probably print a picture with the caption 'Carol's Ghouls.'"

"Nonsense," Eva replied. "It'll be fun. Brie's boyfriends are helping her decorate, turning our barn into a spooky haunted house."

I looked heavenward. "They're friends, and they're men, not boys. Definitely not boyfriends."

Aunt Eva waved away my objection. "Whatever. Carol can judge for herself. She knows Paint and Andy. They were on Zack's team in high school. When does our star arrive?"

"Right after lunch. We'll swing by on our way home from the airport. Give you a chance to say hi before tonight's madness."

Once Carol left, I peppered Eva with questions about what Zack was like before his rise to celebrity status. My aunt started his thumbnail bio when he was a teen and badly hurt in a car wreck.

"It was touch and go whether he'd survive," Eva recalled. "Carol had just lost her husband to cancer. Not sure she could have handled Zack's death. He's her only family."

Eva said Zack began his pro career as a third-round draft pick and spent a decade as a back-up quarterback, shuffled among three teams via trades.

"You know all the recent drama. When the Aces' veteran quarterback tore his rotator cuff early last season, Zack stepped in red hot. Took what had been a lackluster team to the Super Bowl. He felt kind of crummy that his success came at a buddy's expense."

"Well, the press sure loves him," I commented. "Good looking, single, and his Southern drawl doesn't hurt one bit."

Eva nodded. "Too bad the media includes some dodgy tabloids and loony bloggers. Carol says they drive Zack nuts. Make him feel like a hunted animal."

TWO

"That's perfect," I hollered to Paint. "Let Mr. Goblin hover right there."

David Paynter—Paint to his friends—scooted forward on his stomach. His muscled arms dangled from the hayloft as he adjusted Mr. Goblin. When visitors rounded this corner in our Udderly Haunted Barn of Horrors, they'd run into our macabre, eye-level ghoul. I could hear the screams already.

Watching Paint's capable hands at work, I had a fleeting wish he'd tug on a few of my strings. I'd had the pleasure of enjoying his talented fingers and inviting lips up close and personal. With regret, I now kept such temptations at bay. Paint's devilish dark eyes met mine. His face lit up in a wicked grin as he brushed his black hair off his sweaty forehead. Hard to resist.

"Hey, how about my contribution?" Andy asked, pulling my mind from one temptation to another. Andy had posed a scarecrow just outside one of the stalls. The stuffed female dummy's angry pout made me laugh.

"Whoever made the mask nailed it," I said. "An excellent—if somewhat cruel—caricature of our paper's illustrious owner."

"Mollye's the artist," Andy answered. "Snapped a picture of Allie Gerome in mid-rant at an Ardon County Council meeting. She played with the image on her computer, enlarging the bags under her eyes and adding a hint of purple to the woman's double chin."

I chuckled. "A bit unfair. She doesn't look quite that horrid. But I feel no guilt given her paper's vicious smear campaign against Aunt Eva."

Mollye's mask coupled with a long-pronged pitchfork made the one-time goofy scarecrow look truly scary. It appeared ready to spear anyone who ventured near.

Duct tape in hand, Andy strolled out from behind the effigy, giving me another male hunk to admire. Emerald eyes and curly blond hair. Broad shoulders. Andy Green, our veterinarian, boasts lips more addictive than sweet tea. I felt quite certain his bedside manner would prove just as appealing. Too bad I'd never find out.

I briefly dated both Andy and Paint last spring. I'd never believed a woman could fall for two men at the same time. Only I'd gone and done precisely that. How could I choose one of them? They'd both risked their necks to save my hide.

Besides, they'd been best friends forever. I wasn't about to come between them. All of which explains why I spent most nights alone at war with my libido.

After Andy and Paint rescued me from a psychopath, we had a long conversation. I admitted I was attracted to both of them but would date neither. I said I wanted the three of us to be good, good friends, without benefits. At least not the benefits they had in mind.

Unfortunately, I regularly fantasized about said benefits.

"Any other scary stuff to hang or are we done?" I asked, enjoying the decorating task far more than I expected.

Andy brushed hay off his jeans, and my eyes lingered a minute too long on his well-formed derriere. "We're finished," he said. "Think we cleaned out the Halloween supplies at all the area stores. Only thing left was a full-sized skeleton down at Roses."

I nodded. "Glad you passed on it. Hope I never see another skeleton on this farm."

My residency at Udderly Kidding Dairy began the same week Tammy, our pot-bellied pig, unearthed a skeleton. That would be a real, used-to-have-skin-attached-to-it skeleton. It was quickly identified as Aunt Eva's unlamented missing husband.

I heard footsteps and turned.

"What a sorry sight for these eagle eyes."

The open barn door framed the owner of the sultry baritone. My first impression was a very fit specimen of the male persuasion. His T-shirt, tucked into jeans slung low on narrow hips, strained to mold to his solid chest and prominent biceps. Red highlights danced in his ginger hair creating a halo effect. The newcomer stepped forward and a sunbeam spilled through a crack in the barn spotlighting his face and an angry scar that zig-zagged from ear to chin to throat before disappearing under his T-shirt collar.

Not a question in the world. Zack Strong.

The words "Inside Straight" marched across his chest. According to Aunt Eva, Zack's Sin City Aces teammates awarded him the custom shirt after a tabloid questioned his sexual preferences. Sure, he was a pro football player, but he was also thirty-four, unmarried, liked to cook, and refused to divulge any details about his love life. Zack's mom told Eva that the quarterback found the insinuations amusing despite their potential to scare off some endorsement opportunities. He was less amused when scandalmongers ambushed him in men's rooms.

Paint scrambled down from the hayloft. "Eagle eyes? How come you didn't see that open receiver in the third quarter? You cost me points in Magic Moonshine's fantasy football league."

Zack shrugged. His smile fleeting. "I did it to spite you, of course. Heard through the grapevine you'd made a bet. Meant I had to blow the pass."

Andy deserted his stuffed dummy to walk over. "You finally admit it. I suspected it all along: your sole ambition is to screw your friends."

"Yeah, you and all the other crazies. At least I now know it's bad juju to talk back. Just stirs up the idiots."

Paint and Zack grasped right hands and pulled each other into a practiced hug/chest bump. I watched the reunion of the old high school buddies unnoticed and apparently forgotten behind a hay bale and yards of gauzy fake cobwebs.

Once the ritual male back-slapping and phony insults ended, Andy, bless his heart, remembered me. "Zack, you haven't been introduced to Udderly Kidding's newest and prettiest resident. Meet Brie Hooker, Eva's niece."

I stepped out from behind my straw bunker to shake hands with the quarterback I'd heard so much about, but had only seen on television. Strong chin. Piercing blue eyes. White teeth. The jagged scar only served to point up his otherwise flawless features.

Moldy Munster. Did all the thirty-somethings in Ardon County have to look so delectable?

I answered my own question as soon as I recalled a sampling of the less-attractive masculine population. I still shuddered remembering the night Paint escorted me to a biker bar. Bloodshot eyes. Greasy hair. Beer breath. Ugh.

"Brie, delighted to meet you." Zack's huge hand engulfed mine, erasing all thoughts of greasy bikers.

"Glad you could make your mom's party," I said. "Carol is always bragging about you."

"If Mom had told me more about you, I'd have come home sooner." Zack continued to hold my hand.

"Hey," Paint said. "Back away, Sport. No horning in on your old buddies. Andy and I have staked our claims on Brie. She just hasn't decided yet that I'm the most desirable. Only a matter of time. You don't stand a chance."

I figured Paint was kidding, sort of.

"What do you think of our haunted barn?" I waved my hand around at the ghoul-infested beams decked out in cobweb finery. Giant hairy spiders lurked in every other web. Come nightfall, all our decorations would look far less hokey. Especially after we added sound effects.

In one corner I spied a particularly realistic web. Then I watched the absolutely genuine spider occupant harvest a trapped fly. Made me think of Mabel, the farm's quite healthy, very robust black snake. If she made an appearance tonight, I hoped any city folk would assume she was rubber and not try to hurt her. She kept our mice population near zero.

"Not bad." Zack craned his neck to look at the ghoul hanging from the loft. "What's the deal? Pay to enter or pay to exit?"

Andy smiled. "Both. 'Course they won't know that when they come in. Twenty-five dollars to enter. Once they're trapped inside, we'll demand a fifty-dollar donation to let them out."

Zack laughed. "Want an inside man, a reverse bouncer? I'll be looking for somewhere to hide after the speeches end. It gets old, politely answering the same questions over and over."

"You poor thing." Paint mimed brushing tears from his cheeks. "Being famous must be a real burden, especially trying to decide what to do with all that dough. What's your contract—twenty mill? That's like winning the lottery every year."

Zack's smile disappeared. "Money's not everything. Sometimes I wish I'd never left Ardon County. Constant pressure from lots of idiots who think they own you."

He shook his head as if to chase away an unsettling thought, then turned my way and smiled. "Sure as heck if I lived here I'd enter the race to woo Brie."

I blushed. The cell phone in my jean pocket vibrated, saving me the need to reply. I pulled out the phone.

"Hi, Mollye, what's up?"

"Is Zack there?" she asked, breathless.

"Oh, yeah." I glanced over at the newcomer.

Mollye barely let me finish.

"I just got wind that Fred Baxter and Pam North may crash tonight's wingding. Tell Zack he might want to reconsider showing his handsome hide. Things could get nasty."

"What are you talking about?"

"Gotta go. Just tell Zack. He'll know."

THREE

I switched off the phone. "Zack, Mollye wanted to warn you that Fred Baxter and Pam North may show up tonight. She seemed to think you might want to reconsider your appearance."

I watched his expression drop.

"Who are these people?"

Zack groaned and parked his attractive posterior on a bale of hay.

Andy gave Zack's shoulder a brotherly squeeze. "The good ol' days," Andy said. "We just strung up ten ghosts and five witches to pop out and scare folks. We don't need real ones."

"Who are you talking about?" I repeated. "Are they dangerous? Do I need to warn Aunt Eva and Carol?"

Zack sighed. "Fred Baxter the Third claims I killed his son, Quatro. We were barely sixteen when our Jeep slammed into a telephone pole."

The words were matter-of-fact. Zack's face told a different story. The poor fellow still lived that horror.

His fingers feathered over the scar that careened down his throat. "I got this souvenir. My buddy wasn't so lucky. Quatro's dad claims I should have been jailed for homicide, and my mom should have been put behind bars for burying the truth."

Paint walked over to sit on the hay bale beside Zack. "Can't believe Pam's coming," he said, switching the subject to the quarterback's second nemesis. "You knew she was a head case way back in high school. But you still went out with her."

The corners of Zack's lips lifted in an almost smile. "Hey, what can I say? She, eh...made up for her faults in other ways." He turned toward me. "We broke up like once a week. Terrible, terrible fights. But the make-ups—"

Paint snickered. "I believe you claimed Pam made your eyeballs do backflips."

Zack dipped his head and held a hand over his eyes in mock shame. "I was a kid. I had no prior experience with backflips."

"Maybe Pam wants to pick a new fight so you two can make-up like you did in the old days," Paint suggested. "Then again she's told everyone you're a world-class schmuck for tossing her aside soon as you became a hot-shot athlete. I know that's a lie. You were still a walk-on, two-hundred-pound weakling. Hadn't even made the college starting lineup when you dumped her."

"Guilty as charged." Zack shrugged. "Promised I'd be faithful. Didn't happen. Hey, I was eighteen and discovered a whole flock of good-looking coeds who didn't need screaming matches to put them in the mood."

While I found the backstories interesting, my main concern was making sure old grudges didn't ruin tonight's event. "The party's private. We don't have to let this terrible twosome in if they show up."

"Not an option," Zack barked. "Can see tomorrow's *Ardon Chronicle*. 'Carol Stone Refuses to Face Constituents.'" Zack's hand waved as he mimicked writing the headline in the air. "Barring them would only give ammunition to Mom's opponent.

"That's how the *Chronicle*'s owner uses her claws," he continued. "She'd hint Mom was ducking questions about her 'unsavory' past. There's a reason people call her 'Alley Cat.' Let Fred and Pam in if they show. I've sparred with the nastiest of so-called reporters for tabloids and blogs. I can handle anything Ardon County throws at me."

Zack stood. The good old days' reunion cheer had evaporated.

"Great seeing you guys and meeting you, Brie. Time to collect Mom and head home. She claimed my old bedroom for her campaign office. She gets a new office. I get to bunk in the closet-sized guest room. Plus I have to move all the furniture. It's wrong on so many levels."

He sighed dramatically. "Talk to y'all tonight. I'm here till Sunday. Maybe we can do something fun tomorrow. Of course, my contract limits what 'fun' I'm allowed—no touch football, no skiing, no horseback riding. Any activity with injury potential is off limits."

Paint grinned. "So that's why there are no reports of you with a lady?"

Zack laughed. "No, I'm allowed to be with a lady as long as she's petite, pretty and smells good." He turned to capture me in his cobalt gaze. "Brie, if you'd like to trade these dipwads for more mature male company, I'm at your service. Day or night."

Hmmm. The thought of spending an evening with Zack raised goosebumps. This past year I'd been one of about a million women who enjoyed taking note of his tight honey buns every time he ran onto the football field. I conceded men their cheerleaders since their jiggling flesh got much less air time than the hunks on the field.

Maybe it was time to move beyond make-believe. It had been nineteen months since I discovered my fiancé was cheating on me and I broke off the engagement. Maybe I'd do more than admire men on a TV screen if I weren't so pooped most days. Between farm chores and my efforts to renovate Summer Place, the run-down mansion I eventually hoped to turn into a B&B, I had little time for extracurricular activities. Plus the only interested, and interesting, males I encountered—beside my billy goat pals—were Paint and Andy. Off-limits temptations.

After Zack left, Paint and Andy climbed ladders to string up a big vinyl banner, *Carol Strong for a Strong South Carolina*, above the Udderly Kidding Dairy entrance. I directed from below, "A little higher on the left, lower on the right." Then the guys hoisted another banner over the barn door. *Halloween Thrills* appeared in big letters. Below a smaller tag line read, *Scarier than an Editorial in the* Ardon Chronicle.

Though I'd have loved to quiz Paint and Andy with more questions about Zack's past, they were substandard gossip sources. They knew the dirt, but they were his buddies and biased. Mollye, however, would know—and tell—all, including spicy rumors and whatever conspiracy theories Allie Gerome had championed on her rag's opinion page.

My source arrived at five o'clock, just after Paint and Andy headed home to change for our Halloween fundraiser. The men refused to give me a clue about their costumes. Their teasing smirks implied they were quite pleased with their get-ups. I could only imagine.

Moll jangled as she hopped down from the psychedelic van she used to promote her store, Starry Skies. Mom called it a "woo-woo" shop. Starry Skies' inventory included homeopathic remedies, all manner of herbs and oils, astrological doodads, Aunt Eva's goat soap, and Moll's own distinctive pottery. My friend also boosted income doing palm and Tarot readings; though she insisted her psychic offerings were strictly for fun.

"Is that your costume?" I asked as Mollye's brightly colored skirt swirled around her legs. Multiple earrings and bracelets added tinkling sound effects as she moved.

"Heck no. I came straight from work. My costume's in back. Yours, too."

"Little Bo Peep, right?" I figured it was kind of appropriate, though I tended goats not sheep. Why quibble over a baa or a bleat? I also hoped it would be somewhat demure. Leaving my friend to pick a costume invited disaster.

"Nope," Moll said. "And not a peep out of you about my substitute. Best I could do with last-minute leftovers. The previous Bo Peep must have eaten too many lamb chops. She popped out all the important seams in the costume. Would love to have seen that explosion."

"*Leftover Liverwurst*. Quit stalling. What costume horror did you get me?"

Mollye smiled. "You like to swim, right? A mermaid seemed highly appropriate."

How bad could it be? So what if I'd have to mince around all night like a Geisha with my legs and feet confined in a tail? Could be worse, much worse. Madonna. Tarzan's Jane.

"Thanks," I said as she handed me a long, no peek-a-boo garment bag. "Let's go inside so I can get a good look at what you've done to me. How about you? What are you wearing?"

"You'll love it. But I'm not trading. Besides, your mermaid costume wouldn't fit a robust figure like mine." Mollye ran her hands down her sides like she was channeling Beyoncé.

Uh, oh. Did Mollye mean my costume wasn't large enough to fit her or was she saying it was plain skimpy?

It didn't take long to find the answer. Skimpy was too generous an adjective. It made me rethink my aversion to a Madonna, or even a

Tarzan's Jane outfit. Either would have provided more coverage. The mermaid's sequined strapless bra was paired with sequined undies smaller than the lace hanky Grandma Hooker used to carry. Attached to the undies, the gauzy tail would afford onlookers, willing or not, a peek-a-boo look at bare skin from my ankles all the way up to my hoo-ha.

I stripped and shimmied into the costume. Good grief, my boobies and hoo-ha would glow in the dark. The gauzy tail ended in a rubber, fan-shaped fin that made plopping sounds with every move.

"I can't wear this." I shook my head. "Un uh. No way. I'll put on one of Aunt Eva's plaid flannel shirts, wear that stained canvas hat of hers, and carry a rifle. I'll come as Eva, Great Plaid Coyote Hunter."

"The heck you will," Eva said as she entered my bedroom. "That's my costume."

"How can it be your costume, Eva?" Mollye laughed. "You wear that all the time."

"True, but it'll give me an excuse to carry my peacemaker. I hear tell there may be trouble tonight."

Eva finally gave my mermaid attire her full attention and cackled like one of her egg-laying hens. "Perfect. Won't be a man at the party who doesn't approve. But it's a good thing your daddy won't be here. You look gorgeous. Sexy. Go for it."

Mollye pulled a long, blonde wig out of another bag. "If you're really into modesty, you can wear this. Us blondes have more fun." She patted her thick blonde hair that was streaked this week with bright green. I was surprised she hadn't picked orange for Halloween.

"Bet these curls come all the way down to your butt-crack," Mollye added as she shook out the wig. "Not that your butt-crack shows. At least if you don't bend over."

Moll and Eva joined in another round of guffaws. "Oh, don't be a fuddy-duddy," added my friend, who'd accurately nailed the fact she couldn't squeeze into my mermaid suit. At five-foot-six, Mollye had me by two inches, forty pounds, and at least two cup sizes. I was curvy, but my friend's bazooms measured in double-D territory.

Moll was right about one thing. I really did envy her costume. She'd transformed herself into a fruit basket. Perfect for a vegan, though I had to admit, apropos for my zany friend, too. Her pullover costume boasted puffed out cloth apples, bananas, pears, and oranges. The fruits protruded hither and yon. She even had a matching head dress.

"I'll invite the boys to pinch and see what's ripe." She winked. "See my earrings? Strawberries and grapes. I'll carry some real apples and invite any male of interest to take a bite."

With a magician's flair, Moll pulled one last item from her tote bag. The glittery, half-face mask perfectly matched my fishy sequin scales. "Almost forgot. If you want to wimp out, you can go incognito. Leave the mask and wig on to keep the men guessing and drooling."

The fake hair and mask would help. A little. If only I could skip the whole evening.

Too bad I'd promised Aunt Eva and Carol I'd oversee the caterers and make sure no one went hungry or thirsty. Paint would take care of the alcoholic beverages. He'd already set up a tent offering several flavors of 'shine from his Magic Moonshine distillery. I wondered if it would be staffed by the same sexy barmaid who served as a model for the artwork on his truck. If Mollye's bosoms were cantaloupes, hers were...okay, stop, not her fault. Poor woman probably suffered from a bad back. How could she not?

I hoped this party would bring in money for Carol's campaign. Allie Gerome gave barrels of free newspaper ink to Wade Reece, Carol's opponent in the governor's race, while a super PAC paid for ads and radio spots to sell the creep in all of South Carolina's major markets.

All the ads repeated Wade's ridiculous allegations ad nauseam. They painted Carol as a Second Amendment foe, eager to confiscate every six-shooter in South Carolina. Why? Because she opposed public school teachers packing heat in the classroom. Of course the ads failed to mention Carol had her very own concealed carry permit and her son loved to hunt.

I sighed. I'd do what I could to help make Carol's fundraiser a success. Maybe I'd down a few shots of Paint's white lightning to stay warm. This fish-out-of-water would need all the help she could get to make it through an evening dressed in plastic wrap.

How low would the temperatures drop tonight? And how hot would matters get for Zack and Carol if those unwanted guests showed up?

FOUR

Keeping the buffet tables fully stocked doesn't normally require total concentration. But with my feet straight-jacketed by my tail, I was forced to mince back and forth balancing trays. If I didn't watch it, I could easily arrange my own face-plant without any assistance from a billy goat.

Spending way too much time staring at my feet, I had limited opportunities to admire the gathering's ingenious costumes. Still I saw enough to know my attire would not take top honors as most revealing or outrageous. Udderly was packed. If anything, our estimate of two-hundred guests was low. The majority had come fully costumed. The rest made half-hearted gestures at the come-in-costume request.

I saw several raccoon look-alikes. Probably wasn't their plan but that's what happened when they appropriated their kids' Lone Ranger masks. Tiny masks on huge faces. A few folks had even dug through dusty attic chests to resurrect Nixon masks complete with trademark jowls and bushy eyebrows. All the Nixon imposters seemed obliged to parrot the line: "I'm not a crook." If I heard it one more time, I'd scream.

By six o'clock, our Friday night gathering was already packed. Yet, I had no problem picking Paint out of the crowd, even though his face was entirely hidden. Who else would come as a bright red can of spray-paint, complete with a nozzle on top of his head? He approached me and tugged on some gadget near his ear, a puff of air fanned red streamers around his head.

"Oh, my little mermaid, come paint the town with me," he murmured.

"Don't think so," I replied. "I fear your aerosol might be plugged."

"I'm sure we can find several ways to fix that."

"Leave my Lovely of the Sea alone," a deep, easy-to-recognize voice commanded. Definitely Andy, though his head-to-toe beagle uniform with wagging tail provided excellent camouflage.

"Hi, Andy. Hi, Paint. What are the two of you up to?"

"I know what I'd like to do. Dump Andy and cavort down yonder in Eva's pond with a mermaid," Paint said.

The beagle punched the paint can's arm. "Hey, give Brie a break. By now, she's probably been hit on so many times she feels like a piñata."

"Ooh, bad pun." I laughed. "You didn't answer my question. What nefarious activities are you two planning?"

"We're about to open our Udderly Haunted Barn of Horrors," Andy said. "Most people seem to have chowed down and are ready for some fun."

"I'll join you right after Carol's talk. ARGH is sponsoring tonight's fundraiser. Since I'm ARGH's treasurer, the least I can do is pay attention to what Carol has to say."

Andy's eyebrows hitched up. "How did you get roped into being treasurer?"

I sighed. "You know what they say about never missing a meeting? You get volunteered. Since I'm a one-time banker, Eva offered my services when the last treasurer retired to Florida. Actually, I don't mind. I really believe in ARGH's mission. Did you know Lilly co-founded the group?"

Paint chuckled. "I still remember her campaign to name the group 'Ardon for Responsible Growth Here.' Lilly argued ARGH was a perfect acronym since she wanted to scream 'argh' each time she listened to county council bozos defeat any attempt to plan ahead."

I chuckled. "Yep. My aunts always had a decided preference for names that would draw a laugh. Udderly Kidding Dairy? But they never suspected I'd wind up a vegan when they championed my cheesy name. Brie was their compromise between Bridgette and Marie, my grandmothers' names."

"I like your name," Andy said. "It suits you."

I shrugged. "Better than a lot of names they could have paired with Hooker."

Mollye sidled up to Paint and Andy and linked arms with them. "You mean like Happy?" She'd been eavesdropping. Sometimes I thought her large metal earrings were cleverly disguised listening devices.

"Carol's about to give her spiel," Mollye said. "Let's head over."

"We'll visit you boys in a bit. Can't wait to see how people react to our handiwork. Make sure Mollye gets the full treatment. She deserves a good scare. Payback for picking my costume."

Paint's gaze roved from my tail to my mask. "Mollye, you have our undying gratitude."

Mollye took a little bow. "My pleasure, gents," she said, then squeaked like a mouse in a trap when I pinched her rear-end ripe fruit.

Before the program began, Moll insisted we first visit the "honcho" table so she could pay her respects. I followed along even though I'd already completed my "howdy" duties.

Mollye gave the guest of honor's costume a nod of approval. "Love the pack-of-cards theme, Carol."

The candidate, decked out as the queen of hearts, laughed. "Wanted a tie in with Zack's Sin City Aces. Too bad the only costume I could find for him was a Joker."

The woman seated next to Carol stood and hugged Mollye. Linda Rodriguez was Carol's passionate campaign manager. Every time I saw her I admired the striking contrast between her bronzed skin and that cloud of fluffy white hair.

"Hey, Moll," Linda said. "Good to see you. Sure I can't talk you into serving on the board of Ardon's League of Women Voters?"

"Nope, nobody can fill your shoes," Mollye countered.

The brief dossier Eva'd provided made me inclined to like Linda even before we met. Born to immigrant apple pickers in Ardon County, she'd worked like crazy to get a Ph.D. in biology and join Clemson's faculty.

I cocked my head as I considered what I assumed was Linda's biology-inspired costume. Was she a germ or an enzyme?

Mollye next greeted Phil Owens, who co-founded ARGH with Lilly, and Bob Codner, the current president. Aunt Eva and I were in talks with the two men about ARGH serving as trustee for an Udderly conservation easement.

"What's this?" Moll teased Phil, as she tugged on the fake corn silk that spilled around his neck like a stringy ascot.

"I'm an ear of corn." He smiled. "No shucking allowed."

The former pilot made one very tall ear of corn. A lean, fit hiking enthusiast, the only clue to his age—seventy—was his silver hair.

Moll next turned to ARGH's president. "Hey, Bob, how come you didn't come in costume?"

"I did," he answered. "I'm a lumberjack." He put one hand on his hip and another on his head and twirled to show off his plaid wool jacket and frayed jeans.

"What a coincidence that you wear that same costume every day." Moll chuckled.

"Hmm, now that you mention it." Bob's brown eyes twinkled. He was in fact a modern-day lumberjack who owned a large timberland tract and saw mill.

With Moll's greetings out of the way, we searched for vacant seats at one of the picnic tables. Most people had finished eating but were still swilling Magic Moonshine. That encouraged periodic eruptions of raucous laughter. Carol had her work cut out to get them to pay attention.

"Did you spot Zack's jilted high school honey or that Fred Baxter fellow?" I asked Mollye.

She craned her neck to scrutinize faces, at least the ones not covered by masks. "Nope, haven't seen hide nor hair of Pam or Fred."

"You still owe me the complete story. You're a virtual encyclopedia of old scandals."

"Your history lesson will have to wait. The program's about to begin."

Linda tapped the microphone on the mini-stage and the distinctive screech and whompf of irritated electronics focused the attention of all but the very hard of hearing or totally soused.

"Thanks for coming," she said. "We appreciate your support of our distinguished candidate, Carol Strong, who, WHEN elected, will drag our state into the twenty-first century. Let's put our hands together for South Carolina's next governor."

Loud applause erupted as Carol came on stage and hugged her campaign manager. Though both women were average height and weight, the similarities ended there. Carol's skin was so white it almost looked translucent. Whenever I glanced at her well-toned arms, I could easily trace a fine network of blue veins. While I doubted the sixty-year-old's mahogany red hair was natural, it was well done, and provided a perfect foil for her flashing blue eyes.

"I hope Linda's fortune-telling skills are on the money." Her honeyed voice invited listeners in. "Usually the Republican primary decides the election in this very red state. Like many of you, my vote would have gone to Republican primary winner Martin Kelly, if he hadn't died.

"But, after Wade Reece was forced down our throats by a strident minority, I decided to run as an independent."

She paused to scan the quieted audience. "Wade wants to let big oil drill unfettered off our coastline despite warnings of potential disasters and pleas from our shrimpers and tourist meccas. He'd open our state parks and wilderness areas to logging and mining, and run an oil pipe through the middle of a wildlife sanctuary."

She gave the crowd time to digest her words, then added, "What we don't need are dinosaurs like Wade Reece."

A generous round of applause prompted Carol to smile.

Once the clapping tailed off, she raised the mike again. "We're here tonight because we think South Carolina deserves a brighter—"

"Shut your traitorous trap, bitch."

I turned toward the commotion. A black hearse sped down Udderly's drive, flinging gravel before fishtailing to a stop.

For a moment, I was confused. A hearse? It certainly fit with our Halloween theme but why did it have little Confederate flags stuck on the front fenders? It looked like a redneck's request for a last ride.

A man leaned out the passenger side of the hearse, holding a bullhorn. The interloper wasn't alone. The hearse was trailed by two motorcycles and a beat-up truck flying an oversized Stars and Bars.

"Deviled ham! Who is that guy, Mollye?"

"Chester Finley. Shows up at every political meeting and jabbers nonsense. He's the reason County Council imposed a time limit and started using that obnoxious clock. They don't even bring it out if he isn't there. Chester's one of the CAVE men—Citizens Against Virtually Everything."

I watched Chester bring the megaphone back to his lips. “You shame your Confederate relatives, trying to steal our God-given property rights and our guns.”

Okay, his “traitorous” epithet was simply a warm up.

I was glad the bullhorn mostly hid the man’s snarling mouth and wild eyes.

“You have no right to tell us true natives what we can or can’t do on our land,” he yelled. “Our forefathers shed their blood for this land, and there’ll be more bloodshed if you try and—”

Before he could suck in a breath to finish, Carol’s supporters started yelling back, drowning him out. “Get out of here.”... “Who do you think you are, the Ku Klux Klan?”... “Native? Come off it. Was your grandfather a Cherokee?”

I saw movement. Zack ran toward the hearse, looking more like a linebacker than a quarterback. He jerked the passenger door open and tried to grab Chester’s bullhorn.

“If it ain’t the bitch’s bastard. Too bad you didn’t die in that car wreck.”

Chester lashed out with a booted foot. The kick connected with Zack’s thigh and pushed him off balance.

Zack quickly regained his footing and grabbed Chester’s leg, pulling him out of the hearse. The burly loudmouth staggered as Zack snatched the bullhorn.

Chester saw his chance and sucker-punched Zack in the nose. On autopilot, the quarterback returned the favor. Yowzer. Was that bone I heard cracking?

The CAVE men riding the motorcycles started to dismount, and two men jumped from the bed of the truck that brought up the rear. What in blazes? Were we going to have an old-fashioned brawl?

Lights flashed as people snapped pictures. Wouldn’t be long before this went viral on YouTube.

“Zack, stop!” Carol shouted into her microphone. “He’s not worth it. Let him go.”

Zack released the handful of shirt he’d used to haul the cretin to his feet. Then a gunshot got everyone’s attention. Had to be Eva. A minute later my aunt stepped from behind the hearse and into my line of sight.

"Zack, let him go. Chester, get your sorry hide back in your daddy's hearse. You and your little buddies get off my property. Right. Now. If you're here another minute, the next body your father picks up for embalming might be yours. I figure your hunk-a-junk truck broke down again. Did you even tell your daddy what you were planning when you borrowed his funeral home hearse?"

"Lesbo bitch," Chester screeched as he bent to pick up his bullhorn. The man's jeans slipped lower on his hips giving everyone an unwanted view of his butt crack and Spiderman briefs. While one hand swiped at the blood oozing from his nose, the other hitched up his trousers. His butt cleavage thankfully disappeared along with his Spiderman jockeys.

Zack clenched his fists. He clearly wanted to whack Chester again.

The redneck stumbled toward the borrowed hearse. With a snarl, the party-crasher climbed into his Halloween ride. His buddies had long since kick-started their bikes or scrambled back in the truck bed.

Eva kept her shotgun leveled at the invaders as they raced their motors and spun their tires. Gravel kicked up by the tires' reverse spin smacked the hearse's undercarriage. The rocky hailstorm didn't die down until Chester's to-die-for ride backed through the main gate. Did they think the racket made their retreat manlier?

"Who ordered the ghouls?" Carol asked, trying to lighten the mood. "Given the excitement, my son will buy the next round of 'shine from Magic Moonshine. Just hope he hasn't injured his arm. It's better suited to throwing footballs than punches."

There was polite laughter, and Zack yelled, "Drinks are on me."

"We have more entertainment in store—and before you even ask, it's not a boxing match," Carol added. "Be sure to pay a visit to the Udderly Haunted Barn of Horrors, though its thrills may seem a little tame now."

I turned to Mollye. "With free drinks, they'll be lined up six-deep at the Magic Moonshine tent. I'll go help."

My friend shook her head. "Not me. I plan to be drinking not serving. I need it."

I coveted a drink to settle my nerves, too, but I figured Udderly's residents ought to keep their heads clear—and their weapons ready. I posed little danger holding a shotgun. But watch out if I'm armed with a rolling pin. Too bad I could only land a blow if the other person stood stock still in arm's reach. Anyone could outrun me in my stupid mermaid costume.

FIVE

I slipped in the back of the Magic Moonshine tent and told the frantic barmaid to shout orders to me and I'd pour. "Thanks," said Vera, the busty server.

As we fell into a routine, I appreciated the Clemson coed's keen sense of humor. She awarded a zinger to every Dick and Harry who made a suggestive comment.

"That's a big mug. Be careful. Your hands are mighty small."

"Can I see some ID? You look old, but you talk like a pimple-faced teen."

We laughed as the chastened loudmouths slunk away. Thankfully, they were few in number. After fifteen minutes, the line dwindled to less than half a dozen customers. I recognized several faces sneaking back for seconds.

"Think I can handle it now," Vera said.

"Okay." I glanced over at my costumed friend, Mollye, slumped on a stump. I walked over. "Think you've had enough moonshine to qualify as a fruitcake?" I asked. "You know fruitcakes can be stashed in a closet for years without, well, losing a thing."

"I may have marinated a bit, but that just makes me tastier." She smirked. "Anyway, a fish with scales on her boobs should never insult fruit. Let's go visit your Udderly Haunted Barn of Horrors, see what you and your beaus think is scary."

I'd been looking forward to Mollye experiencing our spooky soundtrack and pop-up ghouls. I kinda hoped our surprises might shrivel her grapes and brown her bananas.

As we approached the entrance, a dozen people stumbled out of the barn. Some were running.

"Gotta give you credit," Mollye said. "Those folks look scared. You must have done one heck of a decorating job."

I shook my head. "Something's very wrong."

Andy and Paint were nowhere in sight. At least one of them should have been manning the entrance and taking donations to beef up Carol's campaign fund.

I tried to run, too, though my tail-shortened steps made it feel like I was swimming upstream. As I passed one of the exiting couples, I caught a snatch of conversation. "Do you think he's really dead?"

I shuffle-hopped once I entered the twilight of the barn's interior. While I knew the space like the back of my hand, the eerie lighting and creepy displays forced me to watch my step. I spotted a tall silhouette toward the back of the barn. Paint. The distinctive shape of his fake aerosol headpiece provided a positive ID.

"Paint," I yelled. "What's happened? Is someone hurt?" My heart raced. Could someone have fallen and broken a neck in the darkness?

Paint jerked off his head piece and flung it to the ground as I reached him. His face showed real shock. "It's Zack. Andy just found him." Paint nodded at the adjacent barn stall.

I peered over the wooden divider. Zack's body was spread-eagled, his head turned to the side, one foot bent in an unnatural position. His nose looked crooked, too. Then I saw a sliver of white bone peeking through.

"Oh, no. Is he breathing?"

Zack's head was surrounded by a halo of blood that looked almost black under the dim, pumpkin lights strung from the hayloft. Blood—at least I assumed that's what the blackish goo was—dripped from the long, slender tines of a pitchfork leaning against the barn wall.

Oh, my God. This was no accident.

Andy knelt beside Zack's body. "Someone attacked him with that pitchfork," he said as he looked up at Paint and me. "Think it broke his clavicle, and there's a deep gash in his scalp. His nose may have broken when he fell. He's lost a lot of blood. We need an ambulance. Fast. Brie, call 911."

I patted my hip where my cell phone was normally parked in a pocket. "Oh, no. I don't have my cell." Again I cursed my skimpy costume.

"No worries." Mollye wheezed. Focused on Zack's crumpled form, I hadn't heard my friend come up behind me.

She yanked a phone from a fold in the bosom of her costume. "Last spring, I developed a real fondness for cell phones. Always keep mine handy," she added as she waited for emergency dispatch to pick up.

"What can I do?" I asked.

"I saw Dr. Bowman earlier," Paint answered. "Go find him. He can help Andy till the ambulance comes."

"Good idea. Go," Andy urged.

Mollye squinted into the darkness. "Think the attacker's still here?" Her voice wavered. "He could be hiding."

"Probably long gone," Paint answered. "I hustled everyone I could find out of here. But I'll keep watch. Don't worry about us. Just go."

"Ambulance is on its way," Mollye chimed in as she put away her phone. "Should be here in five minutes. They were right down the road. I'll wait for them outside."

"Be careful. Don't take any chances," I said as I wriggled out of my mermaid tail. I needed to move faster than a waddle. I exited the barn and raced toward the center of the crowd, naked legs pumping, loose strands from my long blonde wig whipping my face. The whistles and catcalls barely registered. A few raised cell phones in my direction. The sequined mask that extended from my forehead to my cheeks chafed, but I wasn't about to take it off. I ran faster hoping to appear as an indistinct streak if anyone tried to post to Instagram.

A familiar plaid shirt came into view. "Eva. Hold up," I yelled.

Oh, hog jowls. Carol stood right beside my gun-toting aunt. I couldn't just blurt out that Carol's only son was unconscious and bleeding on the barn floor.

"What's wrong?" Eva demanded, eyes wide as she stared at me decked out in what looked like a stripper's spangled costume.

"Someone's injured. It's bad, real bad." My words tumbled on top of each other. "Andy's with him. An ambulance is on the way. We were hoping Dr. Bowman could help. Have you seen him?"

Eva pointed. "Over there. The tiger costume."

I turned to run, but an iron grip on my forearm stopped me. "It's Zack, isn't it?"

How did Carol guess? Had I given it away when I tried to avoid her eyes?

I nodded. "Yes. I'm so sorry."

"How? What?" Anguish creased the widow's face.

"Sorry I don't know more. Andy and Paint are with him. They're in the barn."

Carol's hand dropped and she took off in an awkward jog. She shuddered as sobs racked her body. She stumbled and fell to her knees.

Eva caught up and helped her to her feet. "It'll be all right," she whispered. My aunt repeated the words, over and over like a prayer. The incantation echoed in my head as I sprinted on. I had a mission. Shanghai the doctor, take him to the barn. I was glad I had a duty that let me flee Carol's anguish.

Eva said that Zack's car crash twenty years ago had almost done Carol in.

Would losing him now be any easier?

Please, lord, let Zack live. Let it be all right.

SIX

Dr. Bowman and I hustled to the back of the barn. Paint and I scrunched into a neighboring stall to stay out of the way.

"How's he doing?" Dr. Bowman asked as he joined Andy, kneeling on the opposite side of Zack's body.

"Pulse is thready, and his breathing's awfully labored," Andy answered. "I felt inside his mouth. No obstruction. There's a big knot on the back of his head, next to the gash. Someone walloped Zack good. I'd bet on a concussion."

A stray noise made me jump. Couldn't help it. I looked up to scan the barn's dark recesses and the overhead loft.

"How long till the ambulance arrives?" the doc asked.

"Should be here any minute," Paint said.

"Good." The doc turned to look up at us. "Paint, bring the ambulance crew back here, and make sure only EMT and law enforcement come inside."

His order brought home an unwelcome fact: our barn had become a crime scene.

"We need to wait for the EMTs to move him in case there's a spinal injury," Dr. Bowman said as he took Zack's pulse. "He's lost quite a bit of blood. I'm worried there may be injuries we can't see."

The doc barely finished his sentence when we heard sirens. A minute later, Paint ushered in two double-timing paramedics.

Doc Bowman and Andy exited the stall so the first responders could cradle Zack's head and roll him onto a stretcher. His limp body and blanched face didn't look like they belonged to the healthy, hardy Zack who'd punched Chester an hour ago.

"How long has he been unconscious?" one of the paramedics asked.

"I'm not sure. I found him about fifteen minutes ago," Andy

answered.

The second EMT motioned toward the Halloween decorations and feed buckets littering the floor. "Help me move this stuff. We need a clear path to the ambulance."

When they wheeled Zack outside, Mollye and I followed at a respectful distance. I spotted Eva and Carol. They'd pushed their way through the crowd of gawkers. When Carol saw her son, she broke from my aunt's side and raced to Zack.

Carol cringed at the sight of her son's damaged face. "Oh, my God, he's dying, isn't he?"

"No, Carol," Dr. Bowman soothed. "I saw no indication Zack's heart or lungs are damaged. Your son's in tip-top physical shape. He has everything going for him."

Carol tugged hard on the sleeve of a first responder. "Please, I need to ride with him."

"Ma'am, I'll let you ride up front," the paramedic answered.

I recognized him from our brief encounter last spring. Steve? I glanced at his name tag. Yes. Kind and competent Steve.

"I need room in the back of the ambulance to move around," Steve explained. "That will let me do everything possible to help your son."

"I'll be at the hospital as soon as I can," Eva called to Carol as she scrambled into the ambulance's front passenger seat.

Carol didn't even look back.

As the ambulance pulled away, a sheriff's cruiser slid into the space it left near our haunted barn. Two men jumped out—Sheriff Kyle Mason, and Deputy Danny McCoy, Mollye's sometime boyfriend. The new sheriff, a no-nonsense, spit-and-polish professional, appeared to be the exact opposite of his corrupt predecessor, who was now serving a prison sentence.

The sheriff spotted Eva and hurried toward her. As he huddled with my aunt, another cruiser arrived, and two more deputies joined the law enforcement gaggle. Eva pointed the sheriff toward our Udderly Haunted Barn of Horrors gang.

The temperature had dropped below fifty, and goosebumps decorated my all-too-exposed appendages. I wouldn't have been surprised to see icicles dangling from the tawdry remnants of my mermaid costume.

I'd discarded my scratchy half-mask and blonde wig after escorting Dr. Bowman inside the barn. The wig had turned my scalp into an itchy swamp. My newly freed damp curls probably made me look like a Betty Boop stripper.

So far, none of the men had offered me a jacket. Then again, how could they? Andy was wearing a full-body beagle suit, and Paint was encased in a red cylinder with footies. Now that Paint had discarded his aerosol hat, he looked like a grizzled toddler in a scarlet onesie.

As soon as the sheriff finished with us, I planned to run to the cabin and put on real clothes. If that didn't happen soon, I'd steal a blanket from Eva's horse. At this point, warmth more than trumped odor.

Two more cruisers pulled up, ejecting four more deputies into the on-scene excitement. The sheriff rushed over to our first-on-the-scene group. "Eva says you found the victim in a stall at the back of the barn. Did anyone see the attack?"

"No," Andy answered. "Unfortunately. I don't even know how long Zack was unconscious and bleeding before I found him."

"Any possibility the attacker's still inside?"

"It's possible," Paint answered. "I tried to search, but it's dark and there are places to hide, especially in the loft."

"Danny, take those men with you, check it out, and secure the crime scene," the sheriff ordered. "Now let's hear the who, what, and where. Who found the victim?"

"I did," Andy replied. "Paint and I were working the entrance to the Haunted Barn, which was also the exit. We charged twenty-five dollars per person to enter. Then, when folks got ready to leave, we tried to hit them up for an exit fee. All in good fun. No one really had to pay to get out.

"Anyway, Zack wanted to see our handiwork. He peeled off two hundred-dollar bills as his entry fee. Paint and I were busy chatting up Haunted Barn customers, so maybe half an hour went by before we realized Zack hadn't come out."

"You went in after him?" the sheriff interrupted. "Where'd you find him?"

"First time through, I didn't see him," Andy said. "On my second circuit I realized the pitchfork I'd duct-taped to our scarecrow was missing. Then I peeked in the stall behind the dummy. The lighting was poor. Zack was sprawled face down, the pitchfork stuck in his body, up near his shoulder. For a second, I thought Zack was pulling my leg. Then I came closer and saw the blood."

The sheriff's eyes narrowed. "Isn't it kind of odd that no one saw or heard the attack with so many people inside the barn?"

Paint shrugged. "It was dark. The soundtrack we ran through the speakers played loud screams, rattling chains, groans. Even if Zack yelled or moaned, people probably assumed it was part of our scary audio. Whoever did this could have waited for a window of opportunity when no one was around. Most people came through in groups. It wasn't a steady stream."

The sheriff turned back to Andy. "What'd you do after you discovered the body?"

Sheriff Mason sounded brusque. I understood. Time mattered. Plus a media feeding frenzy seemed inevitable given that someone had tried to maim or maybe kill a pro-football quarterback worth millions to his team. The fact that Zack was the son of a gubernatorial candidate would add to the turmoil. Reporters would be all over the sheriff and his investigation.

Andy sighed. "I pulled the pitchfork out of Zack's shoulder and leaned it against the stall so I had room to assess his condition. I'm a veterinarian with medical training. Zack was my main concern, not evidence. I checked his pulse and breathing and tried to staunch the blood from his head wound."

"Did you leave him to get help?"

"No. I heard a noise. Then a giggle. Saw shadows. Realized it was a couple of girls just a few feet away. I jumped up and yelled. They just giggled some more. Thought it was part of our haunted fright skit. I yelled louder. Probably swore. Told 'em it was for real, and a man was going to bleed to death if they didn't move it. Swore again and told 'em to go get the man collecting entrance fees."

Paint nodded. "The girls were hysterical when they found me. Couldn't make sense of what they were saying. So I went to find Andy. Once I saw Zack, I cleared everyone out of the barn. Didn't want someone else to be attacked."

Danny exited the barn. "We didn't find anyone inside."

The sheriff turned back to Paint. "Could the attacker be one of the people you chased out of the barn?"

Paint pinched the bridge of his nose; his eyes closed. "Guess it's possible. Most of the folks seemed to be with friends. Afraid I just assumed the attacker was some crazy loner."

The sheriff's gaze roamed over the barn. "Can you put together a list of the people who went into the barn before the attack?" He doffed his hat and used a handkerchief to swipe at his almost bald head. Sweat beaded on his forehead despite the evening chill.

Paint's head dropped and his shoulders slumped. "'Fraid not, Sheriff. Most people wore costumes and masks. I could ID maybe a third of them. Tonight's guests were a real mix. Even without disguises, I wouldn't have known quite a few of them. We didn't take names, just money."

"Terrific," Sheriff Mason grumbled. "How many possibles are we talking about?"

"At least forty people paid to come in," Andy said. "Like Paint, I didn't keep track. Not sure it matters. Zack's attacker didn't have to arrive or leave through the front of the barn. We barricaded the back door with hay bales, but it would have been easy to sneak through a window. The first people I'd interview are those crazies who follow Chester Finley."

"What? Why would Chester Finley or his friends come after Zack?" the sheriff looked genuinely puzzled.

"Zack slugged Chester a little over an hour ago," Paint began, explaining that the quarterback had decked the idiot in retaliation for Chester's sucker-punch.

"Great, just great." The sheriff sighed. "Andy, you—and you alone—take me back to where you found the victim. No sense contaminating the crime scene more than it already is. The rest of you head to the sheriff's department where an officer can take your statements. Looks to be a long night."

The sheriff briefly glanced in my direction. "You can put on street clothes first, but don't go talking to anyone but our officers. No reporters. Understood?"

"Yes, sir." Grateful and relieved I headed to the cabin to exchange my siren-of-the-sea costume for well-worn jeans and a sweatshirt. I was happy to avoid another look at the crime scene. My mind kept revisiting the blood drip, drip, dripping from the pitchfork's long, sharp tines. I shuddered, thinking about the needle-like ends thrusting into Zack. Had he seen it coming? Did he recognize his attacker?

I prayed Zack would recover quickly. That he'd be able to tell officers which of Chester's maniac followers had attacked him. I shared my friends' suspicions that one of Chester's crew must have sneaked back to even the score with Zack.

But evil isn't always so obvious. There were other possibilities. Could Zack have acquired new enemies in Las Vegas? Or had one of the quarterback's long-time foes stalked him and seized on the barn's shadows to strike?

No one had mentioned seeing either of the homegrown enemies who'd threatened to come and taunt Zack.

Braunshweiger on a bun. Costumes and masks sure complicated things.

SEVEN

I met Eva inside the cabin as she grabbed the keys to her truck. "I'm going to the hospital to be with Carol," she said.

"Is Billy going with you?" I asked.

Billy Jackson, a farrier who shoes our equines, slides his own shoes under Aunt Eva's bed at least twice a week. Both my aunt and Billy are independent cusses, and the informal arrangement suits them, though it sometimes bugs my mom and dad.

"No. I asked him to stay here tonight. I don't want you here alone. He was planning to stay anyway to help with tomorrow's clean-up."

"The sheriff wants me to come to the station, but I'll come back to Udderly as soon as I can," I said. "Billy and I can handle the morning chores if you want to stay at the hospital."

"Good," Eva answered. "Our part-timers should show up in the morning, like always, for Saturday chores. The sheriff said only the horse barn will be kept off limits. That won't interfere with milking the goats or any of our other regular farm chores."

I glanced out the cabin window and saw a sea of headlights.

"Looks like the exodus is going to take a while," I said.

"The sheriff promised his deputies would clear the way for me," Eva said. "They're taking names and contact information before people are allowed to leave. But they'll waive me through."

"Call your folks," she added. "They're bound to hear a news report and worry about you."

My parents were in Iowa for a long weekend, attending some sort of reunion at Iowa State University, where Dad got his PhD and taught while I was growing up. Dad accepted the offer to head the horticultural department at Clemson University after I was in college. Now my folks live in Clemson, not far from the Ardon County line.

"Will do," I promised.

Eva kissed my cheek. "Probably be late morning before I'm back. Take care. Love you."

"Love you, too," I replied.

Eva barely cleared the cabin's doorway when Mollye bustled in. My friend had taken a short detour to have a few words with Deputy Danny, her casual sweetie.

"Thought you'd be changed by now," Mollye said. "Or have you decided to leave on those oversized pasties. They definitely advertise your charms. Danny says reporters, including a TV truck, have gathered outside the gate. The deputies put up a roadblock to keep them out."

I gave Mollye a withering look. "You're the one who suckered me into wearing this."

"Yeah, I did." She laughed as she peeled off her costume, which had a front zipper hidden beneath protruding fruit.

"Lucky I changed clothes here or I'd have been forced to appear at the station as Carmen Miranda—whoever she is. Mom says this Carmen lady used to appear on TV wearing some sort of fruity hat back in the day. Who knew I was so retro?"

I quickly slipped on jeans and a bright orange Clemson sweatshirt. Mollye, a quick-change artist if I ever saw one, was back in her made-for-the-movies gypsy attire. Did I dare tell her that her everyday attire looked retro, too? In this case, sixties hippie.

"Let's take my van," Moll said. "I'll bring you back when we finish. I Imagine Danny will still be here. That'll give me a chance to pump him for info."

Paint met us on the porch and asked to bum a ride to the sheriff's office. He'd driven to the farm with Andy, who was still in the barn with the sheriff.

Paint took shotgun and I squeezed into the backseat amid magical witches' balls, bottles of medicinal herbs, and other miscellaneous boxes that always littered Moll's van. As we maneuvered into the farm's gravel drive, a friendly soul let us cut into the line of vehicles waiting to be released by the officers manning the gate.

"Man, there was a lot of blood." Paint shuddered. "I sure hope Zack's injuries don't kill his career. Goes to show, one minute you're on top of the world, the next some psycho's trying to skewer you like a shish kebab."

"I told the sheriff Zack's attacker was probably one of the CAVE men," Mollye said. "But I can't rule out Pam or Fred. Did you see either of them tonight?"

Paint shook his head. "Doesn't mean they weren't here. Folks arrived at the haunted barn in clusters. Lots of people just handed over money and didn't say a word. A loner or two could easily have slipped in at the tail end of a group of friends. Any tag-alongs would have looked like they were part of the crowd."

"Linda, Carol's campaign manager, took lots of photos as people arrived," I said. "I think she posted the pictures on Instagram and Carol's Facebook page. Maybe if we look through those candid shots, we can draw up a list of attendees."

Mollye hooted. "You do like to do things the hard way, Miss Vegan. All we need to do is check the guest book. People signed in as they arrived."

Paint waggled a finger at Mollye. "You shouldn't poke fun at Udderly's most-accomplished snoop. Brie has a point. Easy to slip by without signing in. Besides the sign-in names could be bogus. Who'd question what name you scribbled if you were dressed like a zombie or an alien? We should look at the photos and the sign-ins."

I sighed. "If our attacker was trying to avoid notice, he—or she—could have opted for a costume that offered a complete disguise. Maybe the pictures and guestbook are both dead ends."

We lapsed into silence until we arrived at the gate, and Moll rolled down the window to speak to the deputy who was freeing party-goers one vehicle at a time.

"Hi, Joe."

Figured. Moll seemed to know all the Ardon County deputies.

"Hey, Mollye," Joe answered. "You're headed to the sheriff's office, right?"

"Yes, and I'm bringing David alias 'Paint' Paynter and Brie Hooker with me so you can check off their names too. Sheriff Mason asked us to head to the station to give our statements."

"Okay," Joe said. "Good luck running the media gauntlet. Reporters are starting to swarm like yellow jackets."

He waved us on, and a state trooper directed us into a breakdown lane on the narrow state road. Media vehicles dotted the verge on both sides of the blacktop.

"Must have called in law enforcement from three counties by now," Paint observed. "Just spotted Pickens County cruisers along with state police vehicles. Hey, I hear a chopper, too. Wonder if State Patrol sent a helicopter? 'Course it might belong to a TV station, though there's not much to take pictures of this time of night."

I glanced out the window. "Maybe the chopper is looking for Chester's hearse or the motorcycles and truck in his gate-crashing parade. Wonder if anyone got their licenses."

"I'm sure plenty of people at Carol's fundraiser recognized all the CAVE gate crashers," Moll said. "They're not exactly low profile. Wouldn't be hard to figure out who owns the vehicles."

"So if one of the CAVE men attacked Zack, would he hang around or put Ardon County a couple hundred miles behind him?"

Mollye shuddered. "I have a feeling he's still close by. And I get the sense he's scared. Feels cornered. That makes him dangerous."

I tended to believe my friend's premonitions were mostly the product of her very creative and over-active imagination, not actual psychic whispers. She admitted as much.

That didn't prevent a shiver from sneaking up my spine.

EIGHT

The Sheriff's Department was located in a fairly new building on the outskirts of the Town of Ardon. I was well aware of its location, having previously been interrogated there as a murder suspect. Being a potential witness was a big step in the right direction.

When we arrived, the parking lot was lit up like Walmart on Christmas Eve. At least five of the vehicles in the jammed lot sported TV call letters or newspaper logos. A dozen people huddled just outside the station entrance. Once access to the scene of the attack was closed off, the news hounds must have drifted here in hopes of sniffing out a lead. They appeared ready to pounce on any possible eyewitness in the hopes of getting a juicy sound bite.

Ardon is a rural county, and Greenville is the nearest sizeable metro area. However, Zack Strong's football fame and Carol's political ambitions meant a gaggle of media stringers, affiliates, and blog tipsters would be working the story. This assemblage just represented the early scouts.

Mollye grabbed a fistful of business cards before she hopped out of the van.

"Really, Mollye?" I groaned.

Paint laughed.

"Hey, I'm not gonna say a word, but it won't hurt to try and tempt 'em to drop by my store for a take-home souvenir."

"You never cease to amaze me, Mollye," Paint said. "Glad you haven't added moonshine or whisky to your inventory. If you were a competitor, you'd probably steal all my Magic Moonshine customers in a month."

Paint used his imposing six-foot-four frame to clear a path for us through the loitering reporters. I heard shouted questions, but, with so much competing noise, the content was gibberish. The only intelligible things I could make out were Carol's and Zack's names.

I wondered if these folks were staking out the sheriff's department in hopes of identifying "persons of interest." That passing thought made me wonder if we might run into Chester or other CAVE men inside.

I pushed hard on the front door, happy to escape the din. A deputy checked off our names and sent us to cool our heels in what appeared to be a squad or meeting room. Rows of uncomfortable looking chairs were lined up facing a large whiteboard at the front of the room.

"Wait here," our escort ordered. "We'll call you in one at a time to take statements. Help yourself to coffee if you like. There's a fresh pot over there."

They called Paint first. Mollye and I poured ourselves coffee which, contrary to popular cop mythology, proved excellent.

Mollye pulled out her cell phone. "I'm going to see what folks are saying and if any pictures have been posted."

She started laughing, not exactly appropriate conduct while waiting for officers to interview you about a horrible assault.

"Shhh," I admonished.

She shoved her screen my way. The image did not tickle my funny bone. The photographer had caught me running practically "neckid" after discarding my costume's fish tail in the interest of speed. Fortunately my blonde wig and half-mask were still in place.

"Did you see the caption?" Moll's braying laugh subsided into periodic giggles.

I quickly scanned the copy. It read: "Hysterical mystery blonde runs from Zack Strong crime scene. Is she the lover Z's kept under wraps?"

I gasped. "Pickled pigs feet. How would anyone get that idea?"

Opening my own cell phone, I started perusing posts, starting with Facebook. Yep, my photo had gone viral. While some posts theorized the mystery blonde was Zack's current lover, others suggested the running woman having a bad hair day was a spurned lover. One post asked, "Did this madwoman attack Zack in a fit of rage?"

"The good news is I saved you with that wig and mask," Mollye said. "Haven't seen a single picture of a bare-faced and wigless mermaid. Too bad you took them off when we were jawing with the sheriff. Imagine someone took photos of you with Mason that will show up sooner or later."

"Wonderful," I said. "So nice to be offered up as a murder suspect again. At least this time law officers won't be promoting the theory. I was quite visible—thanks to you—from the time the Halloween party started. Lots of alibi witnesses."

The most ridiculous, breathless accounts were posted by bloggers and anonymous contributors on digital tabloid sites. Here, I was not only a murder suspect, but there were speculative stories of why I'd become deranged enough to attack Zack. In some, I'd found out he was cheating on me. In others, I was a victim of domestic abuse. The most common? I was pregnant. Great. Hard to get pregnant when you hadn't actually had sex in—oh, no could it be that long?—nineteen long, very long months.

When Paint emerged from the "interview" room, the plainclothes detective called Mollye's name.

Paint sat beside me. I turned off my phone. Wasn't about to show him the posts we'd been scanning on social media.

"So did the officer ask you anything new?" I wondered. "Or did he just repeat the same questions the sheriff already asked us?"

"There was one new twist," Paint said. "He asked me if I'd seen Zack talking on his phone. Zack had a wallet on him but no cell phone. I told him I was pretty sure I'd seen him checking something on it earlier. Apparently it's missing."

"Did he give you any hint of who they think might have had a motive to attack Zack?"

"Not really. Detective Nettles was a year ahead of me at Ardon High. He knew almost as much as I did about any enemies from Zack's high school days. So we zipped right ahead to any recent history between Zack and Chester Finley before tonight's brawl. I couldn't help him out there.

"I told him about the rumor Mollye'd heard that Pam North or Fred Baxter might show. Pretty sure he already planned to check their alibis. His questions did prompt me to wonder who might benefit if Zack never threw a football again. That added one more person to my suspect list."

"Who?"

"Doug Hayes, the Aces' quarterback Zack dethroned. Doug's fully recovered from the injury that sidelined him. Now Doug will have a shot to lead his team again. A chance at a Super Bowl ring and endorsement money."

"Hope the sheriff checks out Doug's alibi."

"He said he would. But I doubt he'll need to. Some media type is certain to track Doug down for comments. It's a huge sports story. The sheriff will know soon enough if Doug's in Nevada or lurking about Ardon County, South Carolina. Besides, the idea's pretty far-fetched. I've met Doug. He's visited Ardon with Zack a couple of times. They seemed real tight."

"But Doug wouldn't need to be here," I insisted. "He could have hired someone."

"Hiring goons is risky," Paint answered. "Doug's smart. Can't see him paying some hoodlum who'd give him up in a New York minute. They always do. And, like I told you, he and Zack are buddies."

I chewed on my lip as I mentally ran through the few minutes I'd spent in the celebrity quarterback's presence. "What about Zack's complaint that some people think they own a piece of him?"

Paint shrugged. "Sounded to me like Zack was saying fame and money aren't everything. May have been trying to make his old teammates feel less jealous. I mean he dropped the subject real quick and went back to ribbing Andy and me. He also turned his charms on you, which didn't make my day."

Paint draped an arm around my shoulder. "Can't pretend I don't notice, Brie. Andy and I talked it over again last week. This 'we musketeers' bit is killing us. We both want you as a friend. But one day some lucky guy will win more than smiles from you. We'd rather it be one of us than some stranger—or the likes of Zack. Won't you reconsider? Date both of us. We can handle it. Promise. Talk to Andy, he's totally on board."

Yowzer. Hadn't seen that coming. An excited tingling in my gut said yippee. My uncooperative brain warned against making an important, emotional decision in the midst of a crisis.

"Will you consider it?"

I took Paint's hand and squeezed it. "I've told you and Andy how much I care about the two of you. I couldn't bear losing either of you as a friend. But I admit I think about my dates with you and Andy. Can't forget them."

Not exactly an answer.

Mollye sashayed back into the squad room. Her visit with the detective proved much briefer than Paint's. I expected my turn would be even shorter since I had nada to add. Once we finished our spooky decorating project late afternoon, I didn't go back inside the barn until I ran in after Zack's attack. What's more, I'd just met the quarterback and I'd never laid eyes on Chester until a few hours ago. I knew zero dirt about anyone with a potential grudge.

It took the detective about a minute to ascertain I was clueless. Fortunately, he hadn't hooked into the blogosphere speculation that I might be Zack's killer girlfriend.

After Detective Nettles asked his last question, I posed one of my own. "Any update on Zack's condition?"

"They're operating now," he replied. "The pitchfork broke his collarbone and tore muscles and tendons. Luckily it was high enough to miss his lung. Then there's the concussion. He also broke an ankle. Probably fell wrong. I understand your aunt's at the hospital with his mom. A deputy is keeping watch to make sure only authorized hospital staffers get anywhere near Zack."

He paused. "Ardon's a small community. My mother taught at Ardon High when Mrs. Strong taught eleventh grade English, and my father bred Udderly's Great Pyrenees guard dogs. Mrs. Strong and your aunt are good people. We'll do all we can to catch whoever did this to Zack. We'll make sure he stays safe."

I smiled. "Thanks." Ardon County might not be a shopping or dining mecca, but it did have its advantages. A tradition of looking out for neighbors was a big one.

"What's the prognosis on the head injury?" I asked.

Nettles shrugged. "He's in surgery. That's all I know. The concussion is worrisome. Naturally we'd like to talk to Zack as soon as we can. If we're lucky, he'll tell us who did this and we can lock the moron up."

When I returned to the squad room, a frowning Paint was pacing back and forth in front of the whiteboard, his cell phone tight to his ear.

Mollye dipped her chin in Paint's direction. "He finally got through to Andy. Not sure what they're talking about but based on his footwork, it doesn't look like happy news."

Paint ended his call. "Mason suggested it would be a good idea if some family friends spent the night at Udderly, just in case. He's leaving a cruiser at the farm entrance, but there are literally miles of unguarded fences for someone to climb."

I frowned, puzzled. "Does he think the attacker might come back? Why would he? Zack's in the hospital, nowhere near Udderly. Or does Mason think the attack was random and a nutcase is still roaming around?"

Paint squeezed my shoulder. The concern in his dark chocolate eyes reminded me how much I treasured his friendship. "I think he's worried some of the CAVE men might show up. Then there are the reporters and thrill seekers who might sneak onto the farm," he said. "Eva told Billy she's sticking with Carol until Zack's out of surgery and stabilized. It's doubtful she'll be home before morning. I'll feel a lot better if I know you and Billy aren't on the farm alone."

Paint's smile was wry. "Brie, do you have any problems with Andy and me bunking at Udderly tonight? Since the sheriff has already asked Andy every question he could think of, he said he can wait until morning to come to the station and sign a statement."

"I'd appreciate the two of you staying."

His smile telegraphed the hope I'd help him stay alert on guard duty by kissing those fine, mischievous lips. I bit my own lip trying to banish thoughts about how pleasurable that could be—and had been once before.

"If you're having a slumber party, I'm in," Mollye announced. "Shirley always opens Starry Skies on Saturdays. I'd already planned on a late night. Unfortunately, I don't think Deputy Danny will be the late-night company I was counting on. You guys will have to do."

Recalling Mollye's tendency to steal the sheets and blankets and tuck them under her ample body when she shared my bed, I knew exactly what slumber costume I'd choose. Flannel PJs and thick wool socks.

Too bad flannel couldn't compare with the kind of warmth Andy or Paint could provide.

Wine-soaked cheese balls. I couldn't quit mulling over Paint's suggestion.

Don't go there, or you'll never sleep.

NINE

As promised, we found a cruiser parked at the entrance to Udderly. Fortunately, it was the only vehicle in sight. No newsies, at least for the moment. Mollye rolled down her window and yoo-hooed. Deputy Danny McCoy immediately opened his door and walked over to the van.

"Hi, sweetie," Moll said. "I'm stayin' here tonight. When's your shift end? Wanna hop in bed with Brie and me when you're done?"

"Mollye!" I rammed my fist into the back of her seat.

"Oh, don't worry. Danny's a one-woman man, and I'm more than enough woman for him. He knows I'm teasing."

Danny looked heavenward. He'd been canoodling with Mollye long enough to shrug off most of her nonsense. "We're all working overtime. Looks like I'll be parked here the rest of the night."

"You poor thing," Mollye cooed. "Best I can do is say I'll try and dream about you. Goodnight, Sweetie."

Danny backed up his cruiser to give our van enough room to pass. I groaned as we drove past all of the fundraiser detritus. Either the officers hadn't let the caterers finish their chores or they'd used the chaos as an excuse to boogie on home. Tables. Tents. Chairs. Trash. At least anything that would blow away had been weighted down or put in garbage bags.

The morning chores were growing.

Udderly's Great Pyrenees guard dogs heralded our arrival with a full-throated canine chorus. Each of these fluffy-white giants tipped the scales between eighty- and one-hundred pounds. They were gentle unless they suspected a stranger intended to harm a member of their "family." That took in all Udderly residents, human and animal. While deciding if a new arrival was friend or foe, they barked up a storm.

The ruckus brought Andy and Billy onto the cabin's front porch.

Billy held Eva's shotgun with the business end pointed our way. He leaned the gun against the porch railing as soon as he recognized the Starry Skies van. Andy shushed the dogs, and they instantly quieted. The vet certainly had a way with animals. Did I dare let him whisper in my ear?

"Glad you're here," Billy said. "Come on in. I made a pot of coffee. Let's catch up fast and hit the hay. Milking and morning chores are just a few hours away."

Cashew, my flirty Teacup Morkie, snubbed me. Instead, the furry powderpuff showered affection on Andy, who'd undoubtedly been feeding her treats. His pockets always bulged with them. As soon as we settled around the kitchen table, Cashew hopped in Andy's lap, licking his fingers to coax them into performing a doggie massage.

Eva's cuckoo clock struck one as we sipped our coffee and shared what little we knew.

"Do you think Zack saw his attacker?" I asked.

Andy shook his head. "My guess is no. Given the scuff marks in the hay, it looked like someone clobbered him on the back of the head and dragged him into that back stall to hide the body."

The comment offered the only addition to what we all knew. Zack remained in surgery with Eva and Carol sitting vigil. If the sheriff had any inkling about the who and why of the attack, he hadn't shared.

I'd warned Mollye that any mention of my photo making Facebook and Twitter rounds would be grounds for serious retribution. While I felt certain the men at the table would eventually see those horrid snapshots, I wanted to postpone the embarrassment until some future date when I wasn't present.

When the first bars of "Dixie" blared, we all jumped.

"Sorry." Paint pulled an iPhone from his jeans' pocket. Having worn street clothes under his paint-can costume, he'd only needed to peel off an outer layer to be properly dressed for the sheriff's interrogation. "That's Mick's ringtone. Why in Hades is he calling at this hour?"

Paint moved away to take the call. Given the size of the cabin, there wasn't much room for privacy unless you went in Eva's or my bedroom and closed the door. The porch was an option, but unpleasantly chilly.

"Are you kidding me?" Paint sounded seriously peeved. "You're asking about Zack to fill out next week's fantasy football lineup? It's one a.m. Are you nuts?"

Paint ended the call without saying another word. "Sorry guys. I'll turn off the ringer."

"Who's this Mick and why is he calling you about Zack and fantasy football?" I asked.

"He went to Ardon High," Paint answered. "A grade behind Zack and Andy and me, but he was on our football team."

"Yeah," Andy added. "Mick only made it on the field in the final seconds of a game if our coach decided there was no way we could lose. But to hear Mick tell it, you'd think he was Zack's go-to receiver. An enterprising local jeweler made up state championship rings for us. Honking big suckers. Mick bought one. After all these years, he still shows it off to anyone he meets. Kinda sad."

Paint claimed one of the table's free seats. "Ever since I set up our Magic Moonshine fantasy football league, Mick drops by the distillery or phones two or three times a week to talk football. He's a fanatic. Stays glued to a computer studying statistics and scouting reports. Mick seemed worked up more than usual tonight. The jerk wanted to know when I thought Zack would be able to play again. Guess he wanted a head start looking at waivers."

"Whoa," I said. "Really? Someone clobbers a hometown football hero, a former teammate, and his first question is when will Zack be back on the field?"

Andy shrugged. "He's not the only guy who takes fantasy football seriously."

"Gals do, too," Mollye added. "One of my brothers started a fantasy league for our family. The men play the women. Last year, we won. Was there any doubt?"

"Is it for bragging rights or money?" Paint asked.

"The winners get something better than cold cash. The losers have to prepare Christmas dinner while us victors twiddle our thumbs and make snide comments. Year-long bragging rights are the biggest prize. Money would be less painful to lose."

"Not for some folks," Andy responded. "There's a ten-thousand-dollar buy-in to enter some of the weekly fantasy pools."

"Does the guy who phoned make those kinds of bets?" I asked. "If I had that much dough at stake, I might make a few desperate calls."

Paint shook his head. "I don't see how Mick could ever scrape together enough money to make a ten-thousand-dollar bet. But I know he's been gambling and losing. I think he's up to his eyeballs in hock."

I yawned. "When I'm not so tired, one of you needs to explain the appeal of make-believe football. Whatever happened to rooting for a favorite team—an actual, real-life combination of players? And why the heck is it legal to play fantasy football for money when it's illegal to play poker online for money?"

"Don't you know? Fantasy football's a game of skill, not chance." Mollye's eye roll told me she was being facetious. "I don't get it. Poker takes real skill. Next time we have a slumber party, I'll deal 'em up and take you boys to the cleaners. Five-card stud suit you?"

"Hey, don't be sexist, Mollye," I objected. "I may not play fantasy football, but I started playing poker as soon as I could count chips. My aunts considered it an essential part of my education."

"Deal," she answered. "We have a challenge. Brie, Eva, and I will arrange a game with you boys and see who wins."

"Can we make it strip poker?" Andy grinned.

Billy shook his head. "The bunch of you can almost match Eva for orneriness. I'm off to bed and I ain't sharing Eva's queen with any of you. Find your own bunk. I don't care where. See you in a few hours."

Andy and Paint stood. Andy carried a dozing Cashew to her favored blanket nest for daytime naps. While she usually slept with me, it wasn't in the cards tonight—poker or otherwise. Mollye could pass as a human Cuisinart steadily churning my blankets and sheets as she thrashed in her dreams. Cashew might be a casualty in that maelstrom.

Paint pulled a quarter from his pocket. "Okay, Andy, let's flip. Winner curls up inside. Loser gets that cot in the barn."

Andy shook his head. "Not tonight. The barn's wrapped in crime scene tape. 'Fraid the loser gets the floor. But I choose heads."

Paint tossed the coin. Chuckling, he showed the result to Andy.

"Hey, I've got a blow-up mattress in the back of my van," Mollye said. "You can use it, Andy, but I'm not gonna pucker up to inflate it."

My eyebrows shot up. "Should I ask why you have an inflatable mattress in your van?"

"Probably not." Mollye grinned and tossed her van keys to Andy.

Paint's mocha eyes locked on mine.

Now why did I think of my favorite flavors—chocolate, mocha—whenever the man gazed at me? Sublimation anyone?

"Maybe we ought to talk Eva into adding a guest bedroom," he said. "We could build a bump-out right next to your room."

"No way, I'm reserving any construction activity for Summer Place. Can't thank you and Andy enough for helping Dad and me with structural repairs. At least now, I can walk inside without worrying a rotting beam might bean me. But I've got miles of drywall to go before it's a viable bed-and-breakfast."

A few years ago, I shared my dream with my aunts. I wanted to renovate a beautiful old mansion and turn it into a B&B that catered primarily to vegans and vegetarians. Shortly before Aunt Lilly's death, my generous aunts bought Summer Place, a gorgeous but derelict architectural gem. They'd planned to restore the property a bit before they surprised me with it on my thirty-fifth birthday, still two years away. Not how things worked out. When Lilly died, I inherited Summer Place in all its splendid decrepitude.

I smiled, thinking about the mansion's white pillars and green carpeted lawn. A nice change from recurring flashbacks to Zack's pale face in a puddle of blood.

"Goodnight, y'all." Mollye waved as she headed toward my bedroom with its too-small-to-share-with-her queen bed.

I gave the boys a salute and followed Mollye. "Goodnight, all."

I was beat. My eyelids were lead weights. But could I shut my mind down with Udderly Kidding Dairy front and center in a new crime puzzler?

Did someone try to kill Zack, or was the goal merely to hurt him and end his career?

I could imagine a CAVE dweller seeking revenge. But while Chester or his buddies were obvious candidates, there were at least two other Ardon County residents who counted themselves among Zack's enemies. I'd met neither.

Could this Pam lady actually drive a pitchfork into a one-time sweetheart? For that matter, was Fred Baxter capable of attacking a fit two-hundred-plus pound athlete? If Baxter's sixteen-year-old son died eighteen years ago, the dad was no spring rooster.

If Zack had seen or heard his attacker coming, I figured he'd have fought back. The blow to the back of his head argued for a sneak attack. Somehow that made the assault seem both cowardly and impersonal. If revenge was the motive, wouldn't the attacker want to see Zack's face? Let him know who was demanding his or her pound of flesh?

Time to sleep. Tomorrow I'd quiz my friends and do a Google search to see what the internet could tell me about Pam and Fred. Maybe I'd even figure a way to meet them in person. As far as I knew, neither suspect had a quarrel with any member of the Hooker clan. No reason for hostility if I innocently made their acquaintance.

TEN

With Billy, Mollye, Andy, Paint, and our part-time Clemson crew all helping, we completed the Udderly morning chores in record time. By nine a.m., we'd also picked up and bagged the evening's debris and divided the resulting trash bags among the visiting trucks for a trip to the Ardon County dump.

"Sure you don't want us to stay?" Mollye asked for the third time.

"No. Zack's attacker is long gone. It's bright and sunny. No place to hide. And I know where Eva keeps her shotgun."

"But last I heard you might miss a target glued to the end of your gun," Andy quipped.

I punched his arm. "Luckily, an unknown marauder wouldn't know that."

After they all boogied down the road, Udderly seemed eerily quiet. I poured myself a cup of coffee and settled in one of the cabin's front porch rockers. I breathed in the crisp fall air, enjoying the peaceful interlude.

The peace lasted less than five minutes. Before my cup was empty, an old Plymouth clunker bumped down the drive and parked near our retail cabin. The car suggested it wasn't a reporter. Either a curiosity seeker or a customer who hadn't bothered to read the store hours posted at the farm's entrance gate.

I stood and started walking. I called to the man as he climbed out of his rusty ride, "Sir, sorry but our store doesn't open until noon. Can you come back then?"

The man jumped, startled.

"Uh, sorry, ma'am, I, uh...lost something last night. Thought I'd come by and look for it."

He doffed his ball cap and nodded at me—the ma'am in question. His eyes refused to meet mine. Instead they focused on his work boots, the left one excavating a hole with the point of its shuffling toe.

His fingers worried the edge of his ball cap. He appeared embarrassed. No, cancel that. He looked like a kid caught in church with a comic book tucked inside his hymnal.

"Afraid you're out of luck," I said. "We picked up the grounds this morning and my friends hauled everything to the dump. Hope we didn't throw away something of value. What did you lose?"

The silence stretched as I stared at his head's shiny dome, much whiter than his tanned neck. I decided he spent a lot of time outside, most of it with the ball cap on. A monk-like ring of baby fine blond hair circled his bald pate. Was he ever going to answer?

"Oh, uh, just a business card," he finally stammered. "Met someone who said they might buy several truckloads of mulch. Uh, I already forgot his name."

I smiled. "Bet you can't describe him either."

"Ma'am?" His head jerked up. His eyes seemed as active as his left foot, dancing back and forth like he was scouting an escape route. Was I that threatening?

"Just figured your prospect was in costume," I added. "Recall how he was dressed? Maybe I know him."

"Don't rightly remember. I know Zack got hurt last night. We went to school together. Will he be all right?"

"Too soon to know. What's your name? I'll let Zack's mom know you asked about him."

"Sorry," he mumbled. "Gotta go. Late for work."

He turned and practically ran to his car.

He looked so innocuous. But his behavior made me wonder. Could he possibly be Zack's attacker?

I memorized his license plate and hurried inside to call the sheriff. He was out but I left a message. The strange encounter left me wondering why he'd come and who he might be. I doubted the sheriff would enlighten me anytime soon. I'd have to ask my friends which of their classmates had gone prematurely bald.

Eva returned around lunch time, exhausted. Airlines could assess a surcharge for the size of the bags under her eyes.

I gave her a big hug. "How's Zack doing? And how is Carol holding up?"

My aunt sighed. "The surgery went well, though the docs won't say if Zack'll be able to play football again. Brain trauma's the biggest worry. They induced a coma and lowered his body temperature to give his brain a better chance to heal. He could be in a coma for days."

"Sounds like it'll be a long haul. You should go to bed, get some rest. The four musketeers—Paint, Andy, Mollye, and me—along with Udderly's regular help have finished all the chores. Nothing you need to do."

"What I need to do is take a shower, change clothes, and go back to the hospital," Eva countered.

I shook my head. "A zombie won't do Carol any good. You need some sleep."

"Well, maybe a short nap."

"Deal. Is there anything I can do to help?"

"Just keep Udderly running and don't eat all the profits. Sooner or later your DNA will kick in. You are descended from a long line of dedicated cheese-aholics. You can't hold out forever."

"Funny. You're really pooped if you've lowered yourself to lame cheese insults. Go to bed. I need your truck to run some errands. I'll leave the keys to my Prius by the door in case there's an emergency."

Eva made a face. "Not sure I want to drive your car. All those dents. People might think I'm the bad driver."

A low blow. My high auto deductible was the reason I hadn't undone the dings inflicted on my Prius when a truck intentionally butted me into a ditch. Dings weren't a priority. Every penny I scraped together went toward Summer Place renovations.

"I'll be back late afternoon to wake you. There's a pot of vegetable soup on simmer. I won't even groan when you muck it up with cheese."

I kissed Eva's cheek and hurried to escape before my aunt could ask what errands required me to drive her pickup truck. This past summer she'd forced me to get comfortable with her elderly Ford's stick shift. While my driving skills now passed muster, I doubted she'd approve of my afternoon destinations.

My first appointment was with Pam North. I'd googled her and found she was an Ardon Realty agent. I had a good excuse to pay her a visit. She'd listed a derelict property right behind Summer Place. The abandoned trailer on that lot was covered with so many vines it could pass as an ancient burial mound. Though I doubted I could scrape together enough cash to buy the property, I had a keen interest in its future.

Since Ardon County had zero zoning, the property's future owners could do whatever they wanted with the land. A chicken farm or landfill in my future B&B's backyard wouldn't exactly lend luster to its allure.

Ardon Realty occupied what looked like an overgrown dollhouse. Colorful pansies nodded from window boxes, while bright green shutters contrasted nicely with the clapboard's fresh white paint.

Since there was no bell, I knocked once and walked in. A woman, the only occupant, sat behind one of two desks in the open space. Pam, I presumed.

"Hi, you must be Brie Hooker. A real pleasure to meet you," Pam gushed as she stood to greet me. She wore stretchy tight pants, and a clingy sweater. A wide belt cinched her wasp waist, emphasizing the hour-glass figure that once made Zack and presumably other high school males drool.

Yet from the neck up the thirty-four-year-old looked like a middle-aged throwback to her mother's or maybe her grandmother's era. Her hair was permed in a tight poodle do and dyed a black that made coal look gray. Heavy makeup failed to hide frown lines that formed sad, pouting sentries around her pursed lips.

"Have a seat," she invited. "You say you're interested in the property I listed behind Summer Place?"

I took the chair opposite her desk. "Yes. What's the asking price?"

"One-hundred thousand."

I almost choked. Somehow she'd answered without giggling at her absurd joke.

"You're kidding."

"Oh, no. Location, location, location. All of us real estate professionals are pleased you're fixing up Summer Place, a genuine, historic beauty. That increases the value of adjacent properties. Plus the lot's so close to Clemson, and you know how our charming campus city is exploding. There's high developer demand for land to build condos, student apartments."

Pam's high-pitched voice made me think she might have had a

career in the opera as one of those sopranos who can shatter glass. Never been a great opera fan.

Stinky blue cheese. All right, maybe her message upped my annoyance at her tone. The sweat equity I was pouring into Summer Place was helping others reap profits on land they'd always treated as a place to dump trash. A year ago, I probably could have bought the seedy lot behind my property for a pittance. Did squinty-eyed Pam truly believe anyone in her right mind would pay a hundred grand for an acre of waist-high weeds and bramble topped with a rusted out trailer?

"You're the listing agent, right?" I asked. "Are the owners eager to sell? What do you think they might accept?"

Pam's blue eyes widened, sure she had a sucker on the line.

She put her hand beside her mouth and whispered. "Confidentially, they're a little strapped. Just between us girls, I think they might accept eighty-five thousand."

I did my best to match Pam's fake smile with a phony-baloney one of my own.

"Really? Is the real estate market that hot?"

"Oh, yes," she chirped. "I've never seen such a seller's market."

"How long have you been in the business?" I asked.

My question gave Pam an opportunity to launch into a litany of her personal triumphs.

"I'm the top-selling agent in Ardon. If I weren't such a devoted wife and mother, I'd belong to Greenville's Millionaire Club—agents who sell a million dollars' worth of property a year. Maybe when I'm no longer stuck running my son to football practice and my daughter to cheerleading."

She breezed on. "My little girl takes after me. I was a varsity cheerleader. Should have gotten a college scholarship. I was just as much an athlete as those girls who ran track."

I might have forgiven Pam her recital of accomplishments as over-enthusiastic salesmanship, if she hadn't added grievance caveats to each accolade.

"Wow, you were a cheerleader? Did you know Zack Strong, the pro quarterback who was attacked last night?"

Pam's eyes narrowed for an instant, then she nodded and tried on a grave expression. "Actually Zack and I were high school sweethearts. If he'd been faithful when he went off to college, we'd be married. Some men seem incapable of appreciating a good woman's love. I felt sorry for Zack even before the attack. Even with all his money, he can't be happy. Maybe this will be a wake-up call. Teach him what's important."

I looked at my watch. "Have to run. But thanks for the information."

She looked up startled. "Do you want me to put in an offer?"

"Uh, no. But keep me posted if the asking price goes down. Way, way down."

As I drove off, I mentally moved Pam pretty far down my potential suspects' list. I hadn't bothered to ask her how she'd spent last night. Whomping Zack upside the head did not seem her style. I sensed she was more into martyrdom than vengeance. Pam wanted everyone to acknowledge what an amazing, selfless woman she was.

She needed people to recognize how much farther she'd have gone in the world if others hadn't wronged her and held her back.

My next stop was Ardon's largest car dealership, Fred Baxter's business. I'd driven past it many times. While the dealership sold four brands of new cars, Toyota wasn't one of them, but Ford was. That's the reason I'd driven my aunt's Ford pickup, which came off the assembly line some years before automatic transmissions became the norm. I planned to coast into one of the service bays and ask the mechanic to check out the funny noise I kept hearing. The funny noise was no joke, though it only happened when I failed to properly engage the clutch.

The first part of my plan went smoothly. The next part was a little sketchy. I figured I'd stroll through the dealership while the mechanic poked under the truck's hood. With any luck, I'd get a look at Fred Baxter, probably in one of those fake I-have-to-ask-my-boss meetings staged to con customers into believing the salesperson was sweating bullets to get them the best deal.

I entered the showroom and paused to look at a Ford Escape. I caught the salesman's approach out of the corner of my eye.

"Can I help you? How about going for a test drive in this little honey?"

Close up, I realized the man was older than the typical salesman. Silver strands threaded their way through thick brown hair. A deep tan couldn't hide the slight loosening of skin around his chin. He stuck out his hand.

"I'm Fred Baxter," he said as we shook. I eased away a bit. His breath reeked of cigarette smoke. Had to be a three-pack-a-day habit.

"I own this dealership. Afraid all my sales associates are tied up just now. But I'd be glad to help. What's your name? What kind of vehicle are you looking for?"

"I'm not in the market for a car right now," I stammered. I wasn't anxious to give my name or get into a lengthy conversation. "I brought a Ford pickup in for service. Just taking a look around while I wait."

Fred frowned. "I don't recall seeing you before. Did you buy your truck here?"

"Uh, no. It's my aunt's. I'm not sure where she bought it."

He smiled. "Who's your aunt?"

Uh oh. No choice.

"Eva Hooker," I answered.

His smile disappeared. "Eva Hooker?"

He fastened his fist around my wrist. "You and your aunt hosted last night's fundraiser for Carol Strong, didn't you?" He kept his deep voice low, almost a whisper, but it scared me more than if he'd yelled.

I nodded. What else could I do?

He smiled. Not the kind of smile that made me think we'd ever be friends. More like the smile an exterminator might get when he saw a mouse heading for a trap.

"We're not going to have a scene," he added. "I'm going to call the service department and put a rush on whatever service is needed. And you're going to sit in the customer lounge and keep your mouth closed until you're called. And you will never come back. Do you understand?"

Alrighty. "Sorry I upset you."

Rage—the icy kind—seemed to radiate from the man's every fiber from his tasseled loafers to his silk tie.

"Oh, by the way, tell Eva I'm praying for Zack. Praying he'll be a vegetable. Justice would be Carol changing her son's diapers for the rest of her life."

Jumping Pepper Jack. Didn't need a second invitation to vamoose. I was darn sure I couldn't coax Mr. Baxter into telling me how he'd spent the prior evening. Time to beat feet.

I sat quietly in the customer lounge until a bewildered mechanic hurried inside to tell me my pickup was ready. I paid the bill—fifty dollars for an unspecified checkup—without protest.

Despite Baxter's frosty vitriol, the man didn't seem like a prime prospect. While he appeared physically capable of attacking Zack, his ire seemed more focused on Carol. Puzzling. I'd have to quiz Eva on that subject.

Either Pam or Baxter could have hired someone to attack Zack. Yet that seemed even less likely than one of them doing the deed in person. Baxter might be able to afford a hitman, but that option seemed too impersonal for him. And, despite Pam's brags on her sales prowess, I doubted she made enough moolah to squander money on righting a long-simmering wrong.

While I wasn't ready to completely cross off Zack's old enemies as possible attackers, I decided the CAVE men deserved more scrutiny. I'd discounted them earlier because the attack seemed over the top as retaliation for a knock-down punch.

But what did I know? The answer was bupkus. Not about Zack's younger days in Ardon nor about his life beyond our county's boundaries. Maybe someone in Las Vegas had a solid reason to hate Zack. A cuckolded husband who wanted to punish a football star who seduced his wife. A psycho who'd become obsessed with Zack.

Then there was the old standby, a profit motive. If Zack died, I wagered his will would leave everything to his mother, and clearly she wouldn't harm her son. But there was also Doug, the Aces' dethroned quarterback. He'd benefit, though he was Zack's friend. I didn't know enough about Vegas bookies, fantasy football fanatics, or celebrity deals to figure out if others might cash in if Zack disappeared from the football field—or the planet.

ELEVEN

At five p.m., I awakened a groggy Eva.

"Good grief, I can't believe I slept away the afternoon," she mumbled as she rubbed her eyes.

She shuffled to the bathroom and I headed to the kitchen. As I stirred my vegetable soup, I could hear her splashing water and muttering. Eva wandered out to our main living area wearing the paw-print flannel nightgown I gave her last Christmas. She still had a washcloth in hand as she poured herself coffee. She took a swallow and dumped the damp washcloth on the kitchen table to free a hand for the phone. Apparently the coffee cup was more important than a potential water mark on the table.

"Calling Carol?" I asked. She nodded.

I eavesdropped on Eva's side of the conversation, which mostly amounted to questions..."Has Zack come out of his coma?...Are you at the hospital?...Have you been home?...Can I bring anything?"

When my aunt hung up, I peppered her with identical questions, anxious to hear Carol's answers.

"Zack's still in a coma in ICU. Since no one knows what miscreant attacked him, a sheriff's deputy is guarding his room. The Sin City Aces also sent a security detail. That hasn't thrilled Sheriff Mason, but the newcomers are accustomed to dealing with media and have stymied most, but not all, reporters trying to sneak up to the ICU floor.

"Allie Gerome is among the exceptions," Eva continued. "That witch isn't even a reporter. She's a vulture. I spotted her lurking in the hallway this morning before I left. Hard to miss. She stuffs herself in too-tight clothes. Must think it makes her look trim. Ha. If the seams of her blouse ever rip, I want to be out of range of her exploding flab. Anyway I caught Allie glaring at Carol through the hospital room's glass window. She looked smug, eager to swoop in for the kill. Venom seems to seep from her every pore."

"Has Carol gone home at all?" I asked

Eva shook her head. "No, but the hospital staff has bent over backwards to make her comfortable. Let her use staff facilities, and one of the nurses loaned her clean clothes."

"How can we help?" I asked.

Eva sipped her coffee. "After supper, I'll run by her house and pick up clothes and incidentals. Keep Carol company for a while. She insists she doesn't want me to spend the night again."

A barking chorus interrupted our chat. I looked out the window. "It's Mollye. Just in time for supper, of course."

In minutes, my friend joined us at the kitchen table. She slapped down a copy of the *Ardon Chronicle*. "That unscrupulous witch is using Zack's attack to revive her old conspiracy theories."

"What are you talking about?" Eva said.

Neither Eva nor I had seen the Saturday morning paper. My aunt refused to subscribe to the *Ardon Chronicle*, saying she wouldn't give a penny of profit to its owner.

I scooted my chair next to Eva's and read over her shoulder. A fairly straight-forward story reported Zack was attacked by an unknown assailant during a Halloween-themed campaign event.

The second "opinion" piece urged authorities to guard against Carol Strong hiding evidence of her son's activities and possible motives for the attack. It cited unresolved questions about the mother's possible obstruction of justice in another investigation involving Zack. The most egregious insinuation implied Zack might have been paid to shave points, which could mean criminal accomplices could be behind the attack.

"Good grief. How can the paper get away with this?" I asked.

Mollye and Eva shrugged.

"Will someone please tell me about Carol's alleged 'obstruction of justice'? Is that why Fred Baxter seems to be angrier at Carol than Zack?"

Eva narrowed her eyes. "Just how did you come to this conclusion about Fred?"

Uh, oh. I'd planned to tell Eva about my afternoon visits, but hoped to do it in more genteel, less interrogation-format style.

"I dropped by his dealership to see if the noise I periodically hear in your truck is anything to worry about," I fibbed. "Fred Baxter introduced himself while I was wandering around the showroom. Once he learned I'd brought your truck in for service, he made it clear that I wasn't welcome, and I made a speedy departure. Apparently any friend of Carol Strong's is an enemy of Fred Baxter."

Eva shook her head. "Well, at least you had enough sense to make a hasty retreat. You'd better not be planning another visit."

"No way," I answered and meant it. "I've learned my lesson. It doesn't pay to call on hostile Ardon residents."

I stood, walked to the stove, and lifted the lid off the vegetable soup. It smelled heavenly. "Besides, I think Fred's a real longshot on any potential attacker list. Paint would have noticed him coming in the barn's front door, and I can't imagine that guy shucking his fancy suit and tasseled loafers to dress like a cat burglar and wiggle through a back window in the barn."

Mollye nodded. "You should have asked. I coulda given you a full report without you tellin' fibs about Eva's fine truck. Fred doesn't need a pitchfork to seek revenge. Not when he's screwing Allie Gerome. She's a big help in the retaliation department."

"What?" Eva and I gasped in unison.

Mollye laughed. "Thought you knew, Eva. Allie the widow and Fred the divorcé have been doing the horizontal samba for at least a year. Way I heard it they took a course for concealed carry together and wound up buying matching Glocks. Neither one of them will leave home without a pistol."

I shuddered. "Wonder if he closes his eyes tight and thinks of free advertising for his dealership every time he boinks her."

"Yuck," Eva said. "I hope he gets lots of free ink. Not what I'd call a fair trade. But they both have a lot of bottled up hate. Guess we ought to be glad Allie prefers maligning her enemies to shooting them."

"I wouldn't be surprised if Fred marries Allie," Mollye added. "She has piles of money."

"Right. Eva told me her development company holds title to big chunks of real estate all across the state."

I set a hunk of cheese and a loaf of bread on companion cutting boards in the middle of the table. "Ladle up your own soup, ladies. Add as much cheese as you like. I'll just start a cholesterol pool and take bets on when your LDL will break the five-hundred barrier."

Once we were chowing down, I returned to Fred's conviction that Carol had done something unforgivable. "So since I've given Scout's honor I won't return to Fred's dealership, will someone tell me why he hates Carol?"

Eva stared down at her soup bowl. "Nobody knows the truth except Carol and Zack. Well, I guess Quatro and Deputy Aaron West knew, too, but they're both dead.

"I never pried. Too much heartache. Whatever the truth may be, it wouldn't have changed my opinion of Carol. Anything she did was out of love. Zack's future could have ended with that horrible car wreck. No way to bring Fred's boy back to life."

"What does Fred think Carol did?" I was still baffled.

Mollye shifted in her chair. "My granny suspects Zack was drunk as a skunk and driving that Jeep when it plowed into a telephone pole, throwing both boys out of the car like wild pitches.

"The way the rumor goes, Quatro, that was Fred the fourth's nickname, died instantly. Deputy West was first on the scene, and phoned Carol right after he called EMS. Fred's convinced she talked West into putting Quatro's corpse in the driver's seat and ditching the liquor bottle he found."

"Why would West go along? A payoff?"

Given my prior dealings with the deceased deputy, I felt certain a bribe would have worked.

Eva stood and carried her empty soup bowl to the sink. "If—and I emphasize if—Carol asked West to do such a thing, she wouldn't have offered money. She was deep in debt, paying off her dead husband's medical bills. West's nephew was a friend of Zack's and a teammate. If—again *if* she interfered—I imagine she argued Zack's grave injuries and guilt would be a high enough price for youthful folly—if he even lived."

"Was there an inquest?"

"Yes, but Fred claimed it was rigged," Eva answered. "Said Quatro would never have driven Zack's jeep. Authorities concluded there were insufficient grounds to doubt the official report."

Mollye shook her head. "Granny thinks Zack's fame has fed Fred's bitterness. The person he blames for his son's death is now a celebrity, rolling in money, living the high life."

"Did blood tests show both boys had been drinking?" I asked.

"If there were blood tests, the results were never made public," Eva answered. "We're talking twenty years ago in a tight, rural community. Back then local newspapers wouldn't publish a story that smeared the reputation of high school football heroes."

"Has Carol ever talked about the accident?" I asked.

Eva shook her head. "No, and I'm not going to second-guess her. Quatro was dead, and Carol wanted to protect Zack. This is ancient, irrelevant history, and no one"—Eva looked directly at me— "should muck around picking at old scabs."

My aunt shucked the light-weight shawl she'd draped around her shoulders while we ate. "Now, if you'll excuse me, I need to get out of my nightgown and get dressed. It's past time for me to head to the hospital."

Mollye helped me put away the leftovers and wash the dishes, by hand of course. Usually the cabin only had one "dishwasher"—me. My aunts had never seen fit to invest in a mechanical version.

We were just finishing our cleanup chores, when Eva re-emerged from her bedroom. At the front door, she started to wave goodbye, then dropped her hand. "Brie, I forgot to mention I spoke with Phil Owens and Bob Codner at the fundraiser before the gatecrashers arrived. I asked them to come by for lunch after church tomorrow so we can talk more about ARGH preparing a conservation easement for Udderly.

"Your folks are flying home tonight, right? Ask them to join us for lunch. I want Iris to hear what Phil and Bob have to say."

"Good idea," I replied. "Mom's reviewed some land trust agreements for clients, and Dad includes information about conservation easements in his courses. I'll issue the invite when I pick them up at the airport."

TWELVE

There's not much to do when you're sitting in an airport cell phone lot, awaiting word on a plane's arrival. I checked out social media and Google, searching for any insights into Zack's lifestyle and potential enemies.

My first stop? Zack's Facebook fan page, now overflowing with get-well wishes and ubiquitous sad-faced emoticons. However, as I scrolled back in time, a number of posts weren't so friendly. Next I tried various Twitter-feed hashtags to see the tone of tweets related to Zack and the Sin City Aces.

Oh, my.

I hadn't watched Thursday's game when the strongly favored Aces lost 28-7. Apparently, the only people Zack made happy with his less-than-stellar performance that night were fans in the opposing camp and gamblers betting against the odds.

While I watched the occasional football game with Dad, I was a hit-and-miss viewer. I didn't have a favorite team. I'd seen a few ESPN stories about Zack, but paid them scant attention since I'd never met the man.

I googled the Sin City Aces and scanned more articles. Tons of choices. The first post I clicked on had an intriguing headline: "New Team Owner Chastises Porker Aces."

A black-and-white photo accompanying the story showed a well-endowed woman wearing a T-shirt with ACES emblazoned across her chest. Underneath the big letters, smaller type read "No Porkers." I wished the picture had been in color. Somehow the woman looked like she'd be white-blonde like Marilyn Monroe.

I read the story. Sala Lemmon, the woman pictured, inherited controlling interest of the Aces when her much-older husband, Ray, passed away eighteen months ago. The will made the minority stockholder, Kate Lemmon, extremely unhappy. Kate, a daughter from a previous marriage, was about the same age as her stepmother.

I laughed out loud when I got to a quote from Sala Lemmon, a Las Vegas showgirl prior to her nuptials.

"When I danced, we worked our buns off to stay in shape," she said. "I expect no less from some candy-ass players, who think blubber qualifies them to waddle on the field. Sure, some positions require extra beef, but there's no excuse for flabby porkers. Now that I own the team, every Sin City Aces player will be physically fit or be gone. If I have to take the field to show them what a real workout looks like, I will."

I startled when my phone beeped. I picked up without looking at the caller ID. I expected Dad's voice. Instead Aunt Eva began talking before I could eke out a hello.

"Ask that lawyer mother of yours a question," she began. "I went to Carol's to collect fresh clothes. Soon as I put her house key in the lock, two men materialized and strong-armed me. Claimed they were security for the Sin City Aces and wanted to know what business I had at the house."

"Well, that's good, isn't it?" I interrupted. "Sounds like extra protection."

"I thought so until they said they were there to take possession of Zack's computer and iPhone. Team property, or so they claimed. Said they needed to prevent the items from falling into the wrong hands."

"That sounds weird," I agreed, "staking out the house instead of contacting Carol. Wonder what they meant by the wrong hands? Would Zack keep football plays on his computer or iPhone?"

Eva made that noise in her throat that indicated she wasn't finished and didn't expect to be interrupted again. "Told them I'd ask Carol's permission when I saw her. Meanwhile, no dice. I wouldn't let them in the house. They walked out of earshot and had a whispered meeting of the minds. I had the same thought you did. Didn't seem a legit approach to seizing Zack's property."

"Want me to ask Mom if Carol's obliged to hand over her son's electronics without his okay?"

"Yes, Carol wants the answer in case Zack's phone turns up. When I told Carol about the men, she was doubly puzzled. Zack left his computer in Vegas, and she had no idea where his iPhone might be. The deputies didn't find Zack's phone at Udderly, even though Paint and some other folks thought they saw him texting on it before Carol's speech. Sheriff Mason wanted the phone to check it for leads."

"Think those men at Carol's house were really security? Did you ask to see ID?"

Eva harrumphed. "Now how would I know if some piece of plastic was legit or bogus? Even if I had a magnifying glass to examine a badge, I still wouldn't know."

My phone beeped. "Eva, Mom and Dad are here. I'll call you after I pick them up."

"Don't bother. I'll be home by the time you get to Udderly. I'm leaving as soon as Carol gets back. The staff's letting her use employee facilities to take a shower and change clothes."

I pulled my Prius into the pick-up area and scanned the brightly-lit sidewalk for Dad since Mom was easy to miss. A skinny lamp post could hide Mom—Iris Hooker, Esquire. A size two, she could shop in the children's department in a pinch, though she'd be hard-pressed to find the boxy suits she wore for court appearances. Mom's the attorney for the City of Clemson. While her five-foot-two stature might be unintimidating, her opponents quickly learn what I discovered as a toddler—you can pack TNT in a small package.

At nearly six-feet tall, Dad—Professor Howard Hooker—was much easier to spot. He was more easy-going than Mom. When I was a kid and forced to fess up to joining in the toilet-papering of the mayor's house, Dad was my preferred confessor. I knew both my parents loved me, and I loved them, but I was definitely Daddy's girl.

Dad waved his arms. I flashed my lights, popped the trunk, and climbed out of the car for the standard round of hugs. As I walked around the bumper, I noticed a woman bustling through the airport doors. Though she wore heels tall enough to trigger my fear of heights, she marched ahead at full speed with nary a wobble. Did I know her? She looked familiar.

She disappeared from view when Dad's bear hug swallowed me. My folks had only been gone five days, but something about airport settings always made people want to demonstrate that their affections hadn't changed.

Mom, next in line, released me from my hug and handed me a shopping bag emblazoned with the Iowa State University seal. "We got you a little something. Didn't want you to forget your heritage."

Whatever was inside the bag felt squishy soft. Definitely fabric. Though I'd never attended ISU, I had more swag from my folks' alma mater than I did from Wake Forest University, my own school. I smiled. "I bet whatever's inside is Iowa State cardinal and gold."

"Can't surprise you, can we?" Dad said, as I pulled out a hooded college sweatshirt. "We figured it would come in handy now that the bite of fall's in the air."

"Thanks." I kissed both of them on their cheeks.

Dad put their luggage in the trunk and opened the front passenger door for Mom. She declined. "You've got the long legs, dear. I'll sit in back."

Dad held Mom's door, then folded himself into the front seat. "Brie, any update on Zack? The news reports haven't provided any concrete information."

As we drove away from the airport, I told them what little I knew, and ended with Eva's question about the cell phone. I couldn't see Mom's expression in the darkened backseat, but I detected a note of hesitation in her answer.

"I don't believe Zack's personal effects would belong to the team unless the Aces purchased the items for official use. And why the big-deal urgency in seizing his phone or computer unless they suspect the devices contain information or images that could damage the team's performance or brand? Makes me wonder whose 'wrong hands' they think might snatch the phone. Other teams? Gamblers? Tabloids?"

I shrugged. "So what's your advice?"

"For starters, Carol should call the owner of the Aces and ask him to identify any team representatives he's sent to Ardon."

Dad cleared his throat. "Actually it's a she. The owner of the Sin City Aces is a woman, Sala Lemmon, and she hasn't exactly been welcomed into the old boys' club."

I smiled. I enjoyed watching college games with Dad, but that was because I wanted to spend time with him, not because of the game. I paid little attention to football, especially pro teams. Dad, however, was an avid fan.

Mom cleared her throat. “Then Carol should contact Ms. Lemmon, and demand some answers, including what interest the team has in Zack’s phone and computer.”

That’s when the ball dropped. That woman on high-heeled stilts at the airport. She looked familiar because I’d just seen her face. In black-and-white newsprint, not color. Sala Lemmon had arrived in Ardon County.

“I don’t think Carol will need to phone Ms. Lemmon. She’s here. I saw her leaving the airport terminal right behind you. It just took me awhile to place her face. My guess is she’s on her way to the hospital.”

Dad nodded. “Probably wants a first-hand report on her investment. Whatever she may think of Zack as a human being, he’s a valuable asset. If his football career is over, she’ll need to make some hard decisions quickly.”

“What kind of insurance does a professional team have to protect against losses like this?” Mom mused.

That thought hadn’t occurred to me, but another had. Maybe Sala Lemmon wanted something more than a first-hand report on Zack’s condition. Maybe she wanted Zack’s phone and computer. That pointed my brain in a different direction.

“Do you suppose whoever attacked Zack took his phone? Maybe he was clobbered because someone wanted something on his phone and didn’t think he’d just hand it over.”

Dad made a low humming noise in his throat as he considered my question.

“That’s possible. But the news reports said Zack was knocked out and then speared with a pitchfork after he was out cold. If getting the phone was the reason for the attack, you’d think the assailant would pocket the phone and hot-foot it out of there. No pitchfork theatrics. That seems awfully vengeful.”

I smiled. “Well, Dad, in your plots the bad guys always try to direct suspicion to others by leaving false clues. Maybe the attacker was just a thug for hire but his employer suggested that he make it look personal.”

While Dad heads Clemson University’s horticultural department, he's a closet crime novelist who constantly tries out potential mystery plots on Mom and me.

Dad chuckled. "You're right, Brie. Maybe the pitchfork is a red herring, though it'll be a very painful one for Zack once he comes out of his coma."

Since none of us seemed to have any more insights into Sala Lemmon's personal visit or the whereabouts of the quarterback's missing cell phone, I changed the subject.

"Eva invited ARGH's president and founder to lunch tomorrow to discuss a conservation easement. She'd like both of you to join her. Are you free?"

I glanced in the rearview mirror and saw Mom nod.

"We have to attend church. The Clemson police chief's daughter is being confirmed but noon should be safe," she said. "Is that all right with you, Howard?"

"Sure, I'll just record the football games to make sure I don't miss anything."

I didn't need to look in the backseat to know Mom was rolling her eyes.

"I hope you're planning to sit in, Brie," she said. "If anything happens to Eva, you inherit Udderly. You need to understand how an easement could affect a sale of the property."

"Eva and I have talked about it. I'd sure hate for Udderly to be paved over for student housing, a shopping mall, or a car dealership. I'm all for the easement. But Eva insisted I sit in. She wants me to totally agree this is the way Udderly should go."

For the rest of the drive to my parents' Clemson home, our conversation covered benign topics: the weather in South Carolina during their absence, their visits with Dad's old colleagues at Iowa State, new construction on campus.

After I dropped off my parents, I headed straight to Udderly. When I walked into the cabin, I caught Eva giving Cashew a treat.

"That's the first and only one, right?" I asked. Any more treats from Eva and Andy, and my dog would look like Tammy, our pot-bellied pig.

Already in her nightie, Eva had the good grace to look guilty and quickly changed the subject. "Are your folks coming tomorrow?"

"Yes," I answered. "And Mom says Carol doesn't need to hand over Zack's phone—if it ever reappears—until she gets some answers from the Aces owner."

"Sounds right." Eva yawned. "I'm tired. Unless we need to blatherskite tonight, I'm off to dreamland."

I kissed her cheek. "No we can blatherskite at first light."

I was tired, too. Before trundling off to bed, I texted Andy and Paint since I'd promised to share any updates on Zack. My report was brief. *Z still in coma. Aces owner at airport.*

Too bushed to work my thumbs into a tither trying to explain all the drama about the missing cell phone, I sent a cryptic request. *Z phone missing. Hunt at Udderly, 2morrow 9a?*

In a flash, both men texted they'd join the cell hunt caper. My final text went to Mollye, who'd feel slighted if she were left out of a scavenger hunt.

I just hoped one of Udderly's critters hadn't decided the phone was a munchie.

Maybe Mollye could use her questionable psychic powers to see if one of the goats had craved an iPhone snack.

THIRTEEN

In theory it was morning. Could have fooled me. Pitch black. Chilly. Nothing seemed to be going right. What did I expect when I hadn't had an injection of caffeine and sunrise seemed a distant promise?

I couldn't find the blasted pail I normally used to feed Rita and scoop up our billy goats' high-energy eats. I rummaged around the milking barn until I stumbled on a substitute, then headed to Duncan's lair.

I crept inside his pen, emptied the feed, and skedaddled.

Whammo!

I pitched forward. Landed hard. My bottom felt as if someone'd hit it with a two-by-four. It took me a second, sprawled in a freshly "watered" (by Duncan) mud patch, for my brain to click in.

The billy goat's de-horned but hard and incredibly bony head had hit me square in the butt. I scrambled up and ran. He wasn't going to get me again.

What was that horrid smell? Ye gods. I breathed through my mouth. Didn't do much to alleviate the smell of my goat pee-soaked pants.

I spotted Aunt Eva's lantern as she stepped out of the milking barn. "You okay?" she yelled as I ran pell-mell toward her.

"No," I answered. "I'm not."

"Peeuw." Aunt Eva laughed. "You idiot, you turned your back on Duncan. What did I tell you? You're not going to bring that stink inside. You smell worse than those tofu concoctions you whip up."

"So what do you want me to do?" I asked, exasperated by her uncompassionate response.

"Strip. Use the outdoor shower behind the milking barn. I'll bring you a towel and clean clothes."

Eva punctuated her shooing motions with loud guffaws.

Grrr.

Scrubbed raw, I'd returned to our cabin, shivering. In late October, daytime temperatures were delightful. Mid-seventies. But come sundown the mercury dived, and it was mid-morning before temperatures climbed out of the forties.

By the time Paint, Andy, and Mollye arrived for the missing iPhone search, I was clean and scent free. Chores complete, I was also fully caffeinated—four cups of java—and ready to rock-and-roll despite a short night and bouts of mind-wandering insomnia.

I'd latched on to the latest coffee research, which suggested a potful wasn't as bad for your health as experts once touted. Good news. I'd given up meat, eggs, and cheese in the interest of a healthy diet, but even we vegans have our limits. Coffee and chocolate were where I drew my dietary line in the sand.

Eva stepped out on the porch to greet the scavengers.

"What's the plan?" she asked. "A grid search?"

"Sounds like a winner," Paint said. "Brie and I will start right outside the barn. Andy, you and Mollye can scour the area where they put the speakers' podium. We can work our way towards each other."

"Not a bad plan, but I think we'll go with girls versus boys. I want the advantage of Mollye's psychic powers," I joked.

What I didn't want was Paint-initiated distractions from the task at hand. The legal moonshiner had quite the talent for flustering me. "Mollye and I will start at the barn."

"What are you going to do, call Zack's phone to see if you hear it ring?" Eva asked.

Andy shrugged. "We could give it a try, but Zack probably switched it to vibrate. Since the fundraiser was his mom's big to-do, I'm betting he was super careful. Having his phone ring while she was mid-speech would have been very uncool."

Paint nodded. "The battery's probably dead anyway. We're not near a cell tower so whatever calls Zack did make ate up a lot of power. If the phone's lost, it hasn't been charged since Friday, and now it's Sunday morning."

Andy pulled out his cell phone. "Well, let's call and see what happens. I've got Zack's number in my directory." A few seconds later, Andy shook his head. "Didn't ring. Went straight to voicemail. Battery's definitely dead."

"Well, good luck with your search," Eva said. "I'm off to make goat fudge. Our inventory is kaput. Tell you what. I'll give a one-pound fudge reward to anyone who finds Zack's phone. Everyone except Brie that is. She'll get a hunk of slimy tofu she can doctor up and try to pass off as chocolate mousse. Ugh. Life's too short."

"Yeah, life tends to be short when you keep shoveling in cholesterol," I countered.

My friends laughed at our tit for tat. My aunt stuck out her tongue as she turned to walk away. After a few steps, she yelled over her shoulder. "Don't forget we have guests coming for lunch, and I suppose we need to feed them."

"I know. Mom and Dad are bringing the grease—a.k.a. fried chicken. I thawed a sweet potato casserole, cut up fruit, and threw together a salad before I left the cabin."

"We're invited, right?" Mollye asked.

"Not this time. Phil Owens and Bob Codner from ARGH are coming over to give Eva more details on setting up a conservation easement."

"Well, rats," Mollye said. "I love fried chicken."

"Help me find the cell phone, and I'll see Eva's fudge and raise it with as much fried chicken as you can chow down in one sitting. I just won't cook it and I'll tattle on you to Riley the Rooster, who may peck you in protest."

"Deal. Riley Roo's my buddy. He loves me," said Mollye.

The crime scene tape was down so the barn was no longer off limits. Mollye and I started inside even though we figured the crime scene investigators had searched all the obvious places. After a few minutes bothering the animals, we moved our search outside. We looked along what we considered Zack's most likely route from head table to haunted sideshow.

Ten feet out, I spotted the missing pail used to feed our mule and billy goats in an unexpected spot. Forced to use a different bucket the last two mornings, Rita had snorted each time her nose bumped its steep sides. I walked over to return the mule's favorite pail to the barn.

Bingo.

"Found it," I shouted. The iPhone's camouflage-style case was a near match with the feed. Lucky I spotted it.

Andy and Paint came running.

"How on earth did the phone land in that bucket?" Paint asked.

"I think I know," Andy said. "There were buckets inside the back stall where we found Zack. Remember how the paramedics wanted everything out of their way, a clear path?"

"Right." Paint nodded. "I helped move stuff."

"Let's make sure it's Zack's," I added, "though I can't imagine another iPhone landing in a feed bucket. We can use my charger to power it up and then call."

"Good idea," Mollye agreed. "Maybe if we look at his text messages we'll find a clue about the attack. Are we detectives, or what?"

"Or what." Andy sighed. "Even if it's Zack's phone, we can't look at texts, downloads, or recent calls without his passcode. He's had so many problems with snoops; Zack was paranoid about being hacked. Said he'd created a doozy of a passcode to defeat even the best black hats, though Paint and I might guess it if we could remember our first day in kindergarten."

Mollye's triumphant expression evaporated. "So can you figure it out? What happened in kindergarten? Do you remember?"

Paint grinned. "I have fond memories of naptime and chocolate milk, but I kinda doubt his passcode is 'napsalot'. Luckily, we don't need Zack's password. We have Zack. He programmed it so he didn't have to fool around keying in a passcode. His thumbprint opens the phone."

"You're right." Andy nodded. "Good. Carol can decide if she wants to open it."

"Eva can talk it over with her," I agreed. "Carol may want to hand the phone over to the Sheriff or Sala Lemmon without yielding to the temptation to peek at Zack's texts."

Mollye shook her head. "I'd sure want to know what made my son's phone such a prize before I gave strangers carte blanche."

Back at the cabin, we plugged the phone in and called Zack's number. The phone vibrated. Definitely his.

"Excellent," Andy announced, smiling in triumph. "Now it's up to Carol. Who's up for going to a dog agility competition in Greenville? One of my former patients, a Jack Russell, is competing. I'll leave about two."

"Sounds like fun," I answered. "A nice break. Two o'clock should work."

"I love dog shows," Mollye said. "It's such a kick to guess which owner belongs to which dog."

"I'm in," Paint added, "even though Lunar would consider such an event beneath him. I may have raised Lunar since he was an abandoned pup, but he's still a wolf. He'd prefer to eat his rivals."

FOURTEEN

Mom and Dad were the first to arrive for lunch, bringing two large, fragrant boxes of fried chicken. Why does grease-coated meat still smell so good? Will my sense of smell ever get on board with my vegan heart?

I transferred the chicken to a tray and popped it in the oven to stay warm while Eva put out a selection of goat cheeses. I brought Mom and Dad up to date on our cell phone find before our guests arrived. I agreed with Eva that phone custody should be Carol's decision.

"Did you let Carol know you found the phone?" Mom asked.

"Yes," Eva replied. "She's going to turn it over to the sheriff after she makes sure there's nothing personal her son would want kept private. I'll take the phone to her after lunch."

Barking dogs announced our guests' arrival. Looking out the window, I watched Bob Codner lever his bulky frame out of the passenger seat of Phil Owens' old but elegant Jaguar. Eva'd told me Phil had bought an abused, fifteen-year-old Jag and restored it the year after he retired. Under the noonday sun, the car's mirror-like finish was almost blinding.

Phil didn't exactly fit the image of someone who tinkers with old cars. Or maybe he did. He had money and time and hated fishing. Phil lived on the banks of Ardon County's Lake Sisel, where retirees' posh homes were slowly edging out former trailers and fishing camps.

Phil, a retired airline pilot, was representative of the silver-haired band of newcomers hated by the CAVE contingent. Phil and Lilly co-founded ARGH when a developer announced plans to build high-rise, high-density condos on the lake, even though infrastructure—roads, water, sewer, fire-fighting equipment—for such a project didn't exist.

Bob, a local, and Phil, a transplant, were fast friends. Both were passionate about protecting Ardon County's ecology, culture, and farmlands from unplanned sprawl.

Eva welcomed both men and completed the introductions. While Mom and Dad had attended ARGH meetings presided over by Aunt Lilly, they'd never formally met either gentleman.

"Let's chat while we eat," Aunt Eva decreed after the handshakes. "I'm hungry."

No one objected. The guests knew Eva well enough to nod assent. My aunt took drink orders while I put plates of steaming chicken on the table. Six was the max our little dining nook could seat without knocking knees.

Once everyone but me had hoisted a chicken part or attacked it with a fork and knife, Mom asked her first question. "Do you think Ardon County will ever get zoning? Wouldn't that eliminate the need for conservation easements?"

Phil shook his head. "Zoning's opposed by slick developers, like Allie Gerome, and the CAVE faction's right-wing fringe. There are also plenty of reasonable locals who want their kids to be able to sell farms or forestland to the highest bidders. They don't want zoning to nix a lucrative offer. Sorry neighbors."

Bob waved a chicken leg as he jumped in. "Of course, the same locals raise a huge stink if someone proposes putting anything that offends them nearby. I know. I'm one of the so-called natives. Native meaning my kin have marked our territory with gravestones for at least four generations. It doesn't mean we have a drop of Cherokee blood."

"What kind of projects trigger local wrath?" Dad asked.

"Group homes for virtually any population segment needing them," Bob added. "Plus any enterprise that violates their morals—shops that sell sex toys, tattoo parlors, even retreats for religions that sound seditious to Southern Baptists."

Phil laughed. "Don't forget the claim that zoning is a United Nations' conspiracy."

Dad's fork clanked on his plate. "You're kidding. Zoning pre-dates the U.N.'s existence by decades."

Bob put down his chicken leg—flesh no longer attached—and shook a finger at Dad. "Howard, logic won't work. The CAVE contingent knows you're a carpetbagger out to steal land anointed with our ancestors' blood. But they reserve even more hatred for locals like Carol and me who think their conspiracy theories are hogwash. That's why Chester and his cronies crashed Carol's fundraiser. They've despised her since she won her first election, a seat on County Council."

"So zoning isn't in the cards?" Mom asked, returning us to her original question.

"We'll get some form of it sooner or later," Phil answered. "It's the later that worries me. We're at a tipping point. Unplanned sprawl can desecrate a landscape before people realize what's happening."

Eva cleared her throat. "And zoning's not a perfect guarantee. Some future County Council could make it meaningless. But a conservation easement's an iron-clad guarantee."

When the conversation segued into tax considerations, my mind wandered. Mom would make certain Eva's trust document was solid. If my tofu creations didn't prompt my aunt to change her will, I would inherit Udderly. I wanted exactly what Eva wanted—Udderly's wooded hills to remain green and unpaved.

Trying to safeguard what you love can be tricky if others feel just as strongly about destroying those protections. That thought brought me back to Carol and Zack.

What could make Zack's phone so valuable? Did Carol have an idea? How far would she go to safeguard it?

FIFTEEN

A few minutes after Eva left for the hospital, Mollye's van pulled up with Paint and Andy already on board. Since her van provided the roomiest option, Mollye'd offered to drive. My Prius certainly couldn't compete.

Mollye rolled down her window and hollered. "Get your fanny in gear. The gents saved the front seat for you. I'm guessing neither wanted to risk being close to me. Afraid their passion might overcome them."

I stepped on the running board and hopped in. "I'm sure that's it. It's all I can do to control myself around you. Hi, everyone."

I'd barely buckled my seatbelt when I heard a phone ring.

"Sorry," Paint said. "I'll put it on vibrate after I see who it is. Ugh. No need to answer. It's that doofus Mick again. Fourth time he's called wanting the inside track on Zack's condition. I know he flew out to Vegas for a game once and Zack played nice guy, introducing him around as a high school pal. But they were never close. I'm guessing Mick's just looking to score insider dope. Every time he calls he sounds a little more frantic, more squirrelly."

Since the Greenville convention center was an hour's drive, it gave me oodles of time to try to pin down why fantasy football was so popular with Mick—and my three buddies. Hey, maybe I was missing great entertainment.

"I'm still not clear. What makes fantasy football so addictive? Enlighten me."

I should have kept my mouth shut. Over the next hour I learned far more than I cared to know. At one end of the spectrum, fantasy football attracted hard-core gambling addicts like Mick. With a ten-thousand-dollar weekly fantasy football option, gamblers could excavate a gaping black hole of debt in no time.

Of course, there were also casual players attracted by camaraderie and the desire to be a winner. Fantasy football made it socially acceptable to gamble, win at something, and crow about their expertise and talent.

Mollye said women loved to show up men in their families—or offices—by proving they were more than capable of mastering football's finer points, studying stats, and reading scouting reports. A lot fairer way to compete than, say, arm wrestling.

"So have we convinced you to join my fantasy football team?" Paint asked.

"Not a chance. Between dairy chores and renovating my someday B&B, free time is a real luxury. Any spare minutes are devoted to sleeping, reading and cooking. I haven't even found time to arrange for Udderly to host the goat yoga classes that have become so popular."

Mollye cleared her throat. "You seem to forget you can do one of the best exercises in bed. I'm sure Andy or Paint would be happy to help."

A backseat duet of "Amen" sounded as we rolled to a stop in the line of vehicles waiting to pay for parking. I groaned and handed Mollye the five-dollar bill Andy had entrusted to me a couple blocks back.

Guess he didn't want to give Mollye additional reasons to take her hands off the wheel. My friend couldn't talk without gesturing, and the need to hold a steering wheel failed to inhibit her. When riding shotgun, my policy was to avoid looking at Mollye. I hoped she'd notice I wasn't paying attention to her gyrations and would return her hands to the wheel. Too bad it didn't seem to work.

The air inside the convention center left no doubt we were attending a canine event. The place smelled like wet dog with a strong undercurrent of urine. Hairs—white, black, brown, short, long, microscopic—were so thick they almost colored the air. Though happy I wasn't allergic, the soupy mix reminded me I'd best breathe through my nose.

We walked around an outer ring, where dogs not on stage were fussed over by their owners. The doggie sweet talk made me giggle. "Now, sweetums, let Mommy brush your tail...I know baby doll. That Chihuahua was a real meanie." I figured I'd hear less cooing at a cutest baby competition. Not that I wasn't occasionally guilty of baby talk with my pup.

Our mission was to locate George, Andy's former Jack Russell patient. I figured we'd found our quarry when a cascade of excited yips greeted Andy's approach. The vet stroked George's head and introduced us to the owner.

"We're on in less than ten minutes," the owner answered. "Go grab seats. I'm so nervous. I hope the crowd noise doesn't terrify George."

"He'll be fine," Andy answered. "Good luck."

Stadium seating circled an agility course more than twice the size of a basketball court. Course obstacles ranged from flexible tubes that looked like oversized ducts for dryer lint to hurdles and teeter-totters. The one that puzzled me looked like a lengthy parking rack for bicycles. "What's that?"

"Weave poles. The dogs weave in and out," Andy answered. "Miss an open space and they lose points."

"So how does this work?" Paint asked. "Are all agility courses the same?"

"No," Andy answered. "Courses have similar obstacles, but the real contest is to see if dogs follow their owners' hand and voice commands to get around a course they've never seen before. Treats or bribes aren't allowed."

"Doesn't look fair to short dogs," Mollye observed.

"They reset the bars for each dog category."

The announcer's voice boomed over the PA system as he introduced the next contestant.

We cheered as the little Pug and her owner gave it their best shot. Unfortunately, the Pug was halfway through a final weave when she succumbed to an overpowering urge to poop. The audience hee-hawed as the owner's shoulders slumped. The woman whipped a plastic baggie out of her pocket, scooped up the deposit, and gave the audience a jaunty wave as she exited with her pet.

Were the owners certifiable? Who had this much time to train a dog? Luckily, I didn't feel I was depriving Cashew. Hard to set bars low enough for a miniature to clear.

"Hey, why don't you train your goats to do this stuff?" Mollye chimed in. "I've seen videos on YouTube. They're even cuter than dogs."

"They're pretty awesome without human coaching. Think I'll leave them to their own tricks."

"Here comes George," Andy said. "Hope he does well."

With one tiny exception—George paused for a second to sniff something—his performance was flawless. Andy gave George a standing ovation. "Pretty good for his first time out."

As he sat back down, Andy frowned. "Paint, look in the aisle at the bottom of the bleachers. See that guy who's scanning the crowd instead of the dogs. Is it Mick?"

Paint looked. "What the hey? Yeah, it's Mick. Think he's looking for me? How would he know I'm here unless he followed Mollye's van? What does he want?"

Stadium lights reflected off the bald man's head. His clothes looked dirty and askew, like he hadn't quite matched his shirt buttons with the right holes. He looked up, and I recognized him. It was the man who'd come to Udderly yesterday morning, claiming he was looking for a lost business card. So that was Mick.

I was about to tell my friends about Mick's visit, when the cell phone in my pocket vibrated. Eva. I had to take the call. My aunt wasn't a casual caller and she never texted.

"Hello," I whispered as I used my hand to muffle the conversation. I hated it when strangers carried on loud conversations that bystanders couldn't ignore. Downright rude.

A second later my "What?" screech betrayed my best intentions. My friends' faces turned toward me like synchronized sunflowers seeking light. They didn't speak until I ended the call five minutes later.

"What's wrong?" Paint asked.

I swallowed hard. "Carol's missing. Eva went to the hospital to deliver Zack's phone. Not a soul beside Zack in his room. Eva questioned the deputy guarding his room and the nurses. They all said the same thing. Carol left the room, saying she needed a fresh dose of caffeine. No one's seen her since. Eva searched every public area in the hospital."

"Maybe a friend dropped by and took her out for some fresh air," Paint suggested.

"Doesn't fly. Carol's car is gone. Eva called her about one to say she was headed her way. She's not answering her phone either. Eva's certain she'd pick up any call, thinking it could be an update on her son's condition."

Mollye frowned. "I'd be freaked if I were Eva. I have an icky feeling. We ought to head back."

"Eva asked us to meet her at Carol's house. She didn't want to go there alone. Not after being greeted by two goons on her last visit. Sorry about the show, Andy."

Andy shrugged. "Not a problem. Eva and Carol take priority."

SIXTEEN

I was so upset by Aunt Eva's news that our sighting of Mick at the dog show fled my mind until we were speeding toward Ardon in Mollye's van. I recounted Mick's furtive visit to Udderly shortly after Zack's attack.

"You called the sheriff, right?" Mollye asked. "Phone him again and tell him Mick was the suspicious guy you scared off your property."

"Can't believe he would attack Zack," Andy said. "But desperate people can do things that are totally out of character."

I turned in my seat to look at Paint and Andy. "Could Mick be involved in Carol's disappearance?"

Paint shook his head. "Can't see how if Carol disappeared a couple of hours ago. Mick had to be at the dog show or en route. He can't be in two places at once, and I'm pretty sure he doesn't have an evil twin."

Our speculation about Carol's possible whereabouts turned to other possibilities. None made much sense.

"Did Eva call the sheriff?" Paint asked.

"Not yet. She's reluctant to report Carol missing when she's only been gone a couple hours. Maybe she just drove off to sit on a park bench. With all these news vultures hanging around, any hint Carol mysteriously disappeared would leak. Eva says her friend would be mortified if people launched a big search when she'd simply unplugged for a bit to scream into a pillow somewhere."

"You said Carol's car was gone?" Andy looked puzzled. "I thought it was still at Udderly. Didn't she ride to the hospital in the ambulance with Zack?"

"She did. A friend swung by Udderly, picked up her car, and delivered it to the hospital. It's nowhere in the parking lot."

Mollye turned onto Carol's street. Instead of stopping at the neat one-story ranch she drove down the block. "Didn't see Carol's car or

Eva's truck," she explained, "just two good-sized goons. Looked like they were coming from Carol's backyard."

"Couldn't miss them," I agreed.

Though scraggly azalea bushes added a bit of greenery to the front entry, the evergreens weren't large enough to provide two hulking males cover as they skulked from the rear of the house. The taller man could have won a Paul Bunyan look-alike contest with his thick black beard and tree-trunk arms. Thank heaven he wasn't carrying an axe. His blond, clean-shaven sidekick was only slightly smaller. I was glad we had them seriously outnumbered.

"Let's wait till those dudes leave or Eva arrives," I suggested. "We don't have a house key, and they don't look like big conversationalists."

I'd barely finished that sentence when Eva's truck appeared in the van's side mirror. Though we were half a block away, I figured Eva had spotted us, too. Mollye's Starry Skies van was next-to-impossible to miss.

Eva parked, but remained in her truck cab as the four of us exited the van and moseyed toward Carol's house. When the burly dudes spotted us, they moved to block the front stoop. Guess they figured there was no point in hiding.

Eva jumped down from her truck and nodded at us. "Glad to see you. Let's go inside, shall we?"

The two men maintained their front stoop blockade.

"What are you doing back here?" Black Beard asked Eva.

"Think I should be asking you the same, sonny. Like I told you the first time, I don't see how my business is any of your business."

Having two muscular fellas in tow seemed to give my aunt extra moxie. Not that she needed a lot of added bravado.

"Who's with you?" the blond bubba asked Eva. My aunt's message hadn't sunk in: she wasn't answering questions.

When Eva started up the stairs, Black Beard lunged forward, going for her arm.

Paint wrapped his own mitt around the guard dog's wrist. "Let her go."

Meanwhile, Andy stepped in front of blondie, and Mollye whipped out her phone. "In one minute, I'm calling my boyfriend. Did I mention he's a sheriff's deputy, and he's on duty? Get lost."

Whether it was Mollye's threat or the prospect of duking it out with two strapping young men, the self-proclaimed Aces' security contingent backed off. In fact, before we opened Carol's front door, they'd hustled to a dark sedan parked two houses down. One had a cell phone pressed to his ear as he slid into the passenger seat. Were they really on the Sin City Aces' payroll? Were they asking Sala's permission to make us disappear?

Like Dad, I read a lot of mysteries.

Eva inserted her key and unlocked the door. Though I was still on the porch as she stepped inside, I had no problem hearing her gasp. The four of us practically trampled Eva as we stampeded inside to see what prompted her reaction.

I gasped, too. Andy had the presence of mind to close the front door and lock it behind us in case the men outside changed tactics. My guess was they didn't need to venture inside to know exactly what the interior of Carol's house looked like.

Chairs toppled. Cushions and pillows gutted; their fluffy innards creating snow-white drifts on the green carpet. Living room bookshelves emptied. Books, spines broken, pages torn, strewn across the floor in no discernible pattern.

It looked like someone had set a giant blender on puree.

Mollye sucked in a breath, most likely to steady her nerves. "Think those two thugs outside did this?"

"Well, it didn't look like this yesterday. Those hooligans would be my top B&E candidates," Eva answered.

Shocked by the ruins, she'd dropped her purse on the floor. She stepped right over it and strode to the center of the room.

Paint carefully zigzagged through the debris to reach a front window. He pulled apart the slats in the window blinds to check the whereabouts of our suspected villains.

"They're gone," he announced. "Whoever they phoned must have told them to book it before we learned what they'd been up to and called 911."

"That is our next call, isn't it, Eva?" Andy asked.

My aunt didn't answer. She marched down the hallway that connected all the rooms in the house. Front room, dining room, and kitchen to the left, bedrooms and baths to the right. All were in shambles though the smallest, guest bedroom had been hit the worst. Zack's suitcase sat empty; its silk lining ripped to shreds. His clothes were strewn across a dismembered mattress.

Eva collapsed on the edge of the shredded catawampus bedding.

"You didn't answer Andy's question," I said. "Shouldn't we get the sheriff?"

Aunt Eva looked up. "Have to, though I feel queasy about making decisions for Carol. But she's missing, so yes, I'll call Sheriff Mason."

"Will you give him Zack's phone?" I asked. "That may be what the maniacs who did this were trying to find."

Eva shook her head. "No. Carol told me she wouldn't hand Zack's phone over to anyone until she was certain it couldn't embarrass her son."

My aunt stared at the four of us huddled near the bedroom doorway and locked eyes with each of us in turn. "No mention of the phone, okay? Not just yet. Not until we find Carol."

Andy cleared his throat. "But the phone might hold some clue about what's happening. Maybe we should unlock it, look at any messages. If there's nothing embarrassing, we hand it over to Mason for his investigation."

Mollye harrumphed and swept her arms wide to encompass the bedroom maelstrom. "Who'd tear things up like this searching for a phone if it didn't hold some juicy secrets?"

Paint nodded. "Agreed. That's if they really were after the phone. We don't know that. Still we owe it to Zack and Carol to find out if that cell offers any clues."

Eva looked about. "Where's my handbag? My phone's in it. Oh, the heck with it, one of you give me a cell. You all have 'em practically Velcroed to your tushes."

I tried to hand Eva my cell, which indeed had been nestled in my back pocket and was still warm from my rump. She waved me off.

"Dial the dang number for the sheriff before you give that hunk-a-junk to me. You know how I hate those touch screens. I'd end up calling Keokuk or Timbuktu."

Once I heard the first ring, I handed the phone to my aunt.

Eva identified herself and asked to speak to Sheriff Mason. We all listened as she dispassionately described the mess we'd found. She also told Mason about Carol's troubling disappearance and her own encounters with muscle bound creeps. She failed to mention she entered Carol's abode with four sidekicks.

When the conversation ended, she tossed the phone to me. "You disconnect. I can never figure out which dang button to push."

"So what now?" Mollye asked.

"The sheriff's on his way, so all of you get going." Eva made a shooing motion. "No reason to mention you were here. Doesn't help a bit in finding who ransacked the place. Go, and take Zack's phone with you. It's still in my purse."

Eva sprang off the mattress, hustled back to the littered living room, and picked her purse off the floor. She unzipped the main compartment, stirred the contents with her hand, and plucked Zack's phone out like it was a Crackerjack prize.

She tossed the iPhone to me. "Now vamoose. All of you."

It felt as if Eva threw me a hunk of ice. The plastic and metal of Zack's phone radiated cold. A shiver ran up my spine.

Did I really want to know what secrets it held?

SEVENTEEN

We piled into Mollye's van and she burned rubber as we zoomed off. I looked in the rearview mirror, scanning the street for any sign of the thugs' dark sedan. I hated leaving Eva alone, not knowing if they were lurking about.

Mollye took one hand off the wheel to reach over and pat my arm. "Don't worry. The sheriff will be there in minutes. No time for the bad guys to accost Eva."

While I didn't believe my friend could tell fortunes, she had an uncanny talent for picking up on other people's emotions in the here and now.

"So where are we going?" Andy asked.

"How about Udderly?" I suggested. "That's where Eva will head as soon as she finishes with the sheriff. I don't think she'll go back to the hospital unless Carol turns up."

I swiveled to speak to the men in the backseat. "You two have someplace else you need to be this afternoon or evening?"

"Not me," Paint said. "No Sunday liquor sales in Ardon County so Magic Moonshine is closed, and Lunar's fenced in the back with plenty of food and water."

"Same for me," Andy replied. "I'd planned to be gone all day. My baby sister, Julie, is animal-sitting the clinic. We only have two in-house patients right now—a parakeet recuperating from a plastic curtain eating binge and a hamster that broke a leg careening off his wheel. Julie will call if there's an emergency."

"Might be a good idea to get our trucks though," Paint added. "Mollye picked us up in the Bi-Lo parking lot. Let's stop so we all have wheels if something comes up. We'll follow you back to Udderly."

"Need any groceries?" Andy asked.

"No, I have enough leftovers from our luncheon to feed everyone."

"Yeah, but are there chicken breasts?" Mollye scoffed. "You promised me all the fried chicken I could eat if I found Zack's phone. In my book that means crispy, crunchy chicken breasts."

I saw no point quibbling over the fact that I found Zack's phone while she stood nearby. After all, she'd driven us to Greenville, and we'd survived her hands-free chauffeuring. I bought a bucket of fried chicken, mostly breasts, at the store's deli counter and dodged out of Mollye's reach when she lunged for the hot, greasy takeout box. "No snacking en route. Keep your hands on the wheel."

By the time our three-vehicle caravan reached the farm, it was six thirty and the sun had all but vanished. As I put our lunch leftovers and chicken re-supply in the oven, my right "cheek" vibrated—my phone, not Zack's, in my back pocket. The switched-off celebrity phone sat mute in the middle of the kitchen table. The ringtone announced Eva was calling.

"I'm on my way," she said. "You're at Udderly, right? Hope none of you wrapped your grubby fingers around anything in Carol's house. The sheriff's dusting for prints. Fingerprinted me to exclude mine. Pretty impressive. Didn't even have to put my fingers in that black goop, just pressed them against a laptop screen."

"I'm getting supper ready," I said. "We'll wait for you."

"Good, I'm starving. There'd better be meat or I might have to chew your derriere."

As soon as I heard Eva's truck, I started putting food on the table. A pile of chicken warm from the oven meant my derriere was safe.

Andy and Paint, who'd been sitting at the table, stood to greet my aunt.

"Sit, sit." She tossed her poncho on the coatrack by the door. "I could eat a hippo."

Despite Eva's dismissal of any need for male chivalry, Andy didn't sit until he'd pulled out a chair for her.

"What did the sheriff make of the mess at Carol's?" Mollye asked as she forked a breast and created a sweet potato moat around her preferred chicken part.

"Kyle Mason isn't the chatty type," Eva answered. "Polite enough, but he doesn't run off at the mouth. I asked questions, got two-syllable replies. But he did seem flummoxed to learn I hadn't a clue about Carol's whereabouts. He asked me to keep quiet about her disappearance. Feared he'd invite a circus if she was declared missing when she might have just taken a privacy breather. The fact that her car was gone seemed to convince him she'd driven off somewhere."

"So is he going to do anything more than twiddle his thumbs?" Paint sounded peeved.

Eva nodded. "At my suggestion, he's going to pay Fred Baxter a visit. Never know when that man will decide his revenge is a dish that's become cold enough to serve. Mason's also assigning a deputy to watch Carol's house. Someone's already on duty at the hospital. If Carol doesn't phone or appear by midnight, he'll treat it as a missing person case."

"What did Mason say about the thugs outside Carol's house?" I asked.

"His deputies are on the lookout for a dark sedan carrying two supersized cretins. But since we never saw a license plate, it's more or less a needle in a haystack. Plenty of dark sedans in Ardon County. And, if it's a rental, it could have been picked up anywhere."

Eva glanced around the table. "What about you geniuses? Any idea how to get Zack's thumbprint and open his phone now that a deputy's making certain he has no visitors?"

"Won't they make an exception for you, Eva?" Andy asked. "Heck, you spent the whole first night there. Surely you're not banned."

"Wrong. The sheriff made it clear I'm included in the ban, at least until Carol returns. He's been getting grief from Sala Lemmon, her step-kid, and now Doug Hayes, who just flew his private plane into our county airport. Mason doesn't want to hear any gripes about favoritism so the rule is nobody enters Zack's room except hospital staff. The sheriff pointed out that as long as Zack's in a coma, he's not gonna care who visits."

Mollye stroked her chin. "I could call Danny and find out who's on hospital duty tonight. If we're lucky, it'll be some deputy Brie's never met. There's been a wholesale turnover at the Sheriff's Office since her run-in with the law last spring. Deputies who grew up here would know me, Andy, and Paint since we're locals, but not Brie."

"So what?" I asked. "My face might not be on a wanted poster, but I'd still be a stranger. The deputy wouldn't let me in."

I frowned, suspecting whatever scheme Mollye was hatching would not thrill me.

Mollye's slow grin reinforced my premonition. "It's Halloween, my dear, and I spotted a darling little nurse costume when I picked up your mermaid get-up."

I awarded her my best stink eye. "Somehow I doubt it matches the uniforms worn by Ardon Hospital nurses. More likely the costume's a translucent white with a mini-skirt that belongs in some grown-up version of 'let's play doctor'?"

"You got me on the fantasy get-up, but you've got the legs to pull it off. Still, I'm sure that costume place has something that would work. Maybe a white coat. You could be a lab tech. And, here's where Eva and I come in. We can create a diversion while you slip by, press Zack's thumb to the screen, and boogie on out. Voila, we unlock those hidden secrets."

Eva's eyes narrowed. "I'm not saying 'no, you're out of your mind'—yet. But what's your definition of a diversion? A belly dance with tinkling bells? Sneaking billy goats inside? Beating out syncopated rhythms on bed pans?"

Mollye giggled. "Hey, your imagination rocks. I'd never have thought of any of those. Just figured we'd pester the heck out of the deputy with a barrage of questions while positioning our ample curves to screen the entrance as Brie sneaks past. If we work it right, he'd just see a nurse's uniform flit by, no face, and certainly not a good enough look for a police sketch."

I crossed my arms over my chest in a forget-it gesture. "And how much jail time is associated with impersonating a nurse and breaching a security perimeter?"

"You worry too much." Mollye grinned.

Eva sighed. "Well, the risk doesn't seem outlandish. It's not like you'd be sneaking in to do the patient any harm. All you want to do is hold his thumb."

"And hack into a phone that doesn't belong to us. One that's wanted by the sheriff and others who are desperate enough to break in and ransack Carol's house searching for it."

"We don't have to make a decision tonight," Paint said. "That costume store won't be open on a Sunday, and I'll bet any stores that sell real uniforms will be closed, too."

Andy cleared his throat. "You're forgetting my sister Julie wears the same kind of scrubs nurses do. Some hospitals dictate color but not style. Anybody notice what color scrubs the Ardon nurses wore?"

We looked blankly at each other. Nurses blended into the institutional background unless they were giving you a shot, waking you to take your blood pressure, or, in a best-case scenario, pretending not to notice the contraband food a loved one snuck in. I noticed nurses' smiles or frowns, not the color of their uniforms.

Eva's eyes screwed shut. "They're pale blue. I've seen them enough lately. Just had to think about it."

"Since I don't care what color Julie wears, she has a rainbow of colors. Imagine blue is one of them. And she used to be about Brie's size."

I frowned. "What do you mean 'used to be' my size? Is she smaller? Maybe her uniforms won't fit."

Mollye laughed. "They'll fit all right. Julie as they say is 'large with child.' Hey, that's even better. We'll make you a prego. Add that blonde wig you had on the other night and even your mom couldn't recognize you."

I wished she hadn't brought Mom into this. She'd brain me for going along with this cockamamie impersonation. Wouldn't matter that our motive was pure as Ivory soap.

EIGHTEEN

In the turmoil following Zack's attack, my mermaid wig literally bit the dust. Once I fetched Doc Bowman, I was only too happy to pull off the prickly wig. Never noticed that it wound up on the ground where folks trampled it, grinding in red clay and other substances I preferred not to identify. Since I never planned to wear the wig again, I hadn't washed it. I brushed it vigorously before I stuck it on my head to become a dirty blonde. A faint odor suggested the genus of the remaining "dirt" particles. My scalp suddenly itched.

My fake pregnant belly was an even bigger costume woe. Paint suggested substituting air pillows for the traditional feather-filled variety to create my expectant mother persona. Paint had a handy supply in his truck since he used the protective air bubbles when shipping moonshine. Andy and Paint, both duct tape fans, used the sticky stuff to create a belt and suspenders to secure the two sheets of the giant bubble wrap around my middle. However, I vetoed duct taping anything to my skin. As a compromise I put on a thin t-shirt before Mollye lowered the sticky assembly over my head.

We'd agreed I should do a walk-by of Zack's room to reconnoiter and give my shills a chance to get in position before I tried to sneak inside. As I strolled down the hospital corridor, I pretended I belonged. Casual gait. No staring straight ahead like a Stepford wife. We'd timed our foray to take advantage of the increased activity that coincides with an approaching deadline for patient visitation. I was happy to see the corridor relatively crowded with loitering family members and friends. In just ten minutes, they'd all be asked to leave. The more distractions, the better. Didn't leave us much time.

A cleaning woman pushing a cart loaded with chemicals walked toward me. She smiled. I smiled. No problems, though I did give the sharp edges of her metal cart a wide berth. Didn't want to chance rupturing an air pillow. I had the feeling the poppity-pop would scare the cottage cheese out of me and anyone nearby.

I ambled past the ICU nursing station without a single "Halt! Security!" alarm. But my biggest test loomed thirty feet away.

A knot of people milled outside Zack's room as I sauntered by on my first pass. I caught a fleeting glimpse of a man scurrying down the hall in the opposite direction. He was bald on top. Some sad remnants of sandy hair circled the back of his head. Mick?

He disappeared and my focus switched to the people immediately outside Zack's room. I recognized Sala Lemmon, who apparently had a bee—or maybe a whole hive—in her bonnet. She'd squared off against another woman, who had her back to me. It seemed I'd arrived at the tail end of a lively shouting match. The deputy on duty was engrossed in their spat and was giving Zack's room scant attention.

Sala's face was bright red. The glare focused on her adversary turned her eyes into angry slits. Made me think of a snake. Her heaving bosom—the apparent result of enraged heavy breathing—had transfixed the deputy. He jumped up from his chair. Did he think he might need to separate the combatants?

Sala pivoted and clipped the other woman's shoulder as she plowed past her headed for a stretch of empty hall. She steamed ahead, straight at me. I looked down at the thermometer in my hand as she stormed by. Wow.

Sala's nemesis then began talking to another woman who'd previously been blocked from my view. Allie Gerome. The newspaper owner appeared to be buddy-buddy with Sala's enemy. Knowing the people Allie invited into her circle of friends, I took an instant, if unfounded, dislike of the stranger.

"You have no right to keep us out of Zack's room," Allie shrieked, her double-chin jiggling as she joined in a tirade aimed at the hapless deputy on duty. "This woman is his concerned employer and I'm press."

Hmm. Maybe Eva and Mollye wouldn't need to be accomplices to my crime.

I hurried to the end of the hall, turned, and started back. No one paid me a bit of attention. As I neared the room, Allie scuttled off alone. Going away from me, thank goodness. Though I wore a wig, I feared Allie might recognize me. Last spring, mug shots of Aunt Eva and me appeared in way too many stories in her newspaper.

Allie's ally remained, but she was jabbering on her cell phone and had ceased harassing the deputy. Right on cue, Eva and Mollye took up diversion duties. The harried deputy barely had time to rejoice at the newspaper owner's huffy departure.

My collaborators positioned themselves so their bodies overlapped, blocking most of the deputy's view. By the time I reached Zack's door, I could only see the deputy's khaki pants. Did that mean he could only see my legs? Maybe the wig and my gas bag tummy were needless props.

I worked to control my breathing as I slipped inside Zack's room.

The deputy didn't notice me until I reached the quarterback's bed.

"Hey," he said. "Didn't see you come in."

I kept my back to him; didn't turn. "Just a quick check on our patient's vitals," I answered sweetly.

I pretended to take Zack's pulse. I figured the deputy had probably watched the same TV scenes of nurses lifting limp wrists that I'd viewed. How would he know the only pulse I could feel was my own, hammering a get-the-pork-rinds-out-of-here message?

I sighed in relief as the deputy reengaged with Mollye and Eva and ceased looking my way. I eased Zack's cellphone out of one of my maternity top's wide pockets and pressed his thumb against the screen. His hand felt as cold as my marble rolling pin. I remembered the heat I felt radiating from Zack when he sat beside me on a hay bale a scant two days ago. Surreal.

I crab walked toward the door. I'd brought a thermometer as a prop and pretended to be engrossed in reading it though it had never touched Zack's lips. I feared the phone would relock before Paint and Andy could check out its contents. My nerves were too frayed to do this again. With my back to the deputy, I sidled out the door and walked toward the elevators constantly rubbing the phone's screen with my thumb to keep it active and alive.

"Hey, you. Stop. I want to talk to you." A woman's voice bellowed behind me.

A nurse who wanted to know who I was? I didn't turn. Pretended I hadn't heard or had decided the woman couldn't possibly be talking to me.

"You, blondie, I said I want to talk to you. Stop."

High heels clicked on the polished floors. Okay, not a nurse. The increasing volume of the stiletto clicks told me I couldn't chance the elevator opening before my pursuer caught up. I flung open the door to the stairwell.

Before the door closed, I heard an "oomph" followed by a string of colorful swear words. Then I heard another voice. "I'm so sorry. Can I help you up?" Definitely Mollye. Still running interference.

I flew down the stairs. Two flights down, I jettisoned the blonde wig and stuffed it between my inflatable belly and my T-shirt. Figured friction would hold it there until I escaped the building.

As I hot-footed it into the hospital parking lot, I spied the getaway car, my Prius, with Andy at the wheel. Paint was holding the passenger door open for me.

"Let's go," I said.

Pop! Whoosh.

"What was that?" Andy asked.

"Me passing gas." I convulsed with nervous giggles. "I popped an air pillow putting on my seat belt."

"Did you get Zack's thumbprint?" Paint asked from the backseat.

"Sure did." I swiveled around to hand him the phone. "It's in your custody now. If it shuts down, you can go back to Zack's room as Dr. Kildare. I'm done."

Paint's fingers managed to caress mine as I relinquished the phone. "We should have at least four hours before it powers down," he said. "Should give us plenty of time to see what we need to see."

As we drove off, I glanced in the rearview mirror. Mollye and Eva were exiting the hospital. We'd come in two vehicles, figuring Mollye's van was all-too-recognizable as a getaway car. Best if the dirty blonde nurse wasn't seen with Mollye and Eva.

"Geez, I can't believe the number of unopened text messages," Paint grumbled. "No wonder Zack was furious someone posted his number in a Twitter feed. Said he'd been inundated ever since with everything from propositions to hate mail."

Andy glanced at Paint in the rearview mirror. "Zack told me he was only opening texts and voice mail from his mom, his agent, and his coach. Probably most of the unopened texts are get well messages that have come in since the attack. Not a help with motive."

"Good point," Paint said. "I'll start with texts that arrived the day Zack was attacked and work backwards."

About five minutes later, Paint mumbled, "Wow. You bad, bad boy."

"You found something incriminating?" I asked.

"Depends on your point of view. I opened a text that read: 'Thought you might find this instructive. A friend.' A video was attached. The first frame showed a nude woman on a bed. Of course, I hit play. Guess you could call it a home movie. At first, the woman was sleeping, partially covered by a sheet, but the leading man was completely 'neckid' and it wasn't long before that sheet disappeared."

His eyes settled on mine. I looked away and rubbed my neck where a warm flush had settled.

Andy jerked around to glance at Paint. "Is Zack the star?"

"Can't say." Paint shrugged. "We only get a rear view of him. Want to see, Brie?"

"No, thank you. Come on, guys. Movie time can wait. I'll pop popcorn if you'll hurry up and get us back to Udderly."

NINETEEN

Our car's dust trail hadn't disappeared when the Starry Skies van pulled into Udderly's drive. Mollye clearly believed her inside track with a deputy would let her skate on speeding tickets. Andy, Paint, and I had just cleared the porch steps, when Mollye's driver side door flew open and she popped out.

"You should have seen that high-heeled hussy's face when she toppled like a dead pine in a thunderstorm." My friend cackled. "Smack. All I did was edge my foot out a teensy bit. Figured you needed a little lead time to escape what with all the griping you've been doing about running less often than you want."

Inside the cabin, we all slid into our usual seats at the dining nook's pine table.

"Who was that woman arguing with Sala? Does anyone know?" I asked.

Eva nodded. "Got a last name. After Mollye tripped her, the deputy helped her up. He called her Ms. Lemmon. She wouldn't be hard to ID in a line up. Her coal black hair stuck up in random clumps. Looked like she'd been electrocuted."

Paint smiled. "Ah ha, mystery solved. You met the minority owner of the Sin City Aces. Give me a minute and I'll google her. Tabloids and sports shows have run dozens of stories about her fight with Stepmom Sala. She's contesting her dad's will. Claims Sala drugged her father and he wasn't in his right mind when he signed his last will."

Paint handed over his phone. "Here's a picture of the woman."

I studied the photo. Kate Lemmon might sport a punk rocker's hairstyle but she dressed like a model for Victoria's Secret. In the photo, she teetered on stilettos that could be twins of her hospital stilts. See-through lace revealed most of the skin covering her bony bod. She looked so thin I wondered if she might be anorexic.

"Did you hear what was said when she was arguing with Sala or conspiring with Allie?" I asked.

"We got in on the tail end. Mostly name calling," Mollye answered. "No juicy details."

"Why do you suppose the stepdaughter tried to stop me? Think she knew I was an imposter?"

"Doubt it," Eva answered. "Imagine she just wanted an update on Zack's condition and thought a nurse who'd just left his room could provide it. She has literally millions of reasons to be interested in the condition of the Aces' star player. It's obvious he's out for this year, but his inability to play next season could cost big bucks."

"Find anything interesting on the phone?" Mollye asked.

"I'd say so," Paint answered. "A short documentary on human mating behavior and Sala Lemmon is one of the stars."

"Let me see." Mollye bounced up and down. "Hey, hand it over."

"I'll pass," I said, excusing myself from the table. "Think I already saw that film in ninth-grade health class. Plus I want to get out of these clothes. My plastic belly's making me sweat."

In my bedroom, I stripped off the borrowed scrubs and considered how best to extricate myself from the phony pregnancy tummy duct-taped to my T-shirt. I finally yanked the whole kit and caboodle—shirt, suspenders, belly—over my head in a single maneuver. Didn't even try to undo the sticky tape.

As I rejoined the group, Mollye's head was moving up and down like she was bobbing for apples. Keeping rhythm with the action on Zack's phone? No need to watch the video clip. I could tell what form of exercise it captured.

Eva glanced at me. "I'm not interested in looking at that home movie either. I'm no prude but it wouldn't feel right to peek at a tush that might belong to someone I once diapered."

I nodded. "I just met the man and I can't help with any derriere ID."

Clearly, Paint, Andy, and Mollye had no such scruples. They passed the phone back and forth, allowing each to sit through the clip several times. They claimed they were studying the surroundings for clues about where and how the video was shot.

"The film's too steady to be handheld," Andy said, "but I don't think a pro set it up. Too jumpy and there's no effort to edit out the frames where the man's adjusting the camera. For a few seconds, the camera swings back and forth as he fiddles with the focus and zoom. Those blurry frames give a glimpse of a nightstand. No framed photos or personal mementos, just a hairbrush, clock, and a couple of pill bottles. Labels turned away."

"No whips, chains, or feathers either." Mollye giggled. "The woman's asleep in bed when the film starts. The guy probably used one of those bendy selfie tripods to attach his phone to something taller than the bed."

"You keep saying 'he,'" Eva interrupted. "You sure it's a man mounting the camera?"

"Uh, yeah." Mollye giggled again. "Next thing we see is a nude male, walking to the bed and climbing on top of the woman. Nice build. Too bad we only see his well-formed backside. Once he's saddled up, there's not much to see besides the writhing bodies and twisted sheets."

"Could have been shot in almost any bedroom," Andy said. "Can't even tell if the nightstand's black or brown."

Mollye grinned. "Well, the colors are plenty vivid in one spot. The tattoo on the man's bouncing butt is inked in red and blue. There's no question who the woman is, and Sala doesn't appear miffed by her wake-up call. Can't say it's Zack in the buff though. Maybe, maybe not. Never catch a hint of profile. We only see him from the back. His hair's light colored, but it could be blond, ginger, even silver. Too murky. Luckily the tattoo's crystal clear on that very fine, pale bottom. The joker from a deck of cards."

Eva glanced at Andy and Paint. "Do tell. Is your buddy's bottom decorated with a joker?"

Andy shook his head. "None of us had tattoos back in high school. But now, who knows? He did come to the fundraiser dressed as a joker."

"Yeah, but his mom picked out the costume," Paint said. "Pretty sure her choice had nothing to do with any tattoo. I haven't had the occasion or desire to see Zack's hairy behind. A few ladies' bottoms, yes, as well as some covered ones I'd like to see neckid."

"Well, who would know if Zack has a tattoo on his backside?"

Mollye asked impatiently. "Can't we just call some of his teammates and ask? I mean those guys take group showers in the all-together, right? Wouldn't someone have noticed?"

Andy and Paint hooted.

"Like they'd tell you if they'd seen Zack's butt," Andy said. "You'd sound like a crazed stalker."

"Yeah, even teammates who aren't fond of each other would think twice about giving up that kind of personal stuff," Paint added. "It would be a betrayal, especially since Zack's in a coma and can't defend himself. That would make tattling even worse."

Andy nodded. "Agreed. No stranger's going to coax that kind of gossip out of anyone who frequents the Aces' locker room."

Eva stood and walked to the coffee pot for a refill. "We're jumping to the conclusion that bobbing butt is the reason everyone's after Zack's cell phone. The text message that accompanies it—'Thought you might find this instructive. A friend.'—isn't exactly a threat. Maybe the leading lady sent it as an invitation. You know, like let's schedule a repeat? People can be very strange."

"Eva's got a point," Andy said. "Maybe this isn't why people are clamoring to get Zack's phone. There's no date stamp so we have no idea when the video was shot. If it actually is Zack, who cares if he and Sala engage in off-the-field calisthenics? They're both single. It would just be a passing titillation for the tabloids."

"They're both single now," I pointed out. "What if that video predates Mr. Lemmon's death? Could evidence of Sala cheating on her husband help the stepdaughter fight the will?"

Andy's fingers slowly shuffled his coffee cup to and fro on his patch of pine table. "I doubt even iron-clad proof of an affair could overturn a properly-executed will. But the video could serve as leverage with the league. It could bring mighty strong pressure to bear on a team owner it felt had violated ethics or morals clauses—maybe force divestiture."

Eva ran her fingers through her curly white hair. "I don't know what to do. If Zack's starring in that bedroom workout, Carol wouldn't want anyone's eyeballs glued to it. But she's not here, and that worries me more than the tabloids getting wind of some bedroom romp. Maybe we should turn the phone over to the sheriff."

I sighed in relief. Last spring I'd learned a hard lesson. Keeping secrets—even for what seemed like good reasons—could have dire consequences. "I agree. Perhaps Mom can turn the phone over to the sheriff and extract a promise that content unrelated to Zack's attack or Carol's disappearance will remain private and confidential."

"Like that's possible," Mollye scoffed. "If enough eyes follow the bouncing buns in that video, somebody's going to blab."

Eva's shoulders slumped. "Nothing I can do to prevent that. But I'm worried sick about Carol. I don't think Zack's in any danger even though Brie was able to sneak inside his room. Who'd want to risk another attack on someone who's already in a coma and under guard? Carol's another story. Where could she be? If something on this phone will help find her, Zack's right to privacy comes dead last."

I nodded. "I'll call Mom now. It is ten o'clock so my folks are probably in bed. But the odds are good they're still reading."

"Do it," Eva said. "No point waiting."

TWENTY

Mom was awake. "We should turn the phone over to Sheriff Mason tonight. I'll call the sheriff soon as your dad and I are in the car. Ask him to meet us at Udderly."

I relayed the news to the kitchen detectives.

Paint stood to leave, then sat back down. "We only read a handful of the text messages and spent zero time looking at Zack's call logs. What's the harm in backing up everything to a Cloud account before we hand the phone over to the sheriff?"

"Do you really need a copy of that bedroom ballet?" Eva challenged. "You seriously think you can come up with a clue that escapes the sheriff?"

"Maybe," Andy jumped in. "Paint and I have been friends with Zack since kindergarten. We know his history. The sheriff's new. He's never even met Zack. We might stumble across something that doesn't make sense, doesn't add up."

Eva shrugged. "Guess it can't hurt. But you'd better be dang sure your backup is secure. I don't want to be blamed for some hacker broadcasting that video."

Paint only needed a couple minutes to create a brand-new account in the Cloud and upload the phone's content. "The password is 25spygoat. Any of us can access the account with that password."

"Why did you pick twenty-five?" I asked.

"Zack's jersey number in high school."

Mom and Dad arrived within minutes of my friends' departure.

"The sheriff should be here any minute," Mom said. "Where'd you find the phone?"

I explained how I noticed the out-of-place feed bucket and looked inside.

"Wonder how the phone wound up in that feed pail?" Dad's

eyebrows knitted together as he tackled a new conundrum.

"Maybe Zack was holding the phone when he got hit and it fell in the bucket," I said. "It was so dark in the barn, the attacker might not have seen it fall, and the feed would have cushioned the sound. The medics ordered a bunch of stuff hauled outside to clear a path for Zack's stretcher. By the time the forensics folks searched the barn, the bucket and phone were gone."

"Do I want to know how you unlocked the phone to see that embarrassing video?" Mom probed. "Did one of you know Zack's password?"

I hoped the look I focused on Eva communicated my desire for a joint confession. My aunt seemed as reluctant as I was to fess up to our hospital charade. But she came clean and assumed her share of guilt for the caper.

"It was the only way we could honor Carol's wishes," Eva concluded. "I just wanted to protect Zack's privacy."

Mom rolled her eyes. "You two. I can't lie for you."

Dad cleared his throat. "But we don't need to share all the gory details. If Mason doesn't ask, we don't need to volunteer information. It doesn't make a whit of difference in his investigation."

We heard a car arrive, heralded as always by our canine chorus. I peeked through the slats in the front window blinds. Not the sheriff, unless he was driving an unmarked car to throw the media off the investigative scent.

The car's driver door flew open. The bony bare legs that emerged clearly didn't belong to the sheriff or, given the red stilettos, to any of Ardon County's female officers.

Cheeses. Had to be the Lemmon stepdaughter. Why was she here? Did someone in the sheriff's department spill the beans this quickly about the phone's discovery?

Thank heaven I'd jettisoned my wig and nurse scrubs the minute we came home. I was thankful our co-conspirators were gone, too. Mollye the Tripper's presence would have given Kate Lemmon one more clue about our hospital scam. I wasn't eager to be fingered as the fleeing nurse.

I turned from the window. I barely had time to warn my family of our caller's identity before she banged on the door.

"Open up," she demanded. "I know you have Zack's phone. Someone used it in this location in the last hour. And we all know Zack couldn't have authorized its use."

Dad opened the door just as the woman launched herself toward a now absent wood barrier. The forward momentum caused her to stumble into Dad, who grabbed her arm to right her.

"Who are you?" Dad demanded. "And why is someone else's phone any of your business?"

The woman employed one of her chicken-wing elbows to shove Dad's arm away. "I'm Kate Lemmon and I own the Sin City Aces. That phone is team property. Where is it?"

My gaze automatically shifted to the phone in question, sitting in the middle of the table like an electronic centerpiece. In plain sight. Would the Lemmon heir spot it and make a grab for it?

"Why don't you have a seat?" Mom advised. "I'm the attorney for the Strong family."

When Kate's attention locked on Mom, Dad casually swept the phone off the table and into his pocket.

"I understand you are the team's minority shareholder," Mom continued. "Before we give the phone to anyone we need to see documentation regarding its ownership and a notarized statement from the majority shareholder that you are authorized to take possession."

"What the hell's with this legal-ass crap?" Kate screeched. "You're not Zack's attorney. I know him. Maybe you aren't an attorney at all. You're the one who needs to show ID. Just who are you working for? Has Sala bought you, too?"

The sounds of another set of wheels crunching gravel brought a temporary truce to the confrontation.

"Ah, that would be Sheriff Mason," Aunt Eva said. "We'll let him sort this out. The sheriff believes the phone might be a help in his investigation. Surely you want the authorities to have all the tools they need to catch Zack's attacker and find out why Carol Strong is missing. Then again maybe you know more than the sheriff on both subjects."

The skin on Kate's forehead creased, as much as possible with what appeared to be a taut, beat-the-wrinkles facelift. "What are you talking about? The Strong woman's missing?"

Either Kate was an excellent actress or Carol's vanishing act came as a total surprise.

Sheriff Mason didn't bother to knock or yoo-hoo before walking inside with Deputy Danny McCoy on his heels. Dad hadn't fully closed the door, and Kate's loud demands probably clued the lawmen they need not stand on ceremony. The officers looked baffled by the unexpected make-up of the kitchen crowd.

Kate Lemmon was first to react. She stuck out her manicured claw to shake Mason's hand. "I'm glad you're here, Sheriff. You can help us quickly straighten out this situation."

Had to give the woman credit. Her patter was smoother than chocolate silk pie.

"These people have taken possession of a cell phone that rightfully belongs to the Sin City Aces organization," she continued. "It contains confidential team data. As the team owner, I'm obliged to safeguard this information."

Kate beamed a smile at the officers. Her teeth so white she could forgo a flashlight on moonless nights. "Of course, I'll be happy to review all content and share any non-team information that might aid your investigation," she cooed. "We're as interested as you are in finding out who attacked our star quarterback."

Sheriff Mason stared down at his shoes, then looked up at the woman. Her expression seemed to communicate both confidence and superiority.

"I'm taking the phone," the sheriff affirmed. "I have zero interest in any confidential team information. My only concern is looking for leads. When we're through with the phone, we'll figure out who it belongs to."

He glanced at Eva, my folks, and me. "Any of you have something to add?"

Mom repeated her claim to be the Strong family attorney and said she'd insist that phone ownership be documented before the sheriff handed it over to anyone. Without evidence to the contrary, Mom contended the phone belonged to Zack and, in the event he remained incapacitated, to his mother.

Dad took the phone from his pocket and handed it to the sheriff.

I bit my lip. Should I clue the sheriff in about the password conundrum? "You may want to keep the phone active for your techies," I offered. "It's password protected."

The sheriff nodded as he handed the cell phone to Danny. I breathed a sigh of relief when he didn't ask the obvious follow-up question: "What's the password?" Perhaps he didn't want Ms. Lemmon to hear the answer.

"We'll see you out," the sheriff told Kate. "Where are you staying? I'll call you if there are any new developments."

The woman hesitated a moment before telling the sheriff that she was staying at the Maison d'Orange in Clemson.

Sheriff Mason shifted his attention to the Hooker clan, all present and accounted for. "I'll be in touch with you, too," he said. "Good night."

Kate's car vanished first. Like she had a choice. The sheriff and deputy herded her down the drive as efficiently as Udderly's Border Collies herded our goats. I watched through the blind slats until all taillights disappeared.

I sighed. "Whew. I'm sure glad the sheriff came when he did. Although I doubt Kate would have pulled a gun to force the issue."

Mom sighed. "No. She's used to ordering peons about and expecting obedience. Too high and mighty to do her own dirty work."

"So why didn't she send some peons to confiscate the phone?" I asked.

"Probably thought her royal presence would be sufficient to make us cave." Dad shrugged. "Did you catch the look on her face when you mentioned Carol was missing? Seemed to be a genuine news flash. I'm inclined to think she's among the innocent on the abduction front.

"But not innocent of some sort of skullduggery," he added. "How did she know Zack's phone had been used by someone here? I doubt Zack willingly supplied her with a 'Find My Phone' app."

I yawned. The adrenaline rush had ebbed, leaving me beat. "Maybe she's telling the truth. Maybe the team bought phones for all the players and pre-loaded them with tracking apps. A good way to keep tabs on their comings and goings without them being the wiser."

Eva tried to stifle a yawn of her own. "We're not going to figure this out tonight. Here's the good news. Reporter snoops, the Lemmons, and any stooges they might have hired should have lost all interest in

Udderly Kidding Dairy's inhabitants. We're in the clear with the law and the lawless. And I'm so tired I'll collapse if I'm vertical five more minutes."

I liked Eva's hypothesis. We'd become yesterday's news. Mom and Dad left, and I headed to bed.

Cashew was already fast asleep, curled in a nest she'd created atop my bed's comforter. Her tail didn't even twitch as I slid between the sheets and jostled her perch.

Despite my own bone deep fatigue, I had a hard time drifting off to sleep. I wondered where Carol might be trying to sleep. Then there was that blasted phone. What made it so valuable? I thought about the boudoir video. What kind of woman would want a permanent record of such a coupling? Hmm. Did she know? Sala was asleep when Tattooed Tush, whoever he was, set up the camera. Maybe the woman had no idea he memorialized their bedroom gymnastics on video.

TWENTY-ONE

Morning seemed to arrive five minutes after I nodded off. Seeing my breath while still in my bedroom convinced me to slip Mom and Dad's Iowa State hoodie over my head. Once I walked outside, I wished they'd brought me a parka.

It had rained in the night. Apparently hard, turning patches of bare ground muddy and slick. I hustled between the barn and feed troughs, careful not to slide in the muck. Tammy the Pig, nestled deep in a mud puddle, greeted me with a friendly oink.

The crisp October air kept my mind focused on two things, staying warm and finishing my chores with record speed. Actually, crisp is a poor description. The cutting wind's long icy fingers kept staging sneak attacks down my neck and up my pant legs.

My final task was to lead Lilly's mule, Rita, and Eva's horse, Hank, to their assigned pasture. We couldn't let Hank and Rita share field accommodations with our goats because the equines were pigs. Sorry, Tammy, guess I should call them gluttons. In fields occupied solely by goats we could fill feed bins to the brim and let the goats eat whenever they got hungry. Goats stop eating once their stomachs are full. Not equines. They'd gorge themselves until they exploded given an endless food supply. That's also why the grass in Rita and Hank's pasture was purposely scraggly.

With the gate secure behind Rita and Hank, I made a beeline for the cabin to secure hot coffee and, I hoped, warm buns (mine).

As I ran lickety-split toward my reward, Mollye's van roared down the drive. What now? My friend wasn't an early riser. If she was up this early, there was a good—make it a bad—reason.

I intercepted Mollye on the cabin steps. Her right fist held the Monday morning edition of the *Ardon Chronicle* in a chokehold. Though she'd scrunched the paper into the shape of a jellyroll, I could make out Carol's name in a front-page headline.

"My considerate next-door neighbor is putting an addition on his house," Moll grumped. "Started hammering at six in the freaking morning. Figured I might as well get up and read the paper."

"Is our local publisher stirring up new trouble?" I asked as I opened the cabin door eager to continue our conversation out of the cold.

Mollye harrumphed. "You could say that."

"What now?" asked Eva, frowning as she poured coffee for herself.

"The paper got wind that Carol's missing," Mollye began. "So, naturally, it's suggesting she and Zack are involved in nefarious activities and had a falling out with fellow crooks. What other reason could there be for the attack on Zack and Carol's disappearance? The *Chronicle*'s editorial urges readers not to vote for a person who's gone missing under 'suspicious circumstances.'"

My aunt sank onto one of the kitchen chairs. I poured cups of hot—thank you, thank you, Eva—coffee for myself and Mollye before joining the twosome at the table.

My aunt unfolded the newspaper and smoothed out the front page. With eyes closed, her fingers scrabbled back and forth across the newsprint as if she were reading braille.

Her eyes suddenly blinked open. "What if Carol's disappearance has nothing to do with Zack's attack? What if someone has a political motive for taking her hostage or..." Eva swallowed hard before voicing her worst fear. "Or killing her? Would any of those CAVE extremists go that far? They're not her only political enemies. The newspaper's editorials are testimony to that."

Mollye's mouth gaped open. Neither my friend nor I spoke. The preposterous idea seemed much less outrageous the longer we considered it.

I shook my head. "Do you really think there's enough incentive for a political enemy to kidnap or kill Carol? We're talking about electing a governor not the president."

Eva used the palms of her hands to rub her eyes. She sighed. "Can't rule it out. I've heard talk about a right-wing militia. The way these jokers rail on talk shows, I wonder what alternate reality they inhabit. They're convinced government is out to get them. To confiscate their guns. Persecute born-agains. Threaten their way of life."

Mollye set down her coffee cup. "But would they murder Carol to make certain she doesn't become governor?"

"Murder is a little hard for me to swallow." Eva shrugged. "But I wouldn't put kidnapping past some of her foes. Or maybe Carol drove off on her own and suffered a stroke or heart attack. That alternative is almost as scary."

"Did the paper mention Chester?" I asked.

"Only that the sheriff hoped to speak with him," Mollye said. "Chester's friends were quoted. Said their buddy left to visit relatives in Oconee County immediately after Zack Strong's—quote unquote—'brutal' attack."

I shook my head and took a deep breath. "Wow. What sterling, unbiased reporting. No wonder you don't take the paper, Eva."

A phone rang—the cabin's land line—Eva's preferred communication vehicle. My aunt jumped up to answer. The phone sat on a small hallway table, a location that made it equally inconvenient to answer from every cabin room. Eva saw no need for multiple telephones.

"Hello." Eva's brows knitted, making me wonder whose voice she'd heard on the other end of the line. But a minute later she smiled. "Wonderful news. I'm on my way."

She hung up and treated Mollye and me to a delighted laugh. "At last some good news. Zack's out of his coma. Looks like he'll make a full recovery. No brain damage. Unfortunately, when he asked for his mom, a nurse hemmed and hawed. That made Zack assume she'd been attacked, too. The doctor wants me to come help calm Zack down. He's in no condition to be riled."

"What will you tell Zack?" I asked. "Any suggestion she might be a hostage is going to make him worry even more."

"I'm not an idiot, you know. I am capable of finesse. I'll assure Zack the authorities are on the case and we're doing everything we can to help."

Eva stood. "Don't forget we're supposed to have lunch at Phil's lake house. Even if I can't make it, you need to go. He invited a dozen folks to celebrate our commitment to an Udderly conservation easement. The luncheon guests all have conservation easements on farms or timber tracts."

As soon as Eva left, Mollye rubbed her hands together in an oh-goody-let's-get-going gesture. She grinned. "I asked myself, now where would CAVE disciples hide Carol if they kidnapped her? The answer came like a bolt out of the blue. And I know how to check it out risk-free."

My baloney detection monitor started pinging. Mollye's plans were like miracle patent medicines, they seemed to offer infinite promise until you realized the side effects could kill you.

"What? You know the location of a militia training ground? Or are you describing a CAVE-owned still or cult stronghold where trespassers get shot on sight?"

"Just listen. Chester and a bunch of fellow losers belong to what they call a hunting club. Not sure they ever bag any wild game but they go there to massacre flocks of tin cans and brag on their weapons—hand guns, shotguns, semi-automatics. They built what is jokingly called a lodge up past Winding Creek. That sorry, run-down excuse for a building is a great hideaway. Only way to reach it is a long drive down a private dirt road. It's miles from any main highway."

"If it's such a great hideaway, how do you know about it?"

"My Uncle Les belonged to the so-called hunt club before he accidentally shot off his big toe. That's when Aunt Ethel confiscated his guns."

"And what's your 'risk-free' plan to check it out? Why wouldn't we be riddled with lead if we so much as poked one of our ten fully-attached toes over the property line?"

"No need for a personal visit. I'll coax Uncle Les into doing it for us," Mollye answered. "If he sees signs Carol's stashed there, we'll alert the sheriff and he can stage a rescue. Uncle Les works a late-night shift so he'll be sleeping now. He cuts off the phone and the doorbell so nothing interrupts his shuteye. I'll call him early afternoon."

Pleased with her spying scheme, Mollye whistled as she vacated Udderly's premises, presumably to give her overheated imagination time to cool before dreaming up another kidnap hideaway we needed to scout. "I'll give you a call after I talk to Les. Toodle-oo."

With a few minutes alone and the morning farm chores complete, I started a pot of split pea soup. The way things were going there was no telling how many people would crowd around our kitchen table come suppertime. After I set the crockpot timer for eight hours, I started a grocery list. Before I could scoot my chair in, Cashew jumped up and claimed my lap, reminding me she was overdue for petting and maybe a little of that baby talk I'd ridiculed at the dog show. I conceded. Every few minutes, I put my list-making on pause to scratch behind her ears and stroke her silky fur. My pup's rendition of contented sighs almost made life seem normal.

I'd just added tarragon to my grocery list when my cell phone played the yodel from the *Sound of Music*'s "Lonely Goatherd." My ringtone for Eva.

I didn't hear it often. If my aunt was using a cell phone, she had good reason. Not just wanting to pass the time and annoy everyone standing behind her in a grocery line.

"Hi, Eva," I said before she could say boo. It always flustered her that I knew who was calling before she spoke. To her that wreaked of black magic or, at least, no-good digital monkey business.

"You sitting down?" Eva's cheerful tone communicated more good news. "Got an update for you."

"Great. How's Zack?"

"Out of danger. He even wangled a release from the hospital tomorrow."

"Wow. Terrific, but isn't that awfully soon? I mean he just woke up."

"The docs wanted to keep him longer, but Zack wants out. Says he can't just laze about in a hospital bed while his mom's missing."

"What did he say about the attack? Did he see who conked him?"

"No. Whoever did it snuck up behind him. Zack was distracted, trying to get a signal on his cell phone, when his lights went out. Now will you quit asking questions and let me talk? Zack's going to stay with us at Udderly. The break-in at Carol's house rules it out as a place to stay. Anyway, his right arm's in a sling to keep his shoulder immobile while the collarbone heals and they're putting a boot on his broken ankle. That means he's gonna need some help."

I thought about the kind of help he might need. "It's fine with me, but I wonder if Zack might feel more comfortable staying with Paint or Andy?"

"Oh, don't be a prude. If Zack needs help with a zipper, I'll give it a tug. Besides, Paint's cabin's too remote, and who knows what noisy critters might be boarding at Andy's clinic."

"Okay," I agreed, "though I'm not sure our animal menagerie is any quieter than Andy's."

"I'll give Zack my room," Aunt Eva continued. "We'll share. I figure you've shared mattress space with Mollye and I take up even less room."

I sputtered. Sleep with my aunt? Un uh, wasn't going to happen. *Hairy Pork Rinds*. I could hear her snores through two sturdy closed doors. Worse, on the nights Billy didn't sleep over, she switched off the lights long before I'd be ready to put down the book I was reading.

"Tell you what." I strived for a cheerful tone. "Let's give Zack my bedroom. I'll curl up on the love seat. It's pretty comfortable. That'll give each of us our own bed. No fighting over covers."

"Fine, if you think that's best." Eva replied in a sing-song voice. Her innocent tone convinced me this sleeping arrangement was her plan from the get-go. It also meant Eva could still share a bed with Billy when the mood struck.

"Anything I need to do to get ready for our guest? When's he coming?"

"Not till tomorrow. Take steaks out of the freezer and put them in the icebox to thaw. Our boy needs protein. Gotta be sick of that namby-pamby hospital food. Why don't you make chocolate mousse? The one you won't tell me what's in it because you think I'll upchuck."

"It's a deal," I said. "You going to be home in time to go to Phil's?"

"Sure. Zack's asleep. No reason to watch him snooze. I'll be home in a jiffy, though I plan to have a word or three with the sheriff before I leave."

TWENTY-TWO

Eva estimated the drive to Phil's would take under thirty minutes unless we got behind a slowpoke. Double-yellow no-passing paint striped the winding country road most of the way to Lake Sisel's shoreline.

With Eva strapped into my Prius's passenger seat, I took advantage of her captive state to pry out a full report on what she'd learned at the hospital. At Zack's insistence, the sheriff let Eva sit in while he interviewed the quarterback.

"Did Zack offer any leads on who might have attacked him—other than Chester or one of his cronies?" I asked.

"No. Claims he doesn't know anyone who hates him enough to try to kill him, end his career, or harm his mom."

"What about the 'adult exercise' video? Did the sheriff quiz him about it?"

Eva nodded. "He did. But Zack never opened the text or its companion video, so he's never seen it. He was answering blind. If Zack had a role in it, he's a good actor. He said for all he knew some fan sent it hoping he'd want to join the fun. He got pretty testy when the sheriff kept pushing. Told him to forget amateur porn and find his mom."

"So our new cabin-mate didn't actually deny the possibility he's in the movie. Did you get the feeling he played a starring role?"

Eva tilted her head to the side. "At first Sheriff Mason gave no clue about the woman's identity. After he said the lady in question was Sala Lemmon, he asked Zack flat out if he might be in the video. Zack took the fifth by zipping his lips. Possibly because it's him. Then again Zack may be protecting someone else. Not my place to judge. I respect Zack for refusing to discuss it."

I tended to agree, though if Zack recorded the video, I hoped Sala had agreed to a recording. Otherwise it felt a lot like exploitation or even blackmail.

"Did Mason give the phone back to Zack?" I asked.

"He's not handing it over to anyone yet. He's following up on threatening texts from unhappy gamblers, including an email from an old schoolmate named Mick. Zack said it was just losers blowing off steam. He added that Mick had sent him more attaboy texts than threats."

"That Mick must be Mick Hardy," I said. "I called the sheriff after he showed up at Udderly acting suspicious. Said he was looking for a business card he'd lost. Wouldn't give me his name, but Paint and Andy pointed him out to me at the dog show. He's been calling Paint fishing for information on Zack's condition. Glad he's on the sheriff's radar."

I glanced at Eva. "You haven't said a word about Fred or Chester and his CAVE cronies. Are they still kidnap suspects?"

"Fred and Chester are in the clear." Eva sighed. "Solid alibis. Fred was in Savannah visiting his sister and Chester was hiding out with kin a couple of counties over. The sheriff thinks Chester burned rubber getting out of Ardon after Zack humiliated him by putting him down with a single punch. Mason seems to view Chester as a grandstanding bully who talks big until someone calls his bluff—not enough guts to attack Zack, even a sneak attack from behind. I tend to agree. But I could still see one of his CAVE men buddies snatching Carol."

Our conversation paused while Eva consulted the Google map I'd printed for her. Though my aunt was serving as my navigator, she refused to follow electronic breadcrumbs on my iPhone. Said she detested the haughty sounds of robotic voices that kept telling you to make a U-turn when you knew darn well your shortcut worked better.

"Take the next left," she said. "Then a right at the entrance to Phil's neighborhood. His house is a big red brick number at the top of the hill."

"We're almost there," I said. "Is that all you learned from the sheriff?"

Eva chuckled. "Didn't say that. Kate Lemmon arrived while the sheriff and I were in Zack's room. She peeked through the glass and saw Zack awake and talking. She tried to barge in but the deputy on guard stopped her. The sheriff asked Zack if he wanted to see Kate. Zack's 'no' was mighty emphatic. Claimed he didn't feel up to talking with anyone but the sheriff and me. My opinion? The 'not feeling up to it' excuse was a bunch of hooey."

I laughed. "Don't blame him. I'd give any old excuse to avoid that bony hyena. How did she take the rebuff?"

"Not well. The sheriff walked outside to personally deliver the message. A lot of huffing and puffing ensued before Kate stomped out of sight. Her exit coaxed a smile out of Zack. No love lost there. But whatever he doesn't like about her he kept to himself."

I made the turn into Phil's neighborhood, a lakeside community with gorgeous homes set on large, mostly manicured lots. Nonetheless, I was pleased to see a plump, gray-haired lady in dirty overalls working a raised-bed garden. Unlike the mountain resort where I almost died last spring, this neighborhood appeared to welcome residents who didn't mind getting their hands dirty planting whatever trees and shrubs struck their fancy.

I slowed to a crawl to make sure I turned into the right driveway. Phil's description of a large brick abode wasn't exactly a foolproof clue. All the houses seemed to include brick in their design, though stone and wood trim, stately columns and bump-outs were different enough to help owners ID their own homes even at night if they were a bit tipsy.

As we inched past a driveway, movement snagged my attention. A tall woman. Platinum hair. Dressed in skin-tight white pants and a loose, lacy top. A firm, tanned body played peek-a-boo through the lace. She walked down the driveway toward a car that had just disgorged two musclemen. Though I only saw their backs, their shapes set off an alarm.

"Look, Eva. Could those guys be our prime B&E suspects? I can't see their faces, but how many men in Ardon are built like sumo wrestlers?"

"It's them all right," Eva answered. "I can see their faces now. Black Beard is one of them."

"Is that Sala Lemmon with them?"

Not sure why I whispered. Our windows were rolled up and we were too far away for the woman or her security thugs to hear.

Even minus her stilettoes, Sala was tall enough to be eyeball to eyeball with Black Beard. Her white-blonde hair fluttered in the breeze.

"Never met the woman, but I've seen her on TV. Kinda looks like her mug." Eva's voice was matter-of-fact, so it startled me when she reached over and clamped her hand around my arm. "You think those two creeps are here to get new orders from their boss?"

"Maybe. Should we pull in the driveway? Confront them?"

Eva shook her head. "No. That's Phil's house next door. Just park behind the other cars. Let's not give ourselves away. Knowing Phil, he chats up his neighbors every time he takes his dog out for a whiz. Bet he can tell us all about his next-door neighbor and how come Sala's a houseguest."

My aunt pulled a scrap of paper from her purse. "At least I can give Sheriff Mason the license plate on the car those cockroaches are driving. Got the number. That tag's a rental. Hand me your phone and I'll call the sheriff. Dang it. They're driving away. I'd hoped Mason could send a car over and nab them while they were chewing the fat."

I parked my Prius in the circular drive. It was the fourth car in. Clearly we weren't the first arrivals. Before we exited, Eva advised the sheriff she'd spotted the men who'd braced her. She gave Mason their tag number, and the location they were last seen. She also informed him they were reporting to Sala Lemmon.

Eva sighed. "Guess that's all we can do. Let's head inside."

Phil opened the front door before we could knock, gave Eva a big hug, and, after a slight pause, hugged me, too.

"Come in, come in. Make yourself at home. You already know everyone."

Know seemed a slight exaggeration. I'd met everyone at ARGH meetings, but only knew the basics one gets with quick handshakes. The ARGH meetings focused on the business at hand, not socializing.

"The first thing I need to greet is the powder room," Eva said.

Okay, I was on my own. Rex and Harriet Billings, who'd inherited a large timberland tract, waved me over. In under a minute, Harriet pointed to a mega-mansion visible from Phil's picture window and told me it was their point-lot home.

I quickly excused myself and strolled over to say hi to Howie Lemcke, a Yankee transplant. Listening to Howie's Boston accent was always a treat. The Army veteran sported a sleek, ultra-modern metal prosthesis and made no attempt to hide it with clothing or fake skin. He'd lost his left leg just below the knee.

"How are things going at your retreat?" I asked. Howie had bought twenty acres of woodland and built several cabins for guests. He was dedicated to helping other wounded veterans adjust to altered realities.

Howie grinned. "We graduated two men last week. Nothing makes me happier."

Phil offered me wine or sweet tea. While I prefer my tea unadulterated, I accepted the sugar-saturated Southern version rather than trouble our host for a glass of water.

When Eva returned from the loo, she instantly became the center of attention, fielding questions about Zack's condition and the search for the missing gubernatorial candidate.

Fancy munchies were set out on tables near floor-to-ceiling windows and I edged over to see if there were any vegan snacks. I nibbled on vegetable sticks while Eva provided updates.

Since Phil's window wall offered an excellent sightline to the neighbor's backyard, I sneaked frequent glances for any sign of activity. I wasn't disappointed. It wasn't long before two women walked outside and claimed lounge chairs. Though November was only days away, a bright sun and no wind had boosted the temperature into the high seventies, prompting the women to do some end-of-season work on maintaining their tans.

Both women were stunners. Sala now wore a tiny white bikini. A great bod for a forty-five-year-old. Heck a great bod for a twenty-year-old. The woman on the adjacent lounge chair could pass for Sala's twin, except her bikini was red and her hair was auburn.

When there was a break in the conversation, I tapped Phil's arm and motioned toward the neighbors' endless horizon swimming pool. "I love to swim. That pool looks so inviting. But why don't your neighbors simply dive off their dock and swim in the lake?"

Phil chuckled. "The neighbor lady's afraid of snakes. Dorothy, she's the one in the red swimsuit, saw one in the lake and refused to dip so much as a toe in the water. Demanded a swimming pool as a condition for buying the house."

"Doesn't she know snakes aren't picky? I doubt chlorine would discourage them from visiting a pool."

"Yeah, I had the same thought. But Dr. Lofland dotes on Dorothy. They're newlyweds. Dorothy wants a pool, she gets a pool."

"What kind of doctor is your neighbor?" Eva asked. Peering out the window, I didn't even realize my aunt had joined me.

"Aren't you happy with Dr. Bowman?" Phil teased. "Should I tell him you're shopping for a new doc? Or are you just being nosy?"

"Yeah, I'm nosy," Eva said. "Just answer the question."

Phil barked a laugh. "He's a plastic surgeon. Neither of you need his services. Besides he doesn't practice here. Went to Clemson as an undergraduate and wanted a second house near the school for football season. He has another vacation house in the Caribbean. His main practice is in Vegas."

Ah ha. That explained the connection. Sala and her late husband had probably hobnobbed in the same social set as the doc and his wife. Who knew? Maybe Dorothy was another dancer who'd snared a mature man with an even more mature bank account.

We sat down to lunch and the talk turned to conservation, land management, and politics. The group expressed a collective fear that Carol's election chances were doomed.

Howie sat beside me at lunch and quizzed me about my work as a chef. He clapped his hands together when I told him I hoped to open a B&B that catered to vegans and vegetarians.

"Would you consider giving cooking lessons at my retreat?" Howie sounded practically giddy. "Most of our wounded vets are single and never learned to cook anything beyond hot dogs and burgers. They eat whatever comes in a can. They really need to eat healthier."

I smiled. This was exactly the type of activity I enjoyed. "I'd love to. But my plate's kind of full at the moment. Maybe after Thanksgiving?"

Howie nodded. "Of course. You have the farm to run and a guest. Sounds like Zack may need help to manage with that broken collarbone. I've enjoyed watching him play football. Be happy to help with rehab while he's in Ardon. I'm a licensed physical therapist."

"Great, thanks for the offer," I answered. His mention of rehab made me wonder how long Zack might stay with us. A week, a month?

His recovery wasn't the only factor. If Carol was found unharmed, he'd move back with his mother.

It wasn't quite two o'clock when the luncheon broke up. Eva checked her usual inclination to stage a footrace to be first out the door. She lingered, making sure we were the last to leave.

Phil walked us to our car. Eva nodded toward the neighboring property. "Phil, we noticed your neighbor has a houseguest. Did you know Sala Lemmon is staying there?"

"Of course," he answered. "It's a small, nosy community. You'd fit right in, Eva. Sala is Dorothy's sister. She's visited the Loflands before. The doc told me Sala flew in as soon as she heard about Zack. Wanted to make sure he received the best possible medical care and security."

Phil's eyebrows scrunched together. "Hey, has Sala contacted you about security now that Zack will be staying with you? What with Carol missing, you could use extra protection. I know you have guard dogs, but it might be prudent to let the Aces pay for some gun-toting guards."

Eva smiled. "Appreciate your concern but we'll be fine. I doubt Sala even knows Zack will be a houseguest. We just found out ourselves. Maybe you can introduce us and we can share the news?"

"Sure, why not? Now's as good a time as any if you're not in a rush to get back to Udderly."

Holy Swiss Cheese. What was Eva up to? Were we walking into the lion's, make that lioness's, den?

TWENTY-THREE

Phil rang his neighbors' doorbell as Eva and I skulked behind him. My cheeks (both sets) clenched. The upper ones faked a smile; the lower ones responded to ye old danger-pucker instinct. What kind of welcome could we expect with Sala giving seek-and-destroy orders to the thugs we'd seen in her driveway?

It took a couple minutes for the door to open. No surprise since we'd seen the ladies lounging out back by the pool. Of course, given the Loflands' apparent wealth, the couple could have employed a maid, a butler, or both to perform door-opening duties.

However, it was Dorothy who swung the carved and polished mahogany door wide. She'd slipped a cover-up over her red bikini. Sister Sala looked on, standing a few paces behind the lady of the house. Sala had donned the lacy see-through top she'd worn while conversing with our B&E suspects. No tight white capris, though. Just long, tanned legs.

Dorothy smiled when she saw Phil. "Hi, neighbor. Noticed all the cars at your place. Wondered what the occasion might be and why I wasn't invited," she teased.

Phil smiled in return, enjoying his neighbor's flirtation. "You know you're welcome anytime. We've been celebrating Eva Hooker's decision to place a conservation easement on a portion of her dairy farm. You may not realize it, but Eva, here"—he nodded at my aunt—"is a good friend of the Strongs. In fact, when Zack leaves the hospital tomorrow, he'll be staying at her farm. I know your sister is concerned about Zack, so I figured Sala would want to meet Zack's new housemates, Eva, and her niece Brie."

I watched Sala's face during Phil's rambling intro. No sign of shock or hostility. Her smile seemed genuinely warm. Huh?

"Well, come on in. Glad to meet you." Dorothy waved us into the mansion's three-story chandeliered atrium. "Sala, I'll let you introduce yourself."

The Aces owner rushed forward. "I'm delighted you stopped by." She ignored Eva's outstretched hand and enveloped my aunt in an embrace that might have been a full-body grapple in a wrestling match. Or maybe she was using the hug as a ruse to check Eva for concealed weapons. The lady was no shrinking violet.

"And you're Brie." She released Eva and turned to size me up. "Glad to meet you."

She started laughing, the kind of braying glee that includes snorts. "Good heavens, you're the mystery mermaid caught in those unfortunate videos following Zack's attack. A new picture of you just surfaced. You were in the crowd sans wig and mask when they loaded Zack in the ambulance. The Internet can be a real pain in the bee-hind. Bet you're glad nobody posted your name."

I glanced over at Phil, whose jaw had dropped. Wasn't sure if it was in response to Sala's raucous laughter or Eva's and my deer-in-the-headlights response.

Once Sala got her hee-haws under control, she turned back to Eva. "I saw you with Carol at the hospital but didn't want to intrude. Can't tell you how happy I am that Zack's awake, on the mend, and making a jailbreak from the hospital. All those shoes squeaking on linoleum and hushed tones creep me out. But I was horrified to hear about his mother's disappearance. What a mystery. Come sit down. Tell me how I can help."

When Sala paused for breath, Phil saw his opening. "I'll leave you ladies to get acquainted," he said. "Need to get home. Promised Helen I'd take care of some chores."

While Phil made his fast getaway, Eva and I found ourselves voluntarily trapped in a posh cage. We followed the sisters into a living room twice the size of our homey Udderly cabin. Sala led us to a grouping of love seats and chairs that's dubbed a conversation area by decorators. The arrangement offered just enough room to cross my legs without kicking the person seated across from me yet promised to let me pick up on every whispered comment.

Not that Sala was a whisperer. Her exuberant greeting and seeming bonhomie had me flummoxed. Had the merry widow been tipping a few? Was she suffering from sunstroke? Had it slipped her mind that the thugs she employed recently tried to intimidate Eva and were the prime candidates for Ardon County ransacker-of-the-year awards?

Sala was definitely an Oscar-worthy actress. Then another possibility snuck into my mind. What if she hadn't sanctioned her employees' strong-arm tactics? Was it possible she didn't know about her starring role in the video that made Zack's cell phone a top prize?

Eva and I sank into the deep suede cushions of a love seat. I scooted forward to avoid being swallowed and immobilized by the fanny-eating, pitcher-plant furniture.

"So you knew Zack was checking out of the hospital?" Eva asked. "Was it on the news? We've been tied up with Phil's luncheon and haven't heard the latest. Any late-breaking developments?"

Sala shook her head. "No announcements. Gunter and Vince, two of our team's security guards, stopped by a couple hours ago to tell me Zack would be released. I'm concerned the attack on Zack was intended to hurt our team's chances of making the Super Bowl. I'm hoping there isn't some looney out there with a hard-on for the Aces—someone who might go after more of our players. Sheriff Mason promised to call if there was any progress in finding out who attacked Zack. The phone hasn't rung."

"So you don't think the assault was personal?" Eva probed.

Sala shrugged. "Maybe, maybe not. I can't ignore the possibility that someone's out to hurt the team. That's why I beefed up security for all our players."

"But if the attack wasn't personal, why is Zack's mother missing?" I sputtered. "Seems like an awfully big, scary coincidence."

"I'm not a big believer in coincidences either." Sala nodded. "But Dorothy tells me Zack's mom is a controversial figure around these parts. Maybe the attack on Zack encouraged some crazy to think he could go after Zack's mother and get away with it in all the confusion."

I glanced at Eva. Her frown said she wasn't buying some multiple villain conspiracy theory. I was dying to ask Sala why everyone wanted Zack's phone, but I didn't know if Eva would approve opening that can of worms.

My aunt cleared her throat. "We met your stepdaughter last

night."

Okay, Eva was baiting the hook and casting her line. Worms ahoy.

"Kate Lemmon came to our cabin to demand Zack's cell phone. Claimed it was team property. Fortunately, the sheriff arrived and took possession, said he hoped the phone might deliver clues about the attacker's identity."

Sala's neck and cheeks turned red, the shade of rage. Was she angry with Eva for bringing up the phone with its neckid images or at her stepdaughter for trying to outfox her?

"That spoiled little maggot."

Guess we had a partial answer.

"'Course I knew Kate had come to Ardon County, but I haven't been able to figure out what kind of game she's playing. Why on earth would she want Zack's phone? I can't imagine how she'd think it would help in her war with me. The way she treated Ray—and me—it's a wonder her dad left Kate anything."

"So you're not concerned the sheriff has Zack's phone?" I asked.

Sala's eyebrows drew together in puzzlement. "No, why should I be?"

I snuck a glance at Eva and took her small nod as a go-ahead.

"A video stored in the phone's memory apparently shows you, uh, sexually engaged with a young man."

"What?" Sala yelled. "You saw this?"

"Uh, no. But after we found the phone, some of Zack's friends searched it for clues that might shed light on the attack. They started with unopened texts and found the video. They were certain you were in it."

"Son of a—" Sala stopped mid-curse and lasered me with a lightning-bolt stare. "And just who was my partner?"

What? Had she participated in so many sexual encounters there was a big field to choose from? My reply came out as a stammer. "My friends...uh, they said they never, uh, saw the man's face."

"But the young man in question had a tattoo on his butt," Eva interjected. "Inked in red and blue. The Joker from a pack of cards."

Sala's face turned a deeper shade of crimson. Her lips drew back in a mockery of a smile. "So that's what that little witch is after. She thinks she can blackmail me. Let her try. She wants a gutter fight, I'll give her one."

Dorothy walked over and wrapped an arm around Sala's shoulders. "I hate that brat. She's shameless."

Weiner warts. I was totally confused. Was this really the first Sala had heard about the cell phone treasure hunt or the video?

"Earlier we saw you talking with two no-neck behemoths in your driveway," Eva said. "They tried to intimidate me and I'm pretty sure they trashed Carol's house searching for that phone. Are you saying you didn't know about it?"

Sala shook free of her sister's embrace. "You're talking about Gunter—the big guy with the black beard—and Vince, the blond? Their only orders are to provide Zack with extra protection and keep me informed. I certainly didn't sanction any break-in." Her barked reply was the human equivalent of a pit bull's growl. "Until now I knew squat about any video much less why it would be on Zack's phone."

Weird as it might seem I believed her. But if Sala hadn't told the meatheads—the men we now knew as Gunter and Vince—to ransack Carol's house, who did? Could somebody else have trashed it?

"Sala, do you suppose your weasely step-worm bribed Gunter and Vince to work off-the-books for her?" Dorothy's eyebrows hitched up as she voiced her theory.

The team owner's glare provided a non-vocal answer.

"Can't tell you how glad I am that you ladies stopped by," Sala said as she stood. "It appears I have business to attend to. Firing Gunter and Vince will be my first step, but it won't be my last. Can I drop by your farm tomorrow to see Zack? I mean if the poor guy's up to it? I'm quite fond of him."

Eva nodded. "If Zack agrees, I'll give you a call. Want to give me your phone number?"

Acting as Eva's secretary, I pulled out my cell phone, typed Sala's name in my address book, then entered the number she dictated.

Did Zack have Sala's number, too? Was he the Joker in the video? Sala hadn't volunteered an answer, and neither Eva nor I had worked up enough nerve to ask.

TWENTY-FOUR

Eva and I jabbered like excited parrots on our drive back to Udderly, tossing out possibilities, rejecting them, then championing alternatives. Yet by the time we turned into Udderly's graveled drive we'd only come to one conclusion: we were more out of our depth than a vegan at a wienie roast. No clue who was on first base let alone who was hiding in the dugout.

As we drove home, the sun disappeared and clouds crowded out the blue. A thick, gray blanket shrouded our piece of the Upstate. October weather seemed as fickle as our billy goats.

I looked heavenward again when I saw Mollye's van occupied my usual parking place in front of our cabin. As we pulled up, my friend leapt from her front-stoop seat and waved. As if we could miss her.

"Thought you'd be here sooner," Mollye chastised as we climbed the steps. "Been waiting half an hour. What's with the deadbolt?"

Eva unlocked the cabin, which was usually left unlocked. "Seemed prudent given all the goings-on," my aunt muttered as we went inside. "Don't mean to be rude, but I need to change into something comfy and run right back out. I promised Zack I'd sneak in some real eats for his dinner; give him a break from institutional slop."

Mollye flopped down at her usual spot at the kitchen table as soon as Eva went to her room. "Hey, I texted you hours ago. How come you never answered?"

"Shut my phone off for the luncheon and, what with all the excitement, forgot to turn it on again." Mollye didn't bite on my excitement teaser. That had to mean she was eager to spill news of her own.

Mollye sighed theatrically. "Called my aunt and uncle. Bad news. Uncle Les is on a fishing trip with buddies down in the Lowcountry. No way he can check out the CAVE hideaway."

I walked over to the refrigerator. "Want something to drink? Iced tea? Apple juice? Water?"

"I should learn to bring my own drinks," Mollye complained. "Never a soft drink and the tea is always minus the sweet. Yuck. Guess I'll settle for apple juice."

I laughed. "Just trying to help you stay healthy."

Eva waved to us as she passed by on her way out the door. "I probably won't be home till eight thirty or so. You're on your own for supper. Don't raid my cheese stash. See you."

As soon as she left, Mollye rubbed her hands together. She'd been biding her time until Eva was out of earshot. "I have an even better idea for scouting that hunting camp than dispatching Uncle Les."

Even better? Translation: even riskier.

"Did you know Andy's first cousin, Larry, is a real estate agent?"

I smiled. "No. Are you thinking we should make an offer on the hunting lodge?"

Mollye folded her arms across her ample chest and tapped her foot. "Let me finish, will you? Larry was the first real estate agent 'round these parts to use a drone for aerial photos. Anyway, last month he bought a new, fancier drone and gave his old model to Andy, who was kind enough to take aerials of my store. I wanted my website to show I had a great location and ample parking. So we have the technology. We'll use Andy's drone to spy on the hunting camp. We can get a bird's-eye view without setting foot on the property."

I took a sip of my unadulterated tea while I considered Mollye's suggestion. Where was the hidden danger? It always lurked somewhere in the fringes of her ideas. "Wait. Didn't you say only one private road led to the camp? Isn't that why you thought it was a perfect hideout? We'd need to drive quite a ways down that road to get the drone within range. That would also put us in range of lookouts and guns."

"You're on the wrong trail. Literally." Mollye's grin grew wider. "The camp butts up to state forest. One of the hiking trails runs real close to the property boundary. We can launch the drone from the hiking trail. Don't have to expose ourselves or put even one eensy, teensy little toe over the property line."

I frowned. "Chester and his pals aren't the types to let a little thing like property lines stop them if they see us. A high-tech spy-in-the-sky would feed right into their paranoia. No telling how they'd react. But my best guess is they'd shoot."

Mollye shook her head. "The drone's itty bitty and real quiet. Fly it above the trees and they'd never see it. Even if they did, they couldn't catch us. The trail is close but it winds along a bluff. They'd have to climb it to get close enough to shoot, and trailhead parking's less than a mile from where we'd launch. We'd be in our car and speeding away before any CAVE men could get their blubber butts in gear."

I still felt queasy. One of Mollye's risk-free suggestions last spring had nearly cut off my oxygen supply—permanently. "Why don't we ask Sheriff Mason to pay a call on the hunting camp?" A reasonable question, but one look at Mollye's face told me she had a rebuttal.

"Thought you might suggest that. The sheriff would need a warrant and there's nothing concrete to justify a search of that camp. Chester hangs out there but he has alibis for both the attack on Zack and Carol's disappearance. Mason's not going to act on my hunch—no matter how inspired—that some CAVE men might be holding Carol captive there."

"Do you even know how to fly a drone?" I asked. "Or have you hoodwinked Andy into helping? It's a Monday. Isn't he at work?"

"No hoodwinking necessary. Andy was just finishing with on-site visits to a couple farms. He's meeting us at the Publix parking lot about now. Told him we'd hook up there so we wouldn't worry Eva. Your boyfriend is all in."

"He's a friend, Mollye. Just like you. A friend."

"Nope, not like me. Our handsome vet is hoping your friendship will include the kind of joint-participation exercise captured on that cell phone."

I dropped the subject mainly because Mollye was right. Andy—and Paint—made it clear that both wanted to be more than pals. I got a dull headache every time I tried to figure some way it could work. For nineteen very long months, none of my calisthenics had taken place in a bedroom. And I really cared for both men, men I could even love.

"You sure we have time for this little escapade before it gets dark?" I asked. "How long does it take to get to the trailhead?"

"Will you quit worrying? We'll get there by five, easy. That'll give us an hour before the sun sets."

TWENTY-FIVE

I looked down at the white gizmo in my lap. The drone looked unimpressive. A spindly toy. Four spider legs linked its compact body's white shell to thin whirlybird rotors.

Andy had offered to drive his vet-mobile, and I rode shotgun. Mollye'd claimed the crew cab to stretch out. Since Andy'd had little warning his truck would have human passengers, my rump was coated in dog hair. Not that I cared if my hiking clothes gained an extra layer of fur.

"Have you taken many pictures with this drone?" I asked.

Andy laughed. "This is my maiden spy outing. I've played with the drone enough to operate it without crashing. Snapped a few aerials for Mollye. Fortunately during my teen years I spent many hours locked in my room playing *Call of Duty*. I also saved the world in *Halo Wars*. Video games offered an excellent escape from my five little sisters. Drone controls work a lot like game controls."

I glanced out the window as we bumped along a dirt fire road leading to the state forest trailhead. Though it was only four o'clock, an overcast sky and the filtering canopy of tall pines combined to create an artificial twilight. Nightfall seemed imminent.

"We're here," Andy said. "I've hiked this trail. Know exactly where we can spy on the CAVE men's bullets-and-beer joint. Our timing's good. Hard to believe but a lot of these morons do work. Mostly manual or manufacturing jobs with four o'clock quitting times. If they're visiting on a weekday, they'll arrive about now."

We walked the muddy trail single file. Not much choice. The narrow, twisty path lay partially within a streambed that only channeled water during gully-washers. Evidently it had recently rained pretty hard here. Shade from the dense pine ceiling could keep the ground wet for days. Clumps of dense mud clinging to the soles of my hiking boots made it feel like I wore ankle weights.

"It's been a long time since I hiked here," Mollye grumbled. "Forgot the trail was better suited to one of Udderly's goats."

After we reached the bottom of a valley, the pine-needled path left the streambed and started climbing. Mollye huffed and puffed as we wound our way up. Soon we were hugging a rocky ridge. The exertion didn't bother me; the drop-off did. Our three-foot wide path had narrowed to maybe eighteen inches. Rock outcrops nudged us toward the outer edge. The mix of pine needles and mud made the slender ribbon of trail slicker than a Teflon frying pan.

"Watch your step," trailblazer Andy called. "A tree's blown over and it's blocking the way."

Oh, goody.

Mollye, second in line in our hiking processional, swore when she reached the tree's carcass. "Too big to step over. Guess I'll have to straddle the slimy bugger."

Great. If long-legged Mollye had to straddle, there wasn't much hope for a shorter Brie.

Mollye grunted as she swung her right leg up. A minute later she sat astride the mossy trunk like she was riding a bronco. Her expression suggested she thought the log might buck.

"Maybe this wasn't such a hot idea. I'm afraid I'll slip if I try to hop down."

"Take my hand," Andy said. "I'll steady you."

Mollye cleared the log hurdle with a little yelp. My turn. I sucked in a deep breath as I looked uphill at the exposed Medusa-like roots of the fallen tree. I had no desire to take in the downhill view. The oak was angled like a park slide that promised an unhappy landing. Sweat popped out on my forehead despite the forest chill. I couldn't move. I searched the obstacle, hoping to see some secret passage that would let me scoot under the log instead of going topside. No. The small amount of daylight between the log and the muddy path couldn't accommodate an anorexic mouse let alone a fond-of-eating chef.

Mollye tittered. "You're afraid of heights? Remember how you gave me the business about fearing I'd drown? Who's petrified now?"

"Can it, Mollye," Andy barked. "You're not helping."

My friend stopped laughing. Her chin dropped. She appeared to be studying her feet. "Sorry, Brie. I mean it. It's just that you're always the brave one." Mollye shrugged. "Guess everyone's afraid of something."

"You don't have to do this." Andy was trying to reassure me with the same tone he adopted to calm frightened animals. "We can all turn back, or you can wait here. Mollye and I can go on, fly the drone, and collect you on our way back. Or you can head back now and we'll meet you at the truck."

Quitting was a real temptation. But I didn't relish the idea of trekking the slip-and-slide trail by my lonesome. I'd seen news clips of rescue workers hoisting hikers who'd fallen into steep ravines. Their strapped-in bodies swayed like crazed metronomes.

Yet I wasn't keen on staying put. What if a bear decided it had dibs on the trail and insisted I step off or be eaten? Okay, I was being silly. Admitting it didn't lower my heartrate.

"I'm coming," I said. "Just don't hurry me."

I sidled up to the toppled monster. Unlike my tall friends, I was too short to swing a leg over and straddle the log. I'd have to drape myself over the trunk and wiggle into position. *Son of a salami.* The moss-slicked trunk was smooth. Not a single burl to serve as a saddle horn in my attempt to giddy-up.

"Give me your hand," Andy said. "I'll pull you over." Only his head and shoulders were visible across the mammoth log.

I shook my head. It wasn't a matter of trust. When scared, I tended to be obstinate about controlling my own fate. I also imagined myself doing a muddy face-plant if Andy pulled too hard. "Thanks, but no thanks. I've got it."

I heaved my body up, draping myself over the log like a sheet on a clothesline. A wet sheet. The sponge-like moss had transferred its reservoir of icy water to my well-worn jeans. Added incentive to get on with it.

I hiked my right leg up as I scrabbled to move my body over the obstacle. *Rip!*

Pickled herring. The strain had proved too much for my old jeans. Cool air tickled my exposed thigh. The denim had surrendered at the seam. Could this get more embarrassing?

"Got you." Andy's hands found purchase under my armpits and

he hoisted me over and upright.

Either my friends hadn't heard (or seen) my worn denim's demise or they had the good grace to ignore it.

"Let's get a move on," Mollye urged. "Need daylight to take pictures."

Her words made me wonder how much daylight remained. Even if we had enough light for the drone to take aerials, would darkness fall before we hiked back to Andy's truck?

"Right, let's move it," I agreed.

TWENTY-SIX

The fallen tree sat close to the top of the ridge. Once past it, we quickly reached the pinnacle and headed downhill. The path widened, providing a little more margin between me and the abyss if I stepped on a shoelace and pitched forward.

Gaps in the pines lining the trail offered glimpses of a small meadow far below. At one spot, a fairly sizeable window opened in the canopy.

This wasn't the kind of flower-speckled meadow that inspires artists. A haphazard collection of weathered wood sat at its center. Calling it a building was a stretch. Blue tarps sagged over the top of the structure. A substitute for a roof after some cave-in? The building wasn't the worst visual offense. A mini mountain of crushed beer cans and empty whisky bottles rose higher than the blue tarps. A hint of foul odor wafted up on a breeze.

"Can you launch the drone from here, Andy?" Mollye panted. "That trail map lies. Feels like we've come five miles."

Andy chuckled softly. "Hiking in woods, especially in the mountains, isn't the same as taking a stroll in a park. Takes a lot more effort—and time—to go a mile. Don't worry, we're nearly to a spot that has a lot fewer trees in the way. That's what we need. This old model doesn't have built-in collision avoidance."

In less than a hundred feet, Andy called a halt where a combination rock and mudslide had toppled most of the pines in the grove below.

He smiled. "I can launch from here. Just need a few minutes to set up."

While giving this section of the trail an unobstructed view of the meadow, the landslide had also bared a six-foot wide rocky outcrop. A perfect overlook though several large boulders still teetered overhead.

Water trickled between the rocks forming half a dozen mini cascades. Our perch didn't exactly feel rock solid.

Andy extracted the drone, its controls, and a screen from his backpack. "The screen will let us see whatever the drone sees," he said.

I never got tired of watching Andy concentrate on a task. His eyebrows scrunched together and tiny lines bracketed his emerald eyes as he focused. His slender fingers effortlessly untangled a rat's nest of wires. I remembered the talent those hands had for gentle caresses.

The mood broke when Mollye plopped down on a semi-smooth rock and rubbed her calves. She sniffed the air, wrinkled her nose, and coughed. "You smell that?"

"Yeah, there's a dead animal near here," Andy answered as he set the multi-whirligig drone on a sheet of hard plastic, a miniature take-off and landing field.

I was impressed as the handsome vet ran our toy spy-in-the-sky through a series of maneuvers, keeping it a few feet off the ground. "I like to make sure everything's working okay before I send her up. But it all looks good."

Mollye stood and walked over to stand beside Andy. "Should it wobble so much?"

"When she's close to the ground, there's more turbulence," Andy replied. "She'll straighten right up when I send her soaring."

"You keep calling that thing a 'she.' Have you named her?" Mollye asked.

Andy looked up from the controls. "Her name's Brie-zy." His eyes found mine. "Named it for you, Brie. Kinda hoping I'd get to show you more of my fine motor skills one of these days."

Exactly my wish a few seconds ago.

Mollye hooted. "Don't think old Andy's talking about a texting demo."

I felt the blush creep up my neck. Had he seen it? Did Andy know I hadn't stopped thinking about his lips, his gentle embrace? "Shhh. Sound carries out here. If there's anyone in that camp, we don't want them to hear us."

Andy grinned. "Sorry. Couldn't resist. Keep looking for some sign you'll relent and let me and my fingers audition for a different role."

He turned back to his controls. The drone lifted up and away.

Andy was right. It performed with considerably more grace now that it was aloft. "Watch the screen," Andy said. "You'll see what Brie-zy's seeing."

As the drone flew closer to the meadow, its camera revealed what looked like a one-hole privy. As it moved toward the edge of the clearing, it pictured a section of ground the privy normally hid from view.

"What's that on the ground?" Mollye ducked her head for a better look at the screen. "Go back and hover over that spot if you can."

Andy fiddled with the twin joysticks. The drone swept right and dropped lower.

"Good Lord, is that a body?" Mollye screeched. "Can you zoom in?"

I crowded in to get a better look at the screen. What first appeared as an indistinct blob on the small monitor came into clearer focus.

"My God, look at his head," I gasped. "Is that Mick? It sure looks like the guy who showed up at Udderly the morning after Zack's attack."

The drone stuttered and the picture turned blurry. "Sorry, a wind gust took her. Didn't react fast enough. I'll straighten her back up. Come in again for a close up."

The drone resumed a position over the body and Andy zoomed in even tighter.

"That's Mick all right, the poor bloke. He isn't passed out. See that knife sticking between his ribs. Good God, who would kill Mick?"

I looked away as fast as I could. Not fast enough. Bile rose in my throat. I fought against the urge to upchuck. Seeing a hunting knife protruding from anyone's chest wasn't the image I'd wanted the drone to catch.

"Any sign someone else is around?" I asked.

"You mean like the killer?" Mollye whispered.

"Don't see anyone," he said. "I'll do another sweep."

I quit looking at the screen and focused on Andy's hands as he worked the joysticks. A dog barked, decidedly angry.

"Dang," Andy muttered. "Think I just screwed the pooch. That's Chester's mutt. I don't often say bad things about a dog. But that mongrel is mean. Sooner rip your throat out than lick your hand. I know that's because of how he was raised, not his fault. Still I wouldn't try to corral him unless I was wearing plenty of padding."

Curiosity drew my gaze back to the screen. The dog, a huge one, barked and growled. Repeatedly it leapt in the air attempting to grab the drone overhead and tear it to pieces.

Bang!

The screen went blank.

Bang!

"Damn," Andy yelled. "They shot my drone!"

Shots? Those were freakin' gun shots?

An adrenaline spike reset my heart to warp speed. My brain sent urgent messages. *Run, you idiot.* My legs weren't getting the message. They'd turned into fence posts...fence posts sunk in a foot of concrete.

"Did you see the shooter?" Mollye squealed. "Is he shooting from inside the building?"

"That's my guess. Didn't see anyone when I did the sweep." Andy hastily jammed the controls and remaining drone paraphernalia into his backpack.

"Forget where the shooter might be now," Andy added. "Where will he be five minutes from now? We need to get out of here. Fast."

"Don't have to tell me twice." Mollye trotted down the trail at a brisker pace than I'd ever seen her move. She looked over her shoulder at Andy and me. "Come on. Hustle it up."

I fought my flight instinct long enough to pull my cell phone out of my windbreaker's zippered pocket. I'd learned my lesson. Always call 911 if you're in trouble and have a chance.

"This is 911. What is your emergency?" The woman's voice was calm. She sounded almost bored.

"We need to report a dead body and someone shooting a gun." My voice seemed to have climbed a couple of octaves.

"You're breaking up," the woman said. "Can you repeat?"

I repeated, and identified the hiking trail.

"Can you stay where you are until help arrives?" she asked.

"No way. We need to get out of here. We don't know the shooter's plans."

Andy grabbed the phone. "We have to go. We'll call again when we're safe."

He ended the call and handed me the phone. Another gunshot rang out. "Whoever's down there is coming after us. Now go."

I stumbled along as fast as I could. I could hear Andy's footsteps behind me. I was afraid to go faster. Tree roots and loose stones seemed to be everywhere waiting to trip me. Couldn't go any slower either or Andy would plow right into me and we'd both go down.

I caught up to Mollye just as she reached the massive tree trunk. I could hear her staccato breathing. Or was it my own? Then another sound registered. Barking. Chester's vicious dog. Was it coming for us?

Another shot rang out.

Fried Pork Rinds.

Mollye cleared the fallen tree with speed and surprising grace.

The log looked even bigger. If I fell on the other side, I would just keep tumbling. Andy wouldn't be there to catch me.

The excited, keening sounds of a canine after prey urged me forward. Amazing how one fear could trump another.

"We'll go together." Andy jettisoned his backpack. Grabbed me round the waist. His boost flung my top half up, over the trunk. *Oomph!* All air escaped my surprised body.

I didn't even see Andy scramble atop the log. He grabbed a handhold on my jeans directly above my hiney. He grunted. My butt and legs sailed up then over.

We collapsed in a tangled heap half on, half off the narrow trail. I squeezed my eyes shut. Tried to fight the nausea.

"Careful," Andy advised.

Careful? I couldn't decide if I was angry or thankful. The man had thrown me like some Scotsman tossing a caber in the Highland Games.

Andy extracted his limbs from mine and lifted me. "Sorry. No time to debate."

Louder barking. A shot added an exclamation point to Andy's logic. I pushed up. Made it to my knees. Swallowed my bile as I staggered upright.

"Come on," Andy urged. "Run."

I began to jog. The steep downhill made my run closer to a controlled stumble. No way could I brake. *Please, please don't let me trip.* Mollye was close. Pitch forward and I'd knock her down like a ten pin in a bowling alley.

The baying hound and his gun-toting companion offered constant reminders. *Focus*. I searched the slick rugged ground for trip hazards. Mollye's wheezes and my own rugged breaths sounded almost as loud as the mutt's barks.

Suddenly the barking stopped. Irritated whines punctuated the hound's snarls and yowls.

Mollye slid to a stop. I stumbled to a halt, too. "I need a second," Mollye said as she leaned against a large rock.

"Sounds like the dog's stymied," Andy huffed as he caught his breath. "Gotta be at that trunk. He's too small to leap over; too big to crawl under. Frustrated as hell. If he wants to follow us, he'll have to backtrack, find a longer way. That'll buy us some time."

I frowned. "What about the gunman? If that tree didn't stop us, it won't stop him. He can lift the dog over a lot easier than you lifted me."

"Good point," he answered. "But I'm betting we have more incentive to keep going than Chester has. Cell phone coverage is spotty up here. If he has a brain, he has to realize we'll try and call for help. If it were me, I'd make it a priority to get the hell away from that clearing and Mick's dead body."

"Hope you're right about him having a brain. Haven't seen much evidence of that."

We reached the section of trail centered within the dry creek bed. Scrambling up it proved even harder than our earlier descent. Halfway up Mollye slipped on a collection of loose gravel and fell to her knees. "Damn, damn. Whose idea was this anyway?"

We helped her up. She winced as she brushed her pant legs. "Do you hear that?"

Andy tilted his head and frowned. "Hear what?"

"Silence." Mollye smiled. "Can't hear that blasted hound and not a single shot fired for at least ten minutes. Think we made it."

Mollye's prediction did little to slow our pace. If Andy was right about the shooter's motivation, we had a similar one—quickly putting as much distance as possible between us and that godforsaken clearing.

When we reached the trailhead, Andy's truck was still the only vehicle. We climbed in. A loud crack sounded. Another shot? Had the gunman caught us?

The heavens opened and the rain arrived in blinding sheets. Not a gunshot. Thunder. Lightning streaked the sky, followed by another wallop of thunder and a prolonged rumble. I rested my forehead against the window trying to see anything through the rain. The thunder seemed to act like a tuning fork; the window vibrated. The tiny hairs on the back of my neck lifted.

"Thank heaven we got off the trail when we did," I said.

"Amen to that," Mollye added.

Andy rammed the truck in reverse. I hoped he could see the edge of the parking lot. I sure couldn't. We slithered along the winding, rutted fire road. Despite the truck's weight, its tires had trouble gripping the dirt roadbed. From what little I could see out the window, the road looked more like river than road. The normal speed limit on these fire roads—fifteen miles per hour—seemed downright reckless.

I glanced at Andy. A death grip on the steering wheel had turned his knuckles white. His eyebrows scrunched together as he tried to see where road ended and ditch began. The whole world turned gray. No visible boundaries. I guessed the darker splotches of gray were tree trunks.

"I think we're almost to the highway," Andy said.

The words had barely left his mouth when he sharply turned the wheel and we skidded to a stop. He'd seen the flashing blue and red lights of a sheriff's van before I had.

We'd almost collided with a rescue vehicle.

TWENTY-SEVEN

I counted my blessings. No crash. No bullet holes. No punctures from the jaws of one of Cujo's descendants. And no tumble into a steep ravine.

My heartbeat cranked down to a near normal rhythm once we stopped. I rested my head against the truck window and tried my meditation routine. *Breathe in, breathe out. Concentrate on each calming breath.*

That didn't keep me from jumping when a hard rap rattled my window.

I could barely make out the officer's face peering out of a rain poncho. The gusty wind had ripped the poncho's hood from his head, and rain pelted every inch of his uncovered hair and skin. Then I noticed what the deputy held in his other hand. A gun. Aimed at me.

"Hands up where I can see them," he shouted over the din of the storm. "All of you. Out of the truck."

I stuck my hands in the air. The officer abandoned the grip on his hood to yank my door open. A second later I was drenched. Wind-spiked rain scoured me. I glanced over my shoulder at Andy, who was sliding out the open driver's side door.

"Officer, I'm the one who called you." Competing with the storm's racket, I raised my voice. "We're not armed. We reported the shooting and the body."

"Get out," he yelled back. "We'll talk once you're in our vehicle."

I guessed the cold rain wasn't improving this dude's mood. He hadn't holstered his gun.

"Okay. But I can't get out of the truck with my hands in the air. I'll fall down. I'm too short, gotta hang on to something."

"Fine. Keep your hands where I can see them."

I grabbed the door handle with my left hand so I could scoot out without turning my back on the officer. Seemed prudent to make sure he had a clear view of my empty hands.

Once I was outside, he patted me down.

"Stay put," he ordered and returned to the truck's open passenger door. "Next," he called. "You in the back. Out now."

"For God's sake, Harry, it's me," Mollye protested as her head popped into view. "Knock off the dangerous felon routine. We're the good guys."

"Mollye?" Harry said. "For heaven's sake. Get your fanny out here and jump in the back of the van. All of you. We got a call about a dead body and some gun-happy creep shooting rounds out here in the sticks. Had no idea who or what."

Huddled in the back of the police van, Andy and I let Mollye serve as our spokesperson. Since she dated a deputy, Moll had a certain built-in credibility, though the officers probably knew she liked to embellish her tales.

We were all dripping wet, but the inside of the vehicle was semi-dry. Harry cranked up the van's heater, and I felt a tiny draft of warmish air. Still I couldn't stop shivering. Andy slipped an arm around me and pulled me close. I sniffed. We both smelled like wet dog. I couldn't wait to get home and strip off my wet, ripped, mud-splattered, dog-hair-coated jeans.

After Mollye wrapped up her story, we took turns answering the deputies' questions. Our most frequent answer: "Don't know." None of us got even a glimpse of the shooter though that didn't stop us from suggesting it had to be Chester given that Andy could ID his dog.

Harry wasn't impressed. "There's more than one mean mutt in Ardon County. You may be a veterinarian, Andy, but I don't believe you can positively identify a dog based on a long-distance look-see and the tone of his bark. Besides, I can't imagine Chester killing his own brother-in-law. His sister would string him up before the law ever could."

"What?" I was confused. "Mick and Chester are related?"

"Mick's sister, Bea, married Chester, so yeah, they're related," Andy added.

Mollye shivered. "I really don't care what you believe. We've told you all we know. Or are you keeping us just so you don't have to respond to any other calls in this monsoon? Come on, let us go."

"No can do," Harry answered. "Sheriff Mason wants us to bring all of you to the station. Ladies, you ride with me. Andy, you can drive your truck. My partner will ride with you. Pull out first and we'll follow."

As we motored to the Sheriff's Office, the rain slacked off, decreasing from torrential to merely drenching. By the time we arrived and sprinted inside the building, we all looked like drowned rodents, hair plastered to our scalps and water dripping from pink noses. The fluorescent lighting made us look even more disreputable if not downright shifty. I hoped Mollye's reputation as a girlfriend would help our street cred.

Sheriff Mason took one look at us and asked an officer to fetch towels. Grateful, we dried off as best we could though there wasn't much we could do about our sopping clothes. I wrapped a soggy towel around my shoulders. I'd have preferred Andy's arms but, following orders, we sat in what I thought of as interrogation chairs. Hard wood, stiff backs. Spaced far enough apart to discourage any contact between suspects.

We told the sheriff everything, including the inciting incident—Mollye's bright idea that some CAVE men might be holding Carol hostage at their hunting hideaway. I lost count of how many times Mason asked us to describe Mick's body, the drone's demise, and our pursuit by a gunman and his hound from hell.

An officer walked into the room and whispered in the sheriff's ear. Mason frowned. "Be back in a few moments." He followed the deputy outside and closed the door.

"Think they nabbed Chester?" Mollye wondered.

"Doubt it. Mason's frown said the latest news flash wasn't good," I replied.

Andy nodded. "I'm with Brie. The sheriff didn't look happy."

We fell silent as we waited for the lawman's return. Restless, Andy stood and started pacing. I was tempted to join in. If nothing else, it might warm me up.

When the door finally snicked open, Mollye muttered, "It's about time. I feel like a wet—" She never finished. We stared open mouthed as Mason ushered in the bedraggled and soaked newcomer.

"Carol," I exclaimed. "My God, are you okay? Where have you been?"

"Take me to Zack," Carol murmured. Her words were slurred. "Someone. Please. I have to get to the hospital. To Zack."

She hadn't answered my questions. My guess? They never registered.

I rushed over and hugged her. Tremors made her arms quiver. Her skin felt like ice. Carol barely seemed to notice me; didn't look at me or even return my hug. But she didn't shake me off either.

The sheriff's eyebrows hitched up. "Mrs. Strong, I'm going to ask you once more. What happened to you? Where have you been? Help us find out what happened. Then we'll take you to the hospital."

Her eyelids flickered and her body sagged. I held onto her arms to keep her from slinking to the floor. Andy rushed over and helped ease Carol into a chair.

Her head dropped and her hands flew up. Her fingers kneaded her temples. "I remember going to the hospital parking lot. Then it's all jumbled. A cold, damp cloth clamped over my mouth. An acrid smell. Loud voices. A scream. I don't know what's real, what's hallucination."

She laughed. Hysterics? The sound wasn't pleasant. "I saw my own body floating outside my Caddy. I tried to start the car and nothing happened. My head feels like it's going to explode. I have to see Zack."

She focused on Mason and whispered, "Please."

Andy knelt beside Carol's chair and patted her arm. He looked up at the sheriff. "She needs to be in the hospital. I think she's in shock. She may be drugged. You can't keep her here."

The sheriff folded his arms across his chest. "Ambulance will be here any second to take her to the hospital. I'd hoped seeing friends might snap Mrs. Strong out of her state—whatever it is."

Might good news do the trick?

"Carol. Zack woke from his coma. He's going to be just fine. He's leaving the hospital tomorrow."

"Zack..." Carol murmured and her eyelids fluttered. She fainted just as two paramedics rushed in.

"Can we go to the hospital with her?" I asked as they lifted her onto a rolling stretcher.

The sheriff shook his head. "No. We're not finished."

The door to the interview room closed, leaving Andy, Mollye, and me alone with the sheriff.

Mason cleared his throat. "I heard back from the unit we sent to that hunting camp Chester frequents. Place was empty. No dog, no shooter, no corpse. No drone either. You sure you're not hallucinating?"

I looked at Andy, then Mollye. *What the Feta?*

"We all saw the same things, Sheriff," Andy said. "I kinda doubt we're victims of some mass hypnosis scheme. We saw what we saw. When you find my backpack, you can check the recording from the drone. It'll prove we're not hallucinating. Surely your men found blood? Signs of a struggle?"

The sheriff shrugged. "You were out in that monsoon. What do you think? Water had pooled six inches deep around that privy. If there ever was evidence of a body or struggle, the water washed it away."

The sheriff looked down at his hands. "Want to know how we located Mrs. Strong?"

We nodded in unison.

"A Good Samaritan spotted her wandering beside the highway turnoff to that hunting camp. She was soaked, incoherent. He bundled her into his car. She kept pleading to be taken to her son. He asked her name...if she was lost. She didn't answer.

"The driver was from out-of-state, had no idea the woman was a missing politician. She was acting so strangely he suspected she'd wandered away from a psych ward. Didn't know what else to do with her so he brought her here."

"What an ordeal," I said. "She was kidnapped. They must have drugged her."

"Maybe," Mason answered. "Then again maybe she's playacting. Could be she's the one who shot at you. I've heard her tell voters she owns a gun and is a better-than-decent shot. Is that true or just campaign rhetoric?"

"What?" Andy practically shouted. "Carol wasn't shooting at anyone. She's a victim. Chester kidnapped her."

The sheriff rocked back on his heels. "Nope. Already told you folks he couldn't have. We confirmed Chester's alibi. He was out of town

Sunday afternoon when Carol disappeared."

"Doesn't mean he didn't kill Mick," Mollye sputtered.

Mason treated us to his best Arctic stare. "If Mick is actually dead, maybe Mrs. Strong killed him. I have to consider all the possibilities."

"You can't really think Carol plunged that knife into Mick?" Mollye threw up her hands. "Then what? She picked up his dead body and hid it before chasing us. Oh, yeah, and with Chester's dog leading the way. And when she was done with all that she sprinted to the road to scam some passerby in the rain?"

The sheriff cleared his throat. "I have no preconceived notion of what happened. Maybe Mrs. Strong did knife this Mick fellow and run. Maybe Chester or one of his buddies came back and removed a dead body. Or maybe you saw someone passed out behind the privy, someone who wasn't really dead and the rain sobered him up. Maybe your corpse got up and walked off.

"Tell me what you *think* you saw one more time. It's too dark and dangerous for my men to search that hiking trail tonight. Come morning I'll send deputies to recover that backpack you say you dropped. They'll look for any signs of a shooter—man or woman."

TWENTY-EIGHT

After Sheriff Mason decided he'd squeezed all the information he could from us, we headed for the hospital. I tried to phone Aunt Eva but got no answer. Probably switched off. Not a shocker.

As Andy pulled into the hospital parking lot, I saw a man, shoulders hunched, puffing on a cigarette in a shadowed enclave at the corner of the building. Though the entire medical campus was declared nicotine-free, it was next to impossible to enforce outdoors—not with frantic people, worried about loved ones, craving a hit.

The man ground his cigarette butt under his heel. Then he cupped his hand around a lighter to fire up another one. The flickering flame lit his face like a spotlight.

"It's Fred Baxter." I nodded toward the man. "What's he doing here? Holding a get-unwell vigil for Zack?"

"If all was right with the world, he'd be waiting to drive his honey Allie home after a forked tongue extraction," Mollye said.

"Forget Fred," Andy said. "It's okay with me if he wants to barbecue his lungs as long as he's not bothering Zack."

Inside, a friendly nurse directed us to Zack's new room outside the ICU.

"Think he's been reunited with his mom yet?" Mollye asked as the elevator doors opened. Down the hall, a dozen-body scrum blocked the entrance to Zack's room. As we got closer, I recognized two sour pusses. Allie and Kate. Fred must be waiting to chauffeur Allie to the next place she planned to infect with hate. Clearly the sheriff's deputy was controlling access, and all members of the hall mob had been turned away. Andy elbowed through the crowd and tapped on the small window set in the closed door.

"Hey, Paint. Tell the deputy we know the secret handshake," he said, trying to get his best friend's attention within the inner sanctum.

Paint opened the door. "Not sure about the three of you." He looked us up and down and grinned. "Maybe we should require showers before letting you inside."

"Showers?" Mollye sputtered. "I'm wetter than a mud wrestler who lasted nine rounds."

Paint laughed. "Yeah, that's exactly how you look."

The guard on duty outside the door looked to Paint for a go-, no-go signal. Paint nodded approval. Apparently he'd been granted the keys to Zack's fiefdom.

Allie screeched an objection as the deputy gave his wave-through pass. "If he's well enough to entertain this riffraff, he's well enough to answer serious allegations," she blustered. "Why has his mother gone into hiding?" She jockeyed to see into the room. "What's she done?"

Kate's head bobbled up and down in approval, but the other media types just looked bored.

"For heaven's sake, they're letting in Hookers!" Allie exclaimed in a last-ditch effort to rally out-of-town media colleagues.

Now that outburst did snap folks to attention. A candy-striper delivering a bouquet next door, fumbled the vase she was carrying. It crashed to the floor. She didn't even look down at the mess. Too focused on our little drama.

"What did you say?" asked a round-eyed reporter for a Greenville paper.

Mollye's laughter pretty well drowned out any other hallway chatter. She waved gaily to the throng. "I'm only an honorary Hooker." She pointed at me. "But she's the real deal."

We ducked inside the private room, and Paint closed the door, shutting out the rabble. Hallway outsiders could still peer through glass windows to see a portion of the room. It felt like a fishbowl.

Zack looked the picture of health. Well, except for the bulging dressings on his head, shoulder, and foot. He lounged on top of the covers wearing silk pajamas in a deep blue that matched his eyes. The left leg of his PJs had been cut off to make room for the bulky soft cast on his broken ankle.

Zack was chuckling over a shared joke with, holy moly, Doug Hayes. I'd forgotten Eva had mentioned the former star quarterback had scored a travel pass to visit his injured buddy. The guys sure were chummy considering he'd soon replace Zack on the field.

Though hard to imagine, Hayes edged out Zack in the handsome department. *Yowzer*. Bronzed skin. Thick fair hair with a little curl at the nape of his neck. A smile so perfect I wondered if he had implants. The intense hazel eyes, a kaleidoscope of green, brown and gold flecks, were the capper. I wasn't much for men who sported a lot of bling, but I forgave him the honking big diamond stud in his left earlobe. Probably part of his fans' style expectations.

Doug stopped laughing and focused his hazel eyes on me. It took a moment for me to pry my gaze away and check out the room's other well-wishers.

Doug and Eva had won the two coveted chairs on opposite sides of Zack's bed. Linda, Carol's campaign manager, leaned against a windowsill. That left foot-of-the-bed, standing-room for Paint, Andy, Mollye and me to squeeze into the tiny space.

"Where have you been?" my aunt scolded. "You look wet enough to grow mold. Have you heard the good news? Carol's back."

"We know," Mollye interrupted. "Is she still loopy?"

"What do you mean *still*?" Zack picked up on the implication. "Have you seen Mom?"

I nodded. "We were at the Sheriff's when they brought Carol in." I glanced at Zack. "She kept begging to be taken to you. Andy thought she might be in shock."

"Your mom seemed to be suffering from amnesia. She couldn't quite sort out what happened to her," Andy added. "Seemed confused about what was real and what might have been hallucination. I think she was drugged."

Zack gripped the rail on the left side of his hospital bed to lever himself upright. He grimaced despite his attempt to favor his damaged shoulder as he moved.

"A doctor let me know Mom was here and seemed in decent health despite exhaustion and short-term memory loss," he said. "The doc promised I could see her as soon as they finished a few tests. He didn't say anything about her being drugged."

"Of course she was drugged." Aunt Eva huffed. "It's not like she's some drunk who suffers blackout spells. Let's pray her amnesia is short-term and she can identify the bastards who kidnapped her."

Zack slunk back against the pillows in his cranked-up bed. "At least she's safe, but I'll feel a lot better when I can see her with my own eyes."

Aunt Eva frowned as she returned her attention to Andy, Mollye, and me. "What were you three doing at the Sheriff's Office when they brought Carol in?"

My aunt's pursed lips told me she'd dog us with questions until we spilled the beans. I decided to speak up. With so many ears in the room, I elected to give a sanitized version of our hike, only mentioning the drone's death by bullet, and my 911 call to report gunfire. I omitted any mention of Mick, being chased by a mutt who could win a Stephen King character contest, and the shooter's attempt to put holes in our running rumps.

I felt certain the sheriff would prefer to be the one to break any news of Mick's demise—that is, if his body was ever found, or if Mason recovered Andy's backpack and an aerial recording that proved we hadn't dreamed the whole escapade.

Eva shook her head. "Glad you just got a soaking and no bullet holes. It's a wonder whoever shot down your drone didn't shoot at you."

"Oh, we were a long way away," Andy said.

Thanks, Andy. Nice deflection.

"So what happened at the Sheriff's?" Paint asked. "Did Carol drive there?"

"Hardly," Mollye said. "Some motorist found her wandering beside a road. Carol woke in her car. When it wouldn't start, she got out and walked. It was pouring, and she got drenched. Plenty reason to be dazed."

I watched Zack's eyebrows knot and decided we shouldn't add to his worries. "She just kept pleading to see you. I'm sure Carol will be fine once you two are reunited and she gets some rest."

I hoped it wouldn't take Carol long to sort through the jumble in her brain. I had the feeling Mason would be keen to hear her explain how she wound up in a parked car near a remote murder scene.

Linda straightened from her perch near the windowsill. "I need to run. I'll try to dodge the reporters. I'm certainly not going to answer any questions about Carol. Even a hint that she's suffering some sort of mental lapse could end her run for governor. The *Ardon Chronicle* would label it mental illness and ride it into the ground. Allie's waiting for just that kind of tidbit."

A stern-faced doctor walked in and scanned the assemblage. "You all need to leave. Mr. Strong needs rest."

"How's Mom?" Zack asked.

The doctor shook his head. "I can only discuss her condition with immediate family. Again, all of you must leave. Security is clearing the hall. This is a hospital, not a bar lounge."

"I'm real sorry we've created such a nightmare for the hospital." Zack smiled at the doctor. "But can my friend Doug stay a couple more minutes? We need a word in private."

The doctor studied the two football teammates for a beat or two before he committed. "Fine. Five minutes."

He then shooed the rest of us toward the door.

"I'll phone you, Eva," Zack called. "Still want you to spring me in the morning."

He glanced at the doctor, then back at Eva. "Maybe you'll get a two-fer. Have you got room for Mom and me?"

"Of course," Eva answered. "Love to have both of you."

I agreed, though I wondered if I'd be sleeping in the barn. Then I shivered, remembering the barn's crime-scene tape had just been ripped down. Plus it was getting danged cold outside.

I glanced over my shoulder for a parting look at Zack and his handsome teammate. Why was Zack so keen to speak with Doug in private? Football or another type of athletic endeavor?

Though the rain had subsided, the bruised color of the clouds looked threatening. Once we reached the parking lot, Linda peeled off to find her car. The rest of us stood in a tight, unmoving knot as if we'd agreed by mental telepathy.

"All of you want to meet at Udderly?" Eva asked. "I'm sure our chef here can figure out how to divide her tofu and loaves to make sure no one goes hungry."

"Sounds great," Paint said. "I'll give you a ride, Brie. Andy had the pleasure of your company this afternoon. It's my turn."

Mollye chuckled. "Andy's been keeping me company, too," she teased. "Want to give me a ride?" She waved her hand. "Just kidding.

Andy, do you mind dropping me back at Publix? I'll start to molt soon if I don't get out of these wet duds."

"No problem," Andy said.

Paint tucked my arm in his as we walked to his truck. "Hope you'll call me for your next spy mission," he said. "I'll buy a drone if that's what it takes."

I smiled. "I'm hoping that's my last drone adventure. You're lucky you missed this one. Andy had to hoist me over a huge log and we fell in a heap. Not pretty."

Paint pulled me closer. "I'm into heaps if you're involved."

He winked at me, and I responded with my usual eye roll. Paint was such a congenital flirt I never knew how serious he was.

As I climbed into his truck, I glanced over at the shadowy building niche where I'd seen Fred Baxter chain smoking. Empty. He was gone. Were he and Allie together? Not sure which was worse, picturing them plotting or under the covers. Under the covers. Definitely under the covers was worse.

TWENTY-NINE

As we drove toward Udderly, I thought about the vultures outside Zack's room.

"What do you think Kate Lemmon wants from Zack?" I asked. "Why is she so eager to talk to him?"

Paint shook his head. "Don't have a clue. But I bet Doug does."

"What are you talking about?"

"Early this afternoon I visited the hospital cafeteria," he began. "Kate and Doug were huddled in a corner. Their faces close enough to engage in eyelash combat. Soon as they saw me they sprang apart like teens caught necking in the backseat of a Chevy."

"Huh. Doug and Zack seem buddy-buddy, but Zack's made it plain he dislikes Kate," I said. "Doug must not share his opinion."

Paint grinned. "How curious are you? I know you're into drones and being chased by Cujo, but my spy craft involves a toasty seat by the fire and a drink. You said Kate's staying at the Maison d'Orange, right? I keep its bar and little souvenir area stocked with moonshine. We can drop by for a nightcap. The owner loves to gossip."

The idea had definite appeal. If I could stay awake that long.

"Maybe," I answered. "Let's see how the evening goes."

Fortunately, the vegan split pea soup started in the crockpot that morning looked like enough to feed the crowd when paired with bread and, for most, cheese. Some days I felt like I was running a B&D. That's a bed and dinner establishment.

Mollye set the table while I put the finishing touches on dinner. Meanwhile, Andy and Paint gave Eva a hand, feeding Lilly's mule, Rita, and Eva's horse, Hank. The equines had been a bit skittish ever since their temporary eviction from the barn during crime scene processing.

Eva made sure all the other animals were squared away with food and clean water.

My aunt and guests filled their soup bowls to the brim and helped themselves to bread. I insisted on being last in line. If the soup ran out, I could always stir-fry veggies and tofu. But it looked like there'd even be enough for seconds. My split pea was thick enough to stand a spoon up in it. I loaded it with onions, potatoes, and lots of carrots as well as split and green peas. For a few minutes, spoons scraping against bowls provided the only sounds.

Usually when this group huddled around the table, it was hard to get a word in edgewise. The silence felt like a dark cloud.

"I keep thinking about what Carol said about a damp cloth over her mouth and her out-of-body experience," Andy said. "My theory? Somebody used a chloroform-soaked rag to put her out and followed up with a drug like Ketamine. I use it to anaesthetize animals when I operate, and I'm very careful about locking it up. It's become a popular drug at raves. Kids misuse it. Though I can't for the life of me understand wanting to experience hallucinations."

"I've heard of it," Paint said. "Maybe from Howie Lemcke. Something about emergency surgeries in the field."

Andy nodded. "Right. It's used to put humans under for surgery, especially when medics have no access to ventilation equipment. Ketamine's less likely than other anesthetics to affect breathing. But it's used less often as a primary anesthetic in hospitals since it can have side effects—like hallucinations, disorientation, and out-of-body experiences. Symptoms like Carol's."

Eva fiddled with her napkin. "I'm sure Carol was drugged. Just hope there's no lasting damage."

"Her ordeal may be over, but Mick is dead." Paint slumped in his seat. "I feel guilty. Maybe if I'd answered his calls he'd be alive. I keep wondering if he was asking for my help. Lord knows he didn't have a lot of friends to turn to."

"Do you think he came to that hunting cabin of his own accord?" Mollye asked as she buttered another hunk of bread. "Uncle Les never mentioned Mick as one of the regulars. 'Course Mick might have gone there looking for Chester. Sorry but I can't see Chester offing his wife's only brother."

Paint sighed. "All I know is Mick seemed obsessed with Zack, and the voice messages he left sounded more and more unhinged. I think Mick either attacked Zack or knew who did."

I frowned as I waved a hand at our three guests. "All of you went to high school with Mick. Was he one of Zack's buddies?"

"Mick was a year behind us, same grade as Chester," Andy answered. "I doubt Mick and Zack ever said more than hi as they passed in the hall. They just didn't run with the same crowd. But a few years ago, Mick scraped together enough coin to go to an Aces game. Zack introduced him around as one of his high school mates."

"You think Mick fantasized he was great pals with the football star?" Mollye asked.

Paint shrugged. "Mick gambled. His sister asked me to talk with him about his gambling. She was convinced he was addicted to online, high-stakes action."

"Did you talk to him?" Mollye asked.

Paint nodded. "Not a very successful conversation. I had the impression he'd been losing big time—at least big time for someone with Mick's income. He seemed all nervous and jerky. Made me wonder if he might be doing drugs. Maybe meth."

"Druggies can get pretty paranoid," Mollye said. "If he was whacked out on meth, he could have lost it and blamed Zack for losing a big bet."

"Guess I can buy that if his brain was fried," Paint answered. "But that doesn't explain why Chester or his hunting buddies would kill Mick. If he was the attacker, I'd think the CAVE men would throw Mick a party. Zack did sock Chester."

Silence descended as we tried to sort through possibilities. Paint walked to the crockpot to help himself to a second bowl of soup. He used the brief recess to jump topics.

"I asked Zack about the sex video. Eva had gone for coffee. Linda and Doug hadn't arrived. Zack still hasn't seen the video, so I provided some color commentary the sheriff omitted when he questioned Zack. It was the first Zack heard about a Joker tattoo on a bare butt."

Paint sat down and paused to slather butter on a slice of bread, acting as if it needed his complete attention.

"Quit toying with us, butthead," Mollye complained. "Inquiring minds need to know. What did Zack say?"

Paint chuckled. "You're so impatient, Mollye. Zack swore his derriere didn't boast a tattoo. He seemed relieved the butt in question couldn't be his. He also seemed annoyed. His reaction made me wonder if he'd also enjoyed the pleasure of Sala's company."

Eva cleared her throat. "No point speculating about something that's none of our beeswax. Did Zack have any idea who sent him the video or why people were frantic to snatch it?"

Paint shook his head. "I suspect he knows who played the male lead. My guess—and it's purely that—is Zack plans to chat with the man."

Mollye grinned. "Okay, if Zack could tell who it was based on the tattoo, the man may be a teammate. Maybe that's why Zack wanted to huddle with Doug. Do you suppose that magnificent butt belongs to Doug? Maybe Sala has a thing for quarterbacks. Couldn't blame her. Look up stud in the dictionary and you might see a picture of both those hunks."

Aunt Eva frowned. "Sala seemed genuinely surprised a video existed. If she's right and her stepdaughter paid those security bozos to break into Carol's house, maybe Kate paid someone to make that video as well."

"Possible, but Kate would be beyond stupid to finance an attack on Zack," Andy said. "If the Aces get to the Super Bowl, the team will rake in megabucks. Even a minority owner would pocket a big chunk of change. Putting Zack on the disabled list would be incredibly dumb."

Mollye waved her soup spoon in the air. "But if Kate didn't commission Zack's attack, who did? Assuming the attack was planned to nab the phone, Kate and Sala are the two with the most obvious motives."

I agreed. "But how would Kate even know there was a video? Zack couldn't have told anyone. He hadn't opened it. Someone had to clue Kate in—either the sender or someone he told. I'm still baffled by the sender's motive unless he was warning Zack that he had claims on Sala."

"That brings up another problem. If the sender wasn't in the video, how did he get a copy?" Mollye asked.

"Maybe the sender wasn't a he," Paint said. "Maybe some woman has it in for Sala. Knowing who sent the video could tell us a lot."

"Any way to ID the sender?" I asked.

"I'll ask the dude who handles our computer security," Paint answered.

A crack of thunder sounded and a sudden gust of wind made the pine trees outside sigh as they swayed, their branches scratching the cabin's metal roof.

"That settles it," Eva said. "I'm off to bed. I need to get up tomorrow and milk goats. Then I'm heading to the hospital to pick up Zack and maybe Carol. If either Strong wants to tell us more about their personal affairs, fine. If not, we'll respect their wishes."

Andy and Mollye rose, too. "Yeah, tomorrow's a weekday." Mollye groaned. "Some customers scheduled Tarot readings with me and I'm expecting deliveries. I'll be at Starry Skies all day. Promise you'll keep me posted. I'm dying of curiosity."

She chuckled. "Business should be brisk. Lots of out-of-towners wandering about, and I'm willing to help them spend money. Maybe I ought to offer reporters Tarot readings, help them figure out how to land a big scoop."

Andy shook his head. "I'm glad reporters don't bring their pets. I've got enough on my plate. Three farm calls tomorrow. I'll be spending the day giving vaccinations to large animals. Sometimes exciting."

Paint lingered, fidgeting with his coat as Andy and Mollye walked out.

"Still up for that nightcap?" He raised our kitchen blinds to check on the storm. A white-hot lightning bolt flared in the glass. Electricity actually raised the hairs on my arm.

"I guess so, if you're sure we won't wash away."

"Not a chance with my truck," he answered.

"Ah, the idiocy—I mean optimism—of youth," Eva countered. "Take your AAA card in case you need a tow, Brie, and don't stay out too late."

Eva twisted the dishtowel in her hands. She looked troubled.

"Would you rather I stayed in tonight?" I asked.

Eva sagged against the kitchen counter. "It's not that. I just hope I did the right thing, inviting Zack and Carol to stay here. What if the people behind Zack's attack and Carol's kidnapping aren't finished? What if I've put you in the line of fire? I love Carol and Zack, but I love you more."

I shook my head. "Sala fired Vince and Gunter. Even if Kate's been paying them off the books, they're probably long gone. I would be. Too dicey."

Paint walked over and gave Eva a hug. "Sheriff Mason's a professional. He'll keep digging. You can count on me, too. I'm an even better shot than Billy."

Eva sucked in a deep breath and rubbed the back of her neck. "Oh, go on, get out of here. I'm just getting old. Still I'd breathe easier if I believed that buffoon Chester and his cronies posed the only danger. There's more to this than some CAVE-man crusade."

Since I hoped to open a B&B, I was eager to see the inside of the Maison d'Orange, a boutique hotel housed in an impressive modern brick building, with six luxurious bed-and-bath suites in each of its two wings.

Paint parked far enough down the circular drive that we wouldn't block the entrance for any late arrivals. We raced to the front door trying to dodge fat raindrops.

Inside, a crackling fire drew me to its side. I was warming my hands when I heard her voice, a French-accented melody. "Paint, so happy you dropped in."

I turned. The woman was striking. Smooth alabaster skin. Large brown eyes. Auburn hair piled in a complicated twist.

En route, Paint had told me a little about Madame Thompson, the widowed owner. After her wealthy husband died, she missed hostessing grand parties. She'd built the estate-like facility to showcase her exquisite taste and hospitality.

The boutique hotel, known for serving a luscious breakfast and afternoon tea, hosted many weddings and special events. It also stocked a bar for after-dinner refreshments. Tough competition for my future B&B, though I hoped vegan and vegetarian fare and lower rates would lure my niche market.

"What can I get my favorite moonshiner and his lady to drink?"

Madame asked.

Paint nodded at me to order. “Do you have coconut cream?” I asked. “If so, I’d like a Kahlua and cream.”

“*Mais, oui,*” she answered.

Paint surprised me by ordering a brandy rather than moonshine. “Product research,” he explained. “Won’t be long before my distillery’s making a variety of whiskies.”

“I’m sure they’ll be wonderful.” Madame Thompson smiled as she prepared my drink.

“Won’t you join us?” Paint asked as we settled at a small table near the fireplace.

“A delight,” she raised an eyebrow as she glanced at me, “if I’m not intruding.”

Madame Thompson was clearly smitten. Though Paint was probably thirty years younger, I got the feeling she’d pursue a dalliance given the slightest encouragement.

Paint brought his hand up to cover mine. His fingers began a gentle massage. Was he signaling I was more than a friend or offering an invitation? Didn’t matter. I wasn’t about to object. The warm connection felt way too good.

As we chatted, Paint proved brilliant at covertly guiding the conversation. In minutes, we learned both Kate and Doug were registered guests. The proprietress also told us about her concern earlier in the day about an unmarked van loitering behind the building. “I was trying to get up my nerve to confront them, when they drove away,” she said.

“Did you see anyone inside?” Paint asked.

She shook her head. “No. The windows were too dark.”

Could it have been Gunter and Vince? If so, was Sala’s intuition right about Kate hiring them?

We heard the front door open, and Madame Thompson levitated to her feet to greet the new arrival. “Oh, Mademoiselle Lemmon,” she cooed. “It’s so cold outside. Won’t you join us by the fire?”

“Don’t turn around,” Paint whispered. “Let’s keep our backs to Kate and hope she goes away.”

“Send a snifter of brandy to my suite,” Kate ordered without so much as a please or thank you. “And I want a limo at nine a.m. to take me to the airport. I'm checking out."

Good. Maybe Gunter and Vince had simply stopped by for a final paycheck. Kate leaving Ardon County had to be good news.

THIRTY

I'm never eager to jump out of bed at five in the morning. This Tuesday was no exception. But, as soon as I walked outside, I could tell the day would be a beauty. Last night's lightning and thunder theatrics cleared the heavens for a Carolina blue sky, no wind, and warmer temperatures. Even our randy billy goats seemed in a mellow mood; no morning stunts as I delivered Duncan and Jordan their special feed.

I whistled as I tackled my chores. My evening excursion contributed to my cheer, though I wasn't certain what made me happier—Kate flying the coop or Paint as thoughtful escort, a taste of what a real date might promise.

With essential dairy and farm duties completed by mid-morning, I worked on a grocery list while Eva phoned the hospital to see if she was breaking out one patient or two. If she needed to bring both Zack and Carol home, we'd swap vehicles. She'd take my Prius; I'd drive her truck to fetch supplies.

Eva looked puzzled when she hung up the phone. "Zack says the sheriff will deliver him and his mom to Udderly around one o'clock."

"Did he say why?"

"Nope, he was very guarded. Maybe the sheriff was in the room. Go ahead and run your errands. I won't need your car. I'll use the break to whip up a batch of cheese."

I headed to the nearest big box superstore, a forty-five-minute drive, to buy two blow-up mattresses. One for me, one for Eva. Better than the cramped love seat. I also needed to stock up on provisions to feed our houseguests. I loved being with people, but it also felt really good to be alone. Silence. No one talking. I didn't even turn on the radio until I was half an hour into the drive. Then I tuned into a local station to see if there was news on any of our mystery fronts.

The pretend sounds of a clattering teletype alerted me, and all other listeners, that a news bulletin was about to begin. "This just in," said a breathless reporter. "This morning the body of a local man, Mick Hardy, was discovered in the trunk of a Cadillac found abandoned near Winding Creek. A knife wound to the chest was the apparent cause of Hardy's death. His body has been taken to Greenville for autopsy. Ardon County Sheriff Mason said it appeared that Hardy, an employee at Jameson Quarry, was killed sometime late Sunday or early Monday. The autopsy should help narrow the time of death.

"The sheriff declined to confirm if the Cadillac containing Hardy's body belonged to gubernatorial candidate Carol Strong. WSSL has learned that Mrs. Strong is the owner of a Cadillac Seville. She was found Monday afternoon walking in the rain near where the car containing Hardy's body was discovered. WSSL will bring you updates as soon as we know more."

Moldy Muenster. Was Eva listening to her radio? No point calling. She wouldn't have taken her cell phone to the barn. Too bad. She'd want a heads up before the sheriff brought our houseguests.

At least Sheriff Mason would now believe my friends and I really saw Mick's dead body. Of course, finding the corpse in the trunk of a Caddy wasn't good news. Carol's car had a roomy trunk. There was no doubt in my mind: Mick's body had been stuffed inside.

But who did the stuffing? I rejected Carol as culprit, and Chester seemed an unlikely candidate unless he'd killed his own brother-in-law. I sure hoped Carol would regain some memory of those missing hours. Looked like she might need to in order to defend herself.

Once I reached the superstore's parking lot, I stayed in the car to phone Mom. While she didn't practice criminal law, she really *was* Carol Strong's family attorney. Mom hadn't fibbed about that when Kate Lemmon tried to bully us into surrendering Zack's phone. Mom would want to know about the new developments. Then she could decide if Carol needed to talk with an attorney sooner rather than later.

Mom's answer? Sooner. Said she'd try to reach the farm before the sheriff arrived with Carol and Zack.

While I sat with my Prius securely in park, I replied to concerned texts from Mollye, Paint, and Andy, letting them know Mom was on the case to protect Carol's legal rights. I finished my shopping as quickly as possible, buying two queen-size air mattresses along with groceries.

While I like to frequent local shops that carry fresh farm-to-table produce, the speed of one-stop shopping trumped my fresh-over-frozen preference.

Back home, I found Eva in the barn. She hadn't heard the news, but was glad I'd called in Mom. We quickly put away the groceries, and wolfed down a quick lunch before we got any more surprises.

At five till one, Mom led a vehicle parade to our cabin. She'd beaten the sheriff to the turnoff by a hair. At least I assumed the unmarked sedan glued to Mom's bumper belonged to the sheriff. I wondered if Mason's incognito ride was designed to spirit the Strongs away without alerting the media. *A girl can hope.*

Eva and I went outside to greet the newcomers. We weren't sure if the sheriff was offering a drop-off taxi service or planned to stay. Mom exited her car and paused at the bottom of the cabin steps. I figured she wanted to see if Zack or Carol needed help and who would come inside.

Sheriff Mason and Deputy McCoy helped their passengers out. Carol, looking—and acting—more like the take-charge woman I knew, shook off the sheriff's arm as soon as she steadied herself. Though Zack's right arm was in a sling and he wore a huge boot to immobilize his broken left ankle, he also waved off assistance. He used a cane, rather than a crutch, to maneuver with his cast-boot.

Eva hugged Carol and awarded Zack a smile. "I'm not gonna hug you and topple us both. Delighted you'll be staying with us."

My aunt turned to the sheriff and deputy. "Did you want to come in?"

"Yes," Mason answered, his tone ominous. "I need to make certain everyone understands the situation."

The cozy cabin wasn't designed for hosting parties. The main living area seated four people comfortably on one love seat and two recliners. Any additional guests had to park their fannies on chairs scavenged from the dining nook. Eva insisted Carol and Zack take the recliners and motioned Mom toward the love seat. My aunt wasn't giving the lawmen preferred seating.

"I'll bring more chairs," I offered. Deputy McCoy, Mollye's beau, followed me to the dining nook and carried two straight-back chairs. I got the third.

Eva settled next to Mom on the love seat. That left the sheriff, the deputy, and me with the hard-bottomed imports. Eva's way of encouraging brevity?

The sheriff cleared his throat. "I think we got Mrs. Strong and her son out of the hospital without any reporters realizing they'd checked out. But sooner or later, they may show up here. I don't have the manpower to keep a guard at Udderly's entrance twenty-four seven. But Mrs. Lemmon informed us that she is making arrangements with an outside executive protection service. We'll have a cruiser do a check every couple of hours. Needless to say you can call 911 any time you need us."

"Thank you, Sheriff," Carol said. "We appreciate your concern."

"You'll be less thrilled with what else I have to say." Mason paused as his gaze bounced between Carol and Zack. "We matched Mick Hardy's fingerprints with ones lifted from the pitchfork. This appears to confirm Mick was Zack's attacker. We also matched your fingerprints, Mrs. Strong, with the knife plunged into Mick's chest. The knife was in the trunk of your Cadillac under Mick's body. That makes you a suspect in his murder. And then there's your very real motive. The man attacked your son."

"What? You're kidding!" Eva blurted.

The sheriff held up a hand. "Let me finish. Please."

Mom put a restraining hand on my aunt's arm to keep her from jumping up.

"We're not charging you, Mrs. Strong, because the urine samples taken when you arrived at the hospital proved positive for Ketamine. That lends credence to your story of waking in your Cadillac and not knowing how you got there."

Carol nodded. "I was so disoriented. Rain pounding on the windshield. I could hear rushing water. I was terrified the car would be swept away. I tried to start it; nothing happened. I saw my body floating outside the car. I thought I was losing my mind. I had to get out, start walking."

Mom broke in. "Is this the appropriate time to question Mrs. Strong? Might she still be feeling lingering effects of whatever drug she was given?"

Mason shrugged. "I'm not a doctor, but I believe your client has told us all she can at this time. I'm not here to question her. Just wanted you to know that some parties are bound to argue that, given the evidence, we should arrest Mrs. Strong for the murder of the man who attacked her son. Her motive was revenge, and she was clever enough to ingest some quantity of Ketamine to fabricate an alibi."

The sheriff stood. His eyes locked with Carol's. "You understand you need to stay in Ardon County, right?" Carol nodded.

"We're hoping the autopsy will pinpoint the time of Hardy's death," he added. "That will be an enormous help in determining a timeline."

"When is the autopsy scheduled?" Mom asked.

"Tomorrow afternoon. We'll share the results as soon as we have them."

Once the lawmen left, Mom said she wanted a few minutes alone with Carol. I knew why. Anything Carol said to Mom was privileged, but if Eva, Zack or I listened in we could be compelled to testify about what was said.

Aunt Eva turned to Mom and Carol. "You're welcome to use my bedroom for your talk. That's your room now, Carol. Zack's staying in Brie's room. Brie and I are sleeping out here. Nice and cozy on new air mattresses."

"Don't be a horse's patoot," Carol snapped. "We're not going to kick you out of your bedrooms. Zack and I will sleep out here." She waved her arm to take in the room's love seat and chairs.

Eva hooted. "You really think Zack can fit on that love seat? Sure as heck he can't get up and down from a blow-up mattress on the floor. Not with that arm and boot. Nope, you two are taking the bedrooms. Besides Brie and I get up at dawn and we need coffee. No sense in us trying to tiptoe around sacked-out guests with our eyes half open."

Mom held her hands up like a traffic cop. "Enough. I already know who's going to win. Right now I need to speak with Carol."

Carol let Eva have the last word and followed Mom to the bedroom. The door closed. Eva excused herself to check on the animals.

"How are you feeling?" I asked Zack. "Can I get you something to eat or drink?"

"I'm fine. Well, except for finding out my attacker was an old high school teammate, and my mother, who's been drugged, is suspected of murdering him. Oh, and we can expect press, since the sheriff can't run interference."

"My head's spinning, too," I agreed. "Do you have any idea why Mick attacked you?"

"Afraid I do." Zack used his left hand to try to fish something out of his pants pocket. A right-hander, he awkwardly seized the object only to have it slip from his fingers. A cell phone fell to the floor. I jumped up to retrieve it.

"So the sheriff gave your phone back to you?" I asked as I handed over the cell.

"Not exactly. Kept the phone as evidence. But one of Mason's techies copied everything to a new phone. Hard to use the blasted thing one-handed. I was going to read you Mick's last text, but his exact words don't matter. He'd bet big on our team winning the last game. We didn't, and he blamed me. He was hopelessly in the red. Don't think he saw any way out. Guess he needed to take his frustration and anger out on someone. I was home, a handy target."

Looking at the cell phone in his hand made me remember Sala. "Do you want to call anyone? Doug? Sala?" I asked. "I can key in the numbers and leave to give you some privacy. I know Sala wants to visit today if you feel up to it. Same for Paint, Andy and Mollye."

"Yeah, I should call Sala," he answered. "For Mom's sake, I'm glad she's offered help with security. Would you mind finding Sala's number in the directory and calling?"

"No problem." I found the entry, hit Send, and handed the phone back to Zack. Then I headed for the door.

"It's okay," Zack said. "You can stay. Don't want to run you out of your own house every time I use the phone."

I shook my head. "It's your home, too. And everybody needs some privacy."

I took a seat in the sunshine on a front-porch rocker and closed my eyes. Relax, I told myself. I was dying to pester Carol and Zack with a boatload of questions. But they deserved a little peace and quiet—for as long as it lasted.

I chuckled to myself wondering if Zack would need any help dressing or undressing. Maybe I'd get a peek at his bare buns to confirm his innocence once and for all.

THIRTY-ONE

I dozed until Mom woke me.

"Looks like someone's pooped," she commented. "Zack says you're welcome to come back inside; he's off the phone."

I yawned. "How'd your talk go with Carol? I'm not fishing for details, just wondering how Eva and I can help."

Mom's right eyebrow lifted. "You mean other than traipsing off in the woods to spy on people who specifically come to that spot to shoot weapons?"

"Yep," I answered. "Other than that."

Mom shook her head. "Carol called her doctors to give me permission to access her medical information. Maybe it'll offer absolute proof regarding how long she was drugged. I'm certain someone dumped Mick's body in her Cadillac then shoved a comatose Carol in the front seat. Definitely a frame-up."

"Are you thinking Chester?"

"If he weren't Mick's brother-in-law, I'd put him at the top of the list," Mom said. "You're sure it was his dog that chased you?"

"Andy was definite, and I wouldn't doubt him on any canine ID. Are you going to represent Carol?"

"Just until the situation becomes clearer. I'll find her a good criminal lawyer if this goes further. But she wants me to hold off on that. Carol hopes to salvage her campaign if she's cleared of any wrong-doing in the next day or two. She fears Allie Gerome's newspaper would equate hiring a criminal lawyer with guilt."

Mom kissed my cheek. "I dropped everything to rush over. Need to get back to the office. Have a plea bargain conference at four o'clock."

When I went back inside, Zack's recliner was as close to horizontal as it could go, and he was snoring. I heard a toilet flush. The cabin's soundproofing was close to nonexistent. A few seconds later, Carol walked into the kitchen where I was washing vegetables for a salad to go with the steaks thawing for the meat-eaters.

"Glad Zack's taking it easy." Carol smiled as she glanced at her son. She kept her voice a tad above a whisper. "Can I help with the salad?"

"That's okay," I said. "You're a guest. Relax."

Carol's answering harrumph sounded a lot like Eva's. "You kidding? All I've done is sleep. Well, actually the docs tell me anesthetics don't exactly put you to sleep. They switch off memory receptors so you won't remember what happens. With Ketamine you can get an extra bonus of hallucinations and dissociative episodes. I'm just happy to know seeing my body outside my Cadillac doesn't make me a candidate for the loony bin."

"So you don't remember being snatched?" I blurted out before I remembered Mom's concern that my aunt or I might be asked to testify about anything Carol uttered.

"I was sitting by Zack's bed when my cell phone rang," she began. "A muffled voice told me to go to my car. The voice—definitely a man's—claimed he knew who'd attacked Zack. He said my son was still in grave danger. Added he wouldn't show if he saw any sign I'd called the cops. He gave me five minutes to meet him or he'd disappear along with the answers I needed to protect Zack from a new attack.

"I was frantic. Since my gun was in my glove compartment I thought I could protect myself. The clock was ticking. I'd just unlocked my car when I sensed someone behind me. I started to turn, never made it. Someone clamped a cloth over my mouth. When I came to, I was blindfolded and gagged, hands and feet tied. I heard raised voices, barking, a scream. Wasn't sure if I was awake or dreaming. Next thing I knew I was slumped over my car's steering wheel in a monsoon. Hadn't a clue where I was."

She smiled at my expression. "Hey, I'm thinking straight enough now to be trusted with a knife. Hand me that cutting board, I'll chop the carrots."

I turned back to the sink. "Have you and Zack had a chance to talk? Does he know what happened to you?"

"Yes, and he filled me in on all the cell phone drama. Don't worry.

No secrets. Ask anything you want. Your mother told me not to say a word about what happened unless she was present. But I'm not afraid to answer anyone's questions. My story isn't going to change."

"I hope you're not planning a press conference," Eva said.

Her voice startled me. Hadn't heard her come in. My aunt must have spotted Zack sleeping, too, because she kept her voice low.

"No, I'm not that daft," Carol said. "Not when I have no answers to the questions they'll ask. Linda will run interference the next couple of days while I'm quote 'recovering from my kidnapping ordeal.' I do plan to hold a press conference Thursday or Friday if the sheriff can vouch for my innocence by then."

A knock on the door prompted all three of us to startle. I peeked out the window. A sporty Mercedes convertible sat in the driveway. Sala Lemmon had come calling. Easy to recognize despite her attempt to travel incognito. She'd tucked her platinum hair inside a ball cap, and donned large mirrored sunglasses to hide most of her face. She'd also traded stilettos for running shoes. However, the black ninja pants and top molded to her body, showing every curve.

As I opened the door, I pressed my fingers against my lips to signal quiet. "Zack's asleep," I whispered.

"No, I'm not." Zack rubbed his eyes. "Just drifted off for a few. Come in, Sala."

The majority owner of the Sin City Aces strode over and smooched Zack, planting a big, fat kiss on his lips before he could maneuver his recliner upright.

I almost giggled, wondering how he'd react. Sort of figured Zack might reconsider sitting up if he could keep that body draped over him. Her ninja-clad breasts definitely grazed his chest.

"Don't get up. Not going to stay long. Just wanted to check on you and your mother."

Sala turned her attention to Carol, abandoning Zack's chair to hustle over and envelop a woman she'd never met in a bear hug. "Mrs. Strong, I'm so happy to see you up and about."

She then embraced Eva and me in turn before any of us had so much as said howdy. She seemed hyper with no ability to drop into a lower gear.

"Have a seat," Eva said. "At least stay long enough to tell us what happened with Gunter and Vince."

"Who?" Carol managed as Sala plopped down on the love seat.

"The team's security men who decided to freelance and perform a little B&E," Eva answered.

Carol still looked bewildered. Clearly she hadn't been brought fully up to speed.

"They're toast." Sala grinned. "Told 'em I wanted to see them. Didn't give a hint that I suspected they'd been working for the Lemmon Twister—one of my more polite names for my stepdaughter. Once we were eyeball to eyeball, I fired them."

Eva clapped her hands. "Good for you."

Sala laughed. "Yeah, I enjoyed myself. Told them their company credit cards had been cancelled and their rental car would be reported stolen if it wasn't returned within the hour. Also let them know I'd informed the sheriff they should be considered prime suspects for the break-in at your place, Carol. If they're smart, they've blown town."

Zack gave her a speculative look. "Doesn't anything scare you? What if those two bruisers had attacked you?"

Sala pushed her sunglasses on top of her head. She wanted to make eye contact. "Guess I forgot to mention. I had a pistol aimed at them when I started my speech. Don't travel with one, but my brother-in-law was kind enough to loan me his."

The tycoon temptress leveled her big brown eyes at Carol. "I've hired an executive protection agency to watch over you and Zack until we have answers to all this madness. The firm's highly reputable and has no affiliation with the Aces or Las Vegas. That means my stepdaughter has less chance than a snowball in Hades of bribing them. Unfortunately, the firm wasn't able to juggle staff instantly. They had another emergency call just before mine. An executive kidnapped on a business trip to Venezuela. Nonetheless, two men will arrive tomorrow afternoon."

"Thank you," Carol said. "It's appreciated."

"Yeah, thanks," Zack added, his tone unusually flat. "Under normal circumstances, I'd decline. I figure I can take care of myself. But I'm banged up and I don't want to take any chances Mom might be snatched again."

Sala took a deep breath. "Good. Now for the humiliating part of my visit. Imagine you've all seen that horrid video by now."

She looked at each of us in turn. She seemed to hold everyone's gaze but Zack's.

"I won't make excuses. Shortly after Ray died, I was in a bad place. Kate was hounding me. I was lonely and feeling sorry for myself. I'd had a few drinks, a few too many, with a man who made me laugh. I thought, 'why not?' My brain took a vacation, but I absolutely had no idea he would film us. That video was not made with my knowledge or permission."

Everyone stayed silent for a moment, then Eva spoke up. "Brie and I chose not to watch that video. Nobody's business. I'm very sorry some man took advantage."

Carol and I nodded agreement. Zack's stony gaze never left Sala's face.

"I hate to ask, but could Sala and I have a few minutes alone?" he said. "We can go out on the front porch. Just give me a second to get up."

The cabin's limitations were quite apparent where privacy was concerned. Even the front porch didn't guarantee acoustic sanctuary, and Zack wasn't easily mobile.

"Stay put," Eva ordered. "I want to show Carol some improvements to our retail cabin." My aunt flicked a glance at me. "And I'm sure Brie has chores to tackle."

I had limited options for leaving "the room" given the cabin's open floorplan. Only the bathroom and bedrooms had doors, and they didn't preclude eavesdropping on any conversation conducted above a whisper. Only our churning clothes washer or spinning dryer, both located on the screened back porch, provided sufficient white noise to prevent eavesdropping.

Okay, dirty laundry here I come.

"Eva's right. I'm going to start a load of laundry. Then I'll finish getting your bedroom ready Zack. Can I get you two anything to drink before I leave?"

"No, thanks," came Sala's and Zack's duet reply. Clearly they wanted me to get lost pronto.

Eva and Carol left, and I walked to the small hall closet that housed our dirty-clothes hamper. Before I could empty it into a basket and clear the back door, Zack's voice boomed, shaking with anger.

"Doug visited me in the hospital. He says that sex tape was your idea. Claimed you sent it to him with an invitation for a repeat performance. I got a copy because Doug's girlfriend found it on his computer. She knew I'd been seeing you and thought I'd want to know what a slut you were."

Yikes. I scurried as quickly as I could and yanked the back-porch door closed behind me. I really didn't want to hear this. Someone was lying. I'd come to like Sala. Didn't know Doug, but he and Zack appeared to be good friends.

Rotten Roquefort. I didn't want to believe Sala'd blessed the video. Didn't want to think Zack's friend was screwing with him either. And I was stunned by the news that Sala and Zack had hooked up. Who else knew?

I started the washing machine, a noisy old clunker, and sat on the porch glider. Cashew, who'd followed me out the door, snuggled in my lap. I stroked Cashew's fur and gently rocked back and forth until I heard the front door bang shut.

"You have to decide who's telling the truth." Sala's sharp parting words were clear as a bell. A car door slammed.

I quietly slipped inside and headed to my bedroom. I wanted to give Zack a little time alone to decompress, and I really did need to shift my dresser to make it easier for Zack to swing his boot-cast up without bumping into it as he climbed out of bed. Then I packed a little overnight bag with clothes and incidentals. I didn't want to knock on Zack's door and barge in to retrieve something when he was sleeping or just wanted time alone.

I was rearranging items to give Zack his very own dresser drawer when Carol and Eva yoo-hooed as they came back inside.

"We saw Sala drive away," Carol said. "She looked upset. Everything okay?"

Curious to hear Zack's response, I returned to the living room and stashed my overnight bag in the corner. I hoped the bag might offer a semi-legit reason for my sudden appearance. Of course, the real reason was nosiness.

Zack lifted his left hand and pinched the bridge of his nose. "I know you're all curious. Might as well talk about the elephants in the room—the video," he paused, "and Sala and me."

I snuck a glance at Carol. She looked flummoxed.

"Don't look so horrified Mom. It's not like there are videos of the two of us." Zack tried for humor but his mother wasn't laughing.

"What about you and Sala?" she demanded.

"We've been seeing each other about six months. Never in public. Kept it real quiet. Neither of us wanted more publicity. And I worried our relationship might be used against you and your campaign."

"Is it serious?" Carol stared at her hands as they smoothed nonexistent wrinkles in her slacks. While I'd seen her stare down political enemies, she couldn't seem to look her son in the eye.

Zack shrugged. "Maybe. I'm not sure after today. She always worried about our age difference, and I didn't want anyone thinking my position on the team depended on my performance anywhere else. Now I've blown it. I doubted her word."

"About what? The video?" Eva asked.

Zack sighed. "Yes. Doug claims Sala asked him to make it. Sala says that's bullshit. At least they both agree it happened before I started seeing Sala. But the when is still a problem. Doug says Sala seduced him while her husband was alive. Told me to watch out for her, that she was a conniving cougar.

"Doug's girlfriend, Kim, found the video on his computer. She sent it to me because Doug told her Sala and I were an item. Apparently, Kim, who's an IT expert, trashed all of Doug's electronic devices to destroy any videos he might have secretly made of their lovemaking. That made the Sala video Kim sent me a collector's edition."

"That's why Kate wanted it so badly," I said.

"I guess." Zack's shoulders slumped. "But how did Kate find out it was on my phone? Kim must have told someone besides Doug. Anyway I can't see how the video helps Kate. It certainly isn't enough for a court to nullify Lemmon's will."

Carol stood. "I'm glad you told us about Sala. Just wish you'd confided in me before this. I'm tired. I'm going to lie down for a while."

She was hurt and disappointed. Everything from the wobble in her voice to her sagging posture said so.

Once Carol departed, Zack turned to Eva and me. "I promised

Sala I wouldn't tell anyone about our relationship. But you needed to know. Please keep this between us."

I felt lucky I wouldn't be sitting at the Udderly dinner table tonight, trying to make casual conversation. Mollye had invited me to try a new Greenville restaurant that had excellent reviews. Since Danny McCoy was working, I was Mollye's date. Eva'd urged me to accept the invitation. "You made salad for our guests, and I'm better than you at grilling steaks. Go on, get out of the house. I can entertain the Strongs. Have fun."

I didn't ask Eva if I should reconsider. Having spent a quiet summer at Udderly Kidding Dairy, all this emotional drama was proving exhausting. A night away sounded ideal. I liked my quiet life, though I often wished my love life weren't quite so quiet.

THIRTY-TWO

I picked Mollye up at five thirty. On the drive to Greenville, she tried her darndest to coax me into gossiping about Zack. I only divulged two things. One, Sala was arranging added security with an executive protection agency, and two, Zack had accepted an invitation from Howie Lemcke to visit his retreat for wounded veterans. I was determined to honor Zack's request to keep his relationship with Sala a secret.

Mollye pulled down the visor, slid open its mirror window, and started applying green eyeshade to match the streak in her hair. "I have a feeling you're keeping your lips zipped about juicier details. But I'm glad you'll have more good men at Udderly. Maybe you should invite one of your new protectors to provide extra cover come nightfall. You're always telling me how important exercise is. Parts of you may shrivel up if you don't give them a workout soon."

I awarded Mollye the standard head shake when she prodded me about my sex life.

She ignored me but skipped to another subject. "I think having Zack visit that veterans retreat is brilliant. Should perk the residents up and lift Zack's spirits, too."

"I agree. Zack asked Doug to join him. Imagine the residents will be ecstatic to shoot the breeze with two football pros. And seeing how Howie has adjusted to his loss of a leg should give Zack real incentive to put his all into rehab."

I didn't mention my misgivings about Zack's decision to invite Doug. Zack had heard two starkly different accounts of the video, one version from his buddy, another from his lover. I figured he'd invited Doug to confront him about the huge 'he said, she said' discrepancies.

We arrived at the restaurant at six thirty. Mollye'd made the reservations but assured me I'd find enough veggie items on the menu to make a meal while she devoured the creamy lobster lasagna the restaurant critic had raved about.

While dining out is oftentimes a challenge for vegans, Mollye was right tonight. The hors d'oeuvres and side menus gave me lots of choices. I ordered a green salad with raspberry vinaigrette dressing, a plain baked sweet potato, and a skewer of grilled vegetables.

When we finally set our forks down, both our plates were empty. "Terrific," Mollye said.

"Agreed, and I think I'll splurge tonight with a little after-dinner treat. I'm going to ask for an Irish coffee sans cream, of course."

"Wow. Sure you can handle that and drive? Your alcohol consumption doesn't worry me. But I figure we'll need to stop two or three times so you can pee. You must have downed a gallon of water with dinner."

I laughed. "Don't worry. I'll visit the ladies' room before we leave."

I looked around to see where the restrooms might be tucked away.

That's when I saw them. My mouth went dry.

"What's wrong?" Mollye asked. "Looks like you've seen a ghost."

She turned and managed a half-hearted wave. I did the same though my stomach had turned sour.

Please don't come over to our table. Please don't introduce your dates.

My mental pleas bombed. Paint and Andy sauntered our way shepherding two gorgeous women—a Swedish-looking blonde and a curvy brunette. They were on a double date.

I pasted on a smile for the introductions. Shook hands with the women. I heard their names but made zero attempt to remember them. I wanted to forget their faces, too, though I knew I wouldn't. The adoring way both women looked at Paint and Andy, suggested someone—okay everyone but me and Mollye—would get lucky tonight.

I forgot all about ordering Irish coffee. "The food is great," I managed. "We were just getting our check. Have to get back to Udderly. We have guests. Enjoy your meal."

I flagged down our waiter as the two men I most wanted walked away with their dates. *Frozen frankfurters.*

Neither Mollye nor I spoke for the first twenty miles. She cleared her throat a couple of times like she was about to break the silence. Then she chickened out. Finally, I decided to gut it out. Silence and Mollye were incompatible entities. Their coexistence made the universe seem out of kilter.

"Sorry I rushed you out of the restaurant," I began. "I know you wanted dessert."

"I understand. Never dreamed we'd run into them. Guess that glowing restaurant review caught their eyes, too."

"Since you greeted everyone by name, I gather you know their dates." I glanced over at Mollye. "Do you like them?"

"Not as much as you." She sighed. "Okay, they're nice. Yvonne, the one with Andy, is a kindergarten teacher; Kristy, Paint's date, is a dental hygienist."

"Have they been dating long?'

Mollye squirmed. "Don't think so. Saw Paint and Kristy out a couple of weeks ago. Hadn't seen Andy with his date before. Hey, I didn't know how to tell you. It's no secret you have the hots for both of them and vice versa but you told them it would never happen. Did you think they'd swear off women in hopes you'd change your mind?"

"I don't know what I thought." I brushed away a tear.

Stop it. This was your decision.

Was it too late to change my mind?

THIRTY-THREE

When I pulled into our drive, I saw lights in the two bedrooms and the main living area. Rats. I was in no mood to chat with anyone.

When I walked inside, I was surprised to see Eva in her PJs and sitting alone in her recliner. Our blow-up beds, sleep-ready with sheets and pillows, consumed most of the living area floor.

"Didn't want to turn out the lights before you got home." Eva kept her voice low as though she believed our guests might be asleep. "Afraid you'd step on me. Hope you're tired. I'm more than ready to call it a night."

"Okay." It wasn't yet ten o'clock but I didn't feel like picking up my book. I was two-hundred pages into a romantic suspense, and there was zero suspense about what the hero and heroine were about to do next. I was afraid I'd substitute Paint and Andy and their dates for the characters in any steamy love scene. *Geesh*. The book's heroine was a school teacher, too.

"Let me brush my teeth and slip on my pajamas," I added. "The lights are on in the bedrooms. Imagine the guests are still awake."

Eva grunted. "Yeah. They've gone to their corners to sulk. I didn't expect them to be angry with each other when I invited them to stay. Dinner conversation was a struggle. Could have used your help, deserter. Hope you had a good time."

She studied my face. "Guess not. What happened?"

I shook my head. "Nothing. Just ran into Paint and Andy on a double date."

Eva got up from her easy chair and gave me a hug. "Sorry, honey, but you had to know it would happen sooner or later. They're healthy young men, not eunuchs. You'd better take a good look at your feelings. Don't just drift. Make a decision. Either you want Paint and Andy as friends or you want one or both as lovers. If you do nothing, it'll be decided for you."

I nodded and hurried to the bathroom so Eva wouldn't see my tears.

Having tossed and turned most of the night, listening jealously to Eva's raucous snores, I was dog tired when my aunt shook me awake. She'd opened the blinds but it was too early for sun to stream through the cabin windows. I was more than ready for Daylight Savings Time to end. I hated it when darkness clung to bigger and bigger chunks of my morning.

I glanced out the window. The gold leaves of the giant hickory tree out front looked black in the moonlight, but a clear sky promised a pretty day. I'd definitely go for a run after I finished my chores. Running cleared my mind, and usually cheered me up. I needed to power up a pile of endorphins today. I could use some serious cheering up.

Eva handed me a welcome mug of coffee. "I told our guests they were on their own for breakfast. There's cereal, fruit, milk and yogurt. Don't feel like you have to cook every meal. I'm not real anxious to gather round the kitchen table with Carol and Zack until they settle their issues."

"Thanks," I said. "I do want to go for a run today, but I can drive Zack to the veteran retreat if you have other things you need to do."

"No, go for your run. I've been promising Howie I'd visit. It's as good a time as any. You'll be alone with Carol. Is that okay? Those security folks Sala promised won't be here until afternoon."

"We'll be fine. Don't think anyone can talk Carol into a secret rendezvous again. Besides your shotgun is nice and handy by the front door. Our Great Pyrenees won't let anyone sneak up on us."

With our morning settled, Eva went off to milk goats and I headed to the horse barn to feed Rita and Hank. After they finished eating, I let them out in a fenced section of woodland rather than a grassed field. Less food to tempt them into pigging out.

Rita and I were getting along a little better. The mule had a very special relationship with Lilly. I remembered how Rita would go still and search for Lilly whenever the mule heard her human's voice. When

Lilly died, Rita didn't understand why she wasn't here anymore. Since I showed up at the same time, she must have thought I was to blame. At least that was Eva's take on Rita's attitude.

The upshot? Whenever I walked behind Rita, she'd swish her tail with pinpoint accuracy to hit me. She'd nip at me, too. Eva urged me to ride Rita. Said she needed exercise. That went about like I expected. First she steadfastly refused to budge. Then she sideswiped every tree she could find, trying to brush off the nuisance on her back.

I hadn't tried to ride her again. But, at Eva's suggestion, I regularly brushed Rita and talked to her just as Lilly used to do. I told her how pretty she was. Murmured that she was a queen amongst mules. Fed her apples and scratched between her long ears. She hadn't tried to nip me in weeks.

Eva and I finished our chores about the same time. When we returned to the cabin, Zack and Carol were dressed, and chowing down on cereal and bananas.

"How about we leave in fifteen minutes?" Eva asked Zack. "That's how long I need to take a quick shower and change clothes."

"Sure." He stood and grabbed his cane. "I'll be ready."

Zack tap-tapped his way to the bedroom and closed the door. I glanced at Carol. Her lips quirked up in a quick smile. "We love each other. We'll be fine. Just need a little more time to sort things out. I want him to be happy. It's just hard to keep from offering unwanted advice when you think someone you love may be making a big mistake."

I nodded. The words Eva spoke last night came back to me. She thought I was making a big mistake.

"If you don't mind, I'd like to go for a run," I said. "Should be gone less than an hour. Your campaign speeches have assured me you're not afraid to use a gun. Eva's shotgun, always loaded, is in the umbrella stand by the door."

Carol's smile brightened. "I'm a much better shot than Eva. Don't worry. I know Udderly's fluffy white guard dogs will give me plenty of warning."

I waited for Eva to clear the bathroom to change into running clothes. With our current living arrangements, I could only robe and disrobe in my new "bed" room if our guests were behind closed doors.

Wearing a pair of new running tights, I gulped down water to hydrate as Eva and Zack reached the front door. "We're invited to stay through lunch," Eva said. "Should be back by two o'clock. You and Carol, stay safe. I'll close and lock the front gate once we go through it. That should discourage any reporters from coming to call."

Two minutes after my aunt and Zack departed, I bid Carol goodbye. Outside I leaned against the hickory tree as I did a few warm-up stretches. A breeze carried the hint of burning leaves, a fall bonfire. The sunny but cool day was made for running. I decided to run through the state forest that bordered the back of the Udderly property. While none of its improved trails ran near us, I enjoyed cross-country jaunts. Okay, not entirely true. I definitely didn't like to run along mountain ridges with steep, vertigo-inducing drop-offs.

My run proved to be exactly the medicine I needed. Lungs and legs pumped, worry and jealousy brain cells switched off. I felt lighter, happier. And I'd made a decision. I knew what I'd say if Paint and Andy inquired about dating again.

Exiting the woods, I slowed my pace. My cool down phase. Almost back home. I checked my watch. Forty-five minutes. Not bad. Hands on my thighs, I bent forward, gulping air and motoring down.

Some of our Great Pyrenees began barking up a storm. What now? I trotted ahead, back on Udderly land. A large black panel van sat inches from the back of my Prius. Slewed sideways, the van's position would make it impossible for my car to back up. Since the front bumper of my Prius sat two feet from the cabin, my ride was completely penned in. *What the Feta?*

Then I saw them. Gunter and Vince had new wheels. They weren't driving their former Aces-funded rental car. But they'd clearly ignored Sala's order to vacate Ardon County. Or had she lied about that? We only had Sala's word she fired them, that she knew nothing about their B&E.

Where was Carol? My heartbeat, which had started to slow, ratcheted up, approaching the hammering pace that warned me to slow down when I'd been running flat-out.

The men thundered up the stairs onto our cabin's front porch.

Get the shotgun, Carol. I yelled the warning in my head. The dogs must have alerted Carol. *Keep quiet.* I knew where our intruders were.

They hadn't a clue where I was. The element of surprise was my only advantage.

Did Carol have Eva's shotgun? She'd told us her pistol remained locked in her impounded Cadillac's glove box.

Just as Gunter and Vince launched themselves inside our living room, guns drawn, I spotted Carol slipping outside the retail cabin. Unfortunately she wasn't toting a shotgun.

How long before they found Carol—and me? Were they here to kidnap or kill? I feared abduction wasn't today's goal.

I waved my arms to catch Carol's attention and pointed toward the wooded paddock where Hank and Rita were corralled. The closest spot to meet up. Its trees, though hardly old-growth forest, offered some cover.

It took under two minutes to cover the space separating us. I opened the paddock gate and we sprinted through. Carol's breath was ragged when she fell into my arms. Hank whinnied at the unexpected invasion and trotted to the farthest corner of the paddock. In contrast, Rita seemed curious. She stared at us, ears twitching, tail swishing. Maybe she was considering a breakout through the open gate.

Could we ride Rita to safety? Would we lose them in the state forest?

Impossible for the killers to follow us in a vehicle, and even with two of us on Rita's back, they'd lose a footrace with our mule.

But would Rita cooperate? My past experiences suggested the notion was daft. The odds stacked heavily against the mule's aid.

The mule and I were now on slightly friendlier terms, but friendly enough for Carol and me to mount her bareback?

"Carol," I whispered, "do you ride? Our best bet is to ride Rita and go for help. If we ride into state forestland, they can't follow us in their van. The few paths aren't wide enough. They'd have to come after us on foot."

Carol's eyes grew wide as she gave Rita a once-over. "Haven't ridden in years and never bareback. Even Lilly described Rita as a stubborn pill. Maybe we should just hide here or try to outrun them on foot."

Wouldn't work. A couple of our Great Pyrenees had decided we weren't paying attention. They'd trotted over to the paddock fence to deliver their intruder alert message up close and personal.

I shook my head, and tried to shoo them away.

"Those big lugs are trying to protect us, but they're bound to give our position. We can't stay here, and I don't think we can outrun bullets on foot."

I eyed Rita. She looked as if she'd been listening. If I could only believe she understood. Unfortunately, I wasn't convinced the half-ton mule would be heartbroken if I disappeared. Would she let two of us climb on?

"Easy girl," I whispered. "You're the most beautiful mule in the world." I pulled her head into a hug, rubbing her face. "You're so good. What a sweet girl."

Scratching under her chin, I slowly backed up, gently luring her over to an old stump. "Now you're going to let me mount you, and then stand still while Carol gets on, aren't you?"

I leapt up, draped myself across the mule like a sack of potatoes, and pivoted on my belly until I could push myself upright. My performance was as far from graceful as it could be without actually suffering some broken bones.

Given that I'd shown style didn't matter, I expected Carol to follow my lead and struggle on board. I looked down. Though Carol's eyes were wide with fear, she seemed stumped.

"Take my hand," I coached. "You can do it. I'll help pull you up."

Carol fastened on to my hand with an iron grip. "Come on, jump," I urged.

She flung herself at Rita. Carol's desperate hold on my hand nearly pulled us both to the ground. She grunted and squirmed. I held on to Rita's mane and clamped my knees into her side to stay upright

"I'm on," Carol said as she wrapped her arms around my waist. A second later I felt her hot breath on my neck.

Hard to believe Rita had stood patiently through our antics. All I could figure was that she sensed our panic and actually wanted to help.

A loud crash startled me as Gunter and Vince burst through the cabin's back door. The ruckus startled Rita, too. She may not have understood their obscenities, but their angry tones were clear. The mule spun left to face the noisemakers, causing Carol and me to slither right. After I stared at the ground for what felt like minutes, knowing my lips were about to kiss dirt, I hugged the mule's neck and pulled us both upright.

The henchmen seemed unconcerned we might hear them. No attempt at stealth. They must have known Carol and I were alone.

Now came the tricky part. We had a fair piece of open ground to negotiate before we reached state forest. That would give our shooters—of unknown marksmanship—better odds of nailing us than skeet shooters had of downing moving targets. A half-ton mule and two adult women were a thousand times bigger targets than clay pigeons.

Still, we had a decent chance if we surprised them. We needed Rita to run like a Porsche, zero to sixty in four seconds.

"Carol, hold on tight and stay low. When I count to three, we'll kick Rita. Grip as hard as you can with your knees. I'll try to guide her with her mane and leg pressure."

"And I thought running for governor was crazy," Carol grumbled. "Okay. Count when you're ready."

I took a deep breath, tightened my grip on Rita's mane, and squeezed hard with my knees. "One...two...three."

I kicked with all my might and heard the thump as Carol did the same. My running shoes and Carol's tennis shoes didn't impress Rita a bit. She simply turned her head so one big eye looked at us. I sensed she was tempted to nip the nearest piece of human flesh. My leg was a convenient target. We were annoying the mule big time.

When another angry shout erupted, Rita's head and ears pivoted back toward the commotion. Apparently the barking dogs and yelling men irritated her more.

Rita had never been big on menfolk. Billy had a heck of a time shoeing her. Andy was the only male she tolerated. Of course, Gunter and Vince didn't know that. While they had yet to locate us, they yelled as they strutted in our direction.

If Aunt Eva was right about Rita sensing she frightened me, I hoped the men's aggressive movements and loud shouts would convince the mule they were up to no good. *Please, Rita, get us out of here.* I thumped her again hoping she'd take the hint. All she did was drop her head a little.

"Those damn dogs were yapping up a storm over here. They gotta be close," the black-bearded Gunter shouted.

"Yep, I can practically smell 'em." Vince laughed. "May have to kill us a few dogs before we find them but we've got plenty of ammo."

"Please Rita," I whispered. "Ready, Carol? One, two, three. Go!"

We kicked. Rita took off like a thoroughbred. We cleared the open gate. What? The mule veered sharply left. Away from the woods. Away from safety.

I had no way to guide Rita. I could barely hang on. Carol slid left, then right. I'd be topless soon if she didn't quit yanking on my clothing.

Vince stood dead ahead. He raised a gun. Aimed it.

Rita didn't slow or stumble. We flew over the thug. He just disappeared under the mule. Carol screamed. The man's agonized cries echoed in my ears. Even louder than my rat-a-tat breathing.

I dared to loosen my grip on Rita's mane to twist slightly.

The mule's slashing hooves had put Vince down. Broken, mangled.

The mule veered again and I almost toppled. Behind me Carol let out a cry as she slid toward the ground. I squeezed Rita's sides with my knees tighter than a hungry boa. If I fell off, Carol and I would both hit the ground. Somehow Carol managed to right herself.

Deviled Ham! Gunter loomed straight ahead. Staring at his downed pal, he faltered. Still he managed to pull the trigger as he dodged the thundering animal. Rita slammed against his body as a bullet whizzed by my ear. I chanced another look.

Gunter was struggling up.

Rita galloped toward the gate on Duncan's pen. The closed gate.

I pulled on her mane. "Stop," I screamed.

Then I braced for impact.

Rita exploded through the boards. Splinters of wood flew like shrapnel. We were inside the billy goat's domain. I couldn't believe Carol and I remained topside. We'd slithered around her broad back like kids on a water slide. Wasn't sure how we'd clung on.

As Rita approached the far side of Duncan's pen, she slowed and circled. Gunter pointed his gun at us.

I prayed. No way could Rita charge Gunter again before he shot her. She was a huge target.

A white blur caught my eye. *Cheeses.* Horny Duncan took advantage of the mangled gate, charging out of his pen. He rammed

Gunter's side. A straight shot to the ribs. The billy drove him to the ground.

"Okay, Rita. Enough fun. Please, please, head for the forest. It's nice and cool in there. Nice and safe."

I pulled on her mane and pressed my sneakers into her sides. Prayed for once the mule would listen before Gunter or Vince scrambled up and started shooting again.

Much to my shock, Rita trotted into the woods. She seemed as serene as a cat snoozing in the sun. Very satisfied with herself.

The woods closed behind us. I listened hard, trying to tune in to any sounds that said the no-necks were coming after us. I heard only chattering birds and the occasional rustle of a tiny animal. I mentally pledged to give Rita a treat every day for the rest of her life.

"My God," Carol said. "I thought we were dead at least three times. First thing I'm going to do when I see Zack is tell him I just want him to be happy. If Sala makes him happy, so be it. I would have hated to leave this world with my son thinking I was mad at him."

"I hear you," I said. "Fear has a way of making us understand our priorities."

A man's voice startled me.

THIRTY-FOUR

"Hey, you, don't you know you can't ride horses here?"

We were approaching a small meadow where a park ranger stood, hands on hips, looking annoyed.

"There are lots of trails for horses in the Clemson Forest, but not here," he continued.

"We know," Carol said. "We're sorry but your trees just saved our lives."

The ranger took a closer look. "My God, you're Carol Strong, what in blazes?"

Fortunately for us and the Park Ranger, Rita seemed to have filled her quota of knock-downs for the day.

"I'm Stu Smith," the park ranger introduced himself as he helped us shimmy down from Rita's tall back.

As soon as Carol finished giving a rundown on our escape, Ranger Smith loaned Carol his cell phone to contact the Sheriff and Zack. We needed to warn our cabin mates not to return to Udderly until the sheriff secured the area.

I eavesdropped on the mother-son conversation while Ranger Smith scrounged up rope for a make-shift lead for Rita. The rope was so frayed I hoped Rita wouldn't consider it an insult, break free, and trot away to demonstrate her disdain.

Carol frowned. "Yes, Brie's absolutely certain they were the same men who skulked around my house and strong-armed Eva."

She gripped the phone tighter as her son spoke.

"Honey, you don't know Sala lied." Carol adopted her political, let's stay calm voice. "Maybe Sala did fire those men and tell them to get lost. Someone else could have paid them more to stay and finish the job. Though I can't imagine what the 'job' might be. What interest could Sala or her stepdaughter have in me? Doesn't make sense."

After Carol ended her call, I used the borrowed cell to phone Andy. I crossed my fingers he could drive his horse trailer over to chauffeur Rita home once the sheriff gave the all-clear. I didn't want to tempt fate by riding Rita back through the woods with no reins or saddle. Andy promised to come as soon as he could.

Ranger Smith invited us to rest in the park office while we waited. At my request, Smith left the door open so Rita could see us. I'd tied the mule's make-shift lead to a split-rail fence that bordered the office.

It appeared neither Carol nor I felt up to initiating small talk. So we sat in uncomfortable silence. At least Ranger Smith had papers to shuffle. After about twenty minutes, the office phone rang.

Smith's "hello" was his last word for several minutes. He just listened and nodded with an occasional "uh huh." Finally, he said, "I'll tell them."

The ranger seemed reluctant to raise his eyes from the office phone and look at us.

"They found an unarmed man dead at your farm. His body was pretty beat up, consistent with being battered by a mule's hooves," he said. "But he didn't die from those injuries. He was shot to death. Looks like the weapon was a shotgun."

"What?" Carol and I managed in unison.

"Both men were shooting handguns," I said.

I pictured Eva's shotgun in the umbrella stand. Had the missing Gunter used it to kill his own partner? Why?

"Hope that doesn't make Brie and me suspects." Carol apparently made the same mental leap. Eva's shotgun had to be the murder weapon. "Just what I need, becoming a person of interest in another killing. Well, it might get me some votes from the gun lobby."

Carol's lips flirted with a smile. "Should have asked Ranger Smith to take a photo of us on Rita. Might have gone viral on YouTube. You'd certainly never see my opponent on any equine, well, except his high-horse."

I walked over to where Carol sat and knelt in front of her. "We can vouch for each other. Those men came to kill us. We just tried to escape. Didn't shoot anyone."

I tried to recall who last handled Eva's shotgun. I'd picked it up to make certain Carol knew where it was.

My fingerprints might be the only ones that were nice and clear if the shooter wore gloves.

The sheriff brought along one of the deputies I'd seen on guard at the hospital. Still didn't know his name.

"Let's head back to Udderly," Sheriff Mason said. "We need you to do a little reenactment."

"Sorry, Sheriff," I said. "I have to wait for Andy. He's bringing a horse trailer to cart Rita back home. Given her day, I'm afraid she might really wig out if I leave her alone with a strange man."

Mason sighed. "Okay."

Despite the sigh, I thought Mason might be happy to have Carol and I separated when we repeated our stories.

Once Carol left with the sheriff, my thoughts turned to Andy. How could I casually broach the subject of his dinner date? I needed to know if the relationship was serious before I blurted out how I felt about him. Well, about him and Paint.

I had no right to be jealous but right had nothing to do with it. Mom would label me "a dog in the manger." At some point, curiosity had prompted me to look up the origin of the phrase. It was a Greek fable about a dog who kept other animals from eating hay in the manger they shared, even though the dog had no desire to eat the hay.

I'd told Andy and Paint I didn't want them as lovers. But I lied. Unlike the fabled dog, I did indeed have an appetite, and I sure as shoot wanted other women to keep their mitts off both men.

Andy jumped down from his truck, picked me up, and swung me around. "Thank God, you're safe. Can't believe someone shot at you, again. When's your birthday? Going to buy you a full SWAT outfit, bullet-resistant vest and maybe one of those storm-the-building shields."

I licked my lips as I stared into his emerald eyes. "Thanks for dropping everything to rush over. You're a sweetheart. Think you can help me coax Rita into the trailer? I have no idea what that stubborn mule might do next."

Andy reached in his pocket, extracted a sugar cube, and untied Rita's lead. She whinnied and draped her big head over Andy's shoulder. Guess she smelled her treat. Andy rubbed her velvety nose, then flattened his palm to reward her with a taste of sugar.

"You have quite the way with women." I strived for a light, teasing tone. "Bring any sugar cubes to dinner with you last night? Or were you the treat?"

Andy's eyes bored into mine. Had my voice hinted at my jealousy? My petty, unwarranted jealousy.

"Brie, darling. If you really think I'm a treat, you can have me any time, any way. It was just dinner. I'm crazy about you. Until I get over you, that's all any date with another woman will be. Problem is I don't want to get over you."

Ranger Smith was standing in the doorway to his office eyeballing us. I didn't care. I felt reckless. Near-death experiences and raging jealousy had obliterated any smidgeon of my good sense. I slid a hand between Rita's head and Andy's cheek and brought my other palm up to bracket Andy's face. I stood on tip toe.

The kiss wasn't sweet. It was hard, possessive. It said I want you here and now. Which might have happened if Ranger Smith and Rita weren't fidgeting bystanders.

When the kiss ended, Andy's green eyes seemed to have darkened. "This is one conversation I want to finish but not here. Let's get you and Rita back home."

By the time we reached Udderly, there were no parking spaces left in front of the cabin. All close-in spots were taken up with three sheriff's cruisers, my Prius, Eva's truck, Sala's Mercedes convertible, and a mystery Hummer, which I presumed belonged to the promised executive protection guys.

Eva's truck didn't surprise me. I figured my aunt and Zack hadn't waited for an all-clear signal and headed for Udderly as soon as Carol ended her conversation with Zack.

However, I was surprised to see Sala's ride. Had she come to see if the thugs had succeeded in making Carol disappear for good? Or was she here to check if the Hummer contingent was in place? I didn't feel confident enough to place a bet either way.

Outside a couple of deputies searched the ground by Duncan's pen. Figured they were looking for any evidence to support our story of gunplay. Everyone else appeared to be inside.

"I'll take care of Rita," Andy said. "Give her a little treat and put her in her stall. You go on, join the crowd. I'll come in soon as I get Rita settled and make sure Duncan's corralled. I don't imagine Eva wants that horny bugger on the loose. She likes to keep her breeds pure, while Sire Duncan doesn't care one bit about a doe's lineage."

I slipped inside the cabin. No one noticed. The crowd was divided into two groups. The sheriff and the hospital-duty deputy huddled with Carol in the main living area, while Eva, Zack and Sala sat at the kitchen table.

I closed the front door and the motion caught Eva's attention. She jumped up, hurried over and gave me a bear hug. "You okay?"

"Yes, thanks to Rita. I'm beginning to believe someone trained her as an attack mule."

Eva loosened her grip. "When confronted with danger, horses always flee. With mules, it's fifty-fifty. They're just as likely to fight."

"I have to check in with the sheriff," I said. "Will join you as soon as I can."

I owed Mason an I'm-here-and-accounted-for appearance. The sheriff had yet to see me since he sat with his back to the kitchen. He jumped when I tapped him on the shoulder.

"Want to talk with me now or should I come back later?"

"Now."

Mason stood and nodded at Carol. "We're done for the moment. I'll take Miss Hooker's statement and check on my men. See if they've found any spent shell casings. Even though Mrs. Lemmon has arranged for security, I'll leave a deputy on guard at the gate for the next twenty-four hours. We will not have a repeat attack. I guarantee it."

"Thank you, Sheriff," Carol said. "I don't want Zack's or my presence to endanger our friends. Can we move back into my house tomorrow?"

Mason bit his lip. "Yes, but let me know when you want to make the move. My deputies and I will escort you."

"Will do," Carol said as she stood. "Thanks again."

"Have a seat." Mason directed me to the love seat. The sheriff and his deputy had rejected Udderly's twin recliners in favor of rockers hauled in from the front porch. My guess was they wanted to sit closer to their interviewees, all the better to intimidate interrogation subjects.

"Okay, tell us what happened," Mason said.

Step-by-step I relived the nightmare, from my shock at seeing the gunmen on my return from a run to our wild mule ride through the forest.

"Let's go outside," Mason said. "Show me where everything happened."

I showed the lawmen where I'd stood when I first spotted the intruders and pointed to Carol's location at the retail cabin. We visited the stump marred with the scuffs we'd made trying to mount Rita. I couldn't remember all the turns in our frantic ride. But the broken gate on Duncan's pen made me marvel once more that we'd stayed on Rita's back.

The sheriff seemed solicitous. His questions endless but gentle. Wasn't sure if that was his style of interrogation, lulling me into thinking we were friends, or if Carol had already convinced him we were the victims.

"Okay," Mason said, after a final question. "That's all I need. We've taken photos. Found a few pieces of brass the shooter missed. We also found a black van abandoned about a mile from here. Ran the plates. It was stolen yesterday."

"Do you have any idea why those men tried to kill Carol and me?" I asked.

"I imagine you were just collateral damage," the sheriff ventured. "But, no, I don't know why they wanted to kill Mrs. Strong."

My head hurt. Who was behind this? Why?

Carol was like family. I couldn't bear the thought of losing her. And Eva? What if she'd been here, caught in the thugs' crosshairs? I shuddered. Fear raised the hairs on my neck.

I shook my head. Don't go down that scary road of "what ifs." We're alive.

We walked back to the cabin. The sheriff cleared his throat.

"For your safety and peace of mind, I'm going to share some information," he said. "We have Chester Finley in custody. We arrested him shortly before those gunmen arrived at Udderly. We're holding

Chester on charges of obstructing justice and accessory to murder."

"Accessory?" I asked. "You don't think he killed Mick?"

"Only Mrs. er Ms. Strong's fingerprints were found on her Cadillac and the knife that killed Mr. Hardy."

Eva interrupted. "For heaven's sake, Sheriff, you're not giving a statement to the press. We know these people by their first names. Can't remember some of these characters' last names. Forget all the Mr., Mrs., Ms. nonsense, just tell your story. We'll all be less confused."

I wasn't sure whether to interpret the look Mason gave Eva as one of gratitude or surrender, but he switched to a first-name narrative.

"As I was saying, only Carol's fingerprints were found on her Cadillac and the knife that killed Mick. However, we were able to lift Chester's prints off Mick's belt and shoes. Chester clearly handled the body, probably dumped it in the trunk, and wiped down the car. But he has a solid alibi for Mick's murder. Autopsy results put the time of death around midnight Sunday. Chester was definitely in Oconee County then."

My head swam. But it kind of made sense. Chester must be covering up Mick's murder for a friend. One of his CAVE men cronies must have killed Mick. But why?

"We tried to speak with Kate Lemmon after we learned about the Udderly shootout, since there appeared to be some suspicion she had a relationship with the former Aces employees who took part in the attack. But we learned she's back in Vegas, no longer in Ardon County.

"We've mounted a full-scale manhunt for Gunter." He tipped his hat. "If he's hiding anywhere around here, we'll find him."

THIRTY-FIVE

Andy returned to the cabin as the sheriff and his deputies took their leave.

"I put Hank in his stall to keep Rita company and coaxed Duncan into the empty paddock and shut the gate. Wish I could stay, but my sister called. Someone brought in a badly injured dog. Gotta go. Walk me to my truck?"

"Sure," I answered. Butterflies fluttered in my stomach. Was Andy going to ask me what my steamy kiss signaled?

When we reached his truck, Andy leaned against the door and snaked an arm around me. "I talked to the deputies," he said as he dropped a kiss on my forehead. "They assured me Udderly is locked up tighter than a drum. You're safe."

"Yep, we'll be fine." I pulled back a smidgeon. "Call or text when you're free and I'll give you an update. Thanks so much for helping with Rita and Duncan."

"My pleasure." Andy gently kissed me again before he freed me from his embrace. The look in those green eyes said the kiss was a hurried one from a lover, not a friend. "I hope to collect my reward later."

As he left, panic set in. What had I done? Had I made a commitment to Andy? A promise of exclusivity? I pictured Paint's black Irish good looks—laughing mocha eyes, black as night hair, and that icing-on-the-cake dimple in his cheek. No, no, he's like eggs Benedict with double servings of hollandaise. Delicious but not at all good for me. I shook my head as I headed toward the cabin. Maybe my unconscious had made my choice for me. But then why did I feel so nervous about seeing Paint again?

Carol and Eva didn't notice me at first. They were returning the heavy front porch rockers to their usual spots. Eva turned and opened her arms wide.

"Come give me a hug. Carol says you saved her life. I'm proud of you, niece. But it makes me dizzy thinking those men might have killed you."

I returned Eva's hug.

Carol sighed. "I'm so sorry Zack and I put you two in danger. We're leaving come morning. Already had Linda announce a press conference for noon tomorrow. We'll hold it on my very own front porch. Don't know if I have any chance of salvaging my campaign, but at least I can get the word out that Zack and I are back home and ready to return to normal life."

Eva didn't argue with Carol about her decision. If I weren't living at Udderly, I bet my aunt would have used her many wiles to convince Carol and Zack to stay. But maybe the Strongs would be safer in town. Carol's house sat on a small lot on a well-lit street. Much easier for the executive protection service and officers to safeguard.

Eva plopped down in one of the rockers. Carol followed suit, letting out a contended sigh. "Join us," Eva invited. "We thought we'd give Zack and Sala a little privacy."

I claimed the third rocker and nodded at the Hummer that was hogging parking space out front. "Did you meet whoever arrived in that monster machine or are invisibility suits the latest style for high-priced gunslingers?"

Eva chuckled. "We met them. A different breed than the no-neck jerks who came gunning for you and Carol. Former Navy Seals. Lean, mean, no-nonsense with 'Yes, ma'am, no, ma'am' manners. They decided to survey the property while the sheriff and his crew were still here. Imagine you'll meet them soon enough."

We rocked in silence a few more minutes. An angry yell broke the peaceful quiet. Our cabin windows weren't thick enough to mute Sala's outburst. "Damn it! Call up the damn video. I haven't seen it either. We'll watch together. Have to if we're going to get past this. Doug claims it was my idea. Says I screwed him while Ray was dying. Well, I'm not afraid to look. Maybe it'll even prove who's telling the truth."

Eva rose. "Think I'll head over to the barn and see how Rita's settled in."

Carol jumped up. "I'll come with you."

The barn was just about the last place I wanted to go. All I wanted was to keep my buns parked right where they were. I was exhausted. But I couldn't stay and eavesdrop on such a personal argument. If the situation were reversed, I'd hope anyone in listening range would get off their butts and move.

I didn't exactly jump up, but I stood.

"I'll head to the retail cabin and check inventory."

That's what I told Carol and Eva. What I meant was I'm going to the retail cabin to sit in a spot where no one can see or bug me. For the hundredth time since I'd come to Udderly, I was oh so glad we only opened for retail customers on weekend afternoons.

"Hi."

I jumped at the baritone voice intruding on my dream. I'd fallen asleep. Head down, drool on chin, comatose-style sleep. I blinked. A man stood in the doorway. He wore neatly pressed khakis and a lightweight jacket with multiple pockets. I rubbed my eyes. Was he here to buy cheese? Then I saw the gun in his holster and remembered. I was hiding out, not minding the store.

"Didn't mean to startle you, ma'am. I'm Jim Haas, one of the men assigned to protect you. It's four o'clock. Your aunt asked me to escort you back to the cabin."

"Good grief. It's four? Lost all track of time. I'm Brie. Nice to meet you."

Jim held the door for me. As we began the short hike back to the cabin, I asked if he and his partner would be joining us for dinner.

"No, ma'am," he answered.

No idle chitchat. Not much of a conversationalist, but I appreciated his cut-to-the-chase operational mode. His cool, calm presence did make me feel safer.

As soon as we reached the steps to the cabin, Jim peeled off with a "Have a good evening" farewell. I didn't see his partner. Probably setting up a sharpshooter nest on Udderly's one sizable hill. I was surprised to see Sala's car parked out front. Wasn't certain if that made me more or less wary of going inside. If Sala was still here, the lovers must have made up, right?

"How's the inventory?" Eva's sarcasm was obvious, but she smiled. "Isn't it kinda hard to count containers with your eyes closed?"

Sala hooted. "Give the girl a break. Not every day she gets to show off her rodeo skills. Know I'd be tuckered out by now if I'd ridden a wild mule bareback."

The team owner sat in the recliner next to Zack's, while Carol and Eva occupied the living room's love seat. I once again dragged a chair in from the kitchen table to join the party.

I wanted to ask, "Did you watch the video?" and "How did you two patch things up?" With a little will power, I kept my lips zipped.

Zack smiled at me. "Mom told me you heard the start of our argument when you were on the front porch. Imagine you're wondering why we haven't killed each other or Sala hasn't stormed off."

Yep, that was exactly what I was wondering.

"Well tell her, Zack," Sala said. "Everybody else knows what's going on."

Zack sighed. "We finally watched that horrid video. While I'd rather not have seen Sala with another man, the video proved Doug, a man I thought was a good friend, lied through his teeth. When Paint described the video, I knew the leading man was Doug. That Joker tattoo on his butt was a dead giveaway. But Paint never mentioned a smaller tattoo on Doug's right arm. Saw just a flash of it in the video, but that's all I needed. He got that tat two months after Sala's husband died. That video couldn't have been shot when Ray was alive. I know because I got the same tat at the same time. Our whole team did. A small Star of David for Stephen Gross, a Jewish teammate killed during a visit to Israel."

Sala reached over and touched Zack's arm. "Doug's been filling Zack's head with lots of ugly lies."

Zack nodded and rolled his eyes. "My 'buddy' played it like he hated being the bearer of bad news, but what are buddies for? When I confided I was seeing Sala, Doug said he saw no reason to even mention their one-nighter to me. Then he claimed Sala sent him a copy and demanded a repeat performance. Threatened to release him from the team if he refused."

Sala chuckled. "Well, Doug was right about one thing. I released him from the team. This very afternoon. In the off season, we picked up a really promising college quarterback in the draft. Told our coaches to get him ready for Sunday's game."

Zack sighed. "Doug's a very convincing storyteller. Mixes a few truths in with his fiction, and reminds you how he hates telling you things that might be hurtful. He admitted conspiring with Kate, who hoped the video along with Doug's testimony would convince the league that Sala's ownership of the Aces could tarnish its image. Kate wanted the league to pressure Sala to divest her shares."

Carol leaned forward. "That sanctimonious bastard. Every time I visited Vegas, Doug told me how lucky he was to have my son as his best friend. What a two-faced jerk. Makes me wonder if Doug didn't hire Mick to attack Zack. Of course, Kate's a candidate, too. But how would either of them even know Mick existed?"

Zack shook his head. "That's easy. A few years back, Mick flew to Vegas for one of our games, and I introduced him around. Doug dazzled Mick. He has a knack for charming people who might have some future use. They both gambled on sports. Imagine that was a common bond. They must have stayed in touch."

Zack paused, using his good leg to push down on the recliner's footrest and sit up straighter.

"Doug begged my forgiveness. Said he happened to be chatting with Mick and casually mentioned he needed something on my phone. Doug shared his doubts I'd give it to him because some woman had poisoned my mind. My good pal swore he had no idea that innocent conversation would prompt Mick to attack me."

Eva snorted. "What a load of bull crap."

"Agreed," Zack said. "But Doug's a great actor. Even squeezed out a few tears when he asked me to forgive him. Swore he didn't realize Mick was unhinged."

I rubbed my temples. I was totally confused. Maybe I was still groggy from my nap, but it seemed like big chunks of the puzzle were missing.

"Can we back up a little?" I asked. "Let's review what we think we know. Doug planned to deliver the video to Kate Lemmon, but Doug's girlfriend wiped all his devices and sent the only remaining copy to Zack's cell. Doug cajoled or paid Mick to snatch Zack's phone, but he failed.

"I get Kate's motive. But what's in it for Doug? Even if Kate ousted

Sala from team ownership, Doug's status wouldn't change. With the team winning big-time with Zack, Kate would be insane to make Doug the starting quarterback. Then there's Carol. Why kidnap her once it was clear she didn't have Zack's phone? Even as South Carolina's governor, Carol couldn't help or hurt Doug or Kate."

Eva nodded. "Brie's questions are good ones. Carol's the biggest disconnect. I can't think of a single reason Doug or the Lemmon brat would kidnap Carol or send Gunter and Vince to kill her."

I sat forward in my chair. "Zack, did you tell the sheriff about Doug's confession that he'd sicced Mick on you?"

"Yes, I made that call right after Sala texted Doug to let him know he'd been released from the team."

"Good," I said. "Wonder if the sheriff has put Doug in the hot seat? Demanded some answers?"

"Doubt it," Sala added. "I knew Doug's private plane was hangared at the county airport. I called to see if it was still there. His Cessna departed at four o'clock. Filed a flight plan for Vegas. Guess he saw little point hanging around Ardon County once he lost Zack as an ally."

Eva stood. "We need to put our brainstorming on pause. Brie, help me finish the chores. Don't worry about fixing supper. Mollye's picking up pizzas. She got alarmed and called Zack when you didn't answer your cell. Shocked the heck out of me, too. Can't recall when that contraption wasn't glued to some part of your anatomy."

"I turn my cell off when I run. There was so much going on, I forgot all about turning it back on once Andy brought Rita and me back to Udderly."

I walked to the kitchen counter where I'd left my phone when I changed clothes. Had I missed calls or texts from Andy or Paint? Wasn't sure I wanted to know, but I forced myself to check. Both men said they planned to attend Carol's press conference and would visit with Zack and me afterward. They were busy tonight. Did that mean another double date? I sent the same brief text to both: *All calm on home front. See U tomorrow.*

"Are we expecting anyone else for dinner, Brie?" Eva asked when I put down my phone. "Andy, Paint, your folks? I'm beginning to think none of them own stoves."

I shook my head. "Think it's just the five of us plus Mollye."

"Afraid you need to count me out," Sala said. "I promised my sister I'd be back at the lake house for dinner. But, if no one minds, I'll drop by for a nightcap. Want to make sure those security guys are earning their keep."

She kissed Zack gently on the lips and her hand lingered a moment on his cheek. I glanced at Carol, who seemed to wince.

Looked like Carol was having a hard time accepting her son's and Sala's relationship. But she had to be thankful for Sala's efforts to keep Zack safe.

THIRTY-SIX

Mollye arrived with three large pizzas. At dinner's end, nary a crumb survived. Even the vegetarian pie, half with cheese, half naked, vanished. With all other options eliminated, Zack had eaten the last two pieces of cheese-less pizza, though he did dust them liberally with Parmesan before chowing down.

During dinner, Mollye's endless reservoir of questions teased out all the news highlights of the day. My friend seemed most surprised by the sheriff's update on Chester.

"Knew it had to be Chester and his mutt chasing us through the forest after he shot down Andy's drone," Mollye commented. "I was certain he killed Mick and kidnapped Carol. Yet I have to believe Sheriff Mason checked Chester's alibi every which way. Still I'm glad the idiot's locked up. Wonder if someone will bail him out."

While we usually sat around the kitchen table for up to an hour after dinner, I shooed everyone but Mollye into the living room. I'd noticed Zack wiggling and shifting his behind. Figured he couldn't get comfy at the table with his arm in a sling and no way to stretch out a leg that ended in a boot-cast. Eva insisted Zack and Carol take the twin recliners, while she settled on the love seat.

While Mollye and I washed and dried the few dishes needed to consume our takeout meal, we eavesdropped on the living room chatter about tomorrow's press conference. I was pleased to learn Linda, Carol's campaign manager, had convinced the sheriff to make a statement. He'd say there was clear evidence the gubernatorial candidate had been abducted and drugged. He'd add she'd been cleared as a suspect in Mick Hardy's murder.

To join the group, Mollye and I needed to drag in chairs or flop on the floor. Knowing my friend preferred sprawl to straight-back chairs, I sat on the floor. Mollye joined me, doing her usual pretzel number on the wide-planked floor. Eva tossed us a couple of throw pillows for leaning.

Suddenly, Mollye scooted toward the loveseat and used the armrest to haul herself upright. "Almost forgot." She hurried to a large canvas bag she'd left by the front door. "Thought I'd bring entertainment as well as eats."

She grinned as she pulled a Ouija board from her bag. "Now, Brie, before you start in, I'm not suggesting the spirit world can tell us who kidnapped Carol. But sometimes we know things that we don't know we know. Wow, there were a lot of knows in that sentence.

"Anyway, if you pull out a Ouija board your subconscious may guide your fingers without you even being aware of what's happening. Sort of your brain's way of yelling at you to pay attention."

Mollye set the elaborate board with its alphabet letters and potential "yes" and "no" responses in the middle of the floor. The board was well used. Mollye and I had played with it plenty when we were teens, giggling at the spirit's supposed answers to such profound questions as whether Janie Vermillion was still a virgin. I wasn't sure why I felt queasy about asking the Ouija board questions about kidnapping and murder.

My friend held up the triangular-shaped planchette used to spell out the answers posed by the person holding it. "Who wants to be first to give it a go?"

"Not me." I scooted a couple feet away from Mollye to make room for any takers.

When no one immediately spoke, I figured Eva, Carol, and Zack might share my unease. Then Eva stood and tapped her foot against my butt. "Scoot over, niece. I'll give it a go."

Eva knelt above the board. "Who would like Carol to disappear?" She tried for a spooky tone as her fingers hovered above the planchette. Once she touched it, the pointer shot straight toward an "A" and then an "L."

"Don't think you need to spell out the rest of the name, Eva," Carol said. "We all know Allie Gerome would like me to vanish and make her candidate a shoe-in. Allie and I occupy opposite ends of the political spectrum on every issue from university funding to drilling for oil off our coast. But while she'd love for me to disappear, it doesn't mean she'd kidnap me."

"Okay, I'll ask the question a different way." Eva placed her fingers back on the planchette and returned the pointer to its 'neutral' position. "Who had the idiotic brainstorm to kidnap Carol?" she asked.

This time the pointer headed to an "F" then an "R" and an "E."

Mollye laughed. "Well, he'd be my first choice, too. Fred Baxter's had it in for you for twenty years, Carol. But you can be sure the sheriff checked his alibi just like he did Chester's. Didn't Mason tell someone Fred was visiting his sister in Savannah when you were snatched? Guess the board's not going to be an ace crime-solver after all."

I chewed my lip. Maybe, maybe not.

"Moll, didn't you tell us that Allie and Fred were doing the nasty? Could they have dreamed up a kidnap caper together? Just because Fred has an alibi doesn't mean he wasn't involved. Remember, Doug was in Vegas when Zack was attacked, but Doug was the catalyst. He made it happen."

Zack nodded. "You're right, Brie. Maybe Allie or Fred paid someone to kidnap Mom. Could have been spur of the moment. Since no one knew who clobbered me or why, Allie and Fred may have figured the sheriff would assume Mom's kidnap was another part of a personal vendetta against me."

A knock at the door surprised us. I struggled up from the floor to answer it, peeking through the blinds first to make certain it wasn't Gunter, the no-neck killer who'd escaped. I'd seen too many movies where the bad guys popped up again and again with jack-in-the-box regularity.

"It's Sala," I announced as I opened the door.

Sala hurried in. "Yeah, I know. I'm back way before it's time for a nightcap. But I was so fidgety when I sat down at the dinner table that my sister got up, grabbed a coupon for Wendy's, and shoved it in my hand. 'Go on back to your goat farm,' she said. 'Pick up a burger on the way. You'll be lousy company if you stay.'"

Zack started to struggle upright in his recliner, but Sala hustled over and gently pushed him down. "I'll join the floor team. What's this? A Ouija board?"

She stuck her hand out to Mollye. "Sorry I'm barging in on the fun. I'm Sala, who are you?"

Mollye laughed and introduced herself as she always did, noting the "e" tacked on to her name's rear end.

Sala smiled. "There are worse things than extra letters. What have we been up to? Trying to communicate with Vince, my former employee, who I hope is roasting in hell? Still can't believe Gunter shot Vince after your mule trampled him."

Mollye spoke up. "Eva just asked the board who'd want to make Carol disappear. We got immediate, no-surprise answers—Fred Baxter, a long-time enemy, and Allie Gerome, our local paper's idiot publisher. Allie and Fred have been seeing each other for months."

Sala laughed. "So why haven't you called Sheriff Mason and told him to arrest the pair? The Ouija board knows all, right? Then, again, I wouldn't eliminate Kate as a suspect. Maybe she thought if she held Carol hostage she could force Zack to play ball in her quest to get me booted as an owner."

I sighed. "Don't know about Kate or Allie, but Fred has an iron-clad alibi. He was in Savannah when Carol was snatched."

"So what about this Allie person?" Sala asked. "You're not being sexist, are you? Why couldn't she be the kidnapper?"

Hmmm. Why indeed?

"Guess I am being sexist," I answered. "I don't think of women as kidnappers and she's old, about sixty."

Eva's eyebrows shot up as she growled. "Old? She's my age. More than a little on the chunky side but that witch is no invalid. I could kidnap someone if I had a mind to, and I'll bet that she-devil could too. How much muscle does it take to chloroform an unsuspecting victim or shove a needle in someone's backside?"

Eva's outburst made everyone chuckle.

Carol's grin faded. "You know Eva has a point. I assumed whoever kidnapped me was male because the caller who lured me to the parking lot was definitely a man. But maybe the caller wasn't near the hospital. The sheriff already determined the call came from a throw-away cell."

I held up my hand. "Wait guys. Before we pin it on Allie, haven't there been regular sightings of said witch the whole time Carol was held hostage? Eva saw her more than once whispering to one of her reporters while she waited like a vulture outside Zack's hospital room. And she was interviewed on the radio about that editorial of hers that urged folks not to vote for a missing person."

Mollye looked at the Ouija board. "Suppose we inquire about Chester's role. If that dolt is totally innocent and simply walked in to discover Carol was a prisoner at his hangout, why would he try to frame her for Mick's murder?"

Sala picked up the planchette. "No need to ask that question. I can spell out Chester's motive without any help from the Ouija board."

She moved the pointer to "M" and quickly pointed to the remaining letters. "MONEY. Perhaps Chester was paid to mind Carol after she was kidnapped. That would have freed Allie to spend all the time she wanted gloating while taking a front-row seat at the hospital to enjoy everyone's angst. I'm thinking we should try to find a money trail."

Gee, why hadn't I thought of that? As a former banker, I'd spent plenty of time analyzing credit reports and all manner of financial transactions. You could tell a lot about a person from their credit reports, spending patterns, and debt.

"I know how to scout for financial information on all the players—Chester, Fred, Allie, Doug, Mick," I said. "But public information only goes so far. I can't look at anyone's personal banking transactions."

Sala gave me a sly, cat-got-the-canary look. A smile played on her lips. "I know people who can take a look-see at just about any bank account. But let's begin with what we honest-but-curious citizens can find."

I walked to the corner of the room, retrieved my laptop, and took it to the kitchen table. By unspoken agreement, Sala and Mollye pulled up chairs on either side of me. Guess they thought I needed wingmen for my financial investigation. Online searches take time. My efforts were no exception. Less than fifteen minutes after I set to work, Eva urged Zack and Carol to head to bed.

"You two have a big day tomorrow. It's obvious you're in pain, Zack, and you have to be exhausted, Carol. Get some sleep. We'll wake you on the off-chance our kitchen forensic accountants solve the crime."

Sala joined in the shooing exercise and reiterated Eva's promise to wake folks if we made some stupendous find.

We focused our first financial inquiries on Doug. Sala knew he bragged about palatial homes in Vegas, Miami Beach, and San Diego, plus a Jaguar, a collection of modern art, and the Cessna he'd piloted out of Dodge once Zack knew he'd been lying.

It didn't take long to discover Doug's Florida and California houses were in foreclosure, and creditors had put liens on his Jaguar and artwork. The man was in serious financial trouble.

The news shocked Sala. "I had no idea. He's been paid millions over the last decade. Where did it go? Can he really be almost bankrupt?"

"Gambling?" I suggested. "Zack said it was one of his common bonds with Mick."

Mollye shook her head. "What a waste. We don't need to look at Mick's finances. Paint already told us Mick admitted he was up to his eyeballs in hock. That angry email Mick sent suggested his losing bet on the last Aces game was the final straw."

"Okay, let's look at Chester," Sala urged.

It took a while but our online inquiries, with help from Sala's sources, eventually yielded gold. While Chester was busy establishing his alibi for Carol's kidnapping with an extended Oconee County stay, he took possession of a brand-new Ford Explorer, Platinum model no less, with a book value of close to fifty-three-thousand dollars. Yet he'd paid the dealer only five grand. In theory, the price was discounted because it was a "demonstrator" model. Yet the twenty-five miles on its odometer at the time of sale didn't quite merit an almost fifty-thousand-dollar discount.

A search of corporate records turned up what we suspected. Fred Baxter's parent company owned car dealerships in three Upstate counties—Ardon, Pickens and Oconee.

Fred must have finagled Chester's windfall. While the transaction might not be a smoking gun, it indicated Fred Baxter paid off Chester for something. My hunch? Keeping Carol on ice.

Mollye found a jar of Paint's peach moonshine and poured nightcaps for the three of us who were still awake. Fortified with moonshine, I began a probe of Allie Gerome's financial empire via corporate tax returns.

The *Ardon Chronicle* was bleeding greenbacks, but the owner could easily afford to keep her hobby horse afloat thanks to fat profits in her energy-related companies. One of the companies forecasted a huge windfall if it gained permission to build a pipeline that bisected a state-owned nature sanctuary. Allie also had controlling interest in another corporation applying to drill for oil off our state's coastline.

"No wonder Allie wants to make certain Carol isn't the next governor," Mollye said. "Carol's been quite outspoken about her determination to find ways to fight both the pipeline and offshore drilling."

I yawned. My wide-open, show-my-tonsils yawn triggered Mollye and Sala to do their own copycat versions. Not Eva. She was already sound asleep on one of our two blow-up mattresses, snoring loud enough to compete with a buzz saw. We'd been at it for hours.

"Think it's time to close up shop," I said. "My eyelids are so heavy I'll need toothpicks to keep them open if we stay up any longer. Anyway, I doubt there's much else we can dig up. Just hope Chester's vehicle bonanza proves enough to convince the sheriff to take a strong interest in Fred and Allie."

Sala surprised me with a kiss on the cheek. "You done good, kid. Sure you don't want to forget about owning a B&B? I could offer you a good paying job in our accounting department."

She turned to Mollye. "You'd be welcome in our front office. Bring your Ouija board and you'd probably beat most of the projections I get from staff on everything from TV revenues to stadium attendance."

Mollye smiled. "I'm pretty happy here, but I'd like to visit Vegas. You ought to stop by my store before you leave. I'm sure I have a piece of pottery with your name on it."

"Sounds like fun," Sala answered. "Maybe Zack and I can swing by after Carol's press conference."

Mollye clapped her hands. "Great. I can do astrological charts for both of you. See you all at the press conference. I'll leave the board here in case we need it again."

When I escorted my sleuthing wing women out, I spotted one of the security men on patrol. I yawned again. Maybe I would sleep soundly, at least for the hours remaining before Eva shook me awake. Then I noticed the Ouija board sitting where Moll had left it on the edge of the table.

I walked over and picked up the planchette. What the heck?

Silently I asked, “Should it be Andy or Paint?

I lifted my fingers off the pointer as soon as it made its first move. The tips of my fingers felt like they’d been burned.

Damn. Damn.

I felt justified in using something stronger than a cheese or meat curse, if only in my head.

THIRTY-SEVEN

The Strongs' move from Udderly to Carol's home in the Town of Ardon proceeded without a hitch. The executive protection agents coordinated the shift like a military maneuver. They commandeered a second Hummer and the two muscular vehicles bracketed my comparatively miniature car as I chauffeured Eva and the Strongs into Ardon around ten a.m.

I checked the sky. Brooding black clouds obliterated any sunlight. As we turned onto the highway, gusty winds tried to bully my Prius with alternating shoves right and left. I hoped the rain would hold off until Carol's press conference was over.

I drove since Eva's truck wasn't an option, and Carol's Cadillac remained in impound as evidence. Zack sat upfront with me to get a smidgeon more legroom. Carol and Eva huddled in the tight backseat.

Zack fired off the conversational football as we tooled down the highway. "Before I went to bed last night, I called Joe Gahan, the Aces' rookie quarterback. Told him I knew exactly how he felt, being handed an unexpected opportunity to strut his stuff. Told Joe not to waste the chance. Coached him a little on what I expected the opposing team to throw at him. Maybe it'll help. Joe's strengths are a lot like mine. He's got a good arm but finding holes and running through them is his forte."

"What happens if Joe turns in a stellar performance?" Eva asked. "Won't you have to compete with him when you're all healed?"

Zack shrugged. "If I ever go back on the field. That's a big if."

"What?" Carol sounded shocked. "You're thinking of quitting football, retiring?"

I glanced at Zack. He'd surprised all of us. He stared out the window and sighed. "I love football. Hope to coach when my time on the field ends. Frankly that time may be now. I had a long talk with the docs before I left the hospital. A lot of damage to my shoulder. They're not certain I'll be able to throw passes again—at least not like I did."

"Why didn't you tell me?" Carol asked. "It must be eating you up."

"Have to admit it's a downer. But my visit with those wounded vets, some of them double amputees, put things in perspective. I've lived my dream. Earned a Super Bowl ring. I may never be a top athlete again but I have plenty of money, and I'm in decent health."

Zack turned in his seat to look at his mother. "I know you're not thrilled about my relationship with Sala, but I love her. The president of France has ably demonstrated that older women make wonderful wives, especially if they're exceptional ladies like Sala."

"You're that serious? You're thinking of marriage?" Carol's questions tumbled out as sputters. She obviously hadn't a clue Sala was a candidate for daughter-in-law.

"I'm more than ready to pop the question," Zack answered. "Don't know how Sala would answer. That's why I plan to wait a bit. She's got enough going on, dealing with the blowback she'll get for releasing Doug and putting in a rookie. Plus I'm sure she'll have to fend off more vicious attacks by her stepdaughter. For Sala's sake—and the team's—I hope Joe scores big time."

Following Zack's shocker announcement, no one uttered a word until Carol's house was in sight. City cops stationed next to barricades lifted them to let us pass. The executive protection agency had arranged for blockades at both ends of Carol's block so police could screen the press and supporters as they arrived for the noon news conference.

Linda smiled and waved from the Strongs' front porch as she watched our little caravan arrive. "Welcome Home" and "Strong for Governor" banners fluttered from the porch railings.

"What a campaign manager," Carol said. "Wouldn't have dreamed of running without Linda's help."

Zack hopped out to open the car's rear door for his mother. "Well, make sure Linda gets what she wants—you as the next governor. Hope you're planning one heck of a speech."

Carol hugged Zack. "I'll try."

As I climbed the porch steps, I hung back, stalling. I realized I didn't want to be reminded of the mayhem we'd found on our last visit to the house. When I forced myself to walk inside, I grinned. The interior looked neat as a pin. Every surface gleamed. A bouquet of roses added a sweet scent to the homecoming.

"Oh, Linda. What have you done?" A grateful tear rolled down Carol's cheek. "The house looks better than it did the day Zack flew in for our Halloween party."

Linda reached over and brushed Carol's tear away. "None of that. You have to show all those potential voters you're the lady of steel. You've been tested by adversity and survived."

The campaign manager slowly turned in a complete circle. "All of this is a thank you from your ARGH supporters. They all pitched in to restore order. Cleaned the place stem to stern and scoured shops for almost-identical replacements of the items trashed by those thugs."

"Are the ARGH folks here yet?" Carol asked. "I need to thank them. What friends."

Linda shook her head. "Everyone's coming around eleven thirty. The sheriff wanted a chance to speak with you in private first. He should be here any minute."

Carol looked alarmed. "He's not backing out of making a statement, is he? I need Mason to make it official that I'm a victim, not a murderess."

Linda bit her lip. "No, no. Don't worry. He just wanted to give you an update."

"Great. New developments," Eva blurted. "We haven't had time to digest the old developments."

"Maybe it's good news," I said. "We're due for some."

As if on cue, Sheriff Mason's cruiser slid into a space in front of the house. There wasn't another car parked anywhere on the block. Local police had convinced Carol's neighbors to move all their vehicles that normally lined the street.

Mason strode into the house with Deputy McCoy, Mollye's beau. The sheriff nodded at the group, then singled out Carol. "I'd like a word in private, ma'am."

"Sheriff, you know all of these folks. Can't you share whatever news you have with everyone? You know they'll find out soon enough."

Mason scrutinized the gathering and shrugged. "All right. But it's important that none of this information leaks, at least until after we make arrests. We've already had two persons of interest flee our jurisdiction, and the individuals we hope to take into custody today have the resources to disappear as well."

Everyone nodded agreement and murmured his or her own version of a secrecy pledge. We were all so anxious to know who the sheriff planned to arrest that we'd have promised most anything to satisfy our curiosity.

"You might as well sit down," he added. "This will take a few minutes."

He leveled a look directly at me. I squirmed a bit under his scrutiny even though I figured I wasn't one of his anticipated arrestees.

"Miss Hooker here did some financial snooping last night—"

Eva cleared her throat and interrupted. "Come on, Sheriff. Don't start with the Miss, Mr. last-name nonsense again. Just spit it out. There are a bunch of us Hookers. Just say 'Brie.'"

The sheriff looked heavenward and started again. "Last night, Sala forwarded me some financial transactions that Brie helped dig up. It looks like Fred Baxter arranged for one of his dealerships to sell Chester a fifty-thousand-dollar vehicle for a tenth of its value. Sala also shared your theory about Fred and Allie collaborating in Carol's kidnap."

The sheriff began to pace as he continued his story. "That new information prompted me to have another go at Chester, who was nice and handy in our jail on charges of obstructing justice and accessory to murder."

"Did Chester give up Fred?" Eva blurted out.

Mason glared at my aunt. "Hold your horses. I don't want to leave anything out. It's important."

"Okay, okay," Eva said.

"After I informed Chester we could prove Fred paid him off, he admitted returning to Ardon to keep an eye on Carol. Said he wasn't told who actually nabbed her or deposited her at the isolated hunting cabin. Chester claims harming Carol was never part of the plan. Fred said he just wanted her to experience a fraction of the suffering he'd felt when Quatro died. He thought it would be poetic justice for Carol to be kept incommunicado, not knowing whether her son had survived his coma or died."

Carol gasped. "Oh, my god. How could anyone nurse that much hate for twenty years?"

Mason nodded. "Chester agreed to keep an eye on you, Carol. But, even though you were tied up, he wasn't about to risk you waking and causing trouble. So he periodically loaded you up with a new dose of Ketamine to keep you out of it. Not Fred's intent. He wanted you fully aware and agonizing over your son's fate. After enough time went by that you couldn't possibly win the election, you were to be drugged and left in your car, alive but broken."

The sheriff leveled another look at me. "Your drone fly-over changed things. Chester had made a beer run. When he returned, he made his first trip to the latrine and found Mick's body. He panicked. Though he had no idea who killed Mick, he figured whoever launched that drone had spotted the body and perhaps him as well. Chester knew he'd be a prime suspect in Mick's death. Not knowing when Mick was knifed, he didn't realize he had an alibi. That's why he tried to frame Carol. He was convinced whoever flew that drone would tell the authorities to search for a body. He didn't want them to find a body on the property or Carol in the cabin."

"So you're planning to arrest Fred today—even though he was in Savannah when Mom was taken from the parking lot?" Zack asked. "Do you know who actually kidnapped her?"

Mason held up his hand. "I was getting to that. Given your suggestion that Allie and Fred might have collaborated, we decided to go over Carol's Cadillac one more time. Most surfaces had been wiped down—once by the kidnapper, again by Chester. We checked every conceivable surface. We found fingerprints on a strip of metal in the door panel. You know, that area where you often find tire pressure requirements. The prints matched those on file for one Allison Gerome, who was fingerprinted when she applied for her concealed carry permit."

"Hallelujah!" Eva exclaimed. "Always knew that witch would go too far someday."

"Why aren't Fred and Allie already in jail?" Carol's voice had a bit of a tremble.

Mason shrugged. "Figured that was obvious. Can't find them. Not at their homes, not at their places of business. We wanted you to be aware of the situation. They may be real nervous, knowing Chester's in jail and could rat them out. He's not exactly a stand-up guy. If either or both of them feel cornered, they could lash out. We've tightened security. But please don't give any of this information away during your press conference or to your supporters. We don't want the pair to discover what we know and bolt. If we're lucky, they'll show up at the press conference to find out why I'm joining you and what I might say about the investigation."

He nodded at Linda. "Your campaign manager, with my approval, has let the press know I'll provide an update."

Holy Havarti. I'd thought the idea of Allie as kidnapper was preposterous—wishful thinking that she'd get caught and wind up in jail. A natural wish given all the trouble Allie and her newspaper had stirred up for Eva. I prayed the sheriff would lock her up and throw away the key. However, even if Allie was arrested, I felt sure she'd make bail before they could turn the key on her cell door.

"What about Doug?" Zack asked the sheriff. "Do you have a warrant for his arrest?'

Mason shook his head. "We alerted authorities in Vegas that we want to talk to him. But there's no direct evidence Doug did anything more than innocently mention to a gambling buddy that he wanted something on Zack's phone. Doug will claim he had no idea Mick was so deranged he'd attack you to steal it."

Eva waved her hand. "Hold it a minute. Doug can make that claim because Mick's dead. Isn't it kind of obvious that Doug had a vested interest in making sure Mick no longer drew breath? That sort of guarantees no one can dispute him."

Mason ran his hand over the bristles on his shaved head. "Listen, folks. Enough. I've said all I can. No more questions. I'll say my piece. Make it clear Mrs. Strong was a victim and reiterate there's no evidence she's done anything wrong."

The sheriff glanced over at his deputy. "Danny and a couple of other officers will be moving through the crowd, on the lookout for Fred and Allie. If they're spotted, we'll try to take them into custody as quietly as possible. We want to avoid a media circus."

Good luck with that. I sensed neither Allie nor Fred would walk away quietly. Based on my one encounter with Fred, he'd seize any opportunity to call Carol a liar. Allie? She'd play the First Amendment card; scream she was being persecuted because the *Ardon Chronicle* courageously reported the truth about the Strongs. She'd say her sole crime was to defend the rights of South Carolinians to hear the truth.

I sensed an ugly storm brewing. Too bad I couldn't think of a single thing I could do to help my friends weather it.

THIRTY-EIGHT

The sheriff ushered Carol and Zack into a corner for a few private words.

Eva turned to Linda. "What can we do?"

She smiled. "Go outside, greet folks, and pray the rain doesn't arrive until after the press conference ends. Our ARGH supporters should be here any minute. The police know to let them through. They're wearing green T-shirts. They'll help keep the crowd as orderly as possible. It'll be a madhouse once the police start letting folks through the barricades. The police will let everyone in unless they happen to be carrying assault rifles or wearing bomber suicide vests."

Eva and I walked out on the porch. I glanced at the sky. If anything, the clouds looked more threatening than before. A large crowd was massed behind the barricades. I spotted the green-shirted ARGH contingent elbowing its way to the front. Phil's apparel combined with the right password convinced the cop on duty to let the green shirts through.

Sala, Mollye, Andy, and Paint weren't so lucky. When they tried to follow, the policeman stopped them at the barricade. I left the porch and hurried over to speak with the harried officer. It was a wonder he had any hearing left, given the chewing out Mollye and Sala were offering. Once I vouched for the foursome as friends of the Strong family, the town patrol officer grudgingly let them enter. I understood his reluctance. People behind the lucky quartet were already yelling, "How come you're letting them go in and not me?"

Sensing the potential for pandemonium as soon as the barricades lifted, I quickly told my friends to keep their eyes peeled for Allie and Fred. I didn't provide details. Just asked them to hail Danny McCoy or one of the other sheriff's deputies if they spotted either of them.

"Who's Danny McCoy?" Sala asked.

"My deputy sweetie," Mollye answered. "He's right over there." She waved at Danny, her bracelets clinking and clanking.

"Hey, that's some tattoo." Sala's eyes were glued to Mollye's arm. "Didn't notice it last night."

My friend proudly pushed the sleeve of her blouse higher so Sala could see the entire tattoo—a full-color reproduction of a quilt square. "My great granny's design," Mollye said. "Seemed a waste that the only way folks could ever see it was to come to my bedroom." She grinned. "I'm somewhat selective about boudoir visitors."

Sala laughed and turned my way. "I know there's only time for a highlights reel, but please tell me, is it good news that we're trying to spot Fred Baxter and Allie Gerome?"

I nodded. "It is."

"Super," she said. "What do they look like?"

Hmm. No time to pull out my phone and hunt for photos on the web. How to describe the pair? I knew I viewed them with jaundiced eyes and had a tendency to project their personality flaws into their physical descriptions. I made an attempt to be somewhat clinical, objective.

I sighed. "Fred Baxter isn't bad looking, rather distinguished. Dapper dresser. Around sixty. I'm guessing he's five-nine or five-ten. Thick brown hair, graying at the temples. Brown eyes. Oh, and a really dark tan."

"What about this Allie person?" Sala asked.

"She's about the same age as Fred. Late fifties or early sixties. Average height. Overweight. A double chin and really plump upper arms. They tend to make her sleeves bind like stuffed sausage casings. But she's not really obese, just lumpy. Never seen the woman in anything but dowdy gray or black pantsuits. Dyes her hair. Imagine she's trying for auburn but the unfortunate color shades toward orange. Big owl glasses. Small, mean, deep-set eyes. Never noticed their color."

Sala's eyebrows shot up. "Wow. I'd hate to hear how you'd describe me."

Paint and Andy, who'd both been eavesdropping, laughed. "Brie's description of Allie was reasonably kind," Andy said. "She didn't mention the woman's laugh—a cackle—always at someone else's expense."

Andy gave me a wistful look. "But Brie does have a way with words."

I pretended I didn't notice his expression. Questioning?

"Should we spread out?" Paint asked. "Increase our chances to spot our two most wanted?"

"Good idea." I agreed, maybe a little quickly. I wasn't eager to be left alone with either Paint or Andy. I felt reasonably sure Andy had not told his best friend I'd relented on my not-a-boyfriend stance—at least as far as Andy was concerned. Ever the gentleman, the handsome veterinarian would think I should decide when and if to deliver the news.

People streamed toward us. The barricades were down, and it looked like the running of the bulls. Reporters, TV crews, swarms of the curious and supporters, all scurried our way, jockeying for positions near Carol's front porch. A huge crowd.

Mollye, Paint, Andy, and I mapped out four different sectors for our hunt-and-identify mission. Before we launched into the incoming masses, I felt a tug on my sleeve.

"Though you painted a vivid picture of Allie, I'd prefer to tag along with you instead of going solo," Sala said. "That way I can point out any probables and wait for you to confirm before calling the cops down on some innocent. Believe me, plenty of men and women could fit your descriptions."

I nodded. "Fine with me. I sort of doubt Fred will show. Allie? Maybe. She'd normally attend an event like this in order to dictate the *Ardon Chronicle* reporter's slant on the story. I know firsthand how she takes quotes out of context to change their meaning. But today? She may be more shy than normal, knowing a co-conspirator is sitting behind bars and might get chatty."

The door to Carol's house opened, and Carol, Zack, Sheriff Mason, and Linda walked onto the front porch. The campaign manager took up her post behind a lectern as the others took seats in the four folding chairs crammed into the space. A chant rose up from the crowd: "Strong for Governor. Strong for Governor." While I didn't hear any "Praise the Lord" shouts, the crowd's mood had a tent revival quality.

Linda looked at her watch, prompting me to peek at mine. It was exactly noon. The campaign manager freed a hand-held mike from its holder. I doubted Carol would stand behind the podium. She never used notes and liked to pace while she talked.

"Thank you for joining us today," Linda began. "What a wonderful occasion—welcoming the next governor of South Carolina and her son, Zack, back home, safe, and on the mend. Let's tell Carol and Zack Strong how happy we are that they've survived not one but two malicious attacks!"

Thunderous applause and whistles filled the air along with louder chants. I was pleased to mostly see—and hear—enthusiastic support. A few detractors had slipped in. I heard one yell, "Liar! Murderer!" He was quickly drowned out.

I scanned the faces of the people who jostled around me, wishing once more that I was taller than five-four. Sala had me by five inches and wore sandals with cork wedges that boosted her height to almost six feet. Maybe she could serve as my periscope.

"See anyone who looks remotely like a match for Fred or Allie?" I urged. "They wouldn't necessarily be standing together."

"Sorry. Not yet," Sala answered.

Carol took center stage. With her arms spread wide, she played conductor, quieting the audience. "Thank you, thank you. I want to win this election. But winning any office can't compare with the blessings I'm celebrating today. The son I love more than anything in this world has awakened from his coma, and I've survived my enemies' attacks—from kidnapping to bullets meant to kill not only me but the friends kind enough to take me in."

Sala nudged me and bent to whisper in my ear. "Talks a little more high-nosed in public, doesn't she?"

I stifled a giggle. Inappropriate, but Sala's comment struck me as funny. Of course, laughing at inopportune times had long been one of my less-endearing traits. At Cousin Robin's wedding, I'd struggled mightily to hold back my tee-hees. Just before the bride and her soon-to-be husband recited their vows, the church organ struck chords that made the wood in our pews vibrate, prompting the stranger beside me to let out one whopper of a fart.

Once again, I scanned the sea of faces in my visual neighborhood. Carol introduced Sheriff Mason to give a selective update on his investigations into Zack's attack, Carol's abduction, and the attempt to frame her as a killer. There were audible gasps as the audience heard for the first time that Chester was being held as a suspect in an attempt to frame Carol for Mick's murder. It was also the first many had heard about an attempt by two gunmen to kill Carol and me.

Mason concluded with standard law enforcement lingo regarding his inability to answer any questions or comment on ongoing aspects of the investigation into the kidnapping effort, Mick Hardy's murder, or the hunt for an unnamed gunman in the shootout at the Udderly corral. Doug, Kate, Fred, and Allie were never mentioned. Mason ended with a comment that he was following up on "very promising" leads.

The sheriff's reference to the missing gunman I knew as Gunter made my skin crawl. Would the killer dare return? Try to add a notch—or two—to his belt in a public setting?

I was about to nudge Sala and tell her to keep an eye out for her former employee, when she elbowed me.

"Have a possibility," she whispered. "A couple that kinda looks like your wankers. She has a piss-poor dye job with frizzy split ends. Looks like she's wearing a clown's wig. Her sour puss could turn hot tamales into icicles. The guy next to her is kind of nondescript, but he does have dark hair with some gray, and his expression says he's either angry or constipated. Don't think they're fans of the Strong clan or the sheriff."

I couldn't see over the intervening heads. Sala watched my unsuccessful attempt to stand on tiptoe for a better view. "Here." Sala slipped off her sandals. "Put my shoes on. They'll give you another four inches."

I was wearing one of my fancier pairs of shoes—backless, slip-on Skechers. No problem to toe them off. But I doubted my wide tootsies could squeeze into Sala's shoes. Andy's and Paint's shoes were a more likely fit.

"Come on, hurry," Sala urged.

We were hemmed in so tightly, I could barely see my feet let alone Sala's vacated shoes. I slipped my feet, socks and all, into her platform shoes and teetered for a moment before I felt confident I wouldn't topple.

Yes, indeedy, Sala had spotted our quarry. Excited, I searched the crowd for Deputy Danny, swiveling right and left like a wound-up bobble head. No luck.

That's when I heard the thunder that arrived almost simultaneously with a flash of lightning. The rumble shook the ground. Not much of an early warning system. The wind came next, driving the cold rain sideways. It drilled into our faces. I squinted, trying to keep sight of Allie and Fred.

People jostled us as they stampeded for cover. The wind added its own buffeting assault. Standing our ground, we seemed to be tackle dummies for runners to plough into as they headed for their cars.

I still wore Sala's platform sandals. When a strong gust forced my head down, I glimpsed one of my abandoned shoes. Someone had kicked it like a soccer ball into a scrum of drenched reporters.

"My shoes are gone," I shouted at Sala over the drumming rain. "I'll kick yours off so you can put them on."

"Forget it, don't waste time. Look for those two where you last saw them. I don't mind walking barefoot so long as some clown doesn't crush my toes."

I plunged into the wet human sea, using a breaststroke type maneuver to separate bodies and push myself forward. The last time I'd worn heels was at Robin's wedding and that was five years ago, so I was somewhat glad the press of bodies helped keep my wavering body vertical.

I heard Carol's voice over the loudspeakers pleading for calm.

I feared I'd lost Allie and Fred in the wet crush when I spotted the woman's soggy mop of hair, even frizzier than normal. Fred had grabbed her upper arm, trying to hustle her to the barricades and beyond. Since his broad hand didn't quite span her pudgy limb, his action was more push than guide. Allie seemed focused on staying upright, a concern I shared.

I'd lurched within a few feet of the pair when Fred spotted me. "It's that Hooker girl barreling our way," he yelled. "Hurry up, Allie."

I desperately searched for Deputy Danny. No luck.

Fred's latest shove made Allie sway. In a desperate attempt to prevent a close-up examination of the pavement, she stumbled in my direction, arms outspread like the wings of a plane attempting to land in a squall. I tried to backpedal but my foreign footwear had other ideas. I pitched forward and collided with Allie.

I saw the panic in her eyes just before she toppled. A second later I lost my fight with gravity and landed full force. Allie's dumpling figure softened my landing. Though I feared Allie's screams might break my eardrums, I was happy she was trapped under me.

I became quite a bit less happy when Allie started pummeling me. Her hands might be pudgy but they packed a wallop.

I wriggled sideways to win a position that pinned my wrestling partner's energetic fists. Then Fred, who remained upright, landed a kick. A direct hit to my ribs. In self-defense, I reached out and grabbed one of his ankles, right above a shiny tasseled loafer. Fred didn't even have time to yell. Went down like a big oak submitting to the indignity of a chainsaw. I wanted to yell "timber."

I started to giggle. Then Fred scrambled to his knees. His shaking hand held a gun. When would I ever learn how to throttle my impulse to laugh when startled? I'd nudged the man over the edge. Though admittedly Fred had been teetering pretty close to the mental brink for a long time.

I yelled, "Gun," just as Deputy Danny launched his stocky self into the fray.

A second later I was coughing and crying as I rolled off Allie's plump body.

Pepper spray. My eyes burned like someone had forced my eyelids open and injected a hundred tiny hot embers. I couldn't spit a word out of my scorched throat.

Pickled pig's feet.

I wasn't the only one hacking out my lungs. I struggled to see through my tears. Did Fred still have his gun? Squinting, I watched Danny bend down and swat wildly in the direction of Fred's doubled-over frame. Danny's eyes, like mine, were little more than slits. As Mom would say the deputy had been hoisted by his own petard. The rain had tightly concentrated the spray, and Danny couldn't escape the blowback.

Fred, who was kneeling when the spray hit, pitched forward to try to protect his eyes. Now he was kissing the pavement. The hands that protectively cupped the sides of his face were empty. One of Danny's windmill swings must have knocked the gun from Fred's hands.

Where was it?

I blinked trying to see through a torrent of tears.

"Think I'll take this into temporary custody if it's okay with everyone," Sala said as she scooped up the gun.

Sala had pulled the tail of her blouse up to cover her nose and mouth. The maneuver revealed her taut stomach and lacy red bra to anyone who could still see. Danny kept blinking but seemed more riveted on Sala's midriff than the gun or Allie and Fred, whose coughs sounded like warnings about emphysema. Neither Allie nor Fred had made a serious attempt to unglue themselves from the wet concrete.

Sheriff Mason, gun drawn, barged into our little tableau like a raging bull.

"What the hell did you do, Danny? Looks like you managed to pepper spray yourself."

Danny coughed. "Couldn't shoot, Sheriff. I could have hit Brie or some bystander. But I had to stop Fred from firing that gun."

"Well, get up," Mason said. "Help me take these two into custody."

Mason yanked Fred upright, patted him down, and slapped on handcuffs with practiced speed. Allie squirmed into a sitting position. Danny reached down to help her stand up, but backed off when she barked, "Don't you touch me. I'm going to sue the Ardon Sheriff's Department for all it's worth."

Mason paid her no heed. He came up behind her and grabbed under her armpits to hoist her upright. His lack of awe and deference incensed her even more. "You don't know who you're dealing with," she screeched.

The sheriff smiled. "Yes, ma'am, I surely do. Allison Gerome, you are under arrest for the kidnapping of Carol Strong..."

While I'd untangled my limbs from Allie's, I hadn't tried to get up. Too busy weeping and choking. Sometime during our melee, the rain stopped. The thunder and lightning that had switched on like they'd been staged for a movie set, switched off once the cameraman yelled, "Cut." The water hadn't disappeared though. A cold river running across the concrete had soaked through my trousers and breached my undies. I began to shiver and shake.

A pair of strong hands pulled me to a standing position. Okay, a wobbling position. I couldn't believe Sala's blasted platform sandals had stayed on my feet. I looked over my shoulder to thank my helper.

Paint grinned.

"Maybe you should start with trainer heels. Don't think you're ready for those big-girl shoes."

Paint's wet black hair glistened. A trickle of trapped water found an escape route and meandered down his cheek. His tongue snaked out and licked a drop that made it to the corner of his oh-so-inviting lips.

Andy's chuckle stopped me from launching another spontaneous smooch. I'd have nailed Paint with this one.

I returned Andy's smile, and awarded Paint with a simple, "Thanks."

Though the crowd had dispersed, cameramen were capturing every frame of the unexpected arrest of Fred Baxter and Allie Gerome.

Sala looked at me. Given that she was barefoot and I wore her heels, we were almost eye level.

"I gave Deputy Danny that Fred guy's gun. So how about you give my shoes back?"

THIRTY-NINE

The Strong house was crowded. Carol had welcomed in all the green-shirted ARGH supporters as well as Sala and the Udderly crew. There weren't quite enough towels to go around so Mollye and I shared. After vigorously rubbing my short hair, I quit dripping. Mollye wasn't as lucky. Her shoulder-length mane stayed plastered to her scalp. The green streak down her part looking like marshland.

I felt claustrophobic in the packed house and a little shaky after my wrestling match with Allie. Linda and Carol were talking campaign strategy with one group. Zack, Paint, and Andy were deep in conversation with Howie Lemcke about his wounded veterans' retreat. Eva had joined a cluster of ARGH members in the kitchen. They were setting out a buffet. Lots of Carol's supporters had brought casseroles and finger foods for an informal homecoming celebration after the news conference. I crossed my fingers there'd be some naked fruit and veggies.

Sala and Mollye stood with me on the fringes of the activity.

"I need some fresh air," I said. "Think I'll go outside for a few minutes."

"Why not?" Sala and Mollye chirped, almost in unison.

Sala laughed. "Can't get much wetter and there's not much prospect of getting dry either unless I strip."

"I'm game if you are," Mollye said.

"No way." Sala chuckled. "Have enough problems defending my reputation without giving my step-worm more ammunition."

We used the two soggy towels we had between us to cover the first porch step. That gave us a place to sit and we could rest our backs against the edge of the porch. Sitting on the damp towel, I looked at the empty street that had been clogged with bodies half an hour before. All signs of law enforcement—town cops and sheriff's deputies—were gone. But the two Hummers hadn't moved.

"Will you keep that executive protection service on the clock now that Doug and Kate have both flown off and Carol's kidnappers are locked up?" I asked Sala.

Elbows on her knees and chin resting in her hands, she stared at the Hummers. "Too soon to call it safe. We don't know for sure who killed Mick. My bet's on Vince and Gunter. Doug must have discovered Mick was wigging out and commissioned Vince and Gunter to prevent him from blabbing. Still it beats me how Doug could come up with enough money to hire a hit."

"Do you think Kate paid them?" I asked. "Paint and I were told about a suspicious van loitering outside Kate's hotel after you fired Gunter and Vince."

Sala shook her head. "No. Can't buy that. My stepdaughter is a slimy piece of work but I can't believe she'd actually pay someone to commit murder."

Mollye stretched out her legs so her ankles rested against the rounded lip of the stair below us. "If Vince and Gunter killed Mick, maybe they had their own motive to get rid of Carol. Doug was in the hospital room when we were talking about Carol trying to sort out what was real and what was hallucination while she was tied up at the cabin. They know she was there when Mick was murdered. Maybe Doug passed along the info and they worried she'd get enough memory back to ID them."

I nodded. "I see where you're going. They might even worry the sheriff coached Carol to pretend she couldn't remember what happened so she'd be protected as a witness until Mason nabbed them. If the pair had already killed one person, they may have thought why take a chance?"

Mollye tapped a finger against her temple. "Pretty good figuring, if you ask me. We're not half-bad at this sleuthing business."

"If we're right, I feel a lot better about Carol's safety. Surely Gunter wouldn't stick around Ardon now that the sheriff has issued a warrant for his arrest as a suspect in the death of his partner. I still shudder thinking about the creep killing his own partner in cold blood."

Sala slowly twisted her neck side to side and up and down. I did that when my shoulder muscles felt like guitar strings tightened to the point of snapping. She'd been under a ton of strain lately.

"I don't know," Sala said. "For Gunter to be convicted of Vince's murder, the prosecution would need eye-witness testimony from you and Carol that Vince was alive when you rode into the woods. Gunter might still have a strong incentive to get rid of both of you."

I shivered. "Let's talk about something other than more murders—especially Carol's or my potential departure from planet earth."

Mollye glanced sideways at me. I was the tomato in our porch step sandwich.

"Not sure you'll be any fonder of the topic I want to bring up," she said. "What the hell's going on between you and Andy? He keeps looking at you like he's expecting some sign, and you keep averting your eyes. Come on, give. What happened?"

I decided I might as well share my predicament. Maybe my friends could offer some good advice. I desperately wanted to keep Andy and Paint as friends. I couldn't bear to hurt either of them. I'd have to learn how to tamp down my jealousy. Deal with the fact they were going to fall in love with other women and move on if I didn't make a decision soon.

Mollye and Sala listened as I described how I'd ended my self-imposed let's-just-be-friends arrangement by impetuously kissing Andy.

"He told me he was crazy about me, and I made it more than clear I hated seeing him with another woman." I sighed. "Then I kissed him. It wasn't a thank-you-for-bringing-over-the-horse-trailer smooch. It was more like a one-more-minute-and-I'll-rip-off-your-shirt kiss. Andy had to interpret it as me waving a starter flag for us to speed down romance lane with no other passengers in our vehicle.

"An hour later I started to panic. I'd been equally jealous seeing Paint with another woman. I knew I didn't want to choose. I was so confused. I even asked that stupid Ouija board, should it be Andy or Paint? The answer didn't help one damn bit. I—"

Mollye broke in. "So now you want to tell Andy you didn't mean it?" My friend's tone was downright hostile. "That poor guy got his heart stomped on by that gold digger who divorced him. You can't hurt him like this."

"Whoa," Sala piped up. "Hold your horses here. If Brie's not sure about going steady, hooking up, or whatever you call it with Andy, she won't do him any favors by pretending she's sure he's the one. That's just stringing him along. It'll hurt worse when that string breaks, and it's bound to when 'what if' gets stuck in her mind. I'm speaking from experience. Be absolutely certain when you say 'yes it's for keeps.'"

I shook my head. "You two didn't let me finish. Want to know the Ouija board's answer? It didn't spell out Andy or Paint. The planchette pointed directly at that 'Good Bye' square. It means I ought to say good-bye to a future with either man."

"Doesn't have to mean that."

I jumped at the deep voice. Andy. How long had he been standing there? What had he heard? *Rotting ribeyes.* Paint stood right next to him. Could it be any worse?

Mollye and Sala excused themselves, deserting me. Yes, it could be worse. I'd have to face this humiliation alone.

"I knew you were freaking out," Andy said. "You've been avoiding both of us. I'm not naïve enough to think a kiss—even a steamy one—means we're engaged."

Paint rolled his eyes. "No need to go into that kiss again. You get cocky every time you talk about it. If I'd been there, she would have kissed me instead, and the decision would have been made."

Paint held up both hands, grinning at me, and my stomach clenched. What were the boys up to?

Andy took over. "Last spring, you told us plain enough. You wouldn't date either of us because you didn't want to choose one friend over another."

Jumping Jerky, sounded like they were easing into a break-up speech. We hadn't even dated. How could they break up with me?

Paint grinned. "You just need more data to make the right choice. Me, of course. So we've come up with a solution. I've even conceded the starting position to my best friend. Next week, date Andy. The week after, date me. Then Andy's up again. Shouldn't take long for you to decide that you and I were made for each other."

Andy chuffed. "Like that's going to happen. I figure after a week with you, she'll come running back to me." He turned to me. "But there is a condition."

"No sex," Paint said. "Nobody gets naked."

Andy nodded. "Whatever clothing starts the date stays on for the duration." Andy paused until he was sure I was looking at him, paying attention. "When this rule breaks, the decision is made."

"The die is cast," Paint added.

Andy laughed. "Cut and dried."

"The horse has left the barn," Paint countered.

"Stop. You guys want to pass me around like a sack of flour?"

"Not for long. Since Andy has week one, I predict a decision an hour into week two," Paint said.

Sala whooped and hollered. She and Mollye had crept back into listening range once they decided there wasn't going to be a shouting match or cryfest.

"Can we take bets? Sounds like Paint's willing to give odds. I envy you, Brie. You gotta say yes. You'd be a blazing idiot not to."

I wasn't sure about that. Wouldn't Paint feel jealous seeing me with Andy? Or vice versa? Especially if we ran into each other.

Yet how could I refuse? The alternative was too bleak—saying goodbye to any chance of finding out if one of them might be the love of my life. They seemed convinced that if I eventually picked one, the other would still be a friend. It was kind of a win, win. At least for me.

I reached out to shake hands, first with Paint, to formally seal the deal.

"You need to understand, we're not in Mormon territory. This isn't a 'brother-husband' kind of thing," he said, still gripping my hand. "Andy and I will see other women on our off weeks."

Can't say I liked the sound of that, but what's fair is fair.

"Understood." I gave his hand a final shake then shook Andy's.

"It's a deal."

Decision made, I felt light-headed with relief. Stiff winds had chased the black storm clouds away turning the sky an optimistic Carolina blue. I took a deep breath. The scents of fall filled the air. A distant bonfire mingled with a promise of hot mulled cider each time the front door opened.

A lot to be said for being alive.

FORTY

While the welcome home party lasted a couple of hours, Paint and Andy left as soon as they finished off one of the apple pies. Though their hours were often irregular, both had afternoon work commitments. Paint was in the process of expanding his distillery to add fine whiskies to his product line. Andy was interviewing candidates for a veterinary tech assistant. His sister Julie had given notice she'd be leaving his practice as soon as her baby arrived. The last time I saw Julie, her departure looked as if it could happen any minute.

Mollye, Sala, and I hung around, helping with kitchen clean-up. Sala and I scrubbed counters while Mollye emptied the dishwasher, making wild guesses about where all the dinnerware belonged. I hoped Carol wouldn't be searching endlessly to find where Moll stuck things. I never let my friend put away dishes at Udderly. We had quite different opinions on "obvious" locations for utensils and cutlery.

After hiding the last spatula, Mollye announced she needed to leave, too. "Have to fire some pottery. Only two weeks left until that big arts and crafts show in Asheville. Want to have new pieces ready. I'm testing some new glazing techniques. Think the results will be gorgeous but it's impossible to know until they're fired."

"Is your studio near here?" Sala asked. "I'd love to see your work."

"Yeah, it's at the back of my Starry Skies store. Would love to have you visit. How about now?"

"Why not? I have nothing else on the agenda." Sala turned to me. "Want to come? You can ride with me and show me the way."

"Sorry," I answered. "I need to drive Eva back to Udderly, and I'm behind on the bookkeeping."

Eva punched my shoulder. Hadn't heard her walk up. "Nonsense I can drive your puny little car back to Udderly. Go on with Sala. Maybe you'll find the perfect present for someone you love. You may recall a certain beloved aunt has a birthday next week."

I laughed. "How could I forget? You remind me twice a day."

"Guess that's settled," Sala said. "Just need to say our goodbyes to Carol and Zack."

A few guests remained. Howie Lemcke was chatting with Zack about his rehab, exercises that might be helpful, and workout duration. Linda, Phil, and Carol were tossing around ideas for a campaign video to be broadcast statewide in a final push for votes.

We wouldn't be missed.

Sala said her piece first, addressing Carol and Zack. "We're leaving now. But those Hummers will stay. Told the executive protection agency to make sure you two have top-notch protection until Gunter's locked up. I'll check in later."

"Can't thank you enough," Carol said.

"Nonsense," Sala answered. "I'm protecting one of our team's top assets."

She awarded Zack with a furtive wink; he smiled back at her. Neither gave the room at large any sign of their romantic entanglement. Guess that would remain secret until post-election—or longer if Sala didn't find a way to end the battle of the will with Kate.

After a chorus of goodbyes, Mollye headed to her Starry Skies van while Sala and I walked to her Mercedes, an SL Roadster. Since my friends arrived after the barricades went up, both vehicles were parked a block away from Carol's house.

"Wow, love your car." I caressed the soft leather as I slid into the passenger seat. Too bad the convertible hard-top was firmly in place. Still I felt a bit like Robin must feel when he gets to slide into Batman's passenger seat.

"Actually it's Dorothy's car. But what are sisters for? I drove it the last time I visited. Liked it so much I bought myself one soon as I got home to Vegas. While this black's classy, I chose fire-engine red. Bet you're shocked."

"Not a bit," I answered. "Red's definitely your color. It'd be my choice, too, if I could swing the payments."

I figured the price tag probably hovered in the hundred-grand range—a purchase range I never expected to roam.

Sala revved the engine. "Should I just follow Mollye's van?"

"Sure. Your roadster could fly by her van, but that might seem impolite."

Sala chuckled. "Don't want to make the woman mad. She might fire us in her kiln."

It took under ten minutes to reach Starry Skies, a tidy cottage Mollye'd converted into a store. The previous owner had unsuccessfully fought construction of a new highway that devoured a good portion of his acreage and transformed his wooded homestead into commercial property.

His loss had been Mollye's gain. The stone cottage had been solid, well-cared for. With a few imaginative touches, she made it look as if it might be a B&B for witches—good, kindly witches. Mollye then added a pottery studio to the back of the cottage-shop. It wasn't visible from the road.

In full glitter, a large sign out front promised Starry Skies was a "New Age & Metaphysical Experience." Sala smiled when she read the billboard. "The store's charming, and so...Mollye. Reminds me of Mollye's quilt tattoo. Old and new."

"Absolutely," I agreed.

Mollye jumped down from her van and unlocked the door. Her hair had finally dried, and she'd resorted to braids to tame her fly-away locks. The resulting hairdo with its green-streaked part and Gretel-style blonde braids had the same jarring effect as her quilt tattoo.

"None of my regular sales people could come in today so I just locked up. Couldn't miss Carol's press conference and welcome home party," she said as she took down her "Closed" sign.

Unlike traditional Open/Closed signs with clock faces that show when a store is scheduled to reopen, the "Closed" side of Mollye's sign featured a witch on a broom. Printed below: "Will reopen when the witch decides to fly back."

Sala started to ooh and ahh as soon as we walked inside. "Don't worry about lost business. Imagine I'll buy enough to compensate. What a fun place."

The team owner made a beeline for one of Moll's pottery pieces near the front of the store. The expression on Sala's face almost matched the looks she bestowed on Zack when she figured no one was watching. Lovestruck.

Easy to understand. I'd bought several pieces for Summer Place. I couldn't really afford them, even with a friend's discount. But I knew they'd be a huge hit with my B&B guests if I ever managed to finish Summer Place renovations.

"I'm definitely buying at least three of these. They're absolutely beautiful." Sala held one of the large pierced vases that were among Mollye's specialties. After the large vases were thrown and air dried, Moll used an electric drill and needle-sharp punches to create a lacy network of different sized holes. Midnight blue and moon glow glazes fired onto the vases readied them for twinkling interior lights. Voila! Mollye had somehow found a way to lock Starry Skies in a vase—metaphysical take-out.

Since I'd visited many times before, I only half listened to Mollye's explanations of her wares. Still it was fun to hear Sala's delighted responses. I loved it when Mollye found new fans of her art, creativity, and whimsy.

Who could resist? Starry Skies had something to strike everyone's fancy. Moll's pottery was the focus of what I thought of as her "gift" section.

Then there was the garden section. I often wondered what Udderly's animals would make of it if I scattered Mollye's light-weight concrete gargoyles about their domains. Her garden assortment also included giant mushrooms and Greek goddesses.

Of course, the metaphysical section—Mollye's Witches-R-Us supply depot—was the showstopper. There were full-moon candles, talking sticks, and willow wands. Plus maybe a hundred glass containers the size of cookie jars chockful of medicinal herbs. Mollye even arranged them in alphabetical order. I watched as Sala picked up a container labeled Hibiscus Flowers, nestled next to Horse Chestnut (chopped).

"Let me show you my studio," Mollye said. "After that, you can start picking goodies and writing checks."

I picked up a witch ball, imagining my aunt's response if I bought her one as a birthday present. The hollow glass balls were a gorgeous swirl of colors. A variety of myths surrounded them, but Mollye stuck with the one that argued the balls were so fascinating and beautiful they acted like magnets to attract their opposites—the evil spirits. Once evil spirits fell within their sphere, the balls captured them and trapped them inside.

"You coming?" Mollye called, pausing at the cottage's former back door, now the entry to her studio.

"In a minute. Going to browse. It's the first year Eva will celebrate a birthday without her twin. Her gift should be something happy."

Once Mollye and Sala left the stone cottage proper and entered the add-on studio, their voices faded away to mere whispers. The cottage's thick stone walls muted sound.

I spotted a gorgeous necklace—not Eva's taste, but definitely mine. It hung from the carved limb of an intricate wooden jewelry tree. I'd bent to free the necklace from its perch when the front door opened.

Figuring I should greet any customers since Mollye was busy, I started to rise up. I froze. Through the intervening aisles I caught sight of coiffed blond hair, a tanned neck and ear, and a sizeable diamond stud. Then I saw the gun.

An involuntary shudder rippled through me. I dropped the necklace. It fell silently on a cottony cloud below the jewelry tree.

No need to see the rest of his face. How? Why?

Spam in a can. He hadn't come to buy pottery.

FORTY-ONE

Doug.

He'd flown off to Las Vegas—or was it just his plane that departed?

I crouched lower, shifted. Found a space to peer through the jewelry tree and assorted jugs and vases. The two-carat diamond in Doug's left ear caught the light. Too bad he had to flaunt his wealth. I might have stood up and greeted a stranger, made an easy target of myself. But the diamond cinched it. The person who'd entered was the enemy not a customer.

He stood still, getting his bearings. His head slowly swiveled right to left as he surveyed the store. I knew his reputation on the field. A tactician. Patient. Always waiting for the right opportunity, the perfect moment.

When he turned my way, I could see his face as well as his coiled body. He looked like a GQ poster boy. Handsome. Poised. Too bad the thin plastic gloves ruined the image. Doug appeared as comfortable with a handgun as he did with a pigskin.

I had to warn Mollye and Sala. Maybe I could yell a warning and distract him at the same time. Put him off balance. I surveyed the merchandise in my vicinity for potential weapons. Okay, if not weapons, annoyances. The pottery vases were too heavy. I couldn't heave one past the next aisle let alone shotput one at his head.

My gaze caught on the sparkling witches' balls nestled in their stretchy display nets. Maybe, just maybe. They were light, and they'd shatter on impact. I could use the nets to swing the balls like those Spanish cowboys wound up their bolas. Yippee ki-yay and let the suckers fly.

I palmed two balls. I'd use both if I didn't have a heart attack or take a bullet after my first heave-ho.

I leapt up and screamed—"Doug's inside! He's got a gun!"—as I swung the ball overhead lasso-style and let loose. The brightly colored orb careened off my intended path like a demented bird. Still it flew.

It smashed into a post two feet from Doug's head. His right arm automatically jumped up to shield his eyes. He yelped. For a few seconds, his gun waved, un-aimed. I took advantage and ran like a gawky chicken, knees bent, elbows spread for balance.

When I reached the end of the aisle, I ducked down and tried to stop hyperventilating. Didn't need desperate gasps to pinpoint my location.

It took me a couple seconds to regain my nerve. *You can do it. Just do it. Fast.*

I bounded up once more and fired my second crystal sphere, while I yelled. "Get out! Call for help."

Though there were dozens of potential obstacles between Doug and me, my second ball sailed past them until gravity finally claimed it. The colorful sphere plummeted to the floor in Doug's general vicinity. I didn't see it land, but mentally applauded the sound effects as it splintered into tiny shards. I crossed my fingers hoping a few flew up to clip Doug.

"Brie! Where are you? Where's Doug?"

Mollye's voice was panicked but clear as a bell.

I swore silently. Capricious as always, the woman hadn't listened to me. Hadn't run out the back door. She—and I presumed Sala—were inside the studio.

Doug's angry growl said my screams and the exploding glass weren't expected. His eyes narrowed as he searched the aisles for some clue that would tell him where I hid.

"Too bad, Brie. Thought it was just Sala and Mollye. Didn't plan on dealing with you, too."

The hair on the back of my neck prickled. It seemed as if Doug was staring straight at me. He must have seen where I'd been when I popped up to throw the second witches' ball. I hadn't crept very far from that spot.

"Don't worry." Doug's voice sounded soothing. "Sala's my first priority. I'll save you for later."

He chuckled. "Too bad you had to warn your buddies. If you'd snuck out, I'd never have known you were here. And your warning was worthless. I barricaded the back door before I came around front. Mollye and Sala have nowhere to go."

Doug calmly walked toward the front door and flipped the sign around so the broom-riding witch proclaimed the store closed. Then he grunted as he struggled to shift a heavy display case far enough to block the front exit.

I scanned the shop for another exit. The cottage windows were small and Mollye's built-in shelves and cabinets surrounded them. No way for me to climb through without hurdling over a hodgepodge of obstacles, exposing my butt to a bullet in the process.

I pulled out my cell phone. I turned off the sound, then dialed 911. I couldn't afford to say anything. Doug was too close. He'd hear me and knew exactly where to aim. Surely Mollye or Sala had also called for help and actually told the operator it was an emergency.

Greasy gopher guts. We were trapped. Witches' balls were no match for a loaded gun, and I figured Doug wouldn't waste much time. He had to figure Sala or Mollye had called 911, whether they had or not.

He'd stuck the gun in his belt to use both hands to budge the heavy display. An opportunity.

I sprinted toward the studio door. Misjudged a turn. The sharp corner of a shelf stabbed me just below my ribs. I swallowed a scream and kept running. The shelf I'd collided with shuddered for a second. Then it toppled. A dozen glass jars filled with medicinal herbs crashed with it. A few extra hurdles for Doug to clear.

I dove for the studio door as if I were trying for a touchdown. A bullet whizzed overhead. Lucky I took the low road.

Gunfire wasn't the only sound. Doug's curses erupted like audible shock waves, followed by complete silence. The silence was scarier.

As I slid through the door, Sala grabbed my arm, and yanked me clear of the doorway.

"All right. You want to die with your friends. Fine. You'll get your wish." The cold, calm voice of the tactician had returned.

I quickly scrambled to my knees. Mollye gave a little wave from where she crouched on the opposite side of the studio door. Good. Doug had no one in his gun sight, and he'd need a howitzer to penetrate the cabin's stone walls. A water pistol would have as much effect as his handgun.

If Doug wanted to shoot us, he'd be forced to come through that door.

Mollye motioned to a large circle of polished metal mounted near the ceiling. She'd installed it to see if anyone entered the shop while she sat molding wet clay at her potting wheel. I nodded that I understood. If I craned my neck, the mirrored surface would let me catch sight of Doug's approach. Mollye couldn't see, but Sala and I could.

A few seconds' warning. Would it be enough?

Doug was a quarterback, used to running past two-hundred-fifty pound mounds of muscle hurling themselves at his legs. If any of us tried to tackle him, he'd swat us off like pesky mosquitoes.

I looked in the reflector. He hadn't moved. Yet I sensed our wait was more likely to be seconds than minutes.

What was his strategy? He had to think it unlikely he could shoot all three of us bing, bang, boom without at least one of us having a chance to try something. But what?

"Weapons?" I mouthed.

I knew Mollye understood. On her side of the doorway, she pointed to a large, open bag filled with white clay powder. She picked up a giant hand scoop, and pantomimed flinging the powder at the doorway.

Yes, indeedy. Timed right the powder would blind him—for a few seconds. What then? He'd start shooting even while he was blind. Sala tapped my shoulder. She'd picked up a gnarly, carved walking stick Mollye used as a prop in her walk-in-the-woodland display. Good.

"What do you think you'll accomplish killing us?" Sala yelled.

"Plenty," Doug answered. "With you dead, Kate takes over. I'm back on the team, and she gives me an advance on a bonus. There's not a shred of hard evidence I did anything wrong."

"Are you kidding?" Mollye screeched. "The cops'll be here any minute. You can't get away. You know Gunter'll rat you out as soon as he's caught. Give it up."

Doug actually chuckled. "Don't think so. Gunter's dead. Couldn't seem to get past me shooting his pal. I played lookout at the Udderly gate when they came after Carol. Once Carol and Brie rode off on that stupid mule, Gunter phoned me. Wanted me to help him load Vince into the van. Gunter was an old grunt. Never leave behind a downed soldier. I preferred a clean getaway."

As I listened to the shouted exchange, I frantically searched the workbench where Mollye pierced holes in those lacy vases. Could I do the same to Doug? Moll's electric drill would do the most damage if the danged cord would reach. But I sort of figured Doug would quickly dodge out of range.

I picked up the largest of Mollye's needle-sharp punches. It would let me continue the attack, no plug to pull free or get tangled. The punches made small holes but they'd sink deep. I could aim for his gun hand.

Lame. I'd taken a self-defense course for women. Knew my smart play. Go for vulnerable spots, bigger targets.

I spotted another weapon. The razor-sharp wire Mollye used to cleanly slice through stacks of wet clay. It looked remarkably like a garrote. Even had a nice wooden handle at each end.

Could I use it? I shuddered. No. I'd hesitate soon as it dug into flesh. Doug would wrestle it away and slice my head clean off.

I glanced in the polished sphere. *Holy ham hocks!*

"Mollye, now!" I shouted as Doug launched himself on a too-short dash.

In seconds, the air filled with white dust. A blinding blizzard. Just as I feared, the dust storm didn't stop him from squeezing the trigger again and again. In the studio's confined space, it sounded like rolling thunder. I flailed away with the punch.

A hot burning sensation. Felt like Doug had stabbed my left arm with a red-hot poker. I felt woozy. I still couldn't see.

I'd tried to close my eyes when Mollye let the dust fly, but I must have opened them too soon. My eyes watered when I tried to peer through the haze. I felt a warm, wet sensation. Blood ran down my arm. The tangy iron smell was the clincher. I'd been shot.

My fear disappeared. Replaced with white-hot anger.

I heard an "ooph." My murky vision cleared enough for me to see Doug falling to his knees.

"Take that you freakin' sleazebag," Sala yelled as she raised her stout hickory weapon to whack Doug again. I scuttled sideways to vacate the general vicinity.

What had been a dust blizzard was now a gentle snowfall as clay particles drifted down on the dark lump I presumed was Doug's body.

Was he getting up? I wasn't sure. Couldn't risk it. I plunged my needle punch into the muddled form. Had no idea what part of his anatomy I hit.

I heard a scream, then a huge hand tightened around my injured arm.

This time I knew who was screaming. Me.

Just before everything went black.

FORTY-TWO

When I came to, concerned blue eyes were searching my face.

Huh? Steve, the paramedic? Why was the guy who'd helped me stave off hypothermia last spring shaking his head? Where was I?

"We have to stop meeting like this," Steve joked. "You'll be fine. But how about staying out of trouble? If you really want to see me, just bring cookies to the hospital."

An adrenaline rush hurtled me back to the present. The horrifying present. I struggled to sit up. "Mollye, Sala—where are they? Are they all right?"

"Fine," Steve answered. "Your friends are fine. Maybe a little worse for wear. Shock'll do that. But you're the only one with a genuine bullet hole. Through and through. The docs will fix you right up."

I looked around. We were outside Mollye's stone cottage. I was belted onto one of those stretcher contraptions that snap into stand-up service like ironing boards with wheels. There were enough swirling red and blue lights for it to look like a club rave. Only thing missing was the blaring music. I caught a glimpse of Sala huddled with Sheriff Mason.

"Ready to go for a ride?" Steve asked. "Time to get you to the hospital."

"No. Wait. Not yet. I need to know. What happened? Where's Doug? Did he escape?"

Steve chuckled. "You mean the football player? Some pro quarterback. Sacked by three women. Won't live that down. Doubt even a prison team will want him."

"Where is he?"

Steve patted my hand, the one that wasn't connected to my gunshot arm. Then he moved to the foot of the stretcher, ready to roll. "Don't worry. He's gone. Left in the first ambulance that arrived. A deputy rode along just in case he came to. One of you ladies beaned him pretty good. Out cold. Probable concussion. Plus something that looked like an ice pick was sticking out of his butt. Bleeding like the dickens."

"I beaned him," Sala said proudly. She'd run over when she saw I was awake. "First swing with that walking stick caught him square in the back. Nailed his head with the second, while you were putting a neat little hole in his tush. Think you may have defaced his joker tattoo.

"Mollye sat on Doug, holding a vase over his head to conk him again if he came around, but he was still out cold when the Sheriff's deputies rammed through the front door. 'Course you were out cold too."

"Where's Mollye? Is she okay?" I asked.

"Fine," Sala answered. "Just needed an eye wash. She got the worst of the blowback when she flung that powered clay. Hey, they won't let me travel with you. I'll meet you at the hospital. Already let Eva know you're fine. She'll call your parents."

Steve and his paramedic buddy rolled my stretcher into the ambulance. "Is this really necessary?" I complained. "Can't I just ride with Sala?"

"Yes, it's necessary," Steve answered. "If you don't like my company, quit playing cops and robbers."

I felt a prick. When I woke the next time, I was inside the hospital. Steve knew something about sharp objects, too. I was just happy he'd nailed my arm and not my butt. Derriere shots hurt the worst.

I tried to sit up in the hospital bed and bumped my arm against the metal bar designed to keep me from rolling onto the floor. *Cursed Colby* that hurt. Okey, dokey. I'd lie still until a doctor or nurse ratcheted my bed up to sitting position or lowered the side rails.

I figured I was near the bottom of the triage list since Steve had patched me up in the field and stopped the bleeding. I chuckled, wondering if I could call and ask Mollye to don a nurse's costume and wig to break me out.

I needn't have worried about an extended stay. I only required stitches, a sling, powerful pain pills, and a few cautions about self-medicating. None of it argued for an overnight stay.

However, the doc's get-out-of-hospital card simply released me into Sheriff Mason's custody. Apparently he'd been pacing circles in the ER waiting room. Mason shooed away the nurse who'd insisted I climb into a wheelchair for the journey to some mysterious outdoor perimeter where hospital liability ended. "I'll take her from here," Mason said.

"Need to get your statement," he added as he wheeled me toward the parking lot. "Sala let your family know I'd be bringing you home."

The wheelchair bounced over a speed bump as he hustled me to his cruiser. "I took a bullet when I was in the Army. Got shot in the leg," he added. "I know it's not fun. But the doc says you won't have any permanent damage."

He opened the passenger side door. "Want me to help you in?"

"No I can manage." The front passenger seat was a big step-up from my previous rides in cop cars. A lot comfier and much better scenery when you didn't have to peer through a metal screen.

Mason asked questions, and I answered as best I could, though the finale after I got shot was a bit murky. Mason didn't run out of questions until we pulled into Udderly's drive. Most of the vehicles parked in front of the cabin came as no surprise: my Dad's Toyota Highlander, Sala's Mercedes, Mollye's van, and three trucks belonging to Eva, Andy and Paint. However, I hadn't expected to see the two Hummers. I was beginning to think the *Ardon Chronicle* had broadcast news of my return.

I chuckled. "Might as well come inside, Sheriff. Answer questions from everyone at once instead of fielding a dozen calls."

He shrugged. "I'll tell y'all what I can. 'Course there's a lot I can't say."

The hugs weren't as robust as usual. No one wanted to give me a squeeze after seeing the left sleeve of my top had been cut off and my arm rested in a sling. The sling didn't quite hide the impressive bandage on my upper arm.

Andy went easy on the hug, but not on the kiss. An on-the-lips, I-mean-it kiss. And I returned the favor. When we finally parted, I felt his hot breath on my neck. "Remember," he whispered. "I'm allowed to kiss you as much as I want. I'm your designated boyfriend for the next seven days."

Paint, who was next in line, rolled his eyes and ceremoniously shook my hand.

Zack joked that since our opposite arms were in slings we could work together in the kitchen to make one whole chef.

Once the greetings ended, Eva insisted I take her recliner. An honor she'd never bestowed on me before.

As soon as everyone seemed satisfied I wasn't going to faint, the sheriff became the center of attention.

"We do have one new piece of evidence," the sheriff said. "Mick Hardy hand wrote a note and left it in his apartment. His sister found it tucked inside a container of leftovers in his freezer. Guess Mick figured she'd be the one stuck cleaning out his fridge if anything happened to him. Mick said he was sorry—for everything. He admitted attacking Zack. Said Doug promised to pay off his gambling debts if he could snag Zack's phone. Apparently he did some meth before he snuck in the barn to give him a little false courage. Didn't think he could go through with it sober.

"He knocked Zack out. When Mick couldn't find the phone, a blind rage overtook him. He saw the pitchfork and stabbed Zack. Once he started coming off the drug high and heard how badly Zack was injured, he was overcome with remorse. But he still didn't have the phone he had to produce for Doug to pay off his debts. That's why he showed up at Udderly the next morning."

Paint shook his head. "What a waste."

Mom focused on Sheriff Mason. "Does Mick's note give you enough evidence to arrest Doug for murder and keep him behind bars?"

"Attempted murder's a lock," he answered. "No way he can lie his way out of the attempt to kill Brie, Sala and Mollye. But will we ever be able to prove he killed Gunter and Vince or that he solicited Mick's murder? Not sure. While he confessed as much to his last batch of intended victims, he'll claim he was merely trying to frighten them and that he only fired his gun after Brie lobbed pottery at him. He's a cagey guy."

Mason nodded at Sala. "Doug just didn't figure he'd have any difficulty eliminating a bunch of women who'd messed up his plans."

Sala spoke up. "How did he think he'd get away with killing us?"

"Imagine he counted on surprise," I said. "Thought he'd walk in and shoot you and Mollye before you knew what was happening. Finish you off before you could call for help."

"Right," the sheriff answered. "When we found your bodies—maybe hours or days later, Gunter would be the presumed killer."

Mollye shook her head. "But Doug boasted Gunter was already dead, that he'd killed him."

Mason gnawed at his lip as he considered Moll's comment. "True. Doug must have felt confident we'd never find Gunter's body wherever he disposed of it. Or, if we found the body, we'd assume Gunter killed you before he was dispatched by some other thug."

"Speaking of fleeing, I thought Doug flew off to Las Vegas," I said. "What happened?"

"He landed his plane in Charlotte, supposedly to refuel," the sheriff explained. "He got off, and his co-pilot flew on to Vegas. Doug rented a car with a fake driver's license and credit card."

"What will happen now to Chester, Fred and Allie?" I asked.

Mason shrugged. "It's my job to catch 'em, not prosecute them. They'll be tried. Not sure what charges the DA will file against Chester. May go easy on him in exchange for his testimony about Fred and Allie's roles in Carol's kidnapping. But I have no doubt juries will send them all to prison for a nice long stretch."

Mason, who'd been seated in a straight-backed chair for his inquisition, stood. "I need to get back. The Ardon County jail is pretty near filled to capacity with Chester, Fred, and Allie in custody pending arraignment. Doug will be joining them soon as the hospital releases him."

"No other villains lurking out there?" Eva asked. "Can life finally get back to normal?"

Mason didn't quite smile, though the corners of his mouth briefly lifted. "Never run out of villains. Always a new batch. But at the moment I know of no bad guys who have you in their sights."

He turned to Carol. "Sure you still want to be governor? Columbia has a lot bigger population than Ardon County. More people translate into more crime. Just statistics. The bigger the barrel, the more chance for bad apples."

Carol shook her head. "If I win, maybe I'll deputize Mollye, Sala and Brie to help out Columbia's law enforcement. Of course, judging by the look on your face, Sheriff, you'd warn your colleagues that such help comes with its own set of problems."

"Don't worry, Sheriff," I said. "I'm not looking for trouble—here or anywhere."

"You never are," Mom muttered. "You still manage to find it."

Andy walked over to my recliner and offered a hand. "Right now, why don't we help Brie fill her plate? Maybe even offer her a shot of Paint's moonshine. We all have something to celebrate tonight."

His green eyes twinkled.

Yes, indeed. I had a boyfriend. Andy this week. Paint the next.

Not sure I wanted this new arrangement to end.

LINDA LOVELY

Linda Lovely finds writing pure fiction isn't a huge stretch given the years she's spent penning PR and ad copy. Linda writes a blend of mystery and humor, chuckling as she plots to "disappear" the types of characters who most annoy her. Quite satisfying plus there's no need to pester relatives for bail. Her newest series offers good-natured salutes to both her vegan family doctor and her cheese-addicted kin. She's an enthusiastic Sisters in Crime member and helps organize the popular Writers' Police Academy. When not writing or reading, Linda takes long walks with her husband, swims, gardens, and plays tennis.

The Brie Hooker Mystery Series
by Linda Lovely

BONES TO PICK (#1)
PICKED OFF (#2)

Henery Press Mystery Books

And finally, before you go...
Here are a few other mysteries
you might enjoy:

THE DEEP END

Julie Mulhern

The Country Club Murders (#1)

Swimming into the lifeless body of her husband's mistress tends to ruin a woman's day, but becoming a murder suspect can ruin her whole life.

It's 1974 and Ellison Russell's life revolves around her daughter and her art. She's long since stopped caring about her cheating husband, until she becomes a suspect in Madeline Harper's death. The murder forces Ellison to confront her husband's proclivities and his crimes—kinky sex, petty cruelties and blackmail.

As the body count approaches par on the seventh hole, Ellison knows she has to catch a killer. But with an interfering mother, an adoring father, a teenage daughter, and a cadre of well-meaning friends, can Ellison find the killer before he finds her?

IN IT FOR THE MONEY

David Burnsworth

A Blu Carraway Mystery (#1)

Lowcountry Private Investigator Blu Carraway needs a new client. He's broke and the tax man is coming for his little slice of paradise. But not everyone appreciates his skills. Some call him a loose cannon. Others say he's a liability. All the ex-Desert Storm Ranger knows is his phone hasn't rung in quite a while. Of course, that could be because it was cut off due to delinquent payments.

Lucky for him, a client does show up at his doorstep—a distraught mother with a wayward son. She's rich and her boy's in danger. Sounds like just the case for Blu. Except nothing about the case is as it seems. The jigsaw pieces—a ransom note, a beat-up minivan, dead strippers, and a missing briefcase filled with money and cocaine—do not make a complete puzzle. The first real case for Blu Carraway Investigations in three years goes off the rails. And that's the way he prefers it to be.

MACDEATH

Cindy Brown

An Ivy Meadows Mystery (#1)

Like every actor, Ivy Meadows knows that *Macbeth* is cursed. But she's finally scored her big break, cast as an acrobatic witch in a circus-themed production of *Macbeth* in Phoenix, Arizona. And though it may not be Broadway, nothing can dampen her enthusiasm—not her flying cauldron, too-tight leotard, or carrot-wielding dictator of a director.

But when one of the cast dies on opening night, Ivy is sure the seeming accident is "murder most foul" and that she's the perfect person to solve the crime (after all, she does work part-time in her uncle's detective agency). Undeterred by a poisoned Big Gulp, the threat of being blackballed, and the suddenly too-real curse, Ivy pursues the truth at the risk of her hard-won career—and her life.

Made in the USA
Lexington, KY
15 July 2018